The

Good

Child's

River

Thomas Wolfe

The

Edited and with an Introduction

Good

by Suzanne Stutman

Child's

The University of North Carolina Press

River

Chapel Hill and London

This book was published with the assistance of the H. Eugene and Lillian Youngs Lehman Fund of the University of North Carolina Press.

FRONTISPIECE:
Portrait of Thomas Wolfe, circa 1935. (By permission of the Houghton Library, Harvard University)

Library of Congress Cataloging-in-Publication Data
Wolfe, Thomas, 1900–1938.
    The good child's river / by Thomas Wolfe ; edited and with an introduction by Suzanne Stutman.
        p. cm.
    Includes bibliographical references.
    ISBN 0-8078-2002-4 (cloth : alk. paper)
    I. Stutman, Suzanne.
    II. Title.
PS3545.O337G66   1991
813'.52—dc20   91-2946
                                    CIP

The paper in this book meets the guidelines for permanence and durability of the Committee on Production Guidelines for Book Longevity of the Council on Library Resources.

Manufactured in the United States of America

95 94 93 92 91 5 4 3 2 1

TO FRED

Contents

Preface, ix

Editorial Policy, xiii

Introduction, 1

"The Good Child's River" by Thomas Wolfe, 31

    I. The Time That Is Lovely, 33

    II. [My Cousin Robert], 85

    III. [My Father on Tour], 100

    IV. [A Baby Is Born], 108

    V. My Father's Youth, 118

    VI. The Three Sisters, 154

    VII. Esther, 178

    VIII. White Fokes, 186

APPENDIX A

Fragments from "The Good Child's River" Ledgers, 209

    I. Even Such Is Time: The Theatre, 211

    II. [May's Story], 236

    III. Even Such Is Time, 243

    IV. Aunt Hugh, 247

APPENDIX B

Fragments of Projected Chapters from "The October Fair,"
"The Good Child's River," and *The Web and the Rock*, 275

    I. Fragments from "The October Fair" Ledgers, 277

    II. Fragments from "The Good Child's River" Ledgers, 281

    III. Fragments from *The Web and the Rock* Manuscript, 287

Bibliography, 291

A section of illustrations follows page 176.

Preface

When I called Paul Gitlin, the executor of the Thomas Wolfe estate, to request permission to edit the manuscript of "The Good Child's River," I asked him, "Does 'The Good Child's River' ring a bell?" Fortunately for me, it did not, which meant that no one had requested this assignment before me. At the time, I did not fully realize the task that lay ahead: years of detective work and several trips to Harvard's Houghton Library would reveal the full extent of manuscript that represents Wolfe's experimentation with an extended story that is totally beyond his own personal experience. I feel that I have been blessed to have had the opportunity to spend so many years of my life with two talented people who have come to mean so much to me: Thomas Wolfe and Aline Bernstein. The pleasure of continuing my work on Wolfe's manuscript has been enhanced by my renewed collaboration with the University of North Carolina Press.

My thanks first and foremost to Paul Gitlin for granting me permission to edit "The Good Child's River," as well as for his unwavering belief.

Richard S. Kennedy, my former adviser at Temple University, has served throughout the years as teacher, mentor, and cherished friend. He has always been there to give advice, to read manuscript, to puzzle over words that seemed at times indecipherable, and to offer guidance on improving the final text, which I have accepted and acted upon. He has made an impression on my life for which I will be forever grateful. His talented and lovely wife, Ella Kennedy, has also provided encouragement throughout the years.

Special thanks to John L. Idol, Jr., and Leslie Field, who read the text for the University of North Carolina Press and made valuable suggestions that I have incorporated into my finished work. To all of my friends and colleagues of the Thomas Wolfe Society—experts all—I express appreciation for their support and expertise: Rena D'Andrea, James Boyer, Andrea Brown, William Brown, James W. Clark, Jr., Alice R. Cotten, David Herbert Donald, Elizabeth Evans, Leslie Field, Phillip Horne, John L. Idol, Jr., Carole Johnston, H. D. Jones, Carole Klein, Klaus Lanzinger, Aldo Magi,

John S. Phillipson, Duane Schneider, Morton Teicher, Thomas Underwood, Frank Wilson, Harold Woodell, and David Wyatt. Aldo Magi and John Phillipson deserve particular thanks from all of us who are devoted to the work of Thomas Wolfe, for they, in creating and nurturing the *Thomas Wolfe Review*, have served and enriched us all.

Thanks to Rodney Dennis and James Stewart of Houghton Library and to their excellent staff for the expert assistance they have offered me over the years, and to Kenneth Carpenter, editor of the *Harvard Library Bulletin*, for his friendship and encouragement.

I would like to thank all of those at Pennsylvania State University who have provided assistance. The Institute of Arts and Humanistic Studies was generous with its grants and facilities, enabling me to complete my work close to schedule. My special thanks to Stanley Weintraub, the director of the institute, who, like Richard Kennedy, has always been there for me, who knows so much, and who offers the best advice; to Dean Theodore Kiffer for his continued support of my projects and for his unwavering integrity, which has been a beacon and an inspiration for so many of us; and to Albert Skomra, formerly associate head of the English Department, who has always offered encouragement. I would like to thank my former and present department chairmen: Christopher Clausen, who did so much for all of us, and Robert Secor, who continues to serve us well. Kenneth Thigpen, the associate head of the English Department, has offered his expertise as well as his special quality of caring. Daniel Walden, so gifted in his own right, has taken the time to foster my work as well as simply being his own quietly wonderful self. My thanks to Margaret Coté, associate dean of Liberal Arts. Thanks to Robert Bernoff, the former C.E.O. at Ogontz, for his years of excellent service and to Moylan Mills, the former dean of academic affairs, for his continuing help. For their support I am also grateful to our fine new administrators, Anthony Fusaro and Irving Buchen, who have supported me 110 percent, and to all of my friends and colleagues at the Ogontz campus— among them F. Lynn Christy, Barry Goluboff, Claire Hirshfield, Natalie Isser, Linda Miller, William Pencak, Lita Schwartz, and Tramble Turner.

To Sandra Eisdorfer, my editor at the University of North Carolina Press, who over the years has become a true friend, thank you for your expertise, your commitment to what you do, and your unwavering consistency of character. To Stevie Champion, my copyeditor, who has offered me invaluable assistance, my special thanks. Thanks to Gene Corbman for showing me the way. William Rossky, who was my first English professor, has served as my inspiration; he is what I want to be when I grow up. I thank him for always being there and for truly changing my life. His family, Evelyn and Ellen Rossky, have become my family; I give thanks for all of their love and encouragement.

Finally, I dedicate this book to my own wonderful family: Edna Turock, my mother; my lovely children, Craig, Robert, Mary, Roni, and Michael, and my beautiful grandson, Geoffy; my beloved husband and best friend, Fred, who makes everything possible; and Samuel Turock, Irene Stutman, and George Stutman. For I believe in angels. And I know that they fly above me and protect me with their wings.

Editorial Policy

As editor of "The Good Child's River," I have attempted to maintain the integrity of the text by presenting this work in a form as close to the original as possible. To minimize reader distractions, I have silently corrected obvious errors in spelling (e.g., "sandwiches," not "sandwitches"; Percy and Steele "MacKaye," not "Mackaye") and have given the most frequent spelling of often-used words that appeared inconsistently (e.g., in the original manuscript "color" also shows up as "colour," "centre" as "center," and "lifetime" as "life time"). For the same reason, street addresses (West Twentieth Street) and geographic regions (North, West) have been capitalized consistently. For the sake of clarity, I have italicized or quoted titles as appropriate, added missing quotations marks, and standardized paragraph indentations.

Otherwise, I have tried to intrude upon the work as little as possible. For example, Thomas Wolfe had his own sense of where commas should be placed. Unless the meaning of a passage was unclear or flagrantly violated the rules of grammar, I have left his punctuation alone. In the rare instances when Wolfe omitted connecting words (or articles) in his haste to get words on paper, I have enclosed such words in brackets. Some chapters in the text were titled by Wolfe, whereas others were not; had he lived to complete the manuscript, he certainly would have named them all. For clarity and consistency, I have added bracketed titles to the unnamed chapters. All brackets in this edition are the editor's; Wolfe used only parentheses.

To preserve the text's authenticity, I have left numerous stylistic idiosyncracies in their original form without comment. These include British and variant spellings; the separation or hyphenation of compound words such as "ear rings," "horse car," "fairy-tale," and "sea-floors"; idiosyncratic capitalizations for emphasis such as "Bridge," "Park," and "Spring"; and dashes used to indicate various punctuation marks. No material has been deleted from the manuscript. Thus, the complete text of "The Good Child's River" as I found it in the Houghton Library is contained within these pages.

As I have restored it, the final text of "The Good Child's River" consists of several portions of manuscript: (1) the original typescripts of "The Time That Is Lovely" (so titled by Wolfe and later edited and renamed "Penelope's Web" by Edward Aswell for *The Web and the Rock*) and "In the Park"; (2) the three five-hundred-page handwritten ledgers entitled "The Good Child's River" that comprise the main portion of text; (3) almost one hundred pages that Wolfe tore from the first "Good Child's River" ledger and used to create "His Father's Earth" before placing them in the first part of *The Web and the Rock* manuscript; and (4) fragments of chapters that Wolfe had written on the manuscripts of "The October Fair," "The Good Child's River," and *The Web and the Rock*. All of this material was initially written and revised by Wolfe sometime between 1930 and 1938, shortly before his death.

As stated in "The October Fair" manuscript, Wolfe intended that "The Good Child's River" would present together in novel form his "Esther stories," told, for the most part, from Esther's point of view. The text appears in the order that Wolfe wrote it—with one exception. I removed the chapter entitled "Aunt Hugh"—because it digressed from Wolfe's stated purpose—and inserted it in Appendix A at the end of this text, along with additional material from "The Good Child's River" ledgers that the author probably would have deleted from his finished work. Fragments from the manuscripts of "The October Fair," "The Good Child's River," and *The Web and the Rock*, representing little kernels and prophesies of what could or might have been, are collected in Appendix B. I believe that, in its present form, this text will give the reader a full perspective of Wolfe's intent and process of creation.

The Good Child's River

Introduction

The History of "The Good Child's River"

The history of the material contained in "The Good Child's River" is long and complex. Part of the huge William B. Wisdom Thomas Wolfe Collection housed at Harvard's Houghton Library, the manuscript of this unfinished novel consists primarily of first-person narrations told from the point of view of his fictional character, Esther Jack, and based on the world of Aline Bernstein, the great love of Thomas Wolfe's life. Early in the pages of "The October Fair" manuscript, Wolfe refers to these first-person narrations as "the Esther stories." Like much of Wolfe's writing, "The Good Child's River" can be considered a work in progress; it not only encompasses the three five-hundred-page handwritten ledgers that bear its name but also survives in a large number of his manuscripts—from "The October Fair" to *The Web and the Rock*. "In the Park" and "His Father's Earth," both extrapolated from the Esther stories and first published separately in 1935, are considered to be two of Wolfe's most masterful creations. "The Time That Is Lovely," the earliest collection of Esther stories written by Wolfe within his huge "October Fair" manuscript, was later renamed "Penelope Web" by Edward Aswell and published in *The Web and the Rock*, as was a revised version of "His Father's Earth." The material from "The Good Child's River" published previously consists of approximately 20 percent of this text and appears here in its original manuscript and typescript form. I have restored this material and have placed it into its original context; therefore, it is significantly different from earlier published versions.

In this work I follow a long line of scholars who have sought to amend the erroneous perceptions about Thomas Wolfe and his works. My intention here is to present a definitive text of "The Good Child's River," that is, the text as Thomas Wolfe wrote it, without exclusion and with a minimum of editorial intrusions. Similarly, other recent editors of Wolfe's manuscripts—among them, John L. Idol and Louis D. Rubin, Jr., in *The Hound of Darkness* and *Mannerhouse*, Richard Kennedy in *Welcome to Our City* and K_{19}, and Francis Skipp in *The Complete Short Stories of Thomas Wolfe*—have returned these texts to their original condition, not only to display Wolfe's works as he alone wrote them, but to restore his reputation as well.

This reputation was tarnished and undercut as early as 1936, when Bernard De Voto, in an article entitled "Genius Is Not Enough," asserted that Wolfe's *Of Time and the River* was actually a collaboration between the author and his editor, Maxwell Perkins. De Voto said that Wolfe needed Perkins to help reduce the cavalcade of words that erupted with volcanic profusion from his brain onto paper without focus or control. This misconception about Wolfe was exacerbated when, soon after his death, *The Web and the Rock* and *You Can't Go Home Again* were published by Harper and Company under the editorship of Edward Aswell. Aswell, working with the huge pile of manuscript that Wolfe had left with him shortly before his death, took it upon himself to cut and paste portions of the text and to make his own additions and alterations without indicating that he had made any changes.

For years, then, Thomas Wolfe's reputation has suffered the assault that, among other charges, his writing was not even his own. Most recently, John Halberstadt, a Yale Ph.D. who wrote his dissertation on Aswell's editing of *The Web and the Rock*, has created a controversy—referred to by some as "Wolfegate"—by asserting that the posthumously published novels are not Wolfe's at all but rather a collaboration between Wolfe and Aswell. Leslie Field disagrees with Halberstadt's thesis, noting in *Thomas Wolfe and His Editors* that although Aswell did indeed make changes and additions, the posthumously published novels were written by Thomas Wolfe and no one else. Richard S. Kennedy in *The Window of Memory: The Literary Career of Thomas Wolfe* and David Herbert Donald in *Look Homeward: A Life of Thomas Wolfe*, like Field, conclude that the posthumous works are those of Thomas Wolfe, not Edward Aswell.[1] My recent review of the manuscripts of the posthumously

1. For a fuller exploration of this controversy, see Halberstadt, "The Making of Thomas Wolfe's Posthumous Novels"; Field, *Thomas Wolfe and His Editors*; "The Web of Illusion and the Rock of Reality" (pp. 388–413) and "Thomas Wolfe's Rough Outline of His Last Book" (pp. 415–37) in Kennedy, *The Window of Memory*; and "Afterword: The Posthumous Novels of Thomas Wolfe" (pp. 464–84) in Donald, *Look Homeward*.

published works leads me to the same conclusion that has been reached by many of my colleagues: the novels attributed to Wolfe are indeed his works.

Thomas Wolfe's meeting with Aline Bernstein aboard the *Olympic* in August 1925 was an encounter that would change his life. Their mutual attraction seemed unlikely, for he was a tall, gangly, and often unsophisticated young southerner, while she was a small, robust, middle-aged Jewish costume and set designer for the New York stage. Nevertheless, from the beginning, these lovers shared a sense of ideality, romance, and destiny. This woman, at once so worldly wise and yet so innocent of vision, gave to Thomas Wolfe the love and support that enabled him to search into the deepest corners of his mind and heart and to bring forth his masterpiece, *Look Homeward, Angel.*

Because Wolfe depended primarily on the events of his own life for the substance of his fictional re-creations, Bernstein provided him with more than simply inspiration: she became a character in the ongoing drama of their love affair and its subsequent stormy dissolution, a relationship that preoccupied Wolfe for several years and that became the major focus of the second half of his posthumously published novel, *The Web and the Rock.* Moreover, based on her life he fashioned the most memorable character of his later works: Helen-Irene-Rebecca-Esther-Jacobs-Feitlebaum-Jack.[2]

It was with Esther Jack that the young hero, David-"Monk"-George-Hawke-Webber,[3] found the blinding love that would transform his world and with it his vision of life. Through her eyes he would gain perspectives he had never imagined, pieces of life that he had never dreamed existed.

But this woman served not only as a lens to the present but also as a conduit into the past, as this "good child" entered into the river of time to re-create her early life and the lives of her mar-

2. These are the various names Wolfe gave to his heroine throughout his manuscripts. For a study of the real life of Bernstein, see Carole Klein's ground-breaking biography, *Aline.*

3. This list encompasses the significant names used for Wolfe's hero throughout his unpublished and published writings. For a review of Wolfe's life and work, see Kennedy, *The Window of Memory,* and Donald, *Look Homeward.*

velous family: her actor father, Joe, her opulent Aunt Bella, her gentle mother, Rebecca, aunts and uncles, and servants and policemen. Further, she would re-create for him, almost like a series of Currier and Ives photographs, life in New York from the 1880s through the turn of the century. In chapter 23 of *The Web and the Rock*, Thomas Wolfe presents an outline of the material he molded into his Esther stories and entitled "The Good Child's River":

> In her stories of her childhood and youth, of her wonderful, wild father who was an actor, of her beautiful, wasteful mother who bit diamonds from her necklace when she needed money, of her fat Rabelaisian Christian uncles who were enormously rich and ate the most succulent foods, which they themselves went to market for every day, poking and prodding at the meat and vegetables, of her beautiful and generous Jewish aunt, of her Christian aunt, of her English relatives, her Dutch relatives, of her husband's German relatives and her visits to them, of Mr. Roosevelt, and of actors, jolly priests, plays, theatres, cafés, and restaurants, of a great number of brilliant and interesting people—bankers, brokers, socialists, nihilists, suffragettes, painters, musicians, servants, Jews, Gentiles, foreigners, and Americans, he began to get fixed in his imagination an opulent and thrilling picture of the city in the Nineties and the early years of the twentieth century.[4]

"Have you read *An Actor's Daughter?*" Aline Bernstein asked Richard Kennedy during an interview. "That was Tom's book. He was going to write my life, you know."[5] With the same magical talent he exhibited in *Look Homeward, Angel*, a fictional re-creation of his own larger-than-life family, Wolfe gave existence to the family of Aline Bernstein/Esther Jack. In addition, he created in Esther herself a total reality of characterization, from her use of language and imagery, often so distinctly feminine, to her natural artistic preoccupation with texture and design.

Early in their relationship these two exuberant personalities spent endless hours re-creating for one another scenes of their childhoods and of the lavish personalities of their families, particu-

4. Wolfe, *The Web and the Rock*, p. 357.
5. Kennedy, *The Window of Memory*, p. 228, n. 74.

larly their wonderful fathers, who served as the heart's warm center for each and who represented all that was best within themselves: the artist's rich intensity and lust for life, appreciation of the world of the senses, and a basic integrity of spirit that taught them to be, above all else, true to their own artistic vision.

Thomas Wolfe described his desire to devour knowledge and experience as Faustian, and indeed it was. He had a fierce hunger to absorb all of the details of Aline Bernstein's early life and to relive her tales and stories through the exquisite focus of her own vision. In this way, he could add her world to his own until it became a part of his own domain. To accomplish this imaginative repossession, Wolfe demanded of her endless details of all that she had seen and experienced. She, delighted that he desired to hear what she was so happy to tell, shared with him her life's story not only because she loved telling it, but also because she possessed an instinctual generosity of spirit. Their relationship was not to remain idyllic, however; later these same stories that Wolfe so loved to hear became for Bernstein simply one more way to keep their faltering love affair together.

When he returned to Europe in 1928, Wolfe called his trip "The Grand Tour of Renunciation." Tired and drained by what he perceived as Bernstein's suffocating presence, he fled to escape her. Yet, once they were separated, he poured out to her all that he was experiencing, from what he physically saw to what he emotionally perceived. His letters were punctuated by declarations of love for her and by his need to retain her as a vital part of his life. Nevertheless, the end of their relationship had been prophesied by his desperate flight in 1928, a pattern he repeated in 1930, when, after receiving a Guggenheim Fellowship for a projected work to be entitled "The October Fair," he once more went abroad.

He arrived in Europe in May 1930. On June 6, he recorded in the front of the first of his many "October Fair" ledgers the pledge that accompanied the official beginning of the great body of work that would remain his major preoccupation until the end of his life: "This book started in Paris June 6, 1930, from notes and fragments which have been collecting for two years. Now I hope with all my heart for courage and strength enough to see it through to its end, on paper as it is in my spirit, to make it as good as I can, and to do it day by day no matter where I am, no matter what despair or loneliness I may feel, and at no matter what cost of flesh or blood or spirit."[6]

Shortly before he left New York, Wolfe had asked Bernstein to record for him details of her early life, and on May 23, 1930, she wrote of her efforts: "I have been writing the events of my life for you, but find it very hard to make it simple. I keep putting down all kinds of extraneous things, first thing you know it will turn into a novel and then I'll have to use it myself."[7] Later in the same paragraph, she wrote the phrase that Wolfe would soon record in his notebook and that, with slight variation, would become the predominant "melody" of Esther Jack's recollections of her early childhood: "Long long into the night I lay awake trying to think how best to tell my story."[8] Years later, after Wolfe's death, she used these words as the proem to her novel, *An Actor's Daughter*. Wolfe himself used them throughout the pages of "The October Fair" as he sought to capture the melody, the memory, and the artistic vision of Esther and her journey into the past. In his final manuscript of the first segment of "The Good Child's River," much of which became the "Penelope's Web" chapter of *The Web and the Rock*, he took poetic license to mold these words into his own design.

For several months, beginning in 1929, Wolfe had been recording in his notebooks material about Bernstein's childhood, material to which he would refer early in "The October Fair" ledgers as "the Esther stories." One of his first comprehensive outlines for "The October Fair" contained two chapter headings directly related to the material concerning Esther's early years: "A Woman's Life," which was at times either a variant of or a companion title for "The Good Child's River," and "Early Sorrow," which served for a brief period as the title for the material later called "In the

6. "The October Fair" ledgers are part of the vast collection of Thomas Wolfe manuscripts housed at Harvard University's Houghton Library. This material is listed under the call numbers bMS Am 1883 (241) to (278). All references to material from "The October Fair" ledgers are contained within these call numbers. For a fascinating account of Wolfe's various writing projects during his Guggenheim year, see chapter 14 of *The Window of Memory*, entitled "Seed Time."

7. Stutman, ed., *My Other Loneliness*, p. 304.

8. Ibid.

Park." On July 31, he had written to Maxwell Perkins, his editor at Scribner's: "I am now at work on a section of 'The Immortal Earth' which has the curious title of 'The Good Child's River.' I like the title and hope you will too when you see the story: it is complete in itself, and very long—a short book—and I will send it to you when it's finished."[9]

Yet although Wolfe labored to conclude "The Good Child's River" project, he was unable to do so, for other current writings were pulling at him as well. In September 1930, he recorded his dilemma in his notebook: "I have started three books and written twenty or thirty thousand words on each—I *must* finish one. Which?"[10] The three works to which he was referring included the material about the love story in "The October Fair," Esther's early life, and a narrative about a trip on the train.[11] For *Look Homeward*,

9. Wolfe, *Letters*, p. 247.

10. Wolfe, *Notebooks*, p. 509.

11. See ibid., n. 15. In her biography, Nowell gives this assessment of Wolfe's work during this period: ". . . his notebook at this time is filled with lists of books or portions of books. Chief among these were *The Fast Express*, or a part of it which he called 'K 19'; 'Antaeus,' or 'The Immortal Earth,' and other sections of his long book, *The October Fair*. There was also *The River People*, which he evidently still thought of as a separate book. There was *The Good Child's River*, which was to describe the early life of Mrs. Bernstein and which he sometimes thought of as a separate book, sometimes as a part of *The October Fair*. . . . And there were also many lists of titles, such as *Early Sorrow*, *Early Harvest*, *Delicate Death*, *Delicate Time*, *The Deep River*, *Call for the Robin*, which he may have intended for *Hunger* or *The Good Child's River*, or for both. Most of these books were basically parts of Wolfe's own long story, in spite of his attempt to divide them into separate units" (Nowell's italics). Nowell, *Wolfe*, p. 181. Of this material, Donald writes: "A good many long fragments, to which he sometimes gave the general title 'Faust and Helen' but more often called 'The October Fair,' formed a fictional account of his affair with Aline Bernstein. Another group of manuscripts, which he named 'The Good Child's River,' was based on the recollections that Aline kept sending him; it reconstructed her life in the years before he met her. To a third category of material Wolfe gave an eighteenth-century title: 'The Strange Life and Adventures of Mr. David "Monkey" Hawke, a gentleman of good family, of his early youth, of his wanderings in America and Europe, and of his remarkable search to find his father, and how he found him.' All three of these stories were incomplete; they were only in a very loose sense interrelated; and each of them, if finished, would run far longer than the average novel." Donald, *Look Homeward*, pp. 245–46.

Angel, he had been able to follow a chronological path, enabling him to retain a tighter focus on his material as well as on his energies. Of his present state, he wrote: "I am all broken up in fragments myself at present and all that I can write is fragments. The man is his work: if the work is whole, the man must be whole."[12] Wolfe would bring his story of the love affair to the fullest conclusion of the three books and leave behind in both "K19" (the train narrative) and "The Good Child's River" a wealth of publishable material; regrettably, he never had the opportunity to complete any of these stories himself.

Wolfe continued his penchant for recording titles for his projected work about Esther's early life. He placed possibility after possibility into his ledger, starring his favorites. Once he had decided, he inscribed his new title, along with its respective quotation, on the page:

The Good Child's River
By
Thomas Wolfe

"By night on my bed I sought him whom my soul
loveth: I sought him, but I found him not."[13]

On the next page of his ledger, he recorded Esther's theme, already altered to satisfy his purpose:

"—Long, long into the night I lay thinking how I
should begin to tell my story."

12. Wolfe, *Notebooks*, p. 494.

13. In one of his notebooks, Wolfe had recorded:

THE GOOD CHILD'S RIVER
The Story of a Woman's Life
By
Thomas Wolfe

THE GOOD CHILD'S RIVER
The Story of a True Woman
By
Thomas Wolfe
O sweeter than the berry, and redder than the cherry!

Kennedy and Reeves inform us that the quotation is a variation from John Gay's *Avis and Galatea*. Wolfe, *Notebooks*, p. 484 and n. 49.

Wolfe's first formally recorded title for "The October Fair" in his ledger indicates that, from the beginning, the stories of his hero and heroine were inextricably woven together. His characterizations of the two and the connection between them were as grand and all-encompassing as the earth itself:

The October Fair
A Vision
The Child, The Mistress, and the Woman
The Son, The Lover, and the Wanderer
The Sea, the City, and the Earth
By
Thomas Wolfe

From August 1930 until February 1931, Wolfe continued working on his Esther stories in "The October Fair." Toward the end of this manuscript, probably around the time he resumed meeting with Bernstein after returning from his Guggenheim trip abroad in March 1931, he began writing sketches that he later incorporated in the three ledgers of "The Good Child's River." Although the first brief outline for this projected material is entitled "Chapter 4," it actually relates episodes from the first chapter of "The Good Child's River" and parallels the beginning of Bernstein's autobiographical novel, *An Actor's Daughter*.

Here Wolfe began to develop the character of Robert, Esther's shy cousin, who stutters and who runs to the theater to tell Joe Barrett, Esther's father, that his first child has been born. By this time Wolfe had begun thinking that he would incorporate "The October Fair" material into his projected work, *Of Time and the River*. Originally, he had intended to include the love story and Esther's stories of her early life in the context of the hero's first year in the city and his expanding vision of life. In the extended outline that he wrote in 1933 and submitted to Maxwell Perkins with his manuscript, he placed Esther's stories in section 8 of *Of Time and the River*, covering the period from October 1925 to June 1926.[14] The first chapter in this section was entitled "The City Again: Meeting with Esther, Esther's House, Beginning of Love Episodes." Chapter 2 was called "Esther's Life and Former History Told in

14. See Wolfe, *Notebooks*, pp. 632–33.

Her Own Dialog."[15] In an early statement of purpose that he recorded in "The October Fair" ledgers, as he continued to work on his plans for "The Good Child's River," Wolfe wrote:

The October Fair
Preface to Of Time and the River

The author had first of all this purpose:
To tell as completely as possible the story of a woman's life from the time of her birth to the end of physical fertility and the apex of her creative power. For this purpose he has chosen to describe a woman whose life fulfilled itself completely in every spiritual and physical activity: in marriage, in children, in love, in art, and finally, as a person living on the earth among two billion other persons.

Although Wolfe continued to write about Esther's youth, he remained preoccupied with the love story. Several variations of David's meeting with Esther aboard ship appear in the ledgers. It was his intention to include the story of Esther's early life as "told in her own dialog" in "The October Fair" manuscript and to contain it within the tale of the hero's first year in the city. In one of his final outlines, Wolfe included virtually all of what would become the "Penelope's Web" material in *The Web and the Rock*, crossing out the title "The Good Child's River" and replacing it with "Delicate Time":

"Long, long into the night"
Letter to Uncles
Daddy & Mother on the ship
Wilkie Collins
Then noted for muh torso
The Good Child's River
—Wilkie Collins
—The Bridge
—Daddy: Enter, Daughter of Desolation—etc.
—Bella—Her House
—Death of Daddy (coming into his room)
—Auntie Kate

15. Ibid.

"The October Fair" ledgers conclude with text related to his episode "In the Park," a section of manuscript that he had originally written soon after beginning "The October Fair." It is interesting to note that Wolfe was not yet satisfied with this material; indeed, as his editors would discover, he was rarely satisfied with what he had written: manuscripts had to be extricated from his grasp—and even then he would continue to think of changes. There is also a variant of the Polonius Potts material, within "The Good Child's River" ledgers, as well as a brief version of Esther's charming letter to her uncles, Fred and John, those wonderful characters who populate her early life. With many of the Esther stories already created, Wolfe was ready to "begin again" his narrative of "the good child" from a new focus, commencing with the day of her birth.

Wolfe had not written or responded to her letters for several months, and shortly after his arrival in New York in March 1931, Aline Bernstein, on hearing of his return, became ill and required hospitalization. When he learned of her illness, he wrote her a letter declaring his love and loyalty and focusing on his writings about her:

> I could never write a word about you or about my love for you in print that was not full of that love I bear you—no matter what bitter things we have said, I remember what was glorious magnificent and lovely, and I remember all that was beautiful and grand in you: all of my hope now and for the future is that I can wreak out of pain, hunger, and love a living memorial for you: I can not think of other men, or reputation, I am living alone with little money, and have forgotten the literary world—but if ever I put down what is in my heart, what I have known and felt, and the glory and magnificence I have known through you—then men all over this earth will be moved by it, and will know that it is true. I shall never do anything that concerns you in any way, never write a word that may concern you, without your seeing it, and your decision in it will be in all ways final. . . . As for me, I shall love you all the days of my life and when I die, if they cut me open they will find one name written on my brain and on my heart. It will be yours.[16]

16. Stutman, ed., *My Other Loneliness*, p. 304.

This letter effected a reconciliation between the two, and they began meeting weekly, often on Thursday, in Wolfe's small apartment in Brooklyn. For a time he worked almost entirely on "The Good Child's River" manuscript—most probably on the second sequence he had begun drafting in "The October Fair" ledgers. He began researching old newspapers and magazines in the New York Public Library in hopes of capturing the flavor of the old New York. In his attempt to re-create the past, he looked up the addresses of Joseph Frankau, Bernstein's father, in the *New York City Directory* and visited the original sites. He examined old photographs of houses that were like those in which Frankau had lived. He read Percy MacKaye's biography, *Epoch*, about the life of Percy's father, Steele MacKaye, the author of the play *Hazel Kirke*; Joseph Frankau, a member of the original cast with Effie Ellsler, also mentioned in "The Good Child's River," played on Broadway at the New Madison Square Theater for several years. In fact, Steele MacKaye had written the part of the comic character "Met" into his play especially for Joe Frankau. Met was Frankau's best role, and *Hazel Kirke* was one of the most successful stage productions of the period. The "wonderful elevator stage" referred to in "The Good Child's River" was indeed one of the marvels of the modern theater.

Bernstein, happy to be included in his life once again, began once more to supply Wolfe with accounts of her childhood, stories that focused on her actor father and her beloved Aunt Nana. Throughout 1931, her letters reflect upon the stories he was writing about her life. In May, she wrote from her home in Armonk, New York:

> I was terribly tired and excited, what you read to me of the book is the finest thing I have ever known. . . . What you read to me was so grand, so valuable so beautiful, that I feel my life is not lost if it can make the stuff for you to work with. I have so much more to tell you. You are writing a book that no one has approached, and I am telling you what no one has told before. . . . —I know that you are of the great people of the world,—and I know I am of the great people of the world, for not age time abuse nor scorification of the heart can change my

love. I can stand upon the heights with you, and I can bear all pain if I can serve you.[17]

She signed her letter "Aline Scheherazade."

In June, she bravely carried on, trying to be—as Wolfe wished—a friend and companion, and nothing more. In the meantime, she continued her journey with him into her past:

I have asked at the Astor hotel if I can go into 218 W. 45th. They will let me know next week.—We will take a trip backwards and maybe find some ghosts. Maybe Nana and Daddy will be there and you can see if they fit [in]to what I have told you. Time backwards maybe is a dream. God bless you, I wish you could have more jolly times, but you will, and this hard time is making the way for it.—I am sure this book will be so beautiful, so grand, and what is more will be such a surprise and revelation to every body.—Your dear old friend. Aline[18]

In another June letter, she mentioned a tea party of her Aunt Nana's, which appeared in Wolfe's outlines as "Nana's Pink Tea" and which Bernstein later described in chapter 3 of *The Journey Down*. In September, she informed Wolfe that she would arrange for him to see a "great collection of prints and photographs of New York City" that she apparently had just heard about. She wrote wistfully: "Maybe you will find a picture with Nana walking down the street, in her tight fitting princess dress. She used to say the dressmaker broke her thumbs smoothing out the wrinkles."[19] Her dedication to him and to his project about her is reflected at the end of her letter: "I haven't been away for so long. But I will do nothing until the book is ready. I love you forever. Aline[.]"[20]

In the fall of 1931, Wolfe showed signs of tiring of "The Good Child's River" material. Although continuing to write about Esther's early life, he began to focus on the life of her father, Joe, and on an autobiographical character he called "Monkey Hawke." Indeed, as "The Good Child's River" manuscript illustrates, their

17. Ibid., p. 329.
18. Ibid., p. 331.
19. Ibid., p. 336.
20. Ibid, p. 337.

personalities had become so interchangeable that in some of the later episodes he replaced the name of Joe with Monkey. His disorganized and somewhat frantic writing at the end of "The Good Child's River" reflects Wolfe's growing distraction. Literally, the story of Joe began to take precedence over that of Esther, a change in direction that eventually led to a dead end. Wolfe had been unable to come to grips with the passions his writings about the love affair had aroused in him; finally, his stories about Esther and her family had reduced him to a state of exhaustion and extreme distress. As Elizabeth Nowell concluded about Wolfe's work on "Death the Proud Brother" and "The Good Child's River," "Both . . . were fine material, but they were both digressions, and for months on end they diverted his time and strength from the writing of his main narrative."[21]

In November Bernstein sent Wolfe a batch of writing so thick that it had to be contained in two large envelopes, but he did not use it; moreover, he gave no indication that he had received this material until after their final breakup in January 1932.[22] In an unsent letter written soon after their separation, he alluded to his Esther stories: "I have a wonderful memory for anything that

21. Nowell, *Wolfe*, p. 202. In *Look Homeward* (p. 246), Donald refers to the significance of the Esther material: "Aline's history was important if only because it would demonstrate that he [Wolfe] could write something other than autobiography—about people he did not know, and about a time before he had even been born." Of the importance for publishing these fragments, he notes (p. 483): "Still another possibility [for Edward Aswell] would have been the publication of several small volumes, each containing a segment of Wolfe's manuscript that was self-contained and in most nearly finished shape. In some ways such little books would have been good for Wolfe's critical reputation. They would have demonstrated that, whatever Wolfe's limitations in crafting a long novel, he displayed a splendid sense of artistry in the short novel of 15,000 to 40,000 words. . . . Years later C. Hugh Holman edited five of *The Short Novels of Thomas Wolfe*, which reminded readers that this was the form in which Wolfe worked best."

22. The batch included a sketch called "Love in Europe," which eventually became the second chapter in Bernstein's book, *The Journey Down*, entitled "The Apple Tree, the Singing, and the Gold"; sketches about her Aunt Nana, later to be found in *An Actor's Daughter*; and the sketch "Mr. Frolich," which became part of her 1933 book, *Three Blue Suits*.

interests me[,] and for 40 or 50000 words I have made a woman called Esther Jacobs talk magnificently."[23] Within a short time, in another unsent letter, Wolfe wrote to Bernstein about her sketches and his own:

> I have not written you about your pieces before because I have been too tired at night to read them. I have read nothing. But tonight I did read them and they are very fine. The one about Nana's Party is grand and you ought to get it published. So is the other one, although I gather there is more to follow— *The Three Blue Suits*. I shall keep them and treasure them, or do whatever you want me to do with them, but I can't use them. I tried to write a piece about you once, but, as you know, it turned out to be no good. Maybe I'll try it again someday, but not for many years. I can't do it now, what I write about it seems to have no reality.[24]

At the end of this letter, he added: "From now on I shall put nothing on paper but what I have seen or known—my vision of life. That's all there is to write about."[25]

During these difficult months Wolfe had come to realize that his material, with its numerous characters and various episodes, was too gargantuan to contain within a single frame. In *The Story of a Novel*, he wrote of this period:

> I was convinced at that time that this whole gigantic plan had to be realized within the limits of a single book which would be called "The October Fair." . . . I would work furiously day after day until my creative energies were utterly exhausted, and although at the end of such a period I would have written perhaps as much as 200,000 words, enough in itself to make a very long book, I would realize with a feeling of horrible despair that what I had completed was only one small section of a single book.[26]

23. Stutman, ed., *My Other Loneliness*, p. 342.
24. Ibid., p. 345.
25. Ibid.
26. Wolfe, *The Story of a Novel*, pp. 53–54.

In August 1931, Maxwell Perkins had asked Wolfe to submit his manuscript "completely finished" by September, to which Wolfe responded:

> I know you are not joking and that you mean *this* September. . . . and whether I have anything that I would be willing to show anyone next September, or any succeeding one for the next 150 years, is at present a matter of the extremist and most painful doubt to me.[27]

But Wolfe and Perkins did agree that a manuscript must be submitted, and Perkins began once again to assist Wolfe in this process of creation.

Wolfe seemed determined to begin anew. On returning to his vast body of previous writing, he began to disconnect and reorganize material. On April 15, 1932, in a letter to his English publisher, A. S. Frere-Reeves, he wrote: " 'The October Fair' will not be one novel, but a series of novels, and each, I hope, complete in itself but all related to a single thing."[28] Although he worked on the first portion, "K 19," for several months, it did not fall together, and in June Perkins informed him that it would not stand as a separate novel. Once more Wolfe began to search his massive manuscript for the key to the puzzle that would enable him to reorganize and "reinvent" his vast body of material in novel form.

Finally, in February 1933, he wrote to his mother that "after all these months of desperate effort and confusion I have seemed to begin to unravel the knot and to have found the way to get started . . . and the whole river now seems to be flowing."[29] As Elizabeth Nowell notes, ". . . he had failed to come to grips with his new book, but had hedged and feinted all around it, writing hundreds of thousands of words of perfectly magnificent material, but material which, for the most part, had got him nowhere."[30] Once he envisioned this "new" work, based on his own vision of life, his restructuring and revision of the manuscript, which would be en-

27. Wolfe, *Letters*, p. 304.
28. Ibid., p. 333.
29. Wolfe, *Letters to His Mother*, p. 196.
30. Nowell, *Wolfe*, p. 216.

titled *Of Time and the River*, although still months in the making, began to come more easily.

"The Good Child's River," however, remained very much in the past, as circumstances kept Wolfe from both the material about the love affair and the Esther stories for several years. Meanwhile, he struggled to contain and to unify his vast "October Fair" manuscript, and in May 1933 he signed a contract with Scribner's for *Of Time and the River*, to be published in the fall. The third section of the novel, "Faust and Helen," was to deal with the love affair. A detailed typescript, which Wolfe delivered to Perkins with the material in late November 1933, indicates that he had decided to include in the story of the hero's first year in the city Esther's account of her early life. Nevertheless, it was determined, principally by Perkins, that because of the inordinate length of the text as well as apprehension about Bernstein's reaction, only the first half of the manuscript would be published under the title, *Of Time and the River*. The material concerning the love story, entitled "The October Fair," dealing initially with the period from 1925 to 1928 and later expanded by Wolfe to include 1929 and 1930, would be brought out at a later date. Since some connection between these two novels was necessary, a new section, book 7, was created and named "Kronos and Rhea: The Dream of Time." This section contains the scene in which Eugene first sees Esther on board ship and instantly falls in love with her.

In the fall of 1935, after the publication of *Of Time and the River*, Wolfe did return briefly to "The October Fair." The chapter outline he recorded in his ledger indicates that he still intended to incorporate "The Good Child's River" in this projected novel. Chapter 7 was to encompass "The Great World: (as it begins to come to him through Esther) 1) the Great World As It Comes to Him through Esther's Stories, References to People she knows, etc."[31] However, unable to come to terms with this material because of the storm of emotion it aroused in him, he soon set it aside once more to work on other projects.

In the fall of 1936, Wolfe resumed work on a new autobiographical novel, "The Vision of Spangler's Paul," much of which later

31. Wolfe, *Notebooks*, p. 768.

became part 1 of *The Web and the Rock*. Stung by critics' negative reaction to the influence of Maxwell Perkins on his published work, and straining to release himself from what he felt to be another entrapping relationship, Wolfe broke with his editor at Scribner's as he had earlier wrenched himself from Bernstein.

After much hesitation and soul-searching, Wolfe finally decided in December 1937 to sign with Harper and to work with the young, southern-born editor, Edward Aswell. The contract with his new publisher was for a book to be tentatively called "The Life and Adventures of Bondsman Doaks." A synopsis of its contents, written in the early months of 1938, again refers to much of the Esther material. In part 5, entitled "The Oktoberfest," #7 in his outline reads: "Time Interlude Again: 'Long, Long into the Night I Lay' etc., the Park, In the Park, the Good Child's River: Esther's reverie." [32]

In the first months of 1938, Wolfe worked furiously on his manuscript, making it increasingly autobiographical. In March, he pulled together much of the material from his previous writings, primarily from "Spangler's Paul" and "The October Fair." After selecting a new title, *The Web and the Rock*, and a new name for his hero, Wolfe set to work again. Finally, on May 11, 1938, he delivered to his new editor a huge package of typescript containing the complete manuscript.

Aswell had a Herculean task in editing the vast maze of material that had been left in his hands by Thomas Wolfe before Wolfe's tragic and untimely death. While varying in the extent of their indictment of Aswell, most Wolfe scholars argue, and I agree, that while he at times moved beyond the boundaries of accepted editorial policy, the posthumous novels generally are true to Wolfe's intent. But the great tragedy remains that we cannot know what Thomas Wolfe would have done with these materials had he lived to complete them. According to Aswell and Wolfe's agent, Elizabeth Nowell, Wolfe was dissatisfied with the material about the love affair and probably would have revised it.

And what of "The Good Child's River," that magnificent "di-

---

32. Ibid., p. 932. In this outline, the editors have written Wolfe's probable misprint, "revelry," and have included in brackets their suggested correction, "reverie."

gression" that took Wolfe away from his autobiographical mode into the world and vision of Esther Jack, giving the author the imaginative wings with which to enter the mind and heart and vision of, not only a child, a female child, but also a Jewish child, this male southern Protestant writer so often accused of anti-Semitism? [33] Was it a digression or merely a prophesy of what new worlds still lay within his imaginative grasp, just waiting to be explored? Would he have finished the tale of Esther and Joe and Bella and the numerous other wonderful characters who populated their world? Would Wolfe, who used everything possible from his giant work in progress, have returned to this novel in his greater maturity and molded it to completion? Like an unfinished symphony, it remains, a tribute to its author and a testimony to what might have been.

"The Time That Is Lovely"

Wolfe's initial segment of text and chapter I of this edition—"The Time That Is Lovely"—begins with a song of lost time and of the tragedy of lost childhood. As in *Of Time and the River*, the river represents the flow of all time—past, present, and future. And as in *Look Homeward, Angel*, the symbol of the water is used to carry the reader back into the lost world of childhood, the "good time," the world of innocence, spontaneity, and "unmindful time." It is important to remember that the voice of Esther, which is consistent throughout this first portion of "The Good Child's River," is the voice of an artist. In recapturing the world of the past, she reveals a perception that is pristine, sensual, and aware of every detail, bringing the reader fully into the picture that is so lovingly sketched. It is the desire of Esther to capture the complexities of memory while retaining the essence of character and experience.

From the beginning, we are introduced to the world around us through the eye of the speaker, who describes all experience with a sense of sound, of music, of awe and splendor that permeates

33. For a detailed discussion of Wolfe's anti-Semitism, as well as his attitude toward minorities in general, see Reeves, *Thomas Wolfe's Albatross*; Klein, *Aline*; and Donald, *Look Homeward*.

these scenes of life. Here is presented childhood at its most enchanting, with Daddy and Bella the beautiful and beloved prince and princess of her world. All is captured with the truth and certainty of childhood, the Platonic sense of knowledge, "like getting back to the place where all things come from." We observe the wonderful whimsy and imagination of Daddy as he dubs his beloved child "Princess Arabella Clementina Sapolio Von Hoggenheim"; the magical ventriloquism in the episode of "the Bridge" and the accent of the Bridge's creator, who sounds like a magical old toy maker out of a child's fairy tale; the exquisite descriptions, Daddy with his hair "like bright sand," the wagons crawling over the Bridge like "tiny dots of men," and Bella, lush and lovely and bigger than life; the beauty of Esther's vision, which enables her, as she explains to Richard Brandell, "to see a forest in a leaf, the whole earth in a single face"; her sense of imagery and design as she describes "knives, flashing with light like a river"; and, later, her awareness of the world of the theater, "a thousand people who have suddenly become a single living creature." This, indeed, was "Esther's vision, as told in her own dialogue."

Edward Aswell made few additions to this text, but he did edit or eliminate passages that either had been printed earlier or contained material he viewed as controversial. He "framed" the chapter, "Penelope's Web," in *The Web and the Rock* by connecting it to the general story line, focusing not only on the theme of the hero's enhanced and transcendent vision as experienced through his heroine's memory and perception, but also on the larger theme of a "new America." Cut from "Penelope's Web" were the odes to time and memory, which already had been published in *Of Time and the River*. Instead of Wolfe's formal separations between passages, Aswell used an extra space to connote the shift in anecdotes. He rearranged passages in order to accommodate more gracefully the parts that he had edited from Wolfe's original typescript. Some small changes, such as substituting "the next year" for "that year," altered Wolfe's original time sequence. Aswell also revised Wolfe's characteristic punctuation, changing several of his colons to periods. Finally, he generally altered names—for example, Uncle Jake, the policeman who gave Daddy a job, became Uncle Bob.

When Esther's vision appeared to waver and to transform itself into one of her creator's digressions, Aswell was careful to edit.

For example, Richard Brandell begins to rant against the "rivals and enemies" plotting against him; perhaps because this episode sounded more like Wolfe than the character, Aswell simply cut the passage. Also deleted from the Brandell material was the manuscript of "In the Park," which Aswell cut from the typescript and the final manuscript presumably because it had already appeared in both *Harper's Bazaar* and *From Death to Morning*. The editor omitted most of Esther's references to the theater and to the ham actor, Atwater, but retained, earlier in sequence and out of context, her humorous recollection of Atwater's pompous phrase, "As for me, I am noted for muh Torso." Excluded were references to the experimental play *The Adding Machine*, as well as several unflattering comments about Jewish actors and playwrights, which sound more like the author's ideas and prejudices than Esther Jack's. Esther's mystically sensuous passage about her nude swimming was eliminated, as was the humorous passage about Miss Titsworth and Mr. Matchem.

For the most part, then, Aswell apparently cut material that he considered to be repetitious, controversial, or out of character for Esther and for Richard Brandell, while maintaining the essence of Esther's persona and her vision of life. Certainly, Wolfe's original transcript gives to this early sequence the fuller, more mythical sense of time and memory that the writer had intended. "In the Park," one of Wolfe's finest works of fiction, enhances the overall picture of lost time and character forever captured throughout this segment. It is interesting that in the published short story version of "In the Park," the convent sequence was excluded. Perhaps Elizabeth Nowell felt that this segment was digressive and, with Wolfe's permission, cut it from the text.

It is fascinating to compare the works of Thomas Wolfe and Aline Bernstein, particularly the way in which each makes use of the same material. In the front of Bernstein's book, *An Actor's Daughter*, is the passage, taken from her earlier letter to Wolfe, that would serve as a vital source to both writers:

> Long, long into the night, I lay awake,
> trying to think how best to tell my story.

Bernstein's account of her life and "The Good Child's River" ledgers begin in the same way: with her birth on a December night in 1881. But there are several differences. In Bernstein's book, in which Wolfe's twelve-year-old Robert becomes ten-year-old Edgar, there are no negative references to the boy's being Jewish—indeed, no such allusions exist anywhere in Bernstein's work. In addition, no mention is made of his stuttering, a condition that Wolfe seems to have established in the creation of his character. Although Bernstein's father was of mixed stock, his mother, the daughter of a respected Connecticut family, had converted to Judaism, in fact, living in a rabbi's house for an entire year until she was fully versed in that faith. In Bernstein's words, her grandmother was "lovely," possessing "dignity and beauty and . . . spiritual value"[34]—a far cry from Joe Barrett's evil mother in Wolfe's version of the tale. Bernstein's grandfather did fight in the Civil War, but he was only slightly wounded, and Joe's father did not die a horrible death. Her mother's mother died after giving birth to her youngest daughter Rachel, or Nana, and the grandfather so negatively characterized in "The Three Sisters" died before Bernstein was born. Nana's husband, Uncle Ben, was also a doctor, but he was Jewish, not Gentile, as Wolfe depicted him, and Nana's married name was Greenfield. Cousin Julia, or Aunt Harriet (Aunt Hugh in "The Good Child's River"), was really a writer, but she had three children, not one, and did not have a tubercular husband on whom she cheated and whom she came to despise.

Bella and Joe, those characters so romantically depicted in "The Good Child's River," are much more realistically, though no less lovingly, portrayed in *An Actor's Daughter* and *The Journey Down*; in her autobiography, Bernstein writes of Nana's morphine addiction and of Daddy's drinking and running around. And Mama, Bernstein's beloved and guiding presence, is given a much more important place in Bernstein's re-creation of her early life than in Wolfe's fictional one. Indeed, Bernstein, who views her father and aunt as both beautiful and flawed, writes of her mother: "Mama should have had a happier life; she should have been married to a different type of man, and although they both loved her, Daddy and Nana should have given more thought to her."[35]

34. Bernstein, *An Actor's Daughter*, p. 6.
35. Ibid., p. 150.

Several episodes receive the same treatment in both works. School was, as Bernstein recounts it, an uncomfortable place; like her counterpart in *Look Homeward, Angel*, the little boy who could at times have been her brother in spirit, she turned from the painful world of reality into the wonderful world of her secret life. She did have a friend named Jean who lived across the street and with whom she walked to school, and her fear of lateness was so great that for a time she woke in the morning fully dressed. She would walk home past Brewster's Carriage Works and the Horse Market, a path similar to the one Esther takes in chapter VII of "The Good Child's River."

As Esther recounts her remembrance of listening to her parents' aftertheater parties, Aline Bernstein recalls listening through the vent to the goings-on in the dining room below. And there *was* an actor named Dixey, who was a friend of Joe Frankau's. The Russian nurse Annushka, referred to in the lovely fragment about Esther's mother's illness (see Appendix B, section II), is named Sister Augusta in *An Actor's Daughter*. The two Catholic priests of "In the Time That Is Lovely" are remembered by Bernstein for their kindness when they came to talk to Mama before she died. Daddy's sister, Aunt Gert, was not a cruel Christian aunt who squandered away the orphan sisters' money, as portrayed in "The Good Child's River," but "one of his sisters who had a big house uptown, with a whole floor we could have to ourselves."[36] The marvelous tea party of "Nana's Pink Tea" in *The Journey Down* is mentioned as well in "The Three Sisters," but the conversation between the two sisters seems a far cry from the way Nana and Mama would really have spoken.

Like Wolfe's Esther, Aline Bernstein spent many magical moments with her father, going to the opera and the theater and to Healy's after the concerts in the summer with a Father Flannery and Father Chris O'Reagan. At the end of *An Actor's Daughter* is her recollection of the automobile ride in the park that each writer was to immortalize. Her vision is no less magical than Wolfe's as she captures the moment of happiness that will live in her heart forever and the pain that immediately follows, for, in truth, her father died that very night: "Never any more, no, no more of those

36. Ibid., p. 207.

little things, I always have this night, this black perfection, flying through the park, cleansed of petty sin by the wind. I had Daddy with me, and the priests, whom I loved, and I had Nana with me already, tomorrow."[37]

What becomes obvious, then, is that Wolfe borrowed liberally from the facts of Bernstein's life in constructing his story. In doing so he created a character who is, like her prototype, unflinchingly honest and gracious and kind, one who is able to express and capture her vision of life through her depiction of her family and her own experiences. But Esther's story is not always Bernstein's story. It must be remembered that although "The Good Child's River" is based on the life and character of Aline Bernstein, Thomas Wolfe created much of what he wrote from the fabric of his imagination.

The vision of Esther is reminiscent of a quote from a Bernstein letter to Wolfe while he was working on the characterization that would immortalize her: ". . . this is what I think," she wrote, "there is nothing in life that cannot be made beautiful."[38] The persona of Esther captures the essence of experience through the sensibility of touch, sound, smell, and sight, all blended with the wonderful genius of imagination. So true is Esther's vision, so vivid is Wolfe's creation, that Esther seems in this chapter of "The Good Child's River" almost truly to have conquered time, to have accomplished what Quentin Compson yearned for: the timeless transcendence into immortality in the creation of the eternal moment.

"The Good Child's River" Ledgers

Three ledgers in Harvard's Houghton Library are entitled "The Good Child's River." In these ledgers, Thomas Wolfe continued the story of many of the marvelous characters that populate "The Time That Is Lovely." The character of Esther is virtually unchanged from this first segment of the text: her consciousness remains the golden thread that binds together past and present, and her exquisite perception of life, often hypnotic in its quiet lyricism, offers the reader a mesmerizing vision not only of the people

37. Ibid., p. 221.
38. Stutman, ed., *My Other Loneliness*, p. 334.

who populate the domain of her memory, but also of New York at the turn of the century. In "The Good Child's River," Thomas Wolfe has "become" the storyteller, the muse, the feminine and often Jewish consciousness that focuses this tale.

Time plays a prominent role in chapter II of this edition, becoming almost a character: "Slowly, solemnly, remote and elfin as time's memory, the small clock in the room below struck out nine strokes of golden sweetness. The sound thronged through the dark and living silence of the house: it was a music sunken in a far sea-depth, and its chime inhabited the house with its phantasmal magic." Like a fairy tale, this story of a rich and buried life continues.

Developed in this chapter are the magic of Bella and Daddy and their importance to Esther's life. The characterization of Robert and his relationship with his Uncle Joe are also significant. Wolfe identified closely with Bernstein's father, Joseph Frankau; he even kept a picture of him on his mirror. In the later segments of "The Good Child's River" manuscript, he occasionally crossed out Joe's name and substituted "I" in its place. Wolfe is careful to point out that Uncle Joe is a Gentile and therefore separate from the Jewish world that exists about him, a world that he can inhabit but with which he can never become fully one.

In the feminine spirit, particularly through the character of Esther, the author is able to enter this "other" world, to travel into the very center of the Jewish experience and its wisdom of the ages. Bella and Aunt Mary, like Esther herself, contain within them knowledge of both joy and sorrow, time and death; through the knowledge of life's experience from time's beginning to its end, they can transcend into exultancy and therefore conquer life. His men are not so fortunate. Joe, among these Jewish women but not of them, can give to Robert only the wisdom of the moment. Though exuberant and gifted and larger than life, he somehow remains an exile, lost and alone, much like Wolfe himself.

In chapter III, Esther creates a memory piece, focusing on the actors and their families and the loneliness they face in the empty waiting rooms of train stations at night. Wolfe fights against his own prejudice toward actors to present Esther's vision of these fantastic grown children who deal in the magic of other people's words and characters. We see them joking and sparring and band-ing together to conquer the silence of the night while waiting for the train that will take them to yet another temporary destination. In this chapter are blended not only Esther's memories of her father, so gracious and joyful, but also Wolfe's own love of trains and the wanderlust of crossing his own glorious America. The vision of the artist and the painter is united into the music of language as Esther reflects on the conquest of the evening and the coming of the new day: "Bright morning sparkled on the tracks, and before my vision the powerful rails bent out of sight like space and music."

Try as he might, Thomas Wolfe was never able to exorcise the demons of prejudice that occasionally overtook him. His description of Robert at the beginning of chapter IV presents a harsh divergence from the characterization of Esther and sounds like her creator instead: "he was only a blur of fat boy face with a carroty twist of red Jew's hair." Robert thinks about his beloved Uncle Joe as he sits in the dark, ignored by everyone around him because of Esther's impending birth. Although Robert seems rather immature for a twelve-year-old and too ready to believe what his uncle tells him, the humor of the segment and the wonderful sparkle of Joe Barrett comes through. Joe's reaction to being told he has a daughter sounds more like the reaction of Thomas Wolfe than the narration of Esther: "My father stared at Robert for a moment: then suddenly he turned his face away into his hand and for a moment he wept bitterly, for joy, for relief, and for sorrow, because a sentence of death was in his heart and he had wanted, as all men do, a son." Yet the magic is recaptured by the end of this chapter as Joe looks upon his daughter. The author takes a moment and, through his artistry, turns it to gold: "Her eyes are two black buttons and they are looking straight at me because she knows I am her father."

"My Father's Youth"—chapter V—weaves together many anecdotes; indeed, Wolfe excels as a short story writer, and throughout "The Good Child's River" he accomplishes his greatest writing when he captures and encapsulates unified moments in time and experience. In this segment, along with his almost totally fictitious account of Joe Barrett's heritage and his bitter harangue against his mother, are two of Wolfe's best stories: the tale of Joe's travels with the circus and the anecdote of the cherry tree.

When I initially read the first five-hundred-page handwritten ledger of "The Good Child's River" manuscript, I noticed that nearly one hundred pages had been removed. Later, acting on a hunch, I returned to the Houghton Library in search of the missing pages. As I had suspected, they were entitled "The Image of the Circus and His Father's Earth" and had been tucked into the first part of the *Web and the Rock* manuscript. Wolfe had extrapolated this material for use as a short story that was published in 1935; it was reprinted in a prizewinning volume of short stories that appeared in 1936. He had taken his manuscript from "The Good Child's River" and had revised the beginning and the end, presenting this material as a unified short story. With further changes, he incorporated it in the account of Monkey Hawke's childhood in the first section of *The Web and the Rock*. It is important to note that it was Wolfe—not Edward Aswell—who inserted this story in *The Web and the Rock*.

Wolfe's ability to take a portion of one manuscript and add it to another, while utilizing the same material as a separate unit, says much about his writing process. All that he wrote was part of a gigantic work in progress, and as its creator and sole owner, he felt no restrictions in using any of this text whenever and wherever the purpose suited him. Because of this practice, Wolfe's works cannot be considered strictly autobiographical or biographical. In his transmogrification, events may have lost their initial chronology; indeed, they may have been restructured entirely. Moreover, many of his characters, while loosely based on actual people, may have evolved into figures who were more fictional than factual.

Wolfe may have written "His Father's Earth"—in this edition, part of chapter V, "My Father's Youth"—in 1931, when he visited his father's family home in Gettysburg, Pennsylvania. Certainly, Joe's connection to the earth—his travels around America and his vitalistic love of the earth and of the earth's bountiful harvest—is in harmony with Wolfe's own love of the land, food, and travel across America and is reminiscent of his own father's rich and natural earthiness. It remains one of the high points of "The Good Child's River."

Second to this story is Esther's fine account of the legend of the cherry tree, also related in chapter V. This, too, is vintage Wolfe—the narrator sounds less like Esther than perhaps some country storyteller unraveling a regional tall tale. Are its characters, Fred and John and their cantankerous father, so lovingly portrayed by Esther, based on Aline Bernstein's uncles? Bernstein did mention her yearly visits to the farm in Connecticut where her father's family lived and the picnics at which they feasted on fresh-caught fish. Again, the reader is reminded of the love of food, its preparation and its consumption, that was shared by Thomas Wolfe and Aline Bernstein.

As Wolfe traveled further into the world of "The Good Child's River," his writing became increasingly disoriented. As revealed in his brief reference to Monkey Hawke in the circus story, he was moving away from Esther and becoming more and more involved with Joe's story, a story Wolfe easily connected with the tale of his other more autobiographical figure, Monkey Hawke, on which he was simultaneously working.

The voice of Esther, which has made its way through the first two-thirds of "The Good Child's River," is virtually lost in chapter VI, "The Three Sisters." This is so even though there is still a first-person narrator and the story of the Goldsmith family is based on actual events. At times, Wolfe approaches the lyricism of earlier passages, as with Esther's wonderful reverie about the finality and completeness of Jewish women. But, for the most part, as Wolfe lapses into dialogue between the two sisters, Bella and Rebecca, the voice of Esther has disappeared, only to reassert itself briefly in the final paragraphs about Bella's love of the fabulous city. Here is Wolfe at his worst: his feelings about women were ambivalent at best, and his attempt to create a lighthearted, flirtatious, and still-innocent young girl borders on total failure, while Bella's observations about both Jews and women embrace the worst forms of stereotype. A later outline of "The Good Child's River" (see Appendix B, section II) indicates that Wolfe considered placing "The Three Sisters" in a different sequence.

The two stories that follow in chapters VII and VIII are dramatically different from "The Three Sisters" in subject and presentation. Although the first, "Esther," is a fragment, it is closely related to the second, "White Fokes," and would probably have been incorporated into the latter by Wolfe had he returned to this material. Beginning with "Esther," there is a significant change from the first person to the third, a tactic that gives the author more editorial control. Wolfe had not used this device since his early sketches in "The October Fair" material. The writing in both stories is superior to that in "The Three Sisters" in that Wolfe moves from the technique of dramatic dialogue back into the story-telling mode, and he once more focuses on Esther.

But what of Georgia Barnhill, who begins her life within these pages as the daughter of a "German couple" and then quickly becomes of southern descent, reminiscent of Faulkner's Eula Snopes: "large, slow, indolent and indifferent, still definitely 'Southern': immensely vain and ignorant, negroid, sensitive and stubborn in resentment, but incapable of deep penetration of the spirit, as ripe and sensual as a peach." Georgia, a displaced southern phenomenon, appears to be more of the earth than of the city. And these "White Fokes"—particularly the slovenly Mrs. Barnhill, who alludes to the family's aristocratic heritage and "a remote, princely, and awful antiquity," consider themselves to be the "true" Americans, better than the "others" who can never really achieve their stature. As Bella wryly notes to Esther: "Oh *it's* the *white fokes*! . . . White fokes don't have to wash. Don't you know that yet? It's only Jews and niggers who get dirty."

Despite its digressions, "White Fokes" is in many ways a powerful story. Esther displays the same consistency of tone and vision that has carried her character through earlier chapters of "The Good Child's River." Here, once again, is the good child, who, unlike Georgia, accepts people of all backgrounds and heritages, for Joe and Bella have raised her in this way, filling the house with people of "sometimes comically varied" backgrounds who have benefited from their "warm hug" on life. Esther is feminine, innocent, and romantic, in contrast to Georgia, who, ripe and sensual, exudes and celebrates the erotic and the sexual.

Esther's disillusionment on her alienation from Georgia and her distress on hearing the cruel and bitter harangue of Mrs. Barnhill is described in characteristically Wolfean terms: "In herself she felt only the desire for joy, wonder, and exultancy—for the discovery of an earth which had once seemed wonderful but had now betrayed her: she felt herself drowning, the only fish that could not swim or breathe in this sea of abject grey misery and dullness of mankind."

It is the exquisite sense of loss that remains with both Esther and the reader—a loss of something precious and irretrievable, a part of childhood, a remnant of the past never to be recovered, which diminishes moment by moment as each of the sadly worn belongings are carried from the Barnhill house.

In her observations and reveries Esther has indeed created a world populated by a varied mix of people and places, a world textured by her own special vision of life. This character, so sensitive and aware, has presented an assortment of personalities, touching each with her own distinct appreciation for his or her individuality and place in the world. It is a world that the reader feels privileged to have entered.

It is interesting that, aside from Esther, whose personality and vision remain consistent throughout except for a few obvious Wolfean lapses, the female characters in "The Good Child's River" are stilted and unnatural. Bella comes alive through Esther's recollections of her, filtered through the focus of her consciousness, but when she speaks for herself in "The Three Sisters" (chapter VI), she becomes an awkward stick figure, a caricature, unsympathetic and unbelievable. The male characters, on the other hand, are much more sympathetically and realistically depicted.

Its flaws and inconsistencies notwithstanding, "The Good Child's River" is a testimony to the talent of Thomas Wolfe. Certainly, Esther Jack is one of his greatest creations, if not the finest character of his later works. Through her unique vision, Esther enables the reader to journey into the world of old New York and to encounter a segment of American life that has been long forgotten. Her re-creation of the beloved characters who populate this world enables us not only to know and love them, but also to cherish the delicate beauty of their lives and their momentary touch upon this earth. "The Good Child's River" is, finally, a celebration of a love that transcended all other emotions and of the unity of vision that Wolfe sought and was able to achieve in his finest works. It is a living tribute to Esther Jack as well as to its creator.

"The Good Child's River"

by Thomas Wolfe

By night on my bed I sought him whom my soul loveth:

I sought him, but I found him not.

I

The Time That Is Lovely

"Long, long into the night I lay—"
  (One!)
"Long, long into the night I lay awake—"
  (Two!)
"Long, long into the night I lay awake, thinking how I should tell my story!"
  (One, two, three, four! One, two, three, four!)
    Time!
O, there are bells and that is time:
  What time is that?
That was the half hour that the bells were striking,
  And that was time, time, time.
And that was time, dark time. Yes, that was time, time that dark hangs above our heads in lovely bells.
Time. You hang time upon great bells in a tower, you keep time ticking in a delicate pulse upon your wrist, you imprison time within the small coiled wafer of a watch, and each man has his own, a separate, time.
    One!
Now in the dark I hear the boats there in the river.
    Two!
Now I can hear the great horns blowing in the river. Great horns are baying in the harbor's mouth, great horns are lowing in the gulf of night, great ships are putting out to sea.
They call! Ships call! The great ships call!
Hark, then: Hear you now! O hark!

The river is a tide of moving waters; by night it floods the pockets of the Earth. By night it drinks strange time, dark time; by night the river drinks proud potent tides of strange dark time. By night the river draws the tides, proud potent tides of time's dark waters that with champ and lift of teeth, with lapse and reluctivity of their breath, fill with a kissing glut the sockets of the land. Sired by the horses of the sea, maned with the dark: they come.

They come! The great night horsemen come! And the horses of sleep are galloping over the land.

Great whistles blow there. Can you not hear great whistles blow there?

(O now I hear the whistles blowing on the river:)

And there are ships there. Do you not hear the ships there?

(O now great ships are going down the river! O now great ships are putting out to sea!)

A harness of light ships is on the water. A thunder of faint hooves is on the land!

And there is time there! Do you not hear dark time there?

(O now I hear dark time there! Strange time, dark tragic time there! O now I hear dark time, strange time, the dark, the moving tide of time as it flows down the river! And in the night time, in the dark there, in all the sleeping silence of the Earth, I hear the river, the rich immortal river, full of its strange dark time. Full with the pulse of time it flows there, full with the pulse of all men living, sleeping, dying, waking, it will flow there, full with the dark and secret moments of our lives it flows there, in the day time, in the dark, drinking with ceaseless glut the land, mining into its tides the earth as it mines the hours and moments of our life into its tides, moving against the sides of ships, foaming about piled crustings of old wharves, sliding like time and silence by vast cliffs of cities, girdling the isle of life with moving waters—thick with the wastes of earth, dark with our stains, and heavied with our dumpings: rich, rank, beautiful, and unending as all life, all living, as it flows by us, by us, by us, to the sea!)

* * *

There, tell me; tell me, there. Where is lost time now? Where are lost ships, lost faces, and lost love? Where is the lost child now? Did no one see her as the tangled shipping? Did no one see her by light waters? By proud cleavages of forgotten ships at Counties Slip, by forgotten fume-flows of light smoke above Manhattan? Lost? Did no one speak to her? Ah, please! Can no one find her, hold her, keep her—bring her back to me? Gone? Just for a moment, I beseech you, just for a moment out of measured, meted, and unmindful time.

Gone? Then is she lost? Can no one bring me back a child? Why should a dog, a horse, a rat bare lips—at "them"—You'll build great engines yet and taller towers, our dust will tremble to far greater wheels; have you no engines then to bring back sixty seconds of lost time?

Then she is lost.

* * *

And once upon a time there was a tiny little girl, and she was a might pretty sweet little girl, too, and she was awfully smart, she learned to write before she was six years old, and she used to write her dear uncles John and Fred letters and they were great fat fellows, God! how those fellows could eat! *the very best* of everything was *just* about good enough for them, and they simply adored her, and she used to call them her Dere Uncle Honeys: We have a Dog called Roy and he is swete but Bella says he is also messy Sister is lerning to talk and she can now say everything and I am taking french lessons and the tetcher says I can now talk it good I am awfuely smart and good and I think of my dere Uncle Honeys all the time wel that is all Sister sends luv and we know our dere Uncle Honeys will not forget us and will bring something luvly yore darling litel Esther.

* * *

O, but that must have been much later after we came back; yes, I think it must have been a year or two later because all I can remember before is a big boat that went up and down and Mama got awfully sick, God, she was white, I got so frightened and began to cry, and Daddy was so lovely: he brought her champagne, I heard him say, "Here, drink this, you'll feel better," and she said, "O, I can't, I can't!" But she did, everyone always did what he wanted them to do; and I had a nurse called Miss Crampton—isn't that a funny name to have?—and at first we lived behind the museum in Gower Street, then later we were in Tavistock Square, and the milkman had a little cart that he pushed before him and he made a funny noise in his throat, and every morning when he came by they let me go out and sit upon the curb and wait for him, and the sun was like old gold and murky looking, and I gave the man some money, two or three pennies and he said in a loud voice, "There you are, Miss, fresh as a dyesy," and he gave me a *tiny* little bottle of cream and I drank it all right there before him, and gave him back the bottle—God! I was proud, I think I was about three or four years old; and then when I asked Daddy why cream cost so much more than milk he said "Because it's so hard for the cow to sit down on those little bottles," and O! I thought that was so wonderful I couldn't stop thinking about it, and Mama told him he ought to be ashamed of himself talking to a child like that, but there was something so wonderful about him, I believed everything he said.

Then later Daddy was away on a tour with [Richard] Mansfield and Mama went with him and they left me with Auntie May: she had a house in Portman Square, God! what a lovely house that was! She was a writer, she wrote under the name of Hugh Trench, isn't that a queer name for a woman writer to have? She wrote a book called *The Heart of Mile-End Mary*, it was all about a kid who grew up in the east end of London, it was damned good: the whole thing was done with the most enormous skill, it was trash, but it was awfully good trash, it's ten times better than that stuff Cousin Rupert writes now, he makes me tired that fellow! He thinks he's hell. We were both about the same age and we had the same governess, we never could get along, we were always fighting; he's just the same as he always was, I don't think people change that way. Auntie May was awfully nice: she always let us have tea with her, I used to love that, all sorts of people came to see her, she knew a great many people; and one day when I came down to tea there was an old man there with a long white beard and I was wearing my little apron, I must have been awfully sweet; and Auntie said "Come here, my dear," and she took me and stood me between her knees, and turned my face toward the old man and God! I was frightened, there was something so strange about it! And Auntie said "I want you to look at this gentleman and remember his name for some day you will know more about him and remember meeting him." Then Auntie said that the old man's name was Mister Wilkie Collins and that he was a writer and I thought that was an awfully funny name for anyone to have and I wondered what an old man like that could write. Then Rupert laughed at me and teased me because I was afraid of Mister Collins. O! he was dreadful! I used to hate him! and I began to cry and Mister Collins got me to come and sit on his knee, and he was really an awfully nice old man, I think he died a year or so after that. He began to tell me some stories and they were simply fascinating but I've forgotten what they were. But God! I used to love his books—O! he wrote some wonderful books: did you ever read *The Woman in White* and the *Moonstone*? Well, they're pretty swell. So then I guess we must have been away two years in all, Daddy was on this tour with Mansfield, and when we got back we all went to live with Bella, I think that was the only time she and Mama were separated, they simply adored each other—well, no, maybe we did not live with Bella at first, Mama still had some of those houses left down on Eleventh Street, so maybe we went there at first, I don't know, sometimes it seems such a long time ago, we moved around so much and sometimes now it all gets confused.

* * *

That was a good time then, for then the sun came out one day and the Bridge made music through the shining air, it was like a song: it soared like flight above the harbor, and there were men with derby hats upon it. It was like something you remember for the first time, it was like seeing something clearly for the first time in your life and down below it was the river: I think it is like that when you are a kid, I am sure it must be just like that, you remember things but they are all confused and broken up and darkness is in them; and then one day you know what day it is, and you know what time it is, and you remember everything you see; and it was just like that; I could see all the masts of the sailing ships tied up below, and they were like a forest of young trees, they were delicate and spare and close together and they had no leaves upon them and I thought of Spring. And a ship was coming up the river, and there was a white excursion boat all jammed with people and a band was playing, and I could see and hear it all. And I saw all the faces of the people on the Bridge, and they were coming toward me and there was something strange and sad about it, and yet it was the most magnificent thing I had ever seen: the air was clean and sparkling like sapphires and out beyond this was the harbor and I knew that the sea was there. And I heard the hoofs of all the horses, and the bells of the street cars, and all those heavy trembling sounds as if the Bridge was all alive: it was like time, it was like the red brick houses that they have in Brooklyn, it was like being a kid in the early nineties, and I guess that was when it was.

The Bridge made music and a kind of magic in me, it bound the earth together like a cry; and all of the earth seemed young and tender, I saw the people moving in two streams back and forth across the Bridge, and it was just as if we all had just been born. God! I was so happy I could hardly speak, but when I asked Daddy where we were going he kept singing in a kind of chant, "To see the man who built the Bridge, who built the Bridge, who built the Bridge, to see the man who built the Bridge, my fair La-dee." "O Daddy, we are *not*!" I said; he was so wild and wonderful, he told so many stories I never knew when to believe him. We sat up front on one of those open cars behind the motorman: the man kept clanging on his bell with his foot, Daddy was so happy and excited, when he got that way he had a wild crazy look in his eye. God! he was handsome! He was all dressed up in a rich dark coat with light grey trousers, he had a pearl in his necktie and a grey derby tilted sideways on his head, it was all so rich and perfect; his hair was like bright sand, it was thick and shiny. I was so proud of him, everyone stared after him wherever he went, the women were simply mad about him.

So when we got over there we got off and walked down a street and went up the steps of this wonderful old house, and an old nigger man came to the door and let us in: he had a white coat on and he was all white and black and clean looking, and he made you think of good things to eat and drinks in tall thin glasses, something with mint and frost and lots of ice in it. And we went back through the house behind the nigger and it was one of those wonderful old houses that are so dark and cool and grand with walnut stair rails a foot thick and mirrors up to the ceiling. Then this old nigger took us into a room in the back of the house and it was one of the most magnificent rooms you ever saw: it was noble and high, and the air from the sea was in it, it had three great windows all open and a balcony outside and beyond that you could see all of the harbor and there was the Bridge where we had come from. It was like a dream: the Bridge soared through the air and seemed to be so near the window and yet it was so far away. And down below us was the river, and the sparkle of the water, and all the ships; and boats were coming in and boats were going out to sea; and there were delicate plumes of smoke above the boats.

And there was an old man in a wheel-chair by the window: his face was strong and gentle, his eyes were grey like Daddy's, but they were not wild; he had enormous hands, but they were delicate and he used them in a wonderful way, and when he saw us he began to smile, he came toward us in the chair, he could not get up out of it: his face had an eager and wonderful look when he saw Daddy, because Daddy was so grand to people, they all loved him and wanted to be near him; he made them feel good. And Daddy began to talk at once and God! I was so embarrassed I just didn't know what to say, I stood there pulling at my dress. "Major," Daddy said, "I want you to meet the Princess Arabella Clementina Sapolio Von Hoggenheim: The Princess has appeared both in the flesh and by proxy here and abroad and before all the crowned heads of Arop, Erop, Irop, Orop, and Urop." "O Daddy!" I said, "I have not!" God! I didn't know what to say, I was afraid the old man would believe it. "Don't listen to her, Major!" Daddy said. "She'll deny it if she can, but you mustn't believe her. The Princess is very shy and shuns publicity: she is hounded by reporters wherever she goes, the gilded youth pursue her with offers of marriage, and unwelcome suitors are constantly throwing themselves out of windows and under the wheels of locomotives when she passes just to attract her attention." "O Daddy!" I said, "they do *not*!" Gee! I just stood there not knowing what to say, and then the old man took my hand in his, and his great hand was so strong and gentle, it closed around my hand and my hand was lost in it and I was not afraid of him; a kind of wonderful joy and strength went through me like a flame: it came out of him, and it was like being on the Bridge again, and then Daddy said, "This is the man who built the Bridge, who built the Bridge, who built the Bridge, this is the man who built the Bridge, my fair La-dee"; and I knew that it was true! I knew the Bridge had come out of him, and that his life was in the Bridge. He could not move, because his legs were crippled, and yet his life soared up out of him; his eyes were calm and steady, yet they leaped through space like a cry and like a glory; he sat in his chair but his great life sang a song, and I knew in my heart that it was true that he had built the Bridge, and I did not think of all the men who had worked for him, and had done what he had told them to do—I only knew that he was an angel and a giant who could build great bridges with his hands, and I thought that he had done it all himself; and I forgot that he was an old man crippled in his chair, I thought that if he had wanted to he could have soared through space and back again just like the Bridge.

I had a feeling of the most unspeakable joy and happiness, it was as if I had discovered the world the day when it was made; it was like getting back to the place where all things come from, it was like knowing the source where all things start, and having it in you, so that there will always be immortal joy and strength and certainty, and no more doubting and confusion. Yes! I knew he was the man who built the Bridge, by the touch of his hand and the great life that soared out of him, but I was so confused that all I could say was, "O Daddy! He did *not!*" And then I turned to him and said "You didn't, did you?" Just to hear him say he did. And he was so grand and gentle, he kept smiling and he kept holding to my hand, he had a German way of talking, I think he had been born in Germany, and he said: "Vell, your fader says I did, ant you must alvays belief vat your fader says because he alvays tells the truth," and he said this in such a solemn way, and then he looked at Daddy and they laughed. And then I said "O you didn't! How *could* you?" And I kept looking at his crippled legs, and they both knew what I was thinking, and Daddy said: "What! How *could* he? Why, he just called out to them when he wanted anything done; he just hollered over and told them what he wanted and they did it." God! it was so silly that I had to laugh but Daddy was so serious, he had such a wonderful way about him that he could make you believe anything he wanted and I said "O he did *not!*" And then I said to the old man, "Did you?" And he said "Vell, your Datty says I did, and you should alvays belief your Datty." "What's that?" Daddy said. "What was the general drift and purport of that last remark, Major?" "I told her," the old man said, "that you are a truthful man, Choe, and she must alvays belief her Datty." Then Daddy threw his head back and laughed in that strange wild way he had: there was a sort of fate and prophecy in it. "God, yes!" he said, "She must always believe her Daddy."

And I went to the window and kept looking at the Bridge and sometimes it seemed so close you could almost touch it, and again it seemed miles away, and they were both watching me; and then I saw the wagons crawling back and forth across it, and little tiny dots of men upon it, and I said, "I don't believe it: the men couldn't hear you holler; it's too far." "All right, I'll show you, then," said Daddy, and he went to the window and put his hands up to his mouth, and he had this powerful magnificent voice, and he could do all sorts of things with it; he could throw it like a ventriloquist and make it come from somewhere else, and he called out in a tone that made the whole room tremble: "HELLO OVER THERE! IS THAT YOU?" Then he would answer in a funny little voice that seemed to come from miles away: "Yes, sir." "WHO GAVE YOU THAT BLACK EYE?" Daddy said. Then the little voice said: "A friend of mine." "HOW'S THE BRIDGE GETTING ON TO-DAY?" Daddy hollered. "Very well, sir," the little voice said. "WELL, TIE UP THEM LOOSE CABLES. WE DON'T WANT NO ACCIDENTS," Daddy said. "All right, sir," the little voice said. "CATCHING ANY FISH?" Daddy hollered. "No, sir," the little voice said. "WHAT'S THE MATTER?" Daddy hollered. "They ain't bitin," the little voice said.

*   *   *

That year Richard Brandell made a production of *Richard the Third*, and he had sent my father tickets for the performance, with a very urgent and excited note asking us to come to see him before the show began. At this time my father had not played in the theatre for almost a year: his deafness had got so bad he could no longer hear his cues and Uncle Jake had given him a job as his secretary at Police Headquarters: I used to go there to meet him every Saturday—the policemen were very nice to me and gave me bundles of pencils and great packages of fine stationery.

Mr. Brandell had not seen my father for several months: When we got to the theatre we went backstage for a few moments before the curtain. As my father opened the door and went into the dressing room, Brandell turned and sprang out of his chair like a tiger: he threw both arms around my father and embraced him, crying out in a trembling and excited voice as if he were in some great distress of mind and spirit:

"Choe! Choe! I am glad you have gome! It's good to zee you!"

When he was excited he always spoke like this—with a pronounced accent. Although he insisted he was English by birth, he had been born in Leipzig, his father was a German: His real name was Brandl, which he had himself changed to Brandell after becoming an actor.

He had the most terrific vitality of any man I have ever seen; he was a very handsome man but at the moment his features, which were smooth, powerful, and, as everyone knows, infinitely flexible, were so swollen and distorted by some revulsion of the soul that he looked like a pig. At his best, he was a man of irresistible charm and warmth: he greeted me in a very kind and affectionate way, and kissed me, but he was overjoyed to see my father, and he stood for a moment without speaking, grasping him by the arms and shaking him gently. In a moment more, however, he began to speak in a bitter voice of "they" and "them"; he thought everyone was against him, he kept saying that Daddy was his only friend on earth, and he kept asking in a scornful and yet eager tone:

"What are *they* saying, Joe? Have you heard *them* talk?"

"All that I've heard," my father said, "is that it is a magnificent performance and that there's no one on the stage today who can come anywhere near you—no! there's no one who can touch you, Dick—and that's the way I feel about it, too."

"Not even His Snakeship? Not even His Snakeship?" Mr. Brandell cried, his face livid and convulsed.

We knew he was speaking of Henry Irving and we said nothing: for years, ever since the failure of his tour in England, he had been convinced that Irving had been responsible for his failure: in his mind Irving was a monster who spent all his time conspiring how to ruin and betray him. He had become obsessed with the idea that almost everyone on earth hated him and was trying to get the best of him, and he seized my father's hand, and, looking very earnestly into his eyes, he said: "No, no! You mustn't lie to me! You mustn't fool me! You are the only man on earth I'd trust!"

Then he began to tell us all the things his enemies had done to injure him: he began to curse and rave against everyone, he said the stage hands were all against him, that they never got the stage set in time, that the time they took between scenes was going to ruin the production. I think he felt his enemies were paying the crew to wreck the show. Daddy told him this was foolish, that no one would do a thing like that, and Mr. Brandell kept saying:

"Yes they would! They hate me! They'll never rest now until they ruin me! *I* know! *I* know!" in a very mysterious manner. "I could tell you things. . . . I know things. . . . You wouldn't believe it if I told you, Joe." Then, in a bitter voice, he said: "Why is it, then, that I've toured this country from coast to coast playing in a new town every night and I've never had any trouble like this before? Yes! I've played in every damned opera house and village auditorium on the North American continent and I always found the stage ready when it was time for the curtain! I've had my scenery arrive two hours before the performance and they always set it up for me on time—Yes! They'll do that much for you in any one horse town! Do you mean to tell me they can't do as well here in New York?"

In a moment he said, in a bitter tone: "I've given my life to the theatre, I've given the public the best that was in me—and what is my reward? The public hates me and I am tricked, betrayed and cheated by the members of my own profession. I started life as a bank clerk in a teller's cage, and sometimes I curse the evil chance that took me away from it. Yes!" he said in a passionate voice, "I should have missed the tinsel, the glitter, and the six day fame—the applause of a crowd that will forget about you tomorrow, and spit upon you two days later, but I would have gained something priceless—"

"What's that?" my father said.

"The love of a noble woman and the happy voices of the little ones."

"Now I can smell the ham," my father said in a cynical tone. "Why, Dick, they could not have kept you off the stage with a regiment of infantry. You sound like all the actors that ever lived."

"Yes," said Mr. Brandell with an abrupt laugh. "You're right. I was talking like an actor." He bent forward and stared into the mirror of his dressing table. "An actor! Nothing but an actor! 'Why should a dog, a horse, a rat have life—and thou no breath at all?'"

"Oh, I wouldn't say that, Dick," my father said. "You've got plenty of breath—I've never known you to run short of it."

"Only an actor!" cried Mr. Brandell, staring into the mirror.

"A paltry, posturing, vain, vile, conceited rogue of an actor! An actor—a man who lies and does not know he lies, a fellow who speaks words that better men have written for him, a reader of mash notes from shop girls and the stage struck wives of grocery clerks, a seducer of easy women, a fellow who listens to the tones of his own voice, a fellow who could not go into the butcher's to buy his dog a bone without wondering what appearance he was making, a man who cannot even pass the time of day without acting. An—*actor*! Why, my God, Joe!" he cried, turning to my father. "When I look into the glass and see my face I hate the sight of it."

"Where's that ham?" said Daddy, sniffing about the place.

"An actor!" Mr. Brandell said again. "A fellow who has played so many parts that he can no longer play his own: a man who has imitated so many feelings that he no longer has any of his own—Why, Joe!" he said, in a whispering voice, "Do you know that when the news came to me that my own mother was dead I had a moment— yes, I think I really had a moment—of genuine sorrow. Then I ran to look at my face in the mirror, and I cursed because I was not on the stage where I could show it to an audience. An actor!—A fellow who has made so many faces he no longer knows his own— a collection of false faces! . . . what would you like, my dear?" he said to me ironically. "Hamlet?"—instantly he looked the part. "Dr. Jekyll and Mr. Hyde?"—here his face went through two marvelous transformations: one moment he was a benevolent-looking gentleman and the next a deformed and horrible looking monster. "Richelieu?"—all at once he looked like a crafty and sinister old man. "Beau Brummell?"—he was young, debonair, arrogant, and a fop. "The Duke of Gloucester?"—and in a moment he had transformed himself into the cruel and pitiless villain he was to portray that night.

It was uncanny and fascinating; and there was something horrible in it, too. It was as if he was possessed by a powerful and fluent energy which had all been fed into this wonderful and ruinous gift of mimicry—a gift which may have, as he said, destroyed and devoured his proper self, since one got fleeting and haunting glimpses between these transformations of a man—a sense, an intuition, rather than a memory, of what the man was like and looked like—a sense of a haunted, lost, and lonely spirit which looked out with an insistent, mournful, and speechless immutability through all the hundred changes of his mask. It seemed to me there was a real despair, a real grief in Mr. Brandell: I think he had been tormented, like my father, by the eternal enigma of the theatre—its almost impossible grandeur and magnificence, its poetry and its magic which are like nothing else on earth—and the charlatanism and cheapness with which it corrupts its people. Richard Brandell was not only the greatest actor I have ever seen upon the stage, he was also a man of the highest quality—he had a lavish and magnificent generosity: it showed in the productions he made and which he set before the public as if he were inviting them to a feast, and it showed in the company of actors he employed. For no matter how he was obsessed with ideas that rivals and enemies were plotting against him, he surrounded himself with the best actors he could find, he drove them furiously, and he exulted in their success as much as if it had been his own.

He possessed almost every gift a great actor should possess, but because of certain poisonous qualities in his nature he was unable to sustain his powers at the pitch at which an artist must work. He had everything else, voice, tradition, physical beauty of the manliest sort, and unsurpassed background in the profession, a glamorous personality, and just enough of the ham actor—enough to hold the gallery.

And yet his spirit was disfigured as if by an ineradicable taint—a taint which he felt and recognized, as a man might recognize the action of a deadly poison in his blood without being able either to cure or control it. He had an astounding repertory of plays which ranged all the way from the great music of *Hamlet* to grotesque and melodramatic trash which he had commissioned some hired hack to write for him. He could play one night in *Hamlet* until it seemed that Shakespeare's genius had found a living voice, that this man knew the remotest depths of Hamlet's spirit, and the next night he would be posturing and grimacing in some grotesque rubbish which had been thrown together in order to display his amazing gift for the characterization of deformed and monstrous people: — he had a whole gallery of horrors—insane old misers gloating at midnight over bags of gold and calling them "my pretties"; lecherous old Parisian rakes in the act of horrible dissolution before one's eyes; hunched backs deformed in body and soul wreaking out their hate upon a world of widows and young girls; criminal spirits plotting the destruction of all mankind—and he would use his great powers in these parts with as much passion and energy as he used in his wonderful portrayals of Iago, Gloucester, or Macbeth.

Like most men who are conscious of something false and corrupt in them he had a kind of Byronic scorn and self-contempt: he was constantly discovering that what he thought had been a deep and honest feeling was only the posturings of his own vanity, a kind of intoxication of self-love, an immense romantic satisfaction at the spectacle of himself having such a feeling, and while his soul twisted about in shame he would turn and mock and jeer himself and his fellow actors bitterly. Thus, he would corner one of them so that he could not escape, and bear down upon him relentlessly:

"Oh, *please* let me tell you all about myself. Let's just sit right down and have a good long talk all about myself. I can see by the look in your eye that you are just dying to hear, but you're too polite to ask. I know you'd love to hear me talk about myself. Of course, you have nothing to say about *yourself*, have you?" He would sneer. "Oh, dear no! You're much too modest! But what shall it be now? What do you most want to hear about first? Would you like to hear about the house I had in Lima, Ohio? Or would you rather hear of Cairo, Illinois? I had them hanging to the edges of their seats there, you know? It was marvelous, old boy! Such an ovation! They stood and cheered for ten minutes! Women hurled flowers at me, strong broke down and wept. Are you interested? I can see you are! I can tell by that eager look in your eye! Now *do* let me tell you some more. Don't you want to hear about the women? My dear fellow, they're mad about me! I had six notes in the mail this morning, three from Boston heiresses and two from the wives of prominent feed and hay merchants in Minnesota. . . . But I must tell you about the house I had in Cairo, Illinois. . . . I was playing in *Hamlet* that night: it's a good part old boy—a little old-fashioned maybe, but *I* fixed that: I had to write a few of the speeches over here and there, but no one knew the difference. I made up some marvelous business for some of the scenes—absolutely marvelous! And my boy they *loved* me! They adored me! I had sixteen calls at the end of the Third Act—they wouldn't let me go, old man: they kept calling me back—until finally I simply had to say a few well-chosen words. Of course, I hated to do it, old boy—you can imagine how I hated it—after all, the play's the thing, isn't it? We're not there to get applause for ourselves, are we? Oh, *dear* no!" he sneered, "—but *do* let me tell you what I said to them in Cairo: I can see you are burning up to hear!"

That night was the last time Mr. Brandell ever saw my father. Just before we left, he turned to me, took me by the hand, and said very simply and earnestly: "Esther, earn your living in the sweat of your brow if you have to; go down on your hands and knees and scrub floors, if you have to; eat your bread in sorrow if you have to—but promise me you will never attempt to go on the stage."

"I have already made her promise that," my father said.

"Is she as good as she's pretty? Is she smart?" said Mr. Brandell, still holding my hand and looking at me.

"She's the smartest girl that ever lived," my father said. "She's so smart she should have been my son."

"And what is she going to do?" said Mr. Brandell, still looking at me.

"She's going to do what I could never do," my father said. He lifted his great hands before him and shook them suddenly in a gesture of baffled desperation. "She's going to take hold of something!" Then he took my hands in his and said: "Not to want the whole earth and to get nothing! Not to want to do everything and to do nothing! Not to waste your life dreaming about India when India is around you here and now! Not to go mad thinking of a million lives, wanting the experience of a million people, when everything you have is in the life you've got! Not to be a fool, tortured with hunger and thirst when the whole earth is groaning with its plenty. . . . My dear child," my father cried. "You are so good, so beautiful and so gifted, and I love you so much! I want you to be happy and to have a wonderful life—" He spoke these words with such simple and urgent feeling that all the strength and power in him seemed to go out through his great hands to me as if all of the energy of his life had been put into his wish.

"Why, Dick," he said to Mr. Brandell, "This child was born into the world with more wisdom than either of us will ever have. She can go into the Park and come back with a dozen kinds of leaves and study them for days. And when she gets through she will know all about them: she knows their size, their shape and color—she knows every marking on them, she can draw them from memory. Could you draw a leaf, Dick? Do you know the pattern and design of a single leaf? Why, I have looked at forests, I have walked through woods and gone across the continent in trains, I have stared the eyes out of my head trying to swallow up the whole earth at a glance—and I hardly know one leaf from another: I could not draw a leaf from memory if my life depended on it. And she can go out on the street and tell you later what clothes the people wore, and what kind of people wore them: can you remember anyone you passed by on the street today? I walk the streets, I see the crowds, I look at a million faces until my brain goes blind and dizzy with all that I have seen, and later all the faces swim and bob about like corks in water. I can't tell one from the other, I see a million faces and I can't remember one. But she sees one and remembers a million: that's the thing, Dick—if I were young again I'd try to live like that: I'd try to see a forest in a leaf, the whole earth in a single face."

"Why, Esther," Mr. Brandell said. "Have you discovered a new country? How does one get to this wonderful place where you live?"

"Well, I tell you, Mr. Brandell," I said. "It's easy! You just walk out in the street and look around and there you are."

"There you are!" Mr. Brandell said. "Why, my dear child, I have been walking out and looking around for almost fifty years, and the more I walk and look, the less I see that I care to look at. What are these wonderful sights that you have found?"

"Well, Mr. Brandell," I said. "Sometimes it's a leaf, and sometimes it's the pocket of a coat, and sometimes it's a button or a coin, and sometimes it's an old hat, or an old shoe on the floor. Do you know what is wonderful? Well, it's the window of a hardware store: sometimes they have nothing but tools, sometimes pots and pans, and one time I saw one that was nothing but knives—they were arranged in all sorts of designs and patterns: in the centre there was a great circle of them, hundreds and hundreds of knives, flashing with light like a river, all flowing into one another—this is one of the most beautiful things I ever saw. Sometimes it's the tobacco stores, the cigars tied up in bundles on the counter, and all of the jars where they keep the pipe tobacco, and the wonderful dark smell of the place. Sometimes it's a little boy, and sometimes it's a girl looking out a window, and sometimes it's an old woman with a funny hat. Sometimes it's the color of an ice wagon, and sometimes the color of an old brick wall, and sometimes a cat creeping along the backyard fence. Sometimes it's the feet of the man on the rail when you pass a saloon, and the sawdust floors, and the sound of their voices and that wonderful smell you get of beer and orange peel and angostura bitters. Sometimes it's people passing underneath your window late at night, and sometimes it's the sound of a horse in the street early in the morning, and sometimes it's the ships blowing out in the harbor at night. Sometimes it's the design of the elevated structure across the street where a station is, and sometimes it's the smell of bolts of new clean cloth, and sometimes it's the way you feel when you make a dress: you can feel the design go out of the tips of your fingers into the cloth as you shape it, and you feel yourself in it and it looks like you, and you know nobody else on earth could do it that way. Sometimes it's the way Sunday morning feels when you wake up and listen to it—you can smell it and feel it and it smells like breakfast; some- times it's the way Saturday night is, sometimes it's the way Mon- day morning feels, you get all excited and nervous and your coffee goes bouncing around inside you; and you don't enjoy your break- fast; and sometimes it's like Sunday afternoon with people coming from a concert—this feels terrible and makes you blue. Sometimes it's the way you feel at night when you wake up in winter time and you know it's snowing, although you can't see or hear it. Some- times it's the harbor, sometimes the docks, and sometimes it's the Bridge with people coming across it. Sometimes it's the markets and the way the chickens smell; sometimes it's all the new vege- tables and the smell of apples. Sometimes it's the people in a train that passes the one you're in: you see all the people, you are close to them, but you cannot touch them, you say good-bye to them and it makes you feel sad. Sometimes it's all the kids playing in the streets: they don't seem to have anything to do with the grown- ups, they seem to be kids and yet they seem to be grown up and to live in a world of their own—there is something strange about it; and sometimes it's like that with the horses too—sometimes you go out and there is nothing but the horses, they fill the streets, you forget about all the people, the horses seem to own the earth, they talk to one another, and they seem to have a life of their own that people have nothing to do with—I'd like to paint a picture of this. Sometimes it's all the different kinds of carriages—the hansoms, the four-wheelers, the victorias, the landaulets; sometimes it's the Brewster Carriage Works on Broadway: you can look in and see them making them down in the basement—everything is very delicate and beautiful, you can smell the shavings of the finest wood and new leather and harness and the silks, the springs, the wheels, and the felloes. Sometimes it's all the people going along the street, and sometimes there's nothing but the Jews—the old men with the beards, and the old women poking and prodding at ducks, and the girls and the kids: I know all about this and what is going on inside them, but it's no use telling you and Daddy— you're both Gentiles and you wouldn't know what I was talking about. Well—there's a lot more: do you give up?"

"Good God, yes!" said Mr. Brandell, picking up a towel from his dressing table and waving it at me. "I surrender! O brave new world that has such wonders in it! . . . Oh, Joe, Joe!" he said to my father. "Will that ever happen to us again? Are we nothing but famished beggars, weary of our lives? Can you still see all those things when you walk the streets? Would it ever come back to us that way again?"

"Not to me," my father said. "I was a Sergeant, but I've been rejuced."

He smiled as he spoke but his voice was old and tired and weary: I know now he felt that his life had failed. All at once, as I looked at him, I had another terrible flash of premonition as I had had one day when I was living with Bella in New Jersey, and he stood waiting for the street car to come, and I could hear the wind blowing in the leaves. His face had got very yellow from his sickness, and his shoulders stooped, his great hands dangled to his knees: as he stood there between Mr. Brandell and me he seemed to be half-erect and simian as if he had just clambered up from all fours. His strange and grotesque figure which had served him so loyally, which had borne so patiently the terrible drive of his hunger, the frenzy of his tormented spirit, and which he had hated so bitterly in his youth, now looked old and tired, and more apelike than ever: even to a stranger it would have been obvious why men had always called him Monkey Hawke. And yet his face was as delicate and wild as it had ever been, it had the strange soaring look—as if it were in constant flight away from a shackling and degrading weight—that it had always worn, and to this expression of uplifted flight there had now been added the intent listening expression that all deaf people have.

It seemed to me that the sense of loneliness and exile, of a brief and alien rest, as if some winged spirit had temporally arrested flight upon a foreign earth, was more legible on him now than it had ever been. Suddenly I felt all the strangeness of his life and destiny—his remoteness from all the life I knew: I thought of his strange childhood, of the mystery of his father's disappearance, and of his years of wandering about the earth haunted always by the thought that some day he would find his father; and finally I thought of the dark miracle of chance which had brought him to my mother and the Jews—an alien, a stranger, and an exile among dark faces; with us but never of us. And I felt more than ever before a sense of our nearness and farness; I felt at once closer to him than to anyone on earth, and at the same time farther from him. Already his life had something fabulous and distant in it; he seemed to be a part of some vanished and irrevocable time.

I do not think Mr. Brandell had noticed before how tired and ill my father looked: he was buried in his own world, burning with a furious half suppressed excitement, an almost mad vitality which was to have that night its consummation. Before we left him, however, he suddenly glanced sharply and critically at my father, took his hand, and said with great tenderness: "What is it, Monk? You look so tired? Is anything wrong?"

My father shook his head: he had become very sensitive about his deafness and any reference to the affliction that had caused his retirement from the stage or any suggestion of pity from one of his former colleagues because of his present state deeply wounded him. "Of course not!" he said. "I never felt better! I used to be Jo-Jo the Dog Faced Actor; now I'm Jo-Jo the Dog Faced Policeman, and I've got a badge to prove it too"—here he produced his police-man's badge of which he was really very proud. "If that's not a step up in the world, what is it? Come on, daughter," he said to me. "Let's leave this wicked man to all his plots and murders: if he gets too bad, I'll arrest him."

We started to go; but for a moment Mr. Brandell stopped us and was silent—the enormous and subdued excitement, the exultant fury, which had been apparent in him all the time, now became much more pronounced: the man was thrumming like a dynamo, his strong hands trembled, and when he spoke it was as if he had already become the Duke of Gloucester: there was a quality of powerful, cunning and exultant prophesy in his tone, something mad, secret, conspiratorial and knowing.

"Keep your eyes open tonight," he said. "You may see something worth remembering."

We left him and went out into the theatre. It was the last time Brandell ever saw my father.

*　*　*

I have wanted to tell about this last meeting between Richard Brandell and my father because of the wonderful thing that happened to both of us later on that evening, and because in my memory, our visit to Mr. Brandell before the performance has always seemed to be an integral part of it, the beginning of it.

When we got out into the auditorium the house was almost full, although the people were still going down the aisles to their seats. Because of my father's deafness Brandell had given us seats in the front row; for a few minutes I watched the people come in and the house fill up, I felt again the sense of elation and joy I have always felt in the theatre before the curtain goes up—I looked at the beautiful women, the men in evening clothes, and at all the fat and gaudy ornamentation of the house; I heard the rapid and excited pattern of the voices, the stir and rustle of silks, the movement, and I loved it all. Then, in a few minutes, the lights darkened, there was a vast rustling sigh all over the theatre, the sound of a great bending forward, and then, for a moment, in that dim light I saw the thing that has always seemed so full of magic and beauty to me; a thousand people who have suddenly become a single living creature, and all the frail white spots of faces blooming like petals there in a velvet darkness, upturned, thirsty, silent, and intent and beautiful.

Then the curtain went up and on an enormous and lofty stage stood the deformed and solitary figure of a man. For a moment I knew the man was Brandell; for a moment I could feel nothing but an astonished surprise, a sense of unreality, to think of the miracle of transformation which had been wrought in the space of a few minutes, to know that this cruel and sinister creature was the man with whom we had just been talking. Then the first words of the great opening speech rang out across the house, and instantly all this was forgotten: the man was no longer Brandell, he was the Duke of Gloucester.

That evening will live in my memory as the most magnificent evening I ever spent in the theatre. On that evening Richard Brandell reached the summit of his career: that night was literally the peak. Immediately after the performance Brandell had a nervous collapse: the play was taken off, he never appeared as Richard again. It was months before he made any appearance whatever and he never again, during the remainder of his life, approached the performance he gave that night.

With the opening words, the intelligence was instantly communicated to the audience that it was about to witness such a performance as occurs in the theatre only once in a lifetime; and yet at first there was no sense of characterization, no feeling of the cruel and subtle figure of Richard—there was only a mighty music which sounded out across the house, a music so grand and overwhelming that it drowned the memory of all the baseness, the ugliness, and the pettiness in the lives of men. In the sound of the words it seemed there was the full measure of man's grandeur, magnificence, and tragic despair and the words were flung against immense and timeless skies like a challenge and an evidence of man's dignity, and like a message of faith that he need not be ashamed or afraid of anything.

> Now is the winter of our discontent
> Made glorious summer by this sun of York;
> And all the clouds that lour'd upon our house
> In the deep bosom of the ocean buried—

Then, swiftly and magnificently, with powerful developing strokes of madness, fear and cruelty, the terrible figure of Richard begins to emerge: almost before the conclusion of the opening speech it stands complete. That speech is really a speech of terror, and sets clearly the picture of the warped, deformed, agonized Gloucester, for whom there was no beautiful thing in life, a man who had no power to rise himself except by murder. As the play went on the character of Richard had become so real to me, the murders so frightful, the lines filled with such music and such terror that when the curtain rose on that awful nightmare scene in the tent, I felt I could not stay there if one more drop of blood was shed. Then, just as the ghosts of the little princes appeared to Richard, just as he starts up crying, "The lights burn blue—" there occurred one of the most extraordinary experiences of my life.

Suddenly, I heard in my ears the faint rumbling of wheels, far, far away, and gradually coming nearer. The king's tent faded from my view and suddenly before my eyes there stretched a long band of hard silvery sand and a calm ocean beyond. The water was of a delicate blue tint known as aquamarine, the sun shone low in the sky from the land side. The beach near the water was perfectly flat, no human had trod there since the tide had washed out.

I felt the land was an island, the beach curved round a high cliff of earth and growth quite far down. Then I heard the wheels come nearer and saw a chariot moving with great speed, drawn by three horses. The rumble of the wheels grew very loud and the chariot, which was of Greek form, came before my vision. It was driven by a woman who filled my being at once with warmth and familiarity. She was of medium height, her head rather small, and her face I can only describe as heart-shaped: it was wide at the temples and tapering to a delicate pointed chin. She had fine, silky wavy hair, bound with a chaplet of leaves made of beaten gold, the chaplet tied at the back with a red-purple ribbon. Neither face nor figure was of the classic type, as we conceive it. The face was beautiful in its own way and touched a chord within me that answered with all the warmth of my nature.

I had known this woman forever. Sometimes a certain set of vibrations will make a crystal goblet ring when nothing has really touched it. That is what this woman did to my heart. If I had come into a room filled with the most beautiful women on earth and among them I had seen her face, I would have exclaimed, "There she is!" She meant home, love, delight to me. Her figure was rounded, but not developed as the Greek statues and not particularly beautiful except for her noble and perpendicular carriage. She handled the reins and horses with a swift sure grace with one hand, and with the other patted the heads of two children who stood at her left side—a girl of about ten, skinny, and a tiny boy of about four, whose eyes just cleared the rim of the chariot. Her dress was ivory white, laced in infinitesimal pleats of that clinging yet flowing material worn by the Greeks. She wore high laced cothurns of white leather, trimmed with gold.

So they raced along, the wind whipping her dress close to her form. The wheels thundered in my ears and the thud of the horses' hoofs upon the hard wet sand. I could see the wheel revolving on the axle. They passed by and soon had turned the promontory of land. She was gone. I felt a sense of irreparable loss, I have felt nothing like it before or since.

Then I became aware of the theatre full of people, I saw the scene on the stage again, and I heard a sound coming from my own throat. My father had taken my outstretched hands in his and was speaking gently to me. The vision, or whatever it was, seemed to me to have lasted fully five minutes, but in reality it must have been much less.

I wrenched my mind from my vision to watch the stage, the play was drawing to its magnificent close, but the dream stayed by me for many days, and for months I would feel that wonderful sense of recognition and love and smell the beach, the sea, the shore, and see everything as clearly as events that passed around me. Then, in [the] course of time, it faded, but from time to time in years to come it would return, as clearly as when first I saw it that night in the theatre.

What do you think it was?

* * *

"Long, long into the night I lay—" (One!). "Long, long into the night I lay awake—" (One, Two, Three, Four!). "Long, long into the night I lay awake, thinking how I should tell my story." O how lovely those words are! They make a music in me just like bells. *One*, Two, Three, Four! One, *Two*, Three, Four! O, there are bells, and that is time: what time is that? That was the half hour that the bells were striking, and that was time, time, time! O that was time, dark time, strange tragic time, that hangs above our heads in lovely bells.

Time! Where are you now, and in what place, and at what time? Now in the dark I hear the boats there in the river: now I can hear the great horns blowing in the river. Great horns are baying at the harbor's mouth, great horns are baying in the gulf of night, great boats are putting out to sea! O now I hear the whistles on the river! O now great ships are going down the river! O now I hear strange time, dark time, strange tragic time, as it flows down the river; and in the night-time, in the dark, in all the sleeping silence of the earth, the river, the dark rich river, full of strange tragic time, is flowing by me, by me, by me, to the sea!

*　*　*

When the show was over that night we went out onto the street and turned up Broadway. We were both so happy and excited that we fairly bounded along: when a wonderful thing happens it seems to make everything in the world look young and new again, and that was the way it was that night. It was one of the first fine days in Spring, the air was cool and delicate and yet soft, and the sky was of a velvety lilac texture, and it was glittering with great stars. The streets outside the theatre were swarming with hansoms, four-wheelers, private carriages and victorias; they kept driving up in front of the theatre all the time and people kept getting into them.

All of the men looked handsome, and all of the women were beautiful: everyone seemed to be as exultant and happy as we were, it seemed as if a new world and new people had burst out of the earth with the coming of Spring—everything ugly, dull, sour, and harsh had vanished—the streets were flashing with life and sparkle, I saw all of it, I felt myself a part of it all, I wanted to possess it all, and there was something I wanted to say so much it made my throat ache, and yet I could not say it because I could not find the words I wanted. I could not think of anything else to say—it sounded foolish, but suddenly I seized my father's arm and cried: "O to be in April now that England's there."

"Yes," he shouted. "Also in Paris, Naples, Rome and Dresden! O to be in Budapest!" cried Daddy. "Now that April's here and the frost is on the pumpkin, and the dawn comes up like thunder out of the night that covers me."

He seemed to have grown young again; he was the way he used to be when I was a little girl and I would knock at his study door and he would call out in a wonderful actor's voice: "Enter, Daughter of Des-o-la-tion into this abode of mis-er-ee."

His eyes sparkled, and he threw back his head and laughed his wild and happy laugh.

*   *   *

. . . . that year I think we were living with Bella; no we weren't, I guess we were living with Auntie Kate—well, maybe we were staying with Bella: I don't know, we moved around so much, and it's so long ago. It gets all confused in my mind now. When Daddy was acting he was always on the go, he couldn't be still a minute: sometimes he was playing in New York, and sometimes he went off on a tour with Mr. Mansfield and was gone for months.

I think that must have been the year before he died; I was about eighteen: I was a beauty. . . . I was like peaches and cream. . . .

In those days when he was acting I used to meet him after the theatre and we would go somewhere to eat. . . . There was a fellow after your heart:—the very best was *just* about good enough for him. . . . New York was awfully nice in those days. They had such nice places to go to—I don't know, they didn't have all this noise and confusion; it seems like another world sometimes. You could go to White's or Martin's or Delmonico's—there were a lot of nice places. There was also a place called Mocks, I never went there. But one of the first things I remember as a child was hearing Daddy come home late at night and say he'd been to Mocks. When he came home, I would listen at the grating of the heater in my room and I could hear him and the other actors talking to my mother: it was fascinating; and sometimes it was all about Mocks. "O, have you been to Mocks?" I thought I heard my mother say. "O, yes! I have been to Mocks," my father said. "And what did you have at Mocks?" my mother said. "O, I had some oysters and a glass of beer and some mock turtle soup at Mocks," my father said.

We used to go to White's almost every night after the show with two priests who were friends of Daddy's: Father Dolan and Father Chris O'Rourke. Father Dolan was a big man with the bluest eyes I ever saw and Father Chris O'Rourke was a little man with a swarthy and greasy face: it was all full of black marks, it was one of the strangest faces I ever saw; it was greasy and almost black but there was something very powerful and sweet about it. He wore the thickest eyeglasses I have ever seen, he was very nearsighted.

The Time That Is Lovely   57

He was a great scholar, he knew the plays of Shakespeare almost by heart—he and Daddy used to tag each other's lines, to see who knew the most: I never knew my father to catch him up but once and that was on a line from *King Lear*, "The Prince of Darkness is a gentleman"—Father Dolan said it came from *As You Like It*.

How those fellows loved to eat and drink: if one of them had to say Mass the next day we had to hurry because you can't eat or drink after midnight if you are saying Mass the next day. Because of this, both these priests would immediately take out their watches and lay them on the table before them when they sat down: Father Chris O'Rourke drank nothing but beer and as soon as he sat down a waiter would bring him a half dozen glasses which he would drink at once. But if these two priests had a glass of beer on the table before them when midnight came, they left it: no matter what it was, no matter whether they'd finished eating or drinking or not, when the stroke of midnight came these fellows quit, if they were going to say Mass the morning after.

Father Chris O'Rourke would eat and drink for almost an hour as if his life depended on it: he was very nearsighted, he wore thick glasses, and from time to time he would seize his watch and bring it up right under his nose while he peered and squinted at it. Because of his own hurry to get through before twelve o'clock, he thought everyone else must be the same way: he was afraid someone would not get fed, and he was always urging and belaboring people to hurry up and eat. Father Dolan loved to eat too, but he was a great talker: sometimes he would get to talking to Daddy and forget to eat: when he did this Father Chris O'Rourke would almost go out of his head, he would keep nudging and poking at Father Dolan and pointing at his watch with a look of agony on his face, leaning over and muttering at him in an ominous sort of way: "You're going to be *late*! It is almost *twelve*!"

"Bedad, then!" said Father Dolan. "I'll be late!" He was a big man, but he had a funny little Irish voice, it was very crisp and jolly and had a little chuckling lilt in it, and it seemed to come from a long way off. "I never saw a man like ye, Chris, to be always thinkin' of his belly: Did the great Saints of the Church spend their time guzzling and cramming, or did they spend it in meditatin' and prayin' an' mortifyin' their flesh? Did ye never hear of the sin of gluttony?"

"Yis!" said Father Chris O'Rourke, "that I have, an' I've also heard of the wicked sin of wanton waste. Shame on ye, Dan Dolan, wit yer talk about the great Saints of the Church: there was niver a great Saint yit that would praise a man fer wastin' what the Lord had set before him. Do ye think I'll sit here an' see good food go to waste whin there's poor people all over the world tonight that's goin' wit out?"

"Well," said Father Dolan, "I've read most of the argyments of the learned reasoners of the Church as well as the damnable heresies of the infidels, all the way from St. Thomas Aquinas to Spinozey, an' in me young days I could split a hair meself wit the best of them, but in all me life I niver heard the beat of that one: it makes Aristotle look like Wordsworth's Idiot Boy. Bedad, if ye can prove that what ye're doin' wit yer gorgin' is feedin' the poor all over the earth, I won't put anything past yer powers of reasonin', Chris—ye could show the Pope that Darwin was a Jesuit, an' he'd believe ye!"

Father Dolan was a very fine, high sort of man: he was very kind and jolly, but he also had a fine mind and he was very outspoken and honest. He loved the theatre, he knew a great many actors, a great many of them went to his Church, and he loved my father. It was because of him that Daddy sent my sister Edith to the Convent of the Sacred Heart in the Bronx: although Father Dolan joked about it and said she was goin' to get canonized some day as the first Jewish Saint, he gave orders that she should not be approached in any way about religion and the Sisters lived up to this to the letter. Daddy and I used to go up to see her every Monday—she was about fourteen at this time—and when we did Father Dolan would usually come along.

One day when we got up to the gate outside the Convent he had to stand for a long time pulling at the bell: it was old and rusty and wouldn't work, presently it gave a rusty kind of jangle far away. The Sister who finally let us in that day was an old woman named Sister Fidelia, she was an old woman with a good face, there was something stern and very grey about her: when she got down to the gate and opened it Father Dolan spoke to her about the bell and told her they must get a new one.

"That is no bell, Father Dolan, as ye should know very well," said Sister Fidelia.

"No, then?" said Father Dolan is his funny little voice. "And what is it, if it's not a bell?"

"It is the Voice of God," said Sister Fidelia.

"Bedad, then!" said Father Dolan as quick as a flash. "God's Voice is gettin' mighty rusty! I'm thinkin' He'll soon be needin' a new one!"

This Convent was a wonderful place: it was a great brick building set up on a hill and it had trees around it: it took us a long time to get there, sometimes, we went up by train from the Grand Central depot, and sometimes we went uptown on the horse cars, we had to get off and change a great deal, and finally we had to climb the hill to the Convent. One time I went there in Winter when there had been a great fall of snow: all of the little girls and the nuns were out-of-doors and coasting down the hill on sleds—the nuns shot past me on a sled laughing, they had their knees drawn up and their skirts tucked in between their knees: it was one of the strangest sights I ever saw.

The Mother Superior at the Convent was named Mother Mary Ursula: she was an enormous woman, proportioned like an Amazon; she was one of the handsomest women I have ever seen and she had a magnificent figure. She was very proud of her figure, she went to see one of the most expensive dressmakers in New York and had corsets made which cost her seventy-five dollars apiece; she would take one or two of the girls with her, and sometimes my sister Edith went.

When we went to the Convent on visiting days we would often meet in the Mother Superior's reception room and have tea—or rather chocolate—with her. She was very fond of Father Dolan and Daddy: when we had chocolate with her, the silver, the china and the linen was of the very finest and costliest money could buy—everything she had was like this—and the chocolate was so thick and rich that the silver spoons stood upright in it. She had come from a very rich Irish family in Brooklyn, I think her name had been Murphy, she had large luminous grey eyes of great depth and beauty; she was a very beautiful woman, and later I often thought of her and wondered what her life had been like.

Well, as I say, when we got to the restaurant the first thing Father Chris O'Rourke would do was to lay his watch upon the table and the first thing Daddy would do was to order two or three bottles of champagne: they used to know we were coming and it would be waiting for us in great silver buckets full of ice. Then Daddy would pick up the menu—it was a great big card simply covered with the most delicious things to eat, and he would frown and look serious and clear his throat, and say to Father Dolan: "What does the Pontifical Palate crave, Dan?"

After the play, that night, we went to Whites and these two priests were waiting for us when we got there. A little later Mr. Gates came in, he's still alive, I saw him on the street the other day, he's getting quite old. He was married to one of the most beautiful women you ever saw, and she was burned to death in an automobile accident. He saw the thing happen right under his eyes: isn't that the most horrible thing you ever heard of? Well, you could tell by the way Mr. Gates walked that he was awfully excited about something: he was another of these great fat fellows, and you could see his old jowls quivering as he came.

"Good God!" said Daddy, "Here comes Bunny with a full head of steam on!"

Mr. Gates began to speak to Daddy half across the room; all of the people stopped and stared at him.

"Joe! Joe!" he said. He had a funny hoarse kind of voice, one of those foggy whiskey voices, I think he drank a good deal. "Joe, do you know what I've done? I've just bought a Horseless Carriage. Come on! You're going for a ride with me!"

"Now wait! Wait! Wait!" said Daddy, holding up his hand just like an actor, "Not so fast, Bunny! Sit down and have a bite to eat first, and tell us about it. When did you do this Desperate Deed?"

"Today." Mr. Gates said in a sort of hoarse whisper, "Do you suppose I've done right?"

He looked around at us with his old eyes simply bulging out of his head and with a sort of scared look on his face. O! We laughed so much about it: Father Dolan began to laugh, and Daddy had to pound him on his back, he got to coughing so!

Mr. Gates was an awfully nice man: he was a great fat fellow, but he was so handsome: there was something so delicate about him, his mouth kept trembling and twitching so when he was excited and wanted to say something, I think that was why they called him Bunny. He had the finest collection of Chinese things I have ever seen, the things he had in that house were simply priceless.

So Daddy said: "Sit down and have something to eat and then we'll see."

Mr. Gates said: "Say, Joe, I've got the mechanic outside here, and I don't know what to do with him."

"You mean you hired him for keeps?" Daddy said.

"Yes," Mr. Gates said, "and I'm damned if I'm not embarrassed! I don't know what to do with him. I mean, what is his social standing?"

"Does he wash?" Daddy said.

"Well," said Mr. Gates, looking at Father Dolan, "I think he uses holy water."

"O Mr. Gates!" I said, "How awful! Right before Father Dolan, too!"

But Father Dolan laughed just like I knew he would: he was a great fat fellow, he was an awfully nice man. Father Chris O'Rourke laughed too, but I don't think he liked it so much.

"I mean," Mr. Gates said, "I don't know how to treat the man. Is he above me, or below me, or what?"

"It looks to me," Daddy said, "as if he were on top of you. I think you've gone and got yourself saddled with a Black Elephant."

Daddy was so wonderful like that, everybody loved him. Mr. Gates was so worried about the driver: it all seems so funny now to think back on it—he didn't know whether the man was to eat at the table with his family, and be treated like one of them or what. There was something so delicate about Mr. Gates: he was big and fat, but a very sensitive, fine person.

"It looks like a neat little problem in social etiquette, Bunny." Daddy said. "Well, let's have him in here for a bite to eat. We'll see what he looks like."

So Mr. Gates went out and got him, and pretty soon he came back with him, and he was really an awfully nice young fellow: he had a little moustache, and he wore a Norfolk jacket and a flat cap, and everybody stared so, and nudged each other, he was awfully embarrassed. But Daddy was wonderful with people, he made him feel right at home. He said, "Sit down, young fellow. If we're going to run an engine we've got to feed the driver."

So he sat down, and we had a marvelous meal: you'd get great juicy chops in that place cooked in butter, and steaks an inch thick, and the most marvelous oysters and sea food.

I know it was pretty late in the season, but we started off with oysters and champagne: I don't think the young fellow was used to drinking. Daddy kept filling up his glass, and he got quite drunk. He was awfully funny, he kept talking about his responsibility:

"It's a terrible responsibility to know that all these lives are dependent on you," he said, then Daddy would fill up his glass again.

"A moment's hesitation in a crisis," he said, "and all is lost."

"A truer word was never spoken," said Daddy, and he filled his glass up again.

"A man must have a clear brain and a steady hand," he said.

"Right you are," said Daddy. "This will make you so steady, son, that you will get practically paralyzed."

Mr. Gates and Father Dolan laughed so much that the tears began to trickle down their cheeks, O we had an awfully good time in those days, there was something so innocent about everything.

Then we all got up to go, and I was really quite nervous: the poor kid could hardly stand up, and I didn't know what was going to happen. Daddy was so happy and excited, there was something so wild about him, his eyes danced like devils, and he threw back his head and laughed, and you could hear him all over the place.

Father Chris O'Rourke had to hold Mass the next morning, and he left us, but Father Dolan came along. We all went outside with the young man being helped along by Daddy and Mr. Gates, and everyone in the restaurant followed us outside, and Mr. Gates told me to sit up front beside the driver. God! I was proud! And Daddy and Mr. Gates and Father Dolan got in behind, how they ever did it I don't know, it must have been awfully small, I think Daddy must have sat on Father Dolan's lap. O yes! I know he did.

And everybody cheered as we started off; the actors followed us out of the restaurant, and stood looking after us as we drove off into the lilac and velvet darkness, and I can still remember how I looked back and saw their smiling and unnatural faces, their bright masks, their lonely and haunted eyes. They kept shouting funny things at Daddy and asking if he had any last messages, and De Wolfe Hopper was there and he ran around pretending to be a horse and neighing, and trying to climb up a lamp post. O, it was thrilling!

So Mr. Gates said, "Whither away, Joe?"

And Daddy said, "To the Golden Gate and may she never stop!"

Then Daddy said to the young fellow who was driving: "How fast can she go, son?" and the young fellow said, "She can do twenty miles an hour without any trouble."

"Downhill, you mean," said Daddy just to tease him, so we started to go and God! I was thrilled! It seemed to me we were flying, I suppose he did go twenty miles an hour, but it seemed like a hundred would now and we passed a policeman on a horse and the horse got frightened and tried to run away and God! the cop was so mad: he came galloping after us and shouted for us to stop, and Daddy laughed just like a crazy man, and said, "Go on! son! Go on! There's not a horse in the world can catch you!"

But the young fellow was scared and he slowed down and then the cop came up and said what did we mean, and where did we think we were, and he'd a good mind to put us all under arrest for disturbing the peace at that hour of night with "that thing"; he kept calling it "that thing" in such a scornful way, and I got so angry at him, I thought it was so beautiful, it was painted the richest kind of winey red, it looked good enough to eat, and I was so mad to think the man should talk that way.

I don't know why it made me mad, but I think the reason must have been that the car didn't seem to me like a thing at all. It's hard to tell you how it was, but it was almost as if the car was some strange and beautiful and living creature which we had never known before but which now gave to all our lives a kind of added joy and warmth and wonder. And I believe that was the way it was with those first motor cars we ever saw. Somehow each one of them seemed different from all the others, each one seemed to have a different name, a separate life and personality, and although now I know they would look crude and funny and old-fashioned, it was all different then. We had never seen or known them in the world before, we had only dreamed or heard they could exist, and now that I was riding in one, it all seemed incredible and unbelievable, and yet gloriously real and strange, as every beautiful thing is when it first happens to you. The car was magical to me as if it had come out of some other world like Mars, and yet the very moment that I saw it I seemed to have known about it always, and it seemed to belong to that day, that hour, that year, somehow to be a part of all that happened that night, and to belong to Daddy and the priests and Mr. Gates, the young mechanic and all the haunted faces of the actors, and to all the songs we sang that year, the things we did and said, and something strange and innocent and lost and long ago. I can remember now the way that old car looked so well that I could close my eyes and draw it for you. I can remember its rich wine color, its great polished lamps of brass, the door that opened in its round, fat back, and all its wonderful and exciting smells—the strong and comforting smell of its deep leather, and the smells of gasoline and oil and grease that were so strong and warm and pungent that they seemed to give a kind of thrilling life and ecstasy to everything in the whole world. They seemed to hold the unknown promise of something wonderful and strange that was about to happen and that belonged to the night, and to the mystery and joy of life, the ecstasy of the lilac dark, as [if] all the smells of flowers and leaf and grass and earth belonged to them.

So I guess that was the reason that I got so mad when I heard the policeman call the car "that thing," although I did not know the reason then. It looked as if the cop was going to run us in, but then Daddy got up off Father Dolan's lap, and the cop saw Father Dolan and of course he got very nice to us: you know nearly all the cops are Catholic; and Mr. Gates talked to him and gave him some money, and Daddy joked with him and made him laugh, and then Daddy showed him his police badge and asked him if he knew Big Jake Dietz at police headquarters, and then I was so proud to see the way the cop came round.

And the cop said for us all to go into Central Park and we could ride all we damn pleased for all he cared, but you wouldn't catch him in one of those things, they'd blow up on you at any moment and then where'd you all be? And Daddy said he hoped we'd all be in Heaven, and what's more we'd take our own priest with us, so there'd be no hitch in any of the formalities, and we all got so tickled and began to laugh and the cop did too, and then he began to brag about his horse and God! it *was* a beautiful horse and he said give him a horse always, that they'd never make one of those things that could go faster than a horse. The poor fellow! I wonder what he'd say now!

And Daddy teased him and said the time would come when you'd have to go to the zoo to see a horse and the policeman said by that time you'd have to go to a junkshop to see a motor car, and Daddy said, "The trouble with us is that we're anachronisms." And the policeman said well, he didn't know about that, but he wished us luck, and hoped we all got out of it alive.

So he rode off and we drove into Central Park and started off as hard as we could go and began to climb a hill when sure enough, we broke down just as the policeman said we would. I never knew just what did happen, I guess the young fellow may have had too much to drink, he seemed wild and excited, but anyway we saw a hansom halfway up the hill in front of us, and he cried out, "Watch me pass them," and did something to the car, and just as we got up even with them and were trying to go by, the car coughed and spluttered and stood still. Well, we could hear the people in the hansom laughing, and one of them shouted something back to us about the tortoise and the hare. And I felt so mad at them and so humiliated and so sorry for our driver, and Daddy said, "Never mind, son, the race may not always be to the swift, but even the hare will sometimes have his day."

But our young fellow felt so bad he couldn't say a word. He got out of the car and walked round and round it, and finally he began to explain to us the way it happened and how it could never happen again in a hundred years. And well you see it was this way, and well you see it was that. And we didn't understand a word of what he was saying, but we felt so sorry for him that we told him he was right. So he began to poke around inside of it, and then he would turn something here and twist something there, and grab the crank and whirl it round and round until I was afraid he was going to wring his arm off. Then he would get down on his back and crawl in under it and bang and hammer at something underneath. And nothing happened. Then he would walk round and round the car again and mutter to himself. Finally he gave up and said he was afraid we'd have to get out of the car and take a hansom if we wanted to get home without walking. So we started to get out, and the mechanic was so mad and so embarrassed at the way his car had acted that he grabbed it and shook it as if it were a brat. And nothing happened.

He gave it one last try. He grabbed the crank like a crazy man and began to whirl it round and round until he was exhausted. And when nothing happened he suddenly shouted out "O damn that thing," kicked it in the tire as hard as he could, and collapsed across the radiator, sobbing as if his heart would break. And I don't know what that did to it or how it happened, but suddenly the car began to chug and wheeze again, and there we were ready to go, and the young fellow with a grin upon his face that stretched from ear to ear. So we went on up that hill and coasted down the next, and now we really seemed to fly.

It was like soaring through the air, or finding wings you never knew you had before. It was like something we had always known about and dreamed of finding, and now we had it like a dream come true. And I suppose we must have gone the whole way round the park from one end to another, but none of us really knew how far we went or where we were going. It was like that kind of flight you make in dreams, and sure enough, just like something you are waiting for in a dream, we came tearing around a curve in the road and there before us we could see the same hansom we had tried to pass upon the hill. And the minute that I saw it I knew that it was bound to happen, it seemed too good to be true, and yet I had felt sure all the time that it was going to turn out just this way. And that was the way it was with all of us, we threw back our heads and roared with laughter, we yelled and waved our hands at all the people in the cab, we went tearing by them as if they were rooted to the earth, and as we passed them Daddy turned and shouted back at them: "Cheer up, my friends, they also serve who only stand and wait."

So we passed them by and left them far behind us and they were lost. And now there was nothing all around us but the night, the blazing stars, the lilac darkness in the park and God but it was beautiful. It was just the beginning of May and all the leaves and buds were coming out, they had that tender feathery look, and there was just a little delicate shaving of moon in the sky, and it was so cool and lovely, with the smell of the leaves, and the new grass, and all the flowers bursting from the earth till you could hear them grow: it seemed to me the loveliest thing that I had ever known, and when I looked at my father, his eyes were full of tears and he cried out "Glory! O glory! Glory!" and then he began in his magnificent voice: "What a piece of work is a man! How noble in reason! How infinite in faculty! In form, in moving, how express and admirable! In action how like an angel! In apprehension how like a God!"

And the words were so lovely, the music was so grand that somehow it made me want to cry, and when he had finished he cried out "Glory!" once again, and I saw his wild and beautiful brow there in the darkness, and I turned my eyes up toward the sky and there were the tragic and magnificent stars, and a kind of fate was on his wild and beautiful head and in his eyes, and the story of all his wandering, his exile, his loneliness was on his brow; and suddenly as I looked at him I knew that he was going to die.

And he cried "Glory! Glory!" and we rode all through the night, and round and round the Park, and then dawn came and all of the birds began to sing. Now broke the birdsong in first light, and suddenly I heard each sound the birdsong made: like a flight of shot, the sharp fast scarps of sound arose. With chitterling bicker, fast-fluttering skirrs of sound the palmy honied birdcries came. Smooth drops and nuggets of bright gold they were. Now sang the birdtree filled with lutings in bright air: the thrum, the lark's wing, and tongue-trilling chirrs arose now. The little brainless cries arose and fell with liquorous liquefied lutings, with lirruping chirp, plumbellied smoothness, sweet lucidity. And now there was the rapid kweet kweet kweet kweet kweet of homely birds, and then their pwee-pwee-pwee: others with thin metallic tongues, a sharp cricketing stitch, a mosquito buzz, while some with rusty creakings, high shrew's caws, with eery rasp, with harsh far calls—all birds that are awoke in the park's woodland tangles; and above them passed [a] whirr of hidden wings, the strange lost cry of the unknown birds in full light now in the park, the sweet confusion of their cries was mingled.

"Sweet is the breath of morn, her rising sweet with charm of earliest birds." And it was just like that and the sun came up, and it was like the first day of the world, and that was the year before he died and I think we were staying at Bella's then, but maybe we were staying at the old hotel, or perhaps we had already moved to Auntie Kate's: we moved around so much, we lived so many places, it seems so long ago that when I try to think of it now it gets confused, and I cannot remember.

*   *   *

That year I was living with Bella, no I wasn't. I guess we were living with Auntie Kate—well maybe we *were* staying with Bella: I don't know, we moved around so much and it's so long ago. It gets all confused in my mind now, Daddy was always on the go, he couldn't be still a minute: sometimes he was playing in New York, and sometimes he went off on a tour with Mansfield or somebody and was gone for months. O you would have loved Daddy! He was so wild and beautiful, everybody adored him. That was the trouble: things came too easy for him, he never had to work for anything. I think that must have been the year before he died; I was about sixteen. God, I was a beauty. I was like peaches and cream, I don't think I've changed much. Don't you think I have a nice face? I think it's a nice face; it's the same as it always was, people don't change much. . . . Daddy was playing in New York that year. Did you ever hear of a play called *Polonius Potts, Philanthropist*? O, it was a wonderful play: Daddy was so good in it—he took the part of Professor McGilligrew Mumps, of Memphis, D.D.: people began to roar as soon as he came on the stage. I have some pictures of him in his make-up: he had a gold wig and long side-whiskers that stuck out like hay, he had on a long frock coat, and he carried a big floppy umbrella that kept coming open whenever he leaned on it. "Mumps is my name, McGilligrew Mumps of Memphis"—then he would pull out a big red handkerchief from his side pocket and blow his nose like a trumpet; he had only to do that to stop the show, the audience would howl for five minutes.

He was so beautiful: the corners of his mouth bent up as if they were trying to smile all the time: when he smiled his whole face seemed to light up. There was something so delicate about it: it was just as if someone had turned on a light. They don't have plays like that any more, I suppose people would think them too simple and foolish. I thought they were wonderful—I don't know, it seems to me people were more simple in those days. Most people are such Smarties nowadays: everyone thinks he has to be saying or doing something smart all the time. They're all so Fancy, they make me tired. Most of the young fellows are such trash: they're all sicklied over with the pale cast of someone else—a little false this and a little not quite that, it's all like imitation shredded wheat. Good heavens, what's the use of trying to be something you're not and throwing away whatever quality you have? God! I wish I could do something else! I'm too good for it! I'm sorry I gave up my painting. The theatre ought to be the richest and most magnificent thing in the world but most of the people in it are such trash. "As for me I am noted for muh torso!" Imagine giving the words and thoughts of a great poet to a fellow like that! Calling himself Atwater when his real name is Weiss! Atwater, my eye! You can't fool me, young fellow, with that Atwater gaff: I'm one of the chosen myself, you know. Atwater! God! The names they give themselves! Reginald Atwater, when you only have to take one look at his nose to hear the ducks quack: you could hang the complete works of Rubens on one side of it, it looks like the front end of the Leviathan coming into the dock. The nerve of him! Yes, I said, but it doesn't matter at all, Mr. Atwater, what looks best on you: the only thing that matters is what looks best on Hamlet ("Aye, in my heart of hearts, Horatio"), and you have *got* to understand that. God, the conceit of him: it didn't even make a dent in him: "I know, I know," he says, "but we must consider the Physique of the actor playing the part." "Yes, but what part are you playing?" I said, "You are not play-ing Atwater, you are playing Hamlet (which is a big lie, of course, he's playing Atwater: He never played anything but Atwater in his life; he couldn't play anything but Atwater), and you must wear a costume that fits the character." "Yes," he says, "but we all have our Points." (Points! God, that fellow has nothing but Points, he's one complete mass of Elbows and Sore Thumbs so far as I'm con-cerned, he makes me sick!) — "We all have our Points," he says, "and we must try to make the most of them. As for me," he says, slapping himself on the breast like a big piece of Ham, God, it just didn't seem possible — "As for me I am noted for muh torso!" "What!" I cried. "What! O what did you say, Mr. Atwater!" I didn't know what to do, it didn't seem real, I just couldn't believe it: I had to get off the stage as fast as I could; when I told Roberta about it I thought she was going to have a fit — it's become a regular say-ing now, when we've got some terrible ham we say he is noted for his torso.

You just can't believe it's true until you see them: I think Robert and Gwen at the League are about the best of the lot, they work awfully hard — she's a nice woman but if you mentioned Mussolini she'd ask you what did he ever play in. That's about as much as they know about anything. . . . I hope I get some good plays to do this year. God, how I hate this thing the League has given me: it's just like a fake masterpiece, you can smell the ham a mile off, all about Mr. X297, and Mr. Z346 and all of them sitting on their rumps in a row wearing masks and working adding machines and saying the same thing; and all the people in the subway wearing masks and chewing gum, and they've got something hidden up in the garret, an idiot boy, or something, that no one can bear to look at and they try to hide it: I don't know what the hell that's supposed to represent, but it's symbolical and significant and you hear screams from time to time. And then everybody goes to Heaven and God and all the angels are wearing masks and they all sing "The Star-Spangled Banner" together and say: "To hell with Russia, to hell with the Jews, to hell with the Niggers," etc.—Good God! Nobody has ever been like that. Mr. X297! It's ridiculous! He read it in a book somewhere, no, I know where he got it: he went to Germany last year and now he's going to write German plays about America, and I suppose next year he'll be writing Russian plays about Peru, and then he'll read another book and write a Siamese play about Chicago.

It makes me sick, here they've got this magnificent thing around them and none of them will look at it, they're all so fancy; and then there's Mr. Joyce and he's almost blind and God he was glad to get that money, he said he was very hard up, and look what he's able to see: there was something so delicate about his face and when I told him I was deaf he looked awfully interested and asked me a lot of questions about it—he wanted to know what it was like being deaf, he said he was writing something about deafness in his new book, I wonder what it's going to be like. God! there was some good writing in *Ulysses*, it was just as if you had got off suddenly into another dimension, and I thought all that about the man looking for his son was magnificent, and then you have this Burke running around with both his eyes and seeing nothing but X247. It makes me tired! "I don't know if you can do it," he says to me, "it's got to be something cr-r-ude"—gee! I had to laugh at him, the spittle sort of dribbled out of the side of his mouth when he said "crude." But isn't that just like them! They sit around on their back-ends and look bitter and think they're being crude. I'd like to tell them a few things! The nerve of that fellow! "Look here, Burke," I said, "I'm designing this show, and you've got to let me do it my own way." "Yes," he said, "but I want to be sure that you really *feel* the thing" (*Feel* it! My God, I felt like telling him it was like a case of chronic neuralgia). "In a play of this sort," he said, "getting the right scenery is most important." "Vell!" I said, "take avay the scenery and vot have you got?" It was an awfully mean thing to say, but it was so funny I couldn't help it: it just sort of popped out of my mouth before I knew it, usually you think of something like that when it's too late, you never think of it at the moment—I was so proud of myself for thinking of it like that, I think it was awfully smart of me, I don't think he liked it very much, I felt awfully good about it.

* * *

But God! the things I'd like to tell these people if I could: I see the most marvelous things every day, and nobody seems to do anything about it. What a shame to let all this richness and beauty go to waste! It seems to get richer and more beautiful all the time, I see the most marvelous colors and shapes of things now that I used not to notice. God, I wish I could write, what a wonderful power it must be to express yourself in words that way, and to be able to tell what you feel and see. Nobody ever asked me what goes on in my mind when I design, nobody ever tries to find out anything about it, but it is the most exciting and beautiful thing. I should like to write a book and tell people all about it, I should like to tell them about the thing that happens inside me and about all the things I see: O it would be a wonderful book! It would have all kinds of things in it that people know nothing about.

First, I should tell them all about the clothes people wear. O yes! everyone thinks he knows all about clothes, especially these rich Christian women who go into Edith's shop but they know nothing about it. I know more about clothes than anyone I have ever seen, and Edith comes next—I should tell them all the things I see on the street every day and how you cannot know what a person is like until you have seen what he is wearing. People are like the clothes they wear, they may think it's all an accident but it's not. The reason they wear the kind of clothes they do is because they are what they are: when you see one of the men with tight lips and a long thin coldlooking nose he will wear a certain kind of clothes, and when you see all these young fellows nowadays with side pockets that slant and pleat at the waist of the trousers, it is because of something in them, there is something sad about it, and then there is the way that actors and preachers and politicians and quack doctors and psychologists dress: everything they wear sort of goes forward, they are turning everything in them out for the world to see. That was the trouble with Atwater when they did the *Hamlet*: Hamlet turns inward and Atwater turns outward, it is hard to make actors understand that—it is their whole life to turn outward and to be seen and observed, they are always putting themselves forward, it simply kills them if this doesn't happen, they have got to have people talk about them and notice them.

You can tell if people turn inward or outward by the clothes they wear, by their shoes, neckties, shirts, socks and hats. People who wear loose clothes and people who wear tight clothes are not the same, and then there are all the colors they wear: this is simply fascinating. The most wonderful people are the old women you see who wear about a million little things: there are a lot of them in England, they live in all those horrible little hotels up in Bloomsbury and places like that, there are also a lot of them in Boston; they have strange faces, they are lost.

Gee! I saw a wonderful old woman in Boston once: it was in a restaurant, she must have had about a thousand little things on, she had a long black dress on and it was all covered with beads and bangles and glittering ornaments. God! it must have weighed a ton! Then she had all sorts of lace things on over that, it all sort of dripped down from her arms, and fell over her wrists, and got into her soup; and then she had a lot of rings and loose bracelets and beads and necklaces, and a whaleboned collar with a lot more lace and ear rings, and all sorts of combs in her hair, and a hat all covered with masses of things, feathers, fruit, birds, God! that woman was a walking museum. I was so excited, it was one of the strangest things I ever saw in my life, there was something so tragic about her, these people are always sad: I got as close as I could to her and tried to hear what she was saying, but I couldn't. I'd have given anything to know what it was: what do you suppose a woman like that can do? Isn't it a strange thing! It comes from something inside them, something all fancy and broken up like beads, something all cluttered up that can't bear to throw anything away and that is smothering in oceans of junk: there was another of them in Lincoln that time Irene and I were travelling together in that car—she lived in one of those old houses near the Cathedral: it was a lively little old house and when I passed by this old woman was having her tea. God, she was wearing more junk than I've ever seen on any one person [in] all my life, and the room where she was was just like that, there must have been a thousand little things in it—little covers for everything, and little jugs and vases and jars and pots and chairs and tables—it was simply fascinating: I forgot where I was and began to stare in through the window and all of a sudden the door opened and the most dreadful woman flew out at me: she was wearing a maid's dress, and she was one of the most cruel and terrible looking people I have ever seen—her face was all red and hard looking, it was like an axe, you could have chopped wood with it; and she rushed at me with her arms above her head as if she were going to kill me: she cried out in the most terrible voice, "You! You!" I guess she was awfully mad because I had been staring in through the window. God! I was scared stiff; I turned and flew.

Then there are the things people wear underneath, I should like to tell about that too, there is something sad and terrible about it: there was that girl at the theatre when we were doing the Revue, she was a dancer, Jackie they called her, God, she could dance! she was just like a streak of lightning, she was an awfully nice kid, she looked like a boy and when she came in there to be fitted for her costume she was wearing man's underwear, these loose white drawers and an athletic shirt: God, I almost had a fit, there was something awfully sad about it, and the poor kid began to cry as if her heart would break; I don't think she knew what was the matter. And then Lou Becker came in, and she weighs three hundred pounds, she has a great behind that looks like a barrel, and she used to wear the fanciest things you ever saw: she came in once with a black cat embroidered on them in the most sugges-tive fashion, it was simply horrible. "O Lou!" I cried, "In heaven's name, what are you doing?" "It's art, darling," she said, "this mod-ern symbolical stuff. Let those read who can." Gee, she was a funny girl. I wish you could have seen her great fat face with a sort of lewd leer on it when she said it: Martha Hart almost had hysterics.

But isn't there something awfully sad about it? I don't suppose the poor fat thing ever had a beau in her life, and she was always talking about it, she had an awfully dirty mind, but some of the things she said were really very funny. And then there's poor old Rapp, and that time she was staying at our house last year and got bronchitis, and we thought she was going to die: she was simply burning up with fever and shivering, and Edith and I undressed her and put her to bed—Good God! would you believe it, she was wearing three pairs of those old fashioned cotton drawers?

"O Rapp!" I cried, "Rapp! In God's name what's the matter?"

"O don't let them see me!" she said, "they're after me!"

"They?" I said, "Who do you mean, Rapp? There's no one here but us."

The poor old thing, she was simply terrified: she told me later she's been afraid for years that some man was going to attack her, and that's why she wears all those things.

God! it's sad: when I first knew her she was a young and very beautiful woman, she had just come from the hospital, and Bella was her first case. Then later, when I had my little Alma, we had her again: that was the time I almost died, she was simply wonderful, and since then she's always come and stayed with us. Isn't it a strange thing: I remember her when she was a very handsome woman, she had lots of beaus, and several men wanted to marry her, and she had this other terrible thing in her all the time, and now she's old and mad, and she thinks everyone is persecuting her and that men are going to attack her; and sometimes it only seems a little while ago since she came to Bella's and then again it seems so long ago that you can't believe it is real.

O yes! And then I would like to write about the way you feel when you have a child and what it was like when my little Alma came, for I had lain on the earth upon green hillsides all that summer with my child inside me, and I felt the great earth move below me and swing westward in the orbits of the sun. I knew the earth, my body was the earth, I grew into the earth, and my child was stirring in me as I lay there on the earth in that green hillside: and Rapp was there and old Dr. Roth—he was a great surgeon, and I seemed to be out of my head. And yet I knew everything that was going on around me: we were living in that house in West End Avenue then, and it was about eleven o'clock in the morning and God! it was hot! It was August and it was hot as hell, and I could feel the heat and hear the people going by in the street, I heard the clank of the iceman's tongs there in the street and the children shouting, and all of a sudden I could hear all the birds singing in the trees outside, and I cried out "Sweet is the breath of morn her rising sweet with charm of earliest birds," and that was the way it was. It was so lovely, God, I was mad with the pain; it is beyond anything you could ever imagine, it becomes a kind of exquisite and unbearable joy, and one part of you, the upper part, seems to be floating around way up about you, and the other part seems chained to the earth, and they are rending and stabbing you with knives, and great waves of it roll over you, and you feel yourself come and go from it, and when it came I kept crying out "For *who* would fardels bear? *who* would fardels bear? *who* would fardels bear?" And I could see Rapp and Dr. Roth moving about through it all, and it was all so strange because their faces bloomed and faded with the pain; and then there was Rapp with her enormous gentle hands that were everlasting and merciful, they were as big and strong as a man's under me, and I was not afraid but I thought I was dying, I was sure I was dying and I cried, "O Rapp! Rapp! Good-bye, I am going," and she said, "O my darling! My dear! You're not! You will be all right!" She loved me so, and God! but I was lovely then, I was so small and lovely then. And then there was something so strange and terrible about Rapp and Dr. Roth, I had never seen them that way before, he was always so gentle, he told me later he was awfully worried but now he was bending over me and barking in my face: "Push! You've got to push, mother! You're not trying hard enough! You've got to try harder than that, mother! Come on, mother! We can't have it for you, you know! Push! Push hard, mother! You're not trying!" And Rapp said, "O she is trying, too," she got so mad at him, and they were both terribly worried, it had been so long, and then it was all over and I was floating on clouds of peace, I was floating in a lovely and undulant ocean of bliss.

And O yes! I should like to write of the times I go in swimming and of my nice toes and feet and my nice legs, and it was that glorious soft day and the water was so clean and sparkling, and they've got that enormous place that goes a mile or more along the shore, and there was no one there, so Lily and I went in without anything on, and I turned over on my back and floated, and God! I seemed to be right in the very middle of the universe: I could see my nice white belly floating there and my legs all short and funny looking with a strange green color on them moving back and forth like fish, and the sea was like a great bed below me, it held me up and my back and arms floated on it, and I looked up in the sky that was so deep and blue and it all seemed to be part of my body, it seemed to fill me and come from me and flow into me; I was the earth and the sea and the sky and all things were born in me and proceeded from me, it was like something that had gone on forever, it was like music, it was like a star, and I should like to tell people how it was, it was like being in love when your lover comes into you.

And Yes! I should like to tell them all about my little Alma, and how tiny she was, she was just a little scrap of a thing, and of the things that child said! Gee, she was a funny kid: we were having tea one day and she came by the door, and we had guests there, and she couldn't have been more than four years old and I called out "O Alma, Alma, where are you going?" And she said, "I am going out, out, brief candle!" O God! I thought they'd kill themselves laughing, but there was something so wonderful about it too: wasn't that a strange thing for a child that age to say? It popped right out of her mouth, I suppose she had heard some of us quoting Shakespeare. And then one time when Edith and I came in we found her doing her lessons: she had all her books around her in the middle of the floor and she was doing her spelling lesson, she was simply biting the word off as if she were scolding it: O-u-n-c-e, ounce! O-u-n-c-e, ounce! O-u-n-c-e, ounce! Then she changed to another one, P-u-a-r-t, quart! P-u-a-r-t, quart! P-u-a-r-t, quart! God, we had a fit! The poor kid thought the "q" was a "p," and whenever anything went wrong after that we used to say, O-u-n-c-e, ounce!—it was like saying damn, only better. Gee, that kid's a scream: you have never in your life heard anything like the way she goes on at the table, we get to laughing so sometimes that we can hardly eat, she says the funniest things you ever heard, I wish I could remember some of them—O yes! The other night we were talking about the house in the country and what name we would call it by and Alma said, "We will call the side that Father sleeps on the Patri-side, and the side that Mother sleeps on the Matri-side, and as for you, Stinkweed"—that's what she calls Joe, they simply adore each other, they say the most dreadful things to each other—"we will call the side that you sleep on the Fratri-side." God, she's so wonderful! She is my darling and my dear, she is my little Alma, she is the most delicate and lovely thing that ever lived.

And yes! And yes! I should like to tell them how it is the mornings I go into Stein and Bamberg's to design, and Mr. Bamberg is walking up and down on big thick carpets, and God! richness and power and goosegrease seem to be oozing out of every pore of him, and there is something so clean and lovely about the place, the workrooms are great airy places with a beautiful light everywhere, and everywhere there are great clean bolts of magnificent cloth piled upon the tables, and the wonderful smell of cloth: I should like to tell about that in the book and the wonderful feeling it gives you—there is something so generous and full of noble dignity about this cloth, it is grand and beautiful and you can do such wonderful things with it, and all the little tailors are sitting crosslegged on their tables with this magnificent cloth all around them and God! how they stink sometimes! I'm sure some of them never take a bath, sometimes it's simply dreadful when you go in there, you could cut the stink with a knife, but it's fascinating to watch them at work. They're very fine workmen, some of them get paid two hundred dollars a week, they have the most delicate and skillful hands, there is something delicate and beautiful about their movements as they draw the thread through or make a knot, it is like a dance.

And yes! I should like to tell them about Rosen's, what a wonderful place it is, with the Grand Duchess Somebody or Other selling perfume as you go in and this Princess Piccatitti selling underwear. God! I think that is the most horrible name I have ever heard, there is something obscene about it, even Edith has to laugh when she says it—if I had a name like that I'd change it to Schultz or something: imagine being called Ophelia Piccatitti, wouldn't that be horrible? Wouldn't it be awful to be one of the Piccatitti children and then have them call you one of the little Piccatittis. We had a girl down at the theatre once by the name of Titsworth, she was an awfully nice girl, she did the props, but God! I almost got hysterics every time I had to say her name, and what made it more awful the stage manager's name was Mister Matchem, and I think he really got awfully fond of her, she was very pretty, there was something terribly sad about it, I am sure the poor girl suffered tortures about her name. I think she liked him, too, but she was sometimes very unkind to him, and I think that was the reason, and one time he was looking for her and asked where she was and I told him she was upstairs in the workshop, and he asked me would I call her, and I went to the stairs and called up, "Miss Titsworth, some-one wants to see you," and she called down, "Who is it?" And I said, "Mr. Matchem," and God! they had to pick me up off the floor, I got hysterical, they carried me to a chair and Louise Morgen-stern was terribly worried, she thought that I was crying, the tears were streaming down my face, and finally when I got so I could talk again, Louise asked me what the trouble was and I said, "Mr. Matchem is looking for Miss Titsworth," and that started me off again. I think Louise was terribly shocked, she could never under-stand anything like that, she was so awfully pure herself, and she said, "Well, I don't see anything funny about that."

Gee, I have to laugh sometimes when I see their names in the social columns, New York must be simply full of these people, where do you suppose they all come from? When you read about it it doesn't seem possible, it is the God damndest thing you ever saw, it doesn't seem real, you think somebody made all the names up: Mrs. H. Stuyvesant O'Toole entertained at dinner last night in honor of the Prince and Princess Stephano di Guttabelli: among those present were the Lady Jessica Houndsditch, Captain the Right Honorable Hugh McDingle, Mr. and Mrs. Van Rensa-laer Weisberg, Count Sapski, R. Mortimer Shulemovitch, and the Grand Duchess Martha-Louise of Hesse-Schnitzelpuss.

But God! doesn't it make you want to laugh! The nerve of that fellow Burke! This ham playwright that they've got! That's another of those names. Nathaniel Burke my eye! Why didn't you go pick a real fancy Christian name while you were about it? — Montmorency Van Landingham Monteith, or Reginald Hilary Saltonstall, or Jefferson Lincoln Coolidge, or something like that? Nathaniel Burke! Can you beat it? He's the greasiest Kike you ever saw: his real name is Nathan Berkovich, I've known his people all my life. The *Menorah Journal* got hold of all our pictures somehow and the first thing you knew there was Joe Aaronson on the left, and me in the middle, and this Burke on the right with a big black headline: *JEWS NOW PROMINENT IN THE ART THEATER*, or something like that. I thought Burke was going to have a fit: he simply turned green. God! He was mad! I think he thought Joe and I had something to do with it, he stormed around and threatened to sue everybody: he wouldn't speak to anyone for days. I thought Joe would die laughing: he threw his arms around me and kept saying: "After all these years, I believe! There *is* a God!" It was really awfully mean of him, he and Burke simply loathed each other: he kept tormenting him for days about it: "By the way, Burke, I was reading a very interesting piece about you the other day in the *Menorah Journal*." Or, "I see where you have broken into print, Burke. There's a very interesting article about your early life and struggles in this month's *Menorah Journal*. Have you seen it yet? I'll send you a half dozen copies," and so on. I really got frightened: I was afraid once or twice that Burke was going to kill him from the way he looked. His face got all swollen and horrible looking. They both think they are God Almighty: Joe is awfully arrogant and in-sulting when he wants to be—I think it's because he's so small and Jewy looking: his face is so dark and discolored I think he wears all those horrible scarfs and neckties to accentuate it—he suffered tor-tures as a child: when he first went to school the teacher and all the other children thought he was a negro. I don't think that he's ever gotten over it: he's really a very fine and sensitive person, a very high grade sort of man. I think that he has the finest intelligence of anyone they have there.

God! I'm glad he's got Virginia at last, she's a nice girl but nobody's ever going to crown her Miss America. I thought he was going to die for a while; his face became simply purple, none of the doctors knew what was wrong with him, I think he got a little crazy. He hasn't got much money, and he went to Europe and began to spend money right and left. I think he got delusions of grandeur, or something: he hired a Rolls Royce and two men up front and drove all through France and Germany buying costumes right and left—he spent over twenty thousand dollars, part of it he charged to the League. I thought Lawrence Weinberg was going to commit suicide: he tried to tell me about it and he began to strangle, they had to give him a drink to bring him around. Now, they have the cutest Jew baby you ever saw.

But God! the nerve of that fellow Burke! I got so tired of his goings on after a while that I said to him: "Look here, Burke. You'd just better be glad you are a Jew. Where would you be if it weren't for the Jews, I'd like to know? That's too bad about you. You've been treated pretty well, I think. Alle Yiddieshae kinder!" I think he hated me for it. I used to know his father and mother, they were such nice old people—the old fellow had a store on Grand Street, he wore a beard and a derby hat, and washed his hands in a certain way they have before eating: There's something awfully nice about old Jews like that. They were orthodox of course, and I think it almost killed them the way he's acted. He won't go near them any more. Isn't it a shame: to throw that wonderful thing away in order to become an imitation Christian?

And then there's Mr. Rosen in his shop walking up and down and giving orders and bowing and shaking hands with people in his striped pants and rich black coat with the pearl in his necktie: he is like a powerful rich bull, he is so well kept and sleek, I always think of a great well fed bull when I see him; and everything about the place sort of purrs with luxury, everything seems so quiet, but everything seems to be going on just the same, and they're calling for Edith all over the place, you hear them asking for her everywhere, and there she is looking like a very elegant piece of limp celery, with that pedometer strapped around her ankle, she told me she walked seventeen miles one day, sometimes she is simply dead when she gets home, the poor thing is as thin as a rail, sometimes she won't say three words during the entire evening, even when there are people coming to dinner, but God she is smart, they couldn't do without her, she is smarter than any of them.

We're fine people. They sneer at us and mock us but we're fine people just the same. "Many a time and oft in the Rialto you have rated me. . . . and spat upon my Jewish gaberdine." Daddy was a Christian but he was so beautiful. He loved all the things we do, he loved food so much, I don't think he could have stood this Christian cooking. I can't imagine him eating the junk one of these little anemic Christian bitches serves up to her husband. . . . I wonder what they give them . . . O yes, I know! . . . I can just see them now with some awful mess on their plate: I can just see Daddy's delicate and sensitive nose turning up in disgust at the sight of it. He could never have stood it. I know. I know now what they give them: Ox-tail soup out of a can with all of the Ox left out of it, picked-up cod-fish with a little dab of that awful white gooey Christian sauce, boiled Brussels Sprouts and a little stale Angel Food cake that the little bitch got at the Bakery on her way home from the Movies. "Come darling! be a nice boy now! You haven't eaten any of your good boiled Spinach, dear. It's good for you, pet, it's full of nice healthy iron, love (healthy iron, your granny! in three month's time he will turn green with the belly ache and dyspepsia. I bet he'll writhe with acute indigestion). No, you bad boy! you can't have anymore creamed chipped beef: you've already had meat three times this month, you've had 6⅜ ounces of meat in the last three weeks, dear, and it's very bad for you: you'll be getting Uric Acid the first thing you know. If you're a good boy, pet, I'll let you have a nice burned up Lamb chop week after next. I've got the most delicious menu all fixed up for the next two weeks. I read all about it in Molly Messmore's Food Hints in the *Daily Curse*—O yum! yum! yum! Your mouth will water all right when you see what I've prepared for you (Yes! and if I know anything about them his eyes will water too!). Next week is going to be Fish Week darling, we're going to have *nothing* but fish, pet, won't that be nice? (O yes! that will be just too Goddam nice for words.) Molly says fish is good for you, Lamb, the body needs lots of fish, it's Brain Food, pet, and if my big boy is going to use that great big wonderful brain of his and think all those beautiful thoughts, he's going to be a good boy and eat lots of fish like his Momma tells him to. Monday, darling, we are going to have imported Hungarian Cat Fish with hen house noodles—and Tuesday, pet, we are going to have roast Long Island suckers with Gastric juice, and Wednesday, love, we are going to have stewed milk-fed bloaters a la Gorgonzola with stink weed salad and Thursday, sweet, we are going to have creamed Cod with chitling gravy, and Friday—is really Fish Day, lamb—Friday we are going—You bad boy! you take that ugly old *fwown* wight off your face. I don't like to see my big boy's beautiful face all *winkled* up by that ugly old *fwown*. Open your moufy now, and swallow down this nice big spoonful of stewed prune juice. There! Now doesn't he feel better? It's good for my darling's bow-wels—O! wake up in the morning feeling just wonderful . . . O what a naughty word! If my pet begins to talk like that Momma spank! She will wash his mouf right out with soap and water! Yes she will! He just mustn't!"

No wonder Daddy got away from them! He could never have stood it! The very best was not quite good enough for him! And that is the way it is with us too. God, these Christians are a fine lot!

I'll take my chances with a Jew any day! Auntie Kate was another of your Christians and look at the way she acted after Daddy died. And now you would think she was some sort of Saint to listen to her talk—all about how much she did for us, how she sacrificed, and so on. It makes me sick! You just wouldn't believe it possible till you see her . . . she is eighty-five and she gets all dressed up in red velvet, red satin slippers, and red heels. Edith and I send her a hundred dollars a month and she's always asking for more: When she wants more money she writes and says she's got to have a new set of false teeth. One year we counted up and we found we'd bought her seven sets of teeth. Fritz simply loathes her: he's been awfully kind and generous to her, but she is so horrible. She was so mean to Edith and me after Daddy died: Daddy left us some money and she spent every cent of it on herself; she was awfully gay, she had a big house and kept a carriage and did all kinds of entertaining. I guess she needed the money and used it as the bills came in. She did dreadful things: she would go away to Philadelphia or someplace for days at a time and leave me in the house without a penny or anything to eat. There was no one I could go to. I couldn't go to Bella: I think she was living out in the country in Jersey that year, or maybe she was in the sanatarium for taking dope—I don't know: everything was so mixed up and unsettled, we were all moving around so much, it all gets confused now.

When Daddy's lawyer, Mr. Siegel, found out what she'd done, I thought he was going to kill her: he told her hanging was too good for her, he said that he would see that she went to prison if it was the last thing that he ever did . . . I think he really meant it. I got awfully frightened, I was only a kid about twenty, and things frightened me more then . . . I had to go get Edith, she was living in that Convent way up in the Bronx, we had to go to Mr. Siegel's office and answer a lot of questions and sign some papers making it all right. We were both of us frightened nearly to death, Edith was only fifteen, she looked just like a little nun: she had great black staring eyes and she never said anything, no one could ever get her to talk. We walked right into Mr. Siegel's office hand-in-hand, and whenever they asked us a question we just wagged our heads. Neither of us was able to speak. Anyway, everything turned out all right and nothing was done about it. Auntie Kate wept and rung her hands and carried on, and said what wouldn't she do for her dear brother's children. O it made you sick! . . . God what those Christians will do for money! The Jews aren't in it!

* * *

They come! Ships call!
Forever the rivers run.
The great hooves come below their manes of darkness.
And the horses of sleep are galloping, galloping over the land.

* * *

Come, mild and magnificent sleep, and let your tides flow through the nation. O daughter of memoried hours, empress of labor and weariness, merciful sister of dark death and all forgetfulness, enchantress and redeemer, hail! Seal up the porches of our memory, tenderly, gently, steal our lives away from us, blot out the vision of lost love, lost days, and all our ancient hungers: Transformer, heal us!

For we are strange and beautiful asleep, we are all strange and beautiful asleep; for we are dying in the darkness, and we know no death, there is no death, in sleep.

O softly, softly the great dark horses of sleep are galloping over the land. The great black bats are flying over us, the tides of sleep are moving through the nation, below the tides of sleep and time great fish are moving. Call!

As from dark winds and waters of our sleep on which a few stars sparely look, we grope our feelers in the sea's dark bed, among the polyped squirms, blind sucks and crawls and sea-valves of the brain, call through the slopes and glades of night's dark water on great fish. . . .

II

[My Cousin Robert]

My cousin Robert sat quietly on the thick carpet of the stair's top step. He was twelve years old; he was a fat earnest little boy who stammered badly. Slowly, solemnly, remote and elfin as time's memory, the small clock in the room below struck out nine strokes of golden sweetness. The sound thronged through the dark and living silence of the house: it was a music sunken in a far sea-depth, and its chime inhabited the house with its phantasmal magic. After the clock stopped striking there was for a time no sound within the house save its faint slow punctual tock.

As my cousin Robert listened he could hear the footsteps of people coming by on the street outside, and the sounds of their voices. They would come nearer on a crest of sound, pass, with laughter and a maze of voices at its apex, and recede into far sounds and silence. From time to time a cab would pass by in the street outside, and Robert could hear the velvet rumble of its wheels and the sound of the horse, moving at a spanking trot as its hooves struck with a sharp metallic ring upon the frosty pavement.

Among these sounds, these living presences of the moment, the horse lived like a timeless spirit, the house lived the time's spirit, remote, withdrawn, everlasting, and phantasmal. The streets of life cried sharply with their voice of *now*, the splendid frosty stars were burning overhead, and no wind blew. Among the metes and marks of mortal time, joined breath to breath, and link to link, the time here spoken of was some sixteen thousand days and nights ago upon this earth, and now the hoof, the wheel, the sound of all the vanished steps and voices, are forgotten; and my cousin Robert is old and fat and sad.

Robert had the plump white freckled skin, the blue eyes and the curly hair of flaming red that one often sees in Jewish children. He was a good hearted and earnest little boy, generous and affectionate, and his feelings were very easily touched. At the present moment he sat alone in the living silence listening to people passing in the street, and he was a little grieved and thoughtful because suddenly he had been forsaken. That night he had had no dinner. On this spacious and luxurious house where Bella lived, and to which he had so often come with his mother as a favored and pampered guest, a disquieting silence, a silence that removed the house from life and detached it from the cheerful hustle of the streets, had fallen. This was the house of plenty, the house where he had so often stuffed his belly with good things, and Bella was the giver of richness and joy. Therefore he had come here with his mother on this night with the old stir of happy anticipation, and now he found himself, inexplicably, deserted and alone.

People were in the house, and there was life and movement in the house, mysterious life and movement of which he was given a few brief glimpses, but from which he was shut out. They had forgotten him. When he spoke to one of them—to Bella, to his mother, to Bella's husband, or to Else, the cook, they answered him carelessly, indifferently, brusquely. Sometimes they made no answer at all. Once when he had spoken to her, Bella had laid her warm glowing hand, that hand that gave out love and plenty, upon his head; it was an absent and affectionate gesture.

Sometimes a door in the hall above would open; there would be a moment's wedge of soft light, a sudden hiss of quiet voices, a sense of quick but subdued movements. These invasions of life and movement upon the animate silence of the house gave to the boy a sense of intense but quiet activity behind the doors which had been closed to him. From time to time someone would pass him swiftly, softly on the way downstairs, sometimes the heavy waddling form of Else would pant swiftly past him up the stairs. Then doors would open and close gently and the house would lapse into its living quiet again, its breathing silence marked by the slow pulse of the clock.

It was not this momentary and unaccustomed silence that now gave Robert this sense of ominous apprehension; his thought leaped to the living and cheerful activity of the season of which bright scraps and flickers came to him from the streets, and of which this house had always been a living part. It was a few days before Christmas, and the presence of the holiday was everywhere visible, in the streets, in the shops, most of all in the mind of a child which gives to this time a sensuous and mysterious quality, which makes all things—earth, air, fire, and water, the texture of men themselves, different in time and quality from other times. A child breathes ecstasy and hope into him at this season, exultancy gathers in him, he lives with an incomparable intensity, there is mystery and joy in the air around him and he cannot endure to have this rapture broken.

Although my cousin Robert was a Jew, he looked forward to Christmas with as much eagerness as any other child: Bella always had a Christmas tree with gifts for everyone and the family would always gather at her house on Christmas day. For this reason Robert was so troubled now by the silence of the house. Also, until that year, he had accepted Christmas as other children do, as a season of gifts and feasting, and he had never questioned its origin or meaning. But, a few days before, when some of the children at school had been talking of the holiday and of what they planned to do, Robert had said he was going to spend the day at his Aunt Bella's. Then one of the boys, a young tough named Rags Cassidy, began to laugh and sneer at my cousin Robert, and said:

"Why, you ain't got no right to even talk about it. Jews don't have Christmas."

When Robert went home that day he told his mother what the boy had said. My Aunt Mary was a very fine woman, but she was not like Bella or my mother, she did not have much humor; she was a very emotional woman and a fancy talker. So when my cousin Robert told her what this Cassidy had said, my aunt clasped him to her bosom and wept and said, "O my son! My little son! Yes! You are a Jew! Tell him you are a Jew! Tell him you belong to a race that has been persecuted and tortured for three thousand years. Tell him that Christ was a Jew—this Christ that they pretend to worship and in whose name they do such cruel things. Tell them the Twelve Apostles were Jews. Tell him the greatest poets and philosophers who ever lived were Jews, that Spinoza and Disraeli and Heine were all Jews."

Robert did not think it would do much good to tell the Cassidy boy these things, but he promised he would try, and the next day when the boy started on him again, Robert said:

"Spinosey and Heinie and the Twelve Apostles were all Jews."

"You're crazy," the Cassidy boy said, "Heine is the name of a Dutchman."

This is what Robert had always thought, too. So he changed the subject.

"Well, Christ was a Jew," he said.

This made the Cassidy boy very mad and he said if Robert said it again he would smash him one. So Robert didn't say it, but he said:

"Well, if he wasn't one, what was he?"

"He wasn't nothing!" the Cassidy boy shouted. "He was the Loid."

Robert did not understand what the boy meant, and he did not say anything until he had spoken to my father. He knew that my father understood everything and did not get excited like Aunt Mary: My father was a Christian, but he was very smart, and he could always tell my cousin Robert things to say that the Cassidy boy could not answer. So when Robert went to see him, my father said:

"What did he say he was?"

"He said he was the Loid," my cousin Robert said.

"He did, did he?" my father said. "Well, if he knows so much, ask him which Loid he means."

My cousin Robert looked doubtfully at my father.

"There are a lot of Loids," my father said. "First of all there is the North German Loid. Then there is the British South African Loid. Then there are all the Loids in the insurance business. Then there is Loid and Taylor's. Then there are all the English Loids: there is Loid Tennyson and Loid Cornwallis and Loid Burgoyne and Loid Halpus. Maybe he means Loid Halpus," my father said. "Ask him if he doesn't mean Loid Halpus."

When Robert told the Cassidy boy what my father had said, the boy got very angry and said that someday he would kill himself a

Jew, but he had no answer to make to the things my father had told Robert to say.

Therefore, my cousin Robert now sat there on the top step thinking of these things, and of Christmas, and on the ominous and forbidding quiet which now filled the house.

Wherever my father and my mother and Bella were, there was richness and joy: for days the house had been alive with a delightful activity, he had seen Bella come in from the streets with her arms loaded with packages, for weeks my mother and Else had been together in the kitchen: they had baked dozens of cakes, pies, tarts, cookies, and loaves of bread. That magnificent house was perfumed now with a dozen strange, rich, and delicate odors—of cinnamon and butter, of spiced fruits and brandied peaches, of preserved ginger brought from China in jars of dark green with heads of woven straw, the Christmas wreathes with their thick stiff leaves of dull green and the red bitterness of their berries. Bella loved abundance and joy, the very best of everything was just about good enough for her, and in addition to the finest meats and fruits and poultry, she loved whatever was rich, rare, and subtle—silks and spices from China, the smoky shawls of India, goblets of thin Austrian glass, the oldest, rarest, headiest wines of the Rhine and Burgundy, the heavy silver chains and lockets of the East, the softest warmest furs of the North—she loved all things that were rich and rare and plentiful in man and nature, she gathered the treasures of the earth about her, and then, because she was the bountiful giver, the source of love and abundance, she gave them out again.

Shall we hear the sound of the hoof and the wheel in the street again? Shall we hear the sound of the foot on the step? And was there any music in that sound? If there was music, is there more to say?

How proud, how sharp, how certain some have been! Where are the lost words now? Some had the medicines for all our griefs and could not heal their own. Of some was said: "How fine, how wise, how subtle." They died, we said that we regretted them, and our memory grew as grey as their own dust. Some used the mockery of limber tongues, some cursed and threatened, and now the mocker and the angry man lie in the earth together. There was no music in their flesh, they brought no joy up to the lintel of a door, and they are lost. They could not help their barrenness, the taste of life was bitter on their lips, and they are lost. They were born without juice or succulence, they grew wise upon the words of others, they knew what they did not know, and they are lost. There was a fashion in disdainfulness, some therefore curled their lips and spoke of nightingales in Jersey City, and they are lost. They could not mock, and so they curled their lips in mockery; they could not weep, and therefore they covered their faces with their hands; they made a skein of words to speak of love, but they had no love, no love, and they are lost. Born without hope or hopelessness, born without love or madness, they breathed the air punctually and moved inglorious flesh about, and they are lost. They hated life and could not die, they could not believe in their own unbelief, they longed to make the semblance of a living man, they had the parts and painted grief or laughter, and they are lost.

But we heard the horses and wheels of Bella's carriage in the street as children, we heard her slow stride on the steps, the glorious undulations of her dress, and our hearts were lifted to our throats with joy, and the sound of the hoof and the wheel will walk in our brain forever. Therefore, can we say more than this of any man when he is dead? Perhaps there are a thousand memories and reasons, ten thousand affirmations or denials, but at the end, the very end, what can we say of him? At the end, the very end, we might say: "He was not wise or faithful; his tongue was cruel and his brain was mad. He was so wrong and so mistaken, he was drunken, wild and foolish, he laid the treasure of his spirit waste, and he brought us pain because we loved him." At the end, the very end, we might say all these things if they were true, but we would not say them, we would not remember them, they would be melted from us like a wisp of smoke, if joy and richness dwelt in him. At the end, the very end, we could say no more than this, for there would be no more to say than this: "Our hearts were lifted to our throats with joy whenever we heard his step outside the door."

There are some people who have this quality of richness and joy in them, they were born with it and it stays with them throughout their life, no matter what they do, no matter what ruin or misfortune falls upon them. Some of these people are rich and some are poor, but it does not matter at all whether they are rich or poor in worldly wealth, such people are really always rich: they have in them a wealth that can never be taken away from them and that makes them richer in poverty than millionaires. My father and my Aunt Bella had this quality more than anyone I have ever known.

At this time Bella was rich. She still had a considerable portion of the property my grandfather had given to his children: this house was part of it. She had also married a doctor who was a wealthy man, and who had a large practice among rich people. She always had plenty of money at this time, and she spent it with the same gesture as a farmer sowing grain: if there was any chink or rift in the comfort of life, any crack or barrenness in the richness of things, Bella stopped it with gold. She could not bear that anyone within sight or touch of her life should want for anything, and her beautiful and opulent hunger soared over the earth and gathered into her house the rarest things: a poor child like my cousin Robert felt, on entering this house, that he had come into magic, that there was nothing within his wish or desire that could not instantly and abundantly be given to him.

Later, when Bella had begun to feel the pinch of money, this was just the same. Whatever she wanted, or whatever anyone else wanted, she got at once. If she wanted a new carriage and horses, and she had no money for them, she would sell a house; if she had no house to sell, she would bite off pearls or emeralds from a necklace, and send a servant out to get money on them from a pawnbroker: once she paid a grocer who had refused her father credit by sending him a diamond bracelet, and if she wanted to wear jewels which she had already pawned, she would retrieve them by sending others in their place.

One might say that it is easy to give to people this sense of joy and richness so long as one has wealth to fling away in this fashion. It is not true. There is no joy in wealth alone: in the hands of meagre and barren people wealth has a dusty color. The real wealth that Bella had burned like a flame inside her, and it never went out. In the last years of her life, when she had lost everything, when she was a ruined and broken old woman, wrecked with drugs, drifting from one cheap lodging house to another, this quality was more triumphant than it had ever been. Wherever she went the people wanted to be near her: the people in these dingy places—the little shop-girls and stenographers, the broken down chorus women, the clerks and book keepers, and those desolate and barren old men and women who carefully eked their meagre candle-end of life out in these houses—were instantly drawn toward her, and they loved her. The story of her ruin, the degradation of the drug, was legible upon her flesh and in her eye, but their vision passed by this at once and they could never see her in this ruined mask again: Bella stood instantly revealed to them as the most beautiful and distinguished woman they had ever known, whatever she touched at once became valuable and beautiful, the dingy little rooms she lived in at once grew glorious when she entered them, and the poor lives of all these little people feasted like starved sparrows on the endless wealth and bounty of her spirit.

When I have spoken of her to people who never met her, I have found that many would not believe me: some laughed at me and said I had a romantic temperament, that exaggeration was natural to me, that my memory had thrown a false glow over her, and that such a person as I described had never lived. Other people would get somewhat annoyed and bitter when I told them about Bella: there were always people who had not had much life of their own because they had nothing to make it with. I have often noticed that such people get angry and sarcastic when told that such a person as Bella has lived upon this earth: Some of them buy their own sterility, they clutch their little delusion of futility because it is all they have, and they feel it gives them a bitter elegance. If it is taken away from them they are deprived of their whole stock-in-trade, they have nothing left: they say that joy and glory have departed from the earth, and when they meet a person like Bella they are finished. They can still speak, but their words sound foolish. Once when I was talking to such people about Bella, a man burst out resentfully:

"Yes, but why? Why? To what end? What was she living for? For what purpose was all this energy and exuberance? What did it all amount to in the end?"

He waited for an answer but I did not answer him because he was a fool and a fancy talker: he really did not want an answer. My words would have had no meaning for him. But I knew the answer.

I knew the answer because I am a Jew and we are born with a knowledge of all the sorrow on the earth. We are so wise because we know at once that we must die. We have been to the wailing wall of love and death for so many centuries, we know so well how to weep and laugh, and we have no time for childish Gentile gabble of futility. We began at the beginning, we have been the master delvers and explorers of living for so long a time that we know! We know! An immense and tragic authority rests upon us. We knew all that at the start, and it was one of us who wrote thousands of years ago: "I gave my heart to know wisdom, and to know madness and folly: I perceived that this also is vexation of spirit." And the same man wrote that the day of a man's death is better than the day of his birth, he wrote that the "fool foldeth his hands together and eateth his flesh," and he wrote that there is nothing better for a man than that he should eat and drink and enjoy good in his labor. He told us to do the work that lay before us with all our might, for there is neither work nor wisdom in the grave, he told us to live with all our heart, and he said that the living know that they shall die, but the dead know nothing. A Jew said this thousands of years ago, he knew the human destiny and what befalls us, and there has never been anything beyond it in courage, in wisdom or in understanding.

Bella knew this. The reason she had so much exultancy and joy in her life was because the sorrow of time and death was in her heart. The reason she lived this life so well was because she knew that she must die. She died a ruined and broken woman but I think she had as great a wisdom in her as any person I have ever known. The wisdom that Bella had was this: that a man can save his life only by saving nothing, that we can hope to live only by giving all the life we have in us to living, that, in the end, whatever is saved is wasted. I know that we must save nothing that we value dearly: our love, our life, our talent, our possessions and our money must be given utterly and fiercely, and I know whoever saves a precious thing is damned and lost. When I think of Bella, I think also of all the people I have known who have lost their lives through saving them: the people who were forever fearful, forever cautious, who never did anything intensely and with all their life and spirit: who always yielded sparingly and by less than half, and who always kept their eye upon half opened doors of safety and retreat. Here were the lovers with strings of compromise and caution on their love, here were half-poets who wrote of their half-lives the flimsy substitutes for passion; here were the quarter-rebels, and the part-adventurers, the bold eye longing for new lands and oceans and the cold withdrawing heart. Here were the frugal cooks, the thrift of crusts and salad leaves, the almost-good economies and the re-worked remnants, here were the people who had never done or felt anything with all their spirit, with all their life and energy—here they were, most of the men and women I have known on this earth, these are the really poor and the truly wretched, the half-hearted, the half-willed, the half-minded! Here, finally, were those who were frugal, mean, stingy with money, devoured by what they had hoarded, destroyed by what they had saved: the men who had saved their gold and wasted their lives.

As I thought of all these people I saw clearly that they, and not people like Bella, were the true wasters and wantons of the earth: these people were the enemies of life, the foes to inspired and mag-nificent living—the cautious, the calculating, the corrupt—and in the end what did they have for all their pains of fear and caution? They had saved, saved, saved, and in the name of God, for what had all this saving been? What had they saved themselves for? For the bitter lips. For the starved eyes and the constricted heart. For ten thousand days of grey awakenings, for the countless repetitions of their weary acts of dressing, feeding, working, for ten thousand nights of lying down to rest, to sleep, to restore their wasted ener-gies for what, for what? For endless turnings of the wheel that ground no grain. For this meagre house of skin and bone that year by year grows dry and yellow with depletion, that unhallowed by love or joy grows old and sick when corrupted to base uses; for this patched up dwelling place, this shabby inn, and for its final thoughts of dusty earth.

No. I know now with an utter certainty that who saves his life shall lose it, and that Bella had been superbly right, triumphant in her ruin, victorious in her death. I heard her say once, with her wild, impatient, fiercely hungry gesture: "God! I'd like to go up all at once in one good blaze—just like a bonfire!" It was the madness of her hunger, but it was right.

When a person has this glorious endowment of energy and joy it is not an exaggeration to say that "nothing else matters." With such a person the simplest act glows with a vital and exultant power, and the most common and familiar things begin to live with a fresh and living glory. About my first memory of Bella was of her smoking a cigarette: I was sitting on the floor of our back parlor, and it was Spring, and suddenly I looked up and I saw Bella looking at me as she lit a cigarette. I can see her slow rich smile, with the faint shadow of her dimple appearing as she looked at me with the deep and living sparkle of her eyes that was so mocking and so tender, I saw her face dip toward the lighted match, and her mouth pucker, I saw her flick the match away, and then she looked toward mother, who was busy with her sewing, and spoke to her. I do not know what she said, but I know it was something about me, and then she looked at me again for a moment, and her great laugh filled the room. I saw the delicate wires of smoke curl from her nostrils, perhaps I did not know then what tobacco was, but all at once I understood that it was one of the most delicious things in the world, that it was a poignant and glorious weed, and that the cigarette which Bella was smoking at that moment was the finest cigarette that anyone had ever smoked. All at once I discovered the earth. In a second the obscure and broken memory of my infancy was flooded with light: the whole world came to life before me, instantly I saw and knew everything. Bella was sitting in the centre of a universe each part of which was pulsing and glowing with her own joy and energy. I saw the spacious and beautiful room, the high white ceiling with its great central bud of plaster, the back windows that were so proud and tall with their clean sunlit curtains fluttering in the breeze, the squares of living sunlight on the floor, the shelves of books, and the warm comfort of the furniture. I saw the strength and delicacy of everything, the wonderful life that pulsed in all these well used objects, the generous and strong design of the furniture, the carelessness, the ease, the whole living texture of the room charged with its own life and the lives of the people who dwelt here.

Everything made one piece with life: my mother's dark head was bent above her flashing needle, she was dark and silent, a flame was burning in her, she was the listener. Sometimes when Bella talked she smiled, and her hand went back and forth. Suddenly I understood that it was morning, before noon, and that my mother had been here in the room all morning and that Bella had come in from the streets. Instantly I understood the bond between the two women, the enormous casualness of a lifetime was between them, but I felt a love and devotion that was deep as life and death, and I understood in what way I belonged to them and why Bella had looked at me and smiled. Now, also, I was aware of the living presence of the season: I saw the first sharp green of city trees with all their lively piercing ecstasy and I knew for the first time the immense youth and sweetness of the back yards of New York. The vital living air fell with such shining purity upon all things, and, imperial, unperplexed, the bird song rose with its proud liquid clarity. At this moment I heard a sudden shout of children playing, the cry struck strong and hard upon the air with the certitude of gravel, and a feeling of the most unspeakable joy and triumph swept across my spirit. The entire earth came to life before my eyes like music, and everything about me lived, and I saw Bella there before me, and I knew wherever she was, there, too, was glory. This was the day that I first saw her clearly, that I remember her, but I knew at once that to be with such a person was to live constantly with a great enchanter who will take us not into charmed kingdoms, but lead us back into the kingdom of this earth, which some have lost and some have never found. The glory of all this joy is that there is no falseness in it: it reveals the wonder of the earth that has never died, and the power to reveal this wonder Bella never lost. That was the reason people loved her and wanted to be near her wherever she went.

Wealth or poverty made no difference in her. If Bella had invited guests to dinner, and she had only two dollars to buy food with, it would have been the same: she would have bought one thing—she would have bought the best steak she could find for two dollars, she would have brought it home, and cooked it herself, her beauty and her richness would have gone into the steak, she would have served it to her guests upon a single platter, and there would have been no more to eat; yet, when the guests had eaten, they would all have felt that they had banqueted.

It was the same with my father. He could touch nothing that he did not glorify. Wherever he went the earth broke into living forms of magic. Whenever these two people come into the memory of my childhood, life takes on its intensest glow of joy and color, and I remember everything: the large sprawl and dusty chaos of living is burned and drawn to a focal clearness, and I see all the world about them in a series of sharp, intensely living pictures, exultant, touched magically by time, and fabulously real.

Often, I have noticed here upon this crowded and fantastic isle which I have known and loved dearly, the strange intensities of time and history. It has been said of us that we have no history and no sense of time because we are so young, but the truth is that our history is vast and immeasurable and we have all lived through a dozen times and lives. The history of a thousand years has been crammed into this compacted grain of rock on which we live, this mite of laden earth on which so many million men have lived and died, and which gathers into its iron grip the nerves and sinews of the world. This is the fabulous earth, the only legendary city: we live at the heart of time and unbelief, and not only the streets of forty years ago seem evocations of a wizard's dream, but the streets of the present moment, the phantasmagoria of the afternoon, the incredible intensity of each moment of the city's life is touched with legendry. To remember the hoof and the wheel in the street again, the tramp and shuffle of a million solid leathers on the pavement, and the faces of the lost Americans of 1893 is to remember charms and strangers on another earth. It is more fabulous than Araby, more remote than the Saxon themes, the young knights and the horses. And yet we lived in it.

Yet, I have seen that many people who have lived here, who, like myself, have known that strange land, have little memory of it now. And I think that I know the reason. Without some glorious image for their minds to cling to, their memory has been dulled and deadened by the shock and glare of the innumerable days. They can only vaguely speak of "then" and "now." For here, the ravenous hours devour their parents, the mind reels in the tempest of each moment, and the city changes like the destiny of a nation behind the dust and violence of each day's attack: the terrible moments cloak the shift and evolution of a history like a screen of battle smoke until one day we wake to see first light again, to hear the constant miracle of birds, as men have wakened from a fever, and we see that the world we knew has changed: the world of little houses that we lived in as children has shrunk and dwindled underneath stupendous towers—already all that world is lost and ghostly and the faces of the people that we knew there are also innocent and lost. Sometimes at night we lie and listen to the sounds of silence and of death, and day by day, in all our living, the people are dropping one by one into the tides of death, until a hundred million nameless little men have died with all the objects that they dwelt with, and we have a new world, and we don't know how it came. The years come, the savage years, the fury-winged years armed with their whips of days, the tens, the teens, the twenties come, a friend says "Were you living here in 1923? What were you doing then?" and for a moment our hearts grow black, we feel as if we had been drowned: before the dusty roar and shock of the unnumbered days, the years have passed by in a blur of chaos, our minds grip to a straw of memory here and there, we say "that time . . . another time . . . one day . . . it must have been the time that you came back." The color of the years grows grey and blurred before the smashing shock of the city days, we remember little, nothing, because our minds are glutted with a million memories. We see, we hear, we taste no more, because our senses have been blunted by satiety, but at times we see ourselves, blind, driven figures in some nameless destiny, unmindful at length of year or day or any destiny save that moment's painful goal, we see ourselves no longer mindful of great towers, no longer conscious of great changes, bewildered soldiers in a battle, the shock troops in the bloody battle lines, choking in [the] dust and tumult of ten thousand days, and at length asking for nothing but an end to all the beat and clamour of the man-swarm, the calm immensity of night again, the sound of silence on the earth, a few familiar things, and the imperturbable splendor of a single star.

For life is more savage than any war: it is not for the million men who are slain in a battle that men should grieve, but for the hundred million men around us who are daily slain by living, and for whom, soon or late, the earth is waiting. We do not grieve that some men die in battle: we simply grieve that all men die, with all their hunger unappeased, with all their purpose gone amort.

My own memory of my youth, however, has remained fresh and vivid. It has not been dulled and blunted by weariness or confusion. I think the reason for this is that our memory thrives upon some vivid, brilliant thing or person, such as Bella or my father: the blur and confusion of time and all the faces are conquered and dominated by our memory of wonderful people. The powerful energy of these lives and the light they cast evokes a thousand other pictures of the world around them, until, through them, we have drawn up out of oblivion a picture of the past that has order and a sharp design. Even after we have grown up, long after the death of these people, the memory of their lives still masters everything they touched, and saves our own from forgetfulness and confusion. We pass along a street where such people lived, or by a house where they once lived, or by a building that has taken the place of the house, and no matter what swarming change, what bewildering complications have occurred in size and number, we can remember the place as it was when we first knew it, and these people lived here, and our lives are given roots in the midst of this city's life that always changes. This is what Bella and my father gave to me.

III

[My Father on Tour]

One of my first memories of my father was of a time when he had taken us along on one of his tours. At first I have a sense, rather than a memory, of one-night stands in little towns. I have a sense of darkness, of weariness, of always being wakened from my sleep to catch a train, of the hotel bus that took us to the station, and of long weary pauses in the waiting rooms of stations while we dozed upon hard benches. I have a sense, rather than a memory, of the dreary attentive silence of waiting rooms at night, of the occasional brief loneliness of steps, of the clatter of a pail upon the floor, the uneven clatter of the telegraph, of figures of time erased and written on a board, of trains that were constantly late. I can remember the sounds of shifting engines in the yard, the slow wear and wastage of the night, the heavy interminable rumble of a freight as it passed by, and the mournful whistle of an engine far away.

And then, suddenly, in the midst of all this eternity of dreary waiting, the morning and my father came together. I can see the first light of the day outside, a wagon from the post office rattles up, and then I see my father, coming toward us with the eager lift and brightness of his smile. I don't know where he had been before; I suppose he had been there with my mother all the time, but I remember him always as he came toward us, and the sun came up outside. Then the other people, the members of the company, began to stretch and yawn, and straighten out their limbs; there was the air of something impending in the station.

We got up then and went into the station lunch room. All of

the actors, the men and the women alike, sat on the stools at the counter, talking and laughing together, and joking with the man who served them. One of the men pointed to some stale railroad sandwiches under a greasy glass cover, and he asked the counter man if those were property sandwiches. Everyone laughed, and so did I, although I did not know what he meant, and his meaning came to me only one day, after I had grown up. Then Mr. Henry T. Dixie said he was sure he had met the sandwiches before; then someone asked what kind of sandwiches they were, and when the counter man said they were ham, everyone roared with laughter. He said they were the same sandwiches that had played in the banquet scene in *Macbeth*. My father then said no, in his clear and magnificent voice: he told Mr. Dixie that he was mistaken and that he had gotten these sandwiches mixed up with some other sandwiches: he said these sandwiches were the ones that had played in *The Black Crook*. Then someone shouted, "No! No! East Lynne! East Lynne!" and the entire company took it up, arguing with one another in a fierce and animated manner about the parts and plays in which these sandwiches had appeared. As the actors talked in this earnest and animated fashion, I became terribly excited and eager to know what they were talking about: I wanted to ask my father questions about it, I did not understand how sandwiches could play a part in anything, and yet I did not want to say so publicly, and betray my ignorance. But I knew that my father would tell me anything that I wanted to know, and I resolved to ask him when we were alone. Suddenly, the dreary ugliness, the dull weariness of the night had gone; I felt excitement and exultant joy. I sat beside my father and mother at the counter and Mr. Dixie came and sat with us. He was a famous actor of that time, and he and my father were devoted friends. My father was studying the greasy menu with his grave and beautiful look, and presently he said to the counter man:

"I see that you have shark upon your menu. Is it in season?"

The counter man was stupefied. "Where?" he said. "Where do you see that?"

"Here," my father said, pointing to a greasy stain.

The counter man looked. "That don't say shark!" he said. "That says broiled mackerel."

"O, excuse me!" my father said. "I thought it was shark."

Mr. Dixie was also looking at the menu, and he said: "How are the snails today?"

"We ain't got none," the man behind the counter said.

"I did not ask you that," said Mr. Dixie in a gentle tone. "I merely asked you how they were."

Thus they talked with the man behind the counter, asking for all manner of strange dishes, pretending to be surprised and shocked because he had no boiled camel's hump or roasted elephant trunk, telling him such things were all the rage in New York at that moment, and that he should keep abreast of the times. The actors sat all along the counter in a row: then bright and rapid chatter filled the cheery little room with gaiety and sparkle: the place took on a life that it had never had before. As I remember it now, I know it was only a dingy little station lunch room in an American town forty years ago, and I know that most of the actors were what actors have always been: vain and trivial show people, quick and shallow, speakers of lines and passions which a deeper sort of person had set down for them, for the most part men without a talent or belief, fascinated by the glare of light, the sham of tinsel, troupers and mountebanks, without wisdom or understanding, who decided destinies so grandly on the stage, but were unable to decide their own lives wisely for a week, never vouchsafed a gleam of the rare immortal glory of the theatre. I have known them so well, and for the most part they are children: vain, jealous, ignorant and ebullient, in a moment utterly cast down or widely hopeful, each a jaded sort of peacock, the grotesque centre of an absurd firmament, at once more funny and more pitiful than the jokes they made. But how brave, how innocent!

As we sat there, the door opened, and a member of the company came in from the station. He had an open telegram in his hand and he came straight toward my father. His name was Rooney: he was a comedian, a singer and a dancer, well known at that time. He loved children and always had something in his pockets—an apple, an orange, or a piece of candy—to give to them: besides that, he taught us little songs and the steps of a dance. When he danced he was like smoke or ashes, or a streak of lightning. Everyone liked Mr. Rooney, and children adored him. He was like a child himself, hot-tempered and generous, vain and sensitive to his deficiencies.

He was totally illiterate: he could neither read nor write, everyone knew this, but it was part of the delicacy of these people never to refer to it or recognize it in any way. When he received a letter or telegram, he always came with it to my father: my father knew that Rooney could not read, and Rooney knew my father knew it, but the pretense was kept up on both sides with perfect gravity. Now Mr. Rooney approached my father, brandishing the telegram with an air of great distress and indignation.

"Read that, Joe! Just read it!" he exclaimed, thrusting the message into my father's hands.

"What does it say, Pat?" my father said as he looked at it. "No bad news, I hope."

"You'll see! You'll see!" said Mr. Rooney. "Just read it, Joe! I can't believe me own eyes, Joe! Just read it out to me, so I can hear it for meself."

My father therefore read the message, and it contained a very good offer to Mr. Rooney to appear in a show that was going to open in New York in the summer.

"Ain't it a shame, Joe? Ain't it a shame?" Mr. Rooney said at once. His mind was very quick and agile and he always had an answer ready. "Did ye ever hear of such hard luck? Hear I am noine million miles away from Broadway with never a hope of gettin' back before St. Swithin's eve!"

My father said it was too bad, but that he was sure we would all be back before the new show opened. When Mr. Rooney had gone, my father looked at my mother for a moment, and then he smiled. I noticed for the first time that his eyes were grey and his hair a complete silvery white. It had been so from his twenty first year. When he smiled it was as if a light had been turned on; his smile had a grave sweet quality, it came slowly and it gave his face a luminous and shining radiance: every line in his face seemed to lift and try to turn upwards. Everyone who knew him always remembered his smile and his laugh: they printed themselves instantly upon the memory and people never forgot them. His smile had a peculiar and grave sweetness, and his laugh always came a moment or two later. His laugh came suddenly and yet with a kind of deliberation, it always came a moment or two after the thing that caused it: he was always telling jokes and stories, he could tell the wildest and most extravagant story, building it up in his mind and adding some new fantasticality to it with every word. And yet he could persuade people that anything he told them was the truth: his eyes burned and sparkled like a demon's when he talked, but he told the stories with an intense and eager seriousness that fascinated everyone and made them believe against belief. I think that when he talked he believed these things himself: when he finished people would be so fascinated and bewildered they could not speak, and it was only a moment or two later, when the conversation had changed completely, that my father would laugh. He would pause suddenly, glance with his grey piercing eyes at his listener, and suddenly laugh softly and gently, including everyone in a glance that was full of humor and affection.

People adored him. They loved him because he had the power to make them feel a sense of beauty and distinction in themselves. They felt this because he believed it of them: he believed in the value and dignity of everyone, and his relations with people were touched with the sense of respect and honor he had for life. He was a man of a higher quality and with a deeper spirit than the other actors. I think they perceived in him a reality which they did not have in themselves, and I think he felt for them the same affection and sympathy that one feels for unhappy children.

I know now how wretched and poor the lives of all these people must have been. There was very little in themselves on which they could depend: everything in them turned outward, they had to secure the applause and attention of the world, or they were lost. They could not be alone. I know also how miserable and shabby was their physical existence. There was at that time among the people of these small towns all over America a legend that the life of the actor was gay, luxurious, and sinful. They were not considered respectable, or fit company for decent people, but the people in these towns regarded them with fascination and awe. As soon as the company appeared in a new town they were marched out by the natives as "show people," and from that time until they left they were the centre of the town's curiosity wherever they went. If they went out in the streets, children followed them about, and men loafing in front of shops and stores would grow silent when they passed. Later these men would nudge and speak behind their backs: "There he goes! There goes that show feller!"

This attention was not always friendly. Hostility and suspicion were mixed with wonder. The women in the company were regarded by the townspeople as prostitutes: if a woman was young and attractive, she rarely escaped the clumsy foulness of some village Casanova. And neither the actors nor the townspeople had any understanding of one another: the conception each had of the other's life was completely legendary. To the townsman the actor dwelt in a world of fabulous and glittering vice. And to the actor the townsman was a yokel, a gullible hayseed. To the townsman the actor was a figure in a melodrama, and to the actor, the townsman was a buffoon in a farce. The actor came from a legendary city called New York: the townsman dwelt in a legendary village called Hicksville. I think that each believed what he wanted to believe about the other: when the actor talked to a native, his manner was glib and bantering in the fashion of the city fellow pulling the leg of the greenhorn.

Although the actors mocked at these small towns and cursed the fate that sent them on these tours, I know they cherished the conspicuous attention they received. It pleased them to hear the whispers, to see the stares and nudges: it gave their poor lives a sense of dignity and importance, a stimulus they could not do without. They talked of the splendid lives and brilliant opportunities that awaited them in New York, they spoke of their past triumphs, for the most part mythical—each had his own tale of fame and glory to relate, but I think that most of them were really grateful in their hearts even for the shabby insecurity of the road. Their city lives had in the main been records of pain and hunger, of rare employments and of long and weary quests for work, of poverty, rebuff, and squalid living.

For what? They did not know: in these dark histories of defeat and disappointment there was a hope of glory they could not forego, a sense of magic which enthralled them and kept them from every other kind of life. And I think of them as I sat there beside my father with a memory that is full of tenderness: I remember the hard, the aching weariness of the night, the distressed and shabby pattern of their lives, the dull monotony and the ghastly ugliness and discomfort of that life of cheap hotels, of long night waits and pauses, and I remember how quickly they could laugh, how little it took to make them merry, with what fierce and reckless courage they brought brightness back, how fiercely their lives fought for ecstasy. We sat there in that dingy room that had grown bright with all our laughter, and presently, as the time grew tense with the hour for the train, the actors got up and went out upon the platform. Bright morning sparkled on the tracks, and before my vision the powerful rails bent out of sight like space and music.

My father lifted me onto an empty trunk and I sat there with my short legs swinging off the edge, seeing the whole earth perfectly at last. The delicate morning light concealed nothing and yet gave a lyrical quality to the immense ugliness of the station tracks and sheds, the freight cars on the sidings, the cindered yard, and the ragged baldness of the warehouse and factory backs. In the intense purity and sweetness of this light there was enormous hopefulness. A man came from the baggage room drawing a heavy truck piled high with mailbags. The actors stood about in groups and talked or walked up and down the platform. There was an extra cut to everything they did or said; it was in all their clothes and gestures, an added vividness and intensity in their appearance that distinguished them from other people: they were like men in vivid masks.

It was early in the Spring. My father was wearing a light overcoat of a rich tan color; it was a magnificent garment that fitted him perfectly, with a bold firm line, and came down almost to his ankles. He had a cane below one arm and now he began to walk up and down the platform rapidly. At the same time Mr. Dixie began to do the same thing. They approached and passed each other from opposite ends of the platform; then, as their mad exuberance gained on them, they began to glare and mutter melodramatically as they passed. Again and again they passed each other in this manner and each time their glares grew fiercer, and their mutterings grew louder. Each time they got closer to each other, until, at length, they bumped together. Then, with a tigerish ferocity, they sprang apart and faced each other.

"Hah!" my father cried in a terrible voice.

"Hah!" cried Mr. Dixie in the same tone.

"Hold, villain, and defend yourself!" my father cried and whipped his cane out underneath his arm as if it were a sword.

"Have at you, dawg! Your hour is come," cried Mr. Dixie, whipping his cane out in the same manner. Then, furiously, their bright canes flashed and struck together in that pure light: with fierce cries and noble imprecations they thrust and lunged and parried; and all the time my father leaped and moved with an incomparable grace, with the proud and beautiful balance, the rhymed precision of his strong delicate figure that had been trained to twist and fall in circuses. Now, they duelled fiercely up and down the platform, they drove each other back and forth, and suddenly my father stopped, struck Mr. Dixie's cane up, and ran him through the body. And Mr. Dixie cried out in a great and moving voice:

O Woe! O, I am dead, dead, dead! Villain, thou hast slewn me!

And he sank upon the platform while the gapmouthed natives stared at him, and the actors cheered, and the train came roaring round the bend and stopped, panting in its hot sides, and the conductor swung down, and all of us got up and went into the train, and there was a smell of old red plush and cinders in it. Then we left that place of night and ugliness, we went out across the country, we moved across the huge and thoughtful earth, we saw its wild rude immensity, its rough pelt still embourned with water, its tangled lakes and undergrowths: we saw the fields and meadows of the nation, the red barns and the old frame houses, the tattered posters of sudden forgotten circuses, the whipping of light wind among coarse grasses, the rude sweet bursting from the earth of April. We saw the moving light that came and went across great fields, the lift, the fall, the sweep and fold and hollow, the lyric ugliness and fecundity of this immense and everlasting earth that can never be remembered, that can never be forgotten, that has never been described, and that lives in our brain and our heart forever: America.

There was no answer to that living earth. There was nothing but immortal joy. These cities were the ugly haunts of children: we scored their grime and rickets off the earth as men score scum away from buried emeralds. The proud voice of the land said "Here!"— we saw the great plantations, and the actors, the children and the wanderers, vivid as the innocence of a print, rolled through the land toward bright retrievements in new towns and better cities.

IV

[A Baby Is Born]

The clock had finished striking, and Robert sat there in the dark clutching his fat knees where the coarse-ribbed stocking covered them: he was only a blur of fat boy face with a carroty twist of red Jew's hair.

Again, a horse sparked down the ringing street, it stopped quite near: there were voices, laughter, and farewells, and the crisp rattle of a Christmas package. The horse moved on, and a door was opened and shut. Silence.

Robert was grieved and lonely, and he hated darkness. He hated quiet. He hated Bella's husband for commanding quiet. Bella's husband was a doctor: therefore, Robert hated doctors.

He decided he would not be a doctor. He would not do anything where one always had to be so quiet and dark. When he grew up he was going to be something where there was lots of light and people. He wanted gaiety and voices and heroic actions. He wanted deeds and sentiments. He wanted love and romance. Robert knew very well what he was going to be. He was going to be an actor like his Uncle Joe. It would be fine to be an actor if one could be like Uncle Joe: he had fine things to say, he always came out on top—well, almost always—and if anyone talked back to him he'd give him one. Robert thought of the Cassidy boy and reflected how well he should like to give him one.

Robert thought he would like to be like Uncle Joe in *Saved at the Switch*. You could hear the thunder of the night express as it came closer and closer, the girl was tied down to the rails so that she couldn't move, with Henshaw gloating over her.

"You fiend!" she cried. "Will you add murder to your other crimes? May heaven forgive you for your black heart's infamy."

Then Henshaw had laughed in a very sinister tone of voice.

"In another minute the night mail will dismember that proud form. You will be strewn to the winds. Yield, girl! Even now it is not too late! Even now you may be saved if you submit to my desire!"

"Never! A thousand deaths were better than the shame you offer me! Villain, if Rodney Whittaker were here your life would pay the measure of this bloody crime."

"Fool! Your fine lover has forsaken you and cares nothing for your pleas. Even now he dallies in the embraces of the Lady Maude."

"You lie! You coward and villain, you lie!" cried Uncle Joe, at this moment leaping down upon him from a twenty foot embankment. In the desperate struggle that followed it was the girl who got rescued and Henshaw who was run over by the first night mail. This was just. This was excellent and good.

Robert had been to see this drama seven times on passes which his Uncle Joe had given to him: he had loved it, loved it, brooded upon it with such fervor that he could now almost repeat each of the splendid speeches line for line. With the familiar intensity of children in their fantasies, the boy had long since broken down the bridge between living fact and melodrama: his fortunes and his own identity had mingled with those of his uncle, and his uncle's with those of the wonderful hero he portrayed; and the sardonic visage of the villain Henshaw had fused insensibly with the Irish toughness of Rags Cassidy. The imperial magic of the theatre had wrought its wizardry in Robert: he had crouched in the enthralled darkness of the gaudy gas-lit houses, his young eye had cherished all the gilded follies—the golden cornucopias, the terrestrial grapes and fat gilt cherubs, the screws and scrolls and painted pilasters, the mellow plushy staleness of the boxes and that splendid painted gas-lit world upon the stage—those unreal and flawless figures of heroism, virtue, villainy, of brashness or gentleness, of spurious motives, and instant solutions. He loved them all, the beautiful figures of the play had become real to him—the splendid defiances of menaced virtue, the proud resolution of heroism, the ringing voice of his uncle, so clear, so brave, so glorious, as he cried "You lie! You coward and villain, you lie!" as he sprang upon villainy—these sentiments and actions were more real to Robert now than all the daily humdrum of house and school.

The beautiful figures of the play had become so real to him that he saw them now not only in the scenes that had been made for them: he saw them in a thousand lives, a thousand plays, he knew the source from which they came and he could project them and himself instantly into any situation. A thousand times he triumphed over Henshaw-Cassidy, a thousand times vile wrongs and tyrannies were requited, a thousand times the beautiful, the sweet, the sad misunderstandings of the lover and his mistress were resolved and rectified. The scenes shifted, but the figures of his world were constant—the troubling perplexity and confusions of the earth, the complexity of human character; the dense and obscure weaving of men's destinies were unknown in this simple and heroic world in which he was always brave, good, and victorious. Here he had the brave grey eye of his Christian uncle, he was never afraid of anything, and he always won.

Yet there were flaws even in this bright world. His Uncle Joe had not always conquered and survived, there had been troubling interludes, parts and speeches that he could not comprehend: grief and disaster had stricken his great hero, he tried to shut the memory from his mind, but it returned now in dark silence. Once he had gone to see his uncle in one of these old plays he did not like. There were a lot of people dressed in old time costumes. All the men wore tights and carried swords and Uncle Joe had been the best of the lot: some of them were always talking big and drawing their swords out, but they were such a skinny, puny lot they could not have killed a rabbit. Uncle Joe had the best build of any of them, but just when things were beginning to get interesting, Uncle Joe got killed. It was not fair, they killed him by a trick. Uncle Joe got into a fight with another fellow who also had a sword and Uncle Joe was getting the best of him as usual when a friend of Uncle Joe's had to butt in and try to separate them. While he was doing this and Uncle Joe couldn't see what was happening, the other fellow stuck his sword clean through him. Robert saw it go in and come out on the other side. It was a mean, sneaking thing to do, nobody but a coward would do it: if he'd stood up like a man and fought fair Uncle Joe would have killed him as dead as a door nail.

Uncle Joe's friend didn't have any business to come in the way he did, and Uncle Joe told him so. He said:

"What did you have to go and interfere for? He got in under your arm when I wasn't looking. If it hadn't been for you I would have killed him by now!"

Of course his friend was sorry for what he did, he said he thought he acted for the best, but that did no good after Uncle Joe had been killed.

Before he died, Uncle Joe had said: "A plague on both your houses," and although Robert had been somewhat puzzled by the phrase at first, Uncle Joe had explained it all to him when he asked about it. It was like this: Robert's mother ran a boarding house on Forty-fourth Street, and two or three years before she had taken the house next door as well because the house she had was too small to hold all the people who wanted to board with her. She had knocked a hole through the walls of the two houses and joined them with a passageway that ran from one dining room to another. Uncle Joe called this passageway the Bridge of Size and when Robert asked him why he called it such a name he said it was because the boarders at his mother's grew to such a great size. So when Robert asked his uncle what "a plague on both your houses" meant, his Uncle Joe had said:

"Well, a plague on one house would not be so bad, would it? But if someone had two houses, like your mother has, it would be a pretty bad thing, wouldn't it, if she had a plague on both of them?"

Robert had never thought about it in this way before, but now he did, and he said, "Yes, it would be."

But still the memory of defeat and woe, the finality of death, made its small pulse of sorrow in his brain. He stirred uneasily. At this moment his dark quiet was broken suddenly, the door opened in the hall, and Bella stood there calling sharply to him.

"Robert!"

He jumped, got quickly to his feet, ran toward her. For a bewildered second he saw the dark design of the room, somberly lighted by a lamp that made a small hot pool of light around it. He was conscious of the moving figures of the doctor and Else, but his glance went straight to the big fourposted bed before him: in the centre of the breadth of bedding he could see my mother propped with pillows, holding her long white arms straight up above her head. What he saw distressed and frightened him, he did not know why: he turned suddenly and walked away toward the stairs, liking it better there. At this moment he heard a thin long wail, remote but penetrating as from another world, and he felt a wave of anger, jealousy and resentment pass over him. Bella called to him again, he walked on stubbornly. Then she came after him, seized him and wheeled him around sharply, gripping her strong warm paws about his arms.

"Robert!" she said with such fierce excitement that he trembled. "Go to your Uncle Joe as fast as you can! Tell him he has a little girl! Tell him that all—everyone—is well! Go! Go quick, boy!"

He stared at her. She gave him a little push and clapped her palms.

"Go!"

Instantly he turned and ran downstairs. The night was cold and frosty but he did not pause to take his hat or overcoat. He ran outside and down the stone steps of the stoop into the street. Then he chugged briskly off, a runner down enormous streets, a tiny speck upon a swarming rock, below the terrible desolation of proud stars, a puny messenger among ten thousand other instant births and deaths, but yet, he thought, the bearer of a mission, life's pulse and heart, the centre of it all—a fat little boy who stammered.

At this time my father was appearing in a play called *Esther Craig*: it was one of the most famous plays of the time, it had run for years and broken records for performances. It was a play about a poor but beautiful and virtuous miller's daughter who loved and was loved by a lord. She was disowned and driven away from home by her stern father who thought no honest girl could love a lord, and after a period of misunderstanding which almost ended in tragedy, she was restored to the arms of her lover once more. It was just such a play as Robert loved: there was never a purer heroine or more noble hero, and, although the play was, to his taste, a little quiet, and somewhat lacking in the more violent action that delighted him, there was an excellent and moving scene at the end where the heroine was hurled into the mill pond by the father and rescued by her lover. My father did not have the hero's part in this play. He took the part of Pittacus Green.

Pittacus Green was the comic figure in *Esther Craig*. I do not think he was strictly essential to the action of the play. All of the great events of the drama could have occurred without him. And yet, I think he was perhaps the most important figure in the play. He acted as a chorus, an interpreter of events, as a confidant, and as a comic force to relieve the tension of tragedy, and to give the whole play the ease and belief of laughter. He was a wonderful character, a creature that could have existed only in this strange world, a kind of Mercutio of melodrama, and my father played him magnificently. The things he said were of often the most extravagant nonsense, but below this folly we could see the shrewd intelligence of a wise and capable man.

My father loved the play and did the part with all the dash and gusto in him: the kind of nonsense in his speeches was exactly to his taste—he was the first character I ever saw to go through the business of inviting himself to sit down and make himself at home, thanking himself, accepting, shaking his own hand. He was always making puns on his own name, Pittacus—"'Tis true, 'tis Pitty, and Pitty 'tis, 'tis true": My father often quoted this, as well as many other speeches from his part. His entrance was wonderful: he came in singing, and leaped across a fence, and then he said:

"At the early age of one minute, I howled to see the world."

The play had run for several years, and my father had appeared as Green so often that all of his friends at this time called him Pit, and at home the children called him Uncle Pit. Therefore when Robert, who ran all the way to the theatre, got there, he was so excited he could not remember my father's real name when the man at the stage door stopped him. All Robert could remember was "Uncle Pit," and when he tried to say that name he could not, because excitement made him stammer badly. When he tried to speak, all he could say was "Pah-pah-pah-pah-pah." The door man spoke roughly to him, and frightened him still more.

"Who are you lookin' for?" the man said. "Don't you know his name?"

"Pah-pah—" Robert said.

"Pah-pah!" said the door man. "I don't know no 'Pah-pah'! Tell me his name! I can't let you in here unless you do."

Robert tried again, but could not say it. He burst into tears because he was frightened and thought he could not deliver Bella's message to my father. At this moment the curtain had just gone down on the second act, and the actors were going to their dressing rooms. One of them heard the child crying, and she came out to see what was wrong. Her name was Effie Ellsler: she played the part of Esther Craig. When she saw Robert, she spoke to him very kindly and persuasively, took his hand in hers, until he got quieter, and asked him who he wanted.

"Pah-pah-pah—" Robert said.

"God!" the door man said. "He's beginnin' again!"

"*Pittacus*!" said Robert like a shot.

"Oh, I know who it is!" Miss Ellsler said, "It's Joe Barrett! And I bet I know what it's about! Joe! Joe! You come with me, boy!"

She took Robert by the hand and led him backstage. My father had just entered his dressing room. When he heard her voice, he rushed out, saw Robert, and fairly sprang upon him.

"What is it, son?" he said. "Is everything all right?"

"Yes!" Robert shouted. "B-b-b-bella says to tell you that you've got a little guh-guh-guh-guh—"

"Oh, you funny boy!" Miss Ellsler screamed. "You've got a little gul-guh! Joe! He means you've got a little girl. Isn't that what you mean?" she said.

"Yes!" Robert yelled. "That's what I s-s-s-said."

Miss Ellsler ran up and down the corridor outside the dressing rooms, knocking at all the doors and shouting: "Joe Barrett's got a little girl." My father stared at Robert for a moment: then suddenly he turned his face away into his hand and for a moment he wept bitterly, for joy, for relief, and for sorrow, because a sentence of death was in his heart and he had wanted, as all men do, a son.

By this time, however, all of the actors, laughing and shouting, were swarming out into the corridor. They slapped my father on the back, they shook his hand, they made jokes and congratulated him. My father stood among them smiling like a man who has been dazed: he spoke to them without knowing what he said.

Suddenly Robert saw the actors clearly for the first time in his life. Here were the living presences of these heroic figures whose courage and beauty he had so often admired. What he now saw, as for the first time he shared a common earth and air with them, filled him with fear and horror. The bright staring faces of the actors shone with a heightened and obscene splendor, a mockery of life and energy; between their blue lids and leaded brows their eyes glittered with an unnatural and deathlike animation. The child shrank back before the stripped vision of this moment. Below the crude harsh color of these masks, the faces of the actors peered forth like imprisoned men: he saw the weary imperfection of the flesh, he saw how old and scarred and worn their faces were, and a knife was driven through his faith forever.

Now, too, he noticed the battered visage of this backstage world: he saw stored flats of dingy scenery, the canvas stained and coarse, the crude scrawls and blots of paint, which, from the front, could make such splendor, he saw the tangle of strings and ropes, the shabby gaslit corridor and the dressing room doors with their rough lettering.

Presently, when the actors had gone back to their rooms, his uncle led him into one of them. It was a hot little room, brightly lit, with flames of gas, with two dressing tables densely covered with pots of paint, cream, pastes and unguents. At one of these tables a man sat with his face almost buried in a small bowl which held a substance that had been ignited and now gave forth a coil of smoke with a choking heavy odor. The man had loosened his cravat, and opened his shirt at the throat: he was gasping the smoke into his lungs, his ribs panted like a dog's, and his breath came with a wheezing constriction. Robert recognized him as the man who played the youthful and heroic lord: he gazed at him now with pain, pity and disgust as he gulped down the choking fumes in an effort to regain his strangled breath. As they entered, my father seemed to recover somewhat. He said:

"How is it, Tom? Are you any better?"

"No," the man said, without looking up from his bowl.

"Can I do anything for you?"

The man shook his head and continued to draw the heavy smoke into his lungs. In a moment, in a rapid gasping voice, he said:

"Baby . . . come?"

"Yes," my father said.

"Mother . . . all . . . right?"

"Yes."

"Boy?"

"No," my father said, "girl."

The man said nothing: he continued to breathe with hoarse labor. In a moment without glancing up, he stretched his hand out toward my father. My father seized it, pressed it warmly, held it for a moment. There were tears in his eyes, for in that simple gesture was a whole history of his life among these people. Then he talked to Robert gently and quietly, and had a full account of all the boy could tell. When Robert had finished my father kissed him and told him he was a good boy: he gave him a dollar also, and told him to go home and say to Bella he would come as soon as he could. It was now time for the third act: the call boy had just come by and knocked, and some of the actors were already on their way to take their places. As they came past my father's, they knocked or thrust their heads in shouting, "Come on, Come on, father! Come on!" Then they went on down the passage laughing. The man at the table raised himself with a gesture full of pain and weariness, and for a moment he stared fixedly at his visage in the mirror.

"Christ!" he said.

Then he buttoned his shirt and began to adjust his collar and cravat again. Robert went out into the corridor: the sound of the man's hoarse and labored breathing followed him.

As Robert went along the corridor several actors passed him rapidly going toward the stage. For ten minutes that world of legend, of rewards and punishments, and of calculated motives in which they dwelt had been suspended, and during this brief time the other world—the world in which men are born and die and draw their breaths in labor—had shown its dark visage, and now the child was retiring to his world again, the actors to theirs, but which one chose the happier way, by which way lay the greatest wisdom and fulfillment, what man knows?

The child went out into the streets again. It was a cold sharp Northern night of frosty magnificence. The vast dark continent of heaven blazed with myriads of glittering stars. Before the theatre the cabs were drawn up in rows: the drivers stood in groups and talked, hitting their whips upon the stone, and the horses, beneath their heavy blankets, breathed vital smoke and stamped their ringing hooves upon the pavements. A great many people were still ahead: the stores were brightly lighted, and some were still open. The shoppers streamed along the pavements loaded with Christmas packages: from time to time the crowded horse cars jaunted past with a sharp rhythmic jingle of bells. The Christmas wreaths, with their stiff leaves of dull green, and their little red berries, already hung in some of the crisply curtained windows of the houses.

Robert went on more slowly than he had come, no longer toward some brilliant foreseen goal: he was a little boy with love and kindness in his heart, he wanted beauty and glory, but somehow, he did not know in what way, something went amiss: Robert went on along the streets of life, he got rich and fat and bitter, he had a wife whom he despised, and two worthless daughters. He did not foresee it.

Later that evening, as soon as his work was done, my father rushed out of the theatre, jumped into a cab, and was driven furiously homeward. The great stars glittered overhead, filling his heart with joy and ecstasy, his spirit was united to the timeless universe, he was annihilated and he saw nothing but glory everywhere, and he could hear the sounds of boats out on the river. When he got home he ran into the house and up the stairs. Bella held me in her arms, and when my father saw me, he cried:

"Her eyes are two black buttons and they are looking straight at me because she knows I am her father."

Outside the boats were blowing in the harbor, and great ships were putting out to sea.

V

My Father's Youth

My father, Joseph Barrett, was a Gentile: he came from a family which had been well known in New England for many generations. He was born in the town of Brantford, Connecticut, where his father owned a general store. It was one of those wonderful country stores in which everything could be bought from oil lamps to yellow cheese, from calico to coffee, from a boiled shirt to a tub of butter. Upon the long wooden counters every variety of thing was piled, and one was aware of the clean smells of boiled cloth—of cotton, wool, silk, and linen; of the coarse sweet leather of thick brogans and creaking harnesses; and rows of rakes, hoes, shovels, forks, and nails. My grandfather, Samuel Barrett, was a man of considerable wealth for those times, but his feeling against slavery was so intense and bitter that it outweighed any material consideration: at the outbreak of the Civil War he sold his store as soon as he could, and helped organize the first regiment of volunteer troops to go to the war from Connecticut.

At this time my father was a child of six or seven years. He was the youngest of three children: he had a sister who was twelve and a brother who was nine. During the war they all lived on a farm outside of town which belonged to his uncle. The uncle could not go to the war because he was too fat, he weighed over three hundred pounds: he stayed on the farm and took care of all of them. He was very good to them: he was a wonderful man, and later I shall tell of him and of his two sons, John and Frederick Barrett.

When the war was over, my grandfather returned in such poor health he could not go back into business: he had some money left and he took his family to New York to live. At this time my father was eleven years old.

Three years after the family moved to New York my father's brother died of typhoid fever. My grandfather died four years later: the manner of his death was so horrible that it cast a shadow over my father's entire youth. During the war my grandfather had been wounded in the knee at the battle of Antietam: the army surgeons who removed the shot did their work badly and apparently never got all of it out. The wound never healed, a festering kind of gangrene set in, and for years my grandfather literally died by inches. At first his right leg was amputated in an effort to save his life. But apparently none of the surgeons of that time knew how to check the advance of this poison which ate its way into his vitals. Perhaps they know no more about it now. My grandfather was literally cut to pieces: year by year he endured a series of terrible amputations on the stump of his leg. The family lived constantly below this menace of death and horror. Their lives were absorbed by it. They watched the progress of the disease with the terrible fascination with which trapped prisoners might watch the progress of a train of fire toward an explosion which they are powerless to touch. And in the midst of all his horrible suffering, daily watching the death of his own body, able almost to reckon to the month the time of his death, my grandfather looked on life with love and joy; his great laugh filled the house.

My father did not often talk to me about him. I think his memory of his father's suffering and death was so painful he did not like to speak of it. But I know that he loved him dearly. Whenever he spoke of his father, even with the most casual reference, I noticed a remarkable change in his expression: my father had the most luminous and penetrating eyes of anyone I have ever known. They were of a living and powerful grey; one instantly noticed their magnetic and vital quality: Whenever my father felt deeply about anything, the pupils of his eyes would widen and darken until they were smoke-black. This always happened when he spoke of his father. He told me his father was the bravest man he had ever known. He told me that even before one of these terrible operations his father would make jokes with the surgeons. He told me that once his father had said to them:

"Well, what's it going to be this time? Another cut off the joint?"

When the doctor said it would be, my grandfather replied:

"You know, doc, I don't mind these cuts off the joint so much, but when you begin carving off rump steaks I'm going to holler."

He died in unspeakable agony. In the four days before his death, the surgeons operated twice, the last time without an anaesthetic. My grandfather would not cry out: his effort was so great his teeth bit completely through his lower lip. After his death they had to pry his teeth apart.

For months, it seemed, there had been little of the man to keep alive except his magnificent spirit. His body was leprous from head to foot. Almost immediately after his death there was a powerful odor of decomposition. The doctors urged immediate burial. In spite of this, my grandmother, who was a fanatic Methodist, refused. She refused to bury him in New York: she insisted on taking the body back to Connecticut for burial. Furthermore she insisted on services in both places, on the terrible death-watch and barbarous prolongation of Christian burial. Finally, she refused to allow embalming. She had an obscene shame and terror of nakedness, even the nakedness of dead bodies: even before her husband she had never unclothed her body, and as a young woman she had given instructions that, in the event of her death, her own body should not be touched by undertakers, and, if possible, should not be fully exposed to anyone. She now insisted that her husband's body be treated the same way.

My father told me the whole story once, but never referred to it again. At the time of his father's death, he said, he was eighteen years old. And at this time all of the bitter accumulation of years of dislike and misunderstanding came to a head. He felt that his mother could have done much more than she did to ease and comfort the last years of his father's life. He said she had never in her life uttered a word of love and tenderness for anyone: apparently she had always been convinced that life was evil, that men were bad, and that her husband was what she called a "sinner." My father said she felt this way about him because, like all his family, he liked good food and drink, and the gaiety and joy of living. He had never shared in her church-going activity—in her fierce devotion to what she called "The work of the Lord." After he returned from the war, and the family came to New York to live, he never went to church at all. During this time he was, of course, dying by inches, and his indifference to the church infuriated her: she exhorted him upon his evil-doing, besieged him with ministers and church people who tried to prevail on him to "come back to the fold," and she never lost a chance to remind him he was dying and must lose no time if he wanted to repent and save his soul.

"I think she liked to see people suffer," my father told me. "Nothing else seemed to give her any pleasure."

My grandfather loved music and had a fine voice: my father would sit beside him for hours while he sang the songs he had learned as a soldier—the great marching songs of the Civil War, the campfire songs, and a great many jolly and rollicking songs that were then popular but have now been forgotten. He would sing them keeping time with the foot of his good leg, until my father knew them all, and they could sing together. The one hymn that he seemed to like best was "The Battle Hymn of the Republic": When he came to the line "Oh! be swift, my soul, to answer Him, be jubilant, my feet!" his eyes would glow with joy, his good leg would fairly dance upon the floor, and his maimed stump would jerk up and down briskly under the impulse of his feeling, and finally his voice would lift triumphantly on the magnificent line, "As he died to make men holy, let us die to make men free." And once he said to my father: "That would really be worth dying for, wouldn't it?— to make men free." When my father asked him if that wasn't what men had died for in the Civil War he laughed, and said: "Yes. Free for the surgeons and the worms." In his youth he had been very bitter against the South because of slavery, but now his bitterness seemed to have vanished completely: he spoke of the ability and courage of the Southern troops and of the campaigns of Lee and Stonewall Jackson with as much pride and tenderness as if they had belonged to his own side. I think this change in feeling must have come during the war, because I still have a remarkable letter which he wrote to his brother, Wesley, the one that was called Uncle Bud, the great fat fellow I have mentioned:

"Most of the boys down here," he wrote, "have had about enough of this war, but I see that the women and preachers back home are determined to fight it out to the bitter end. I never saw such a bloodthirsty lot as these women and preachers are: they just seem to live on fighting and it looks like they're not going to give the rest of us much peace until they've got the rebs all mashed up into jelly. For my part, I never felt so peaceable in my life, I've had enough fighting to do me from now to Kingdom Come, I could be friends right now with almost anyone, I could be friends with a reb or a preacher. I've got a good idea: in the next war why don't they let the women and the preachers do the fighting? It seems to me that they ought to let these people fight who enjoy fighting, and let the rest of us who want to be peaceable stay at home and make the crops. They could put all the women on one side and all the preachers on the other and let them fight it out to their heart's content.

"Bud, I've been having dreams about you. Have you still got that big fat belly? I've been telling some of the boys about it and they say, by God, they don't believe I'm telling them the truth, they say they're coming home with me to see it when the war is over. My own gut is rammed up against my backbone: they're like twins, I don't know if I'll ever get them apart again, but if I do I'm going to see to it they stay strangers as long as I live. Anyway, we're better off than the rebs: I was talking to one we took prisoner the other day and he said they'd been eating so much parched corn on his side some of the fellows had begun to crow like roosters. He said one of them came by him down the road the other day running for all he was worth. When he asked him where he was going this fellow flapped his arms a couple of times and cackled right in his face. When the man got so he could talk he said he'd eaten so much corn the hens thought he was a rooster: he said every hen in Virginia had been after him, he said they wouldn't leave him alone, and with that he let out another cackle, flapped his arms, and let out down the road with six big Donnecker hens right after him. Now, Bud, do you believe that fellow was telling the truth? Well, Bud, you take care of yourself now and that big belly. When I come home I want to look at it and feel it and see if it is real.

"Your brother,
"Sam Barrett"

From this letter, with its reference to "women and preachers," I believe that my grandfather must have been thinking of his wife and her church friends, and my father told me this was true. I think anyone could see from reading this letter that the man who wrote it was brave, kind, and wise: his feeling about war is the feeling that many people have today and that we have come to think of as "modern," but I think that my grandfather and my father must have been very much alike in this respect: they were such men as belong to no particular time, but are able to live for themselves and by themselves. They are able to get wisdom out of living without being very much influenced by the custom of the moment. My father had this power more than anyone I have ever known.

There was another cause for the bitter feeling between my father and his mother. After the family came to New York, he went frequently with his father to the theatre. My grandfather loved the theatre and had committed to memory the entire plays of Shakespeare. By his fourteenth year my father knew more about these plays than most educated people ever know: they read or declaimed the speeches to each other, and they set each other a task of tagging lines the other began. Once my father caught him up in a mistake, and he said it was the proudest moment of his life. During the war my grandfather had become a good friend of an actor in his regiment (of this man I shall speak later), and now, in New York, he knew a great many people in the theatre. He knew the great actor Booth, and he knew Joseph Jefferson. Many of these people came to see him at his house: when they did there was laughter and music and punch in the parlor. My grandmother refused to take any part in these gatherings: she thought that her house was polluted by the presence of such people, and she reviled and insulted her husband for having such friends. At that time, the actor was almost a social outcast: he lived a wretched wandering life on the fringes of society; even the few distinguished artists like Booth and Jefferson never won the full acceptance to which their talents entitled them. To millions of church people like my grandmother, the actor was a depraved and evil man, and the theatre the devil's dwelling place. My grandmother was convinced that this was true, yet, she could boast at the same time that she had never been in a theatre in her life.

A year before her husband's death an incident occurred which enraged her, and helped to hasten the final breach with her son. My father at this time was only seventeen, but for years, from the first time his father had taken him into a theatre, he had felt the complete fascination of its magic and he had already resolved that this was the life he wanted and the life he was going to follow. In this desire his father agreed, and wanted to help him. That year, accordingly, he was given his first chance. His father's war-time friend, of whom I have spoken, was a man named Clark: Mr. Clark was an actor who had played in many parts and had also been a manager of several theatres. Mr. Clark, therefore, got my father a small part in a play that was soon to open: it was a melodrama and in one scene there was a thrilling fight between two groups of hoodlums. My father was given the part of leader of one of these gangs, and he was given a single speech of three short words. My father was supposed to rush out on the stage at the head of his gang, glare fiercely at the other leader when he saw him, throw up his fists in a fighting attitude, and run forward crying: "Now for it!"

As every actor knows, it is often more difficult to play a small part well than to play a big part. When the actor is given only one or two short speeches, he is likely to be oppressed by a feeling that he must make every syllable and situation count, that there cannot be the slightest flaw or slip in his execution. As a consequence he is often strained and unnatural in his delivery of a few words, whereas if the words were only a fragment of a larger part, he could deliver them with perfect ease and naturalness.

During the course of rehearsals my father was repeatedly told to accent the second of his three words—that is, to say "Now *for* it!" Invariably, however, perhaps because he had been warned so often and erred through trying to avoid error, he would deliver his three words with the accent, thus bounding up upon the last: "Now for *it*!" Finally, the director, out of patience, told him curtly he would be discharged if he did not deliver his speech correctly on the night of the dress rehearsal. My father was heartsick and desperate at the prospect: he strode up and down backstage for hours repeating "Now *for* it!" thousands of times, until he thought it was rooted in his brain beyond possibility of error. On the night of the dress rehearsal, however, he failed again. He rushed out on the stage, shouted "Now for *it*!" and then, turning to the director, he burst into tears and begged the man to give him another chance. To his stupefaction everyone roared with laughter, and the director told him to say his speech in any way he pleased. Thereafter, he always got it right: the play ran for several weeks and he performed creditably.

My grandmother had known nothing of this. When Mr. Clark had got the job for him, my father and my grandfather agreed to say nothing to her about it. But my father's absences from home on the evenings aroused her suspicion: when she asked him what he was doing, he told her. She flew into a terrible fit of temper, told him he was on the road to hell, and insisted that he give up his work at once. He refused; she then turned upon her husband, demanded that he compel the boy to stop, but he would not do this: he stood by his son and told her he should do as he wished. After the play had finished its run, my father made no effort to find new employment in the theatre, knowing that it would cause new tirades and invectives and that his father, now enduring the last hours of his agony, would have to bear the brunt of her bitterness and hate. But she never forgave either of them for it: she thought that both of them were damned and lost, and the harsh weight of her tongue was turned upon her husband to the end.

But now that he was dead, and his house was filled with these people his wife brought there from her church, my father could not endure this obscenity of mourning. It did not seem to him as if his father had died: it seemed that life had died, that the house in which they lived had died, that the corrupted body there belonged to death, was itself death, and had never had a union with his father's life. He remembered his father's bright living eye, his great laugh, and the superb purity and courage of his spirit, which had lived life with such fierce joy, and had been trapped to die there in that corrupted flesh whose evil stench had, even in the last months of his life, polluted the air about him. And now that this corrupted carcass should be cherished hideously by this woman to do duty to these rusty mourners in place of the bright spirit they could never know was not to be endured: my father went to her and begged her to have it taken from the house at once and buried. She refused: I think she must have been insane because she told him that this odor of putrefaction came from evil living, and that the road which he was travelling would lead him to the same decay.

My father went almost mad: he went out and walked the streets like a man who has been struck at the base of the brain and has no knowledge of what he is doing. Toward dark, however, he composed himself somewhat and went to see his father's friend, the actor, Clark. When my father had told his story to Mr. Clark, the man got up, took his hat, and told my father to come with him. They went directly to my grandfather's house: when they got there full dark had come, dim lamps were burning, and they could hear the voices of the mourners filled with their lust of pain and darkness. When Mr. Clark went into the house, he asked my grandmother if she would let him speak to her in private: immediately she denounced him and ordered him out of the house. My father protested at this, he told her Clark had been one of his father's best friends and that he had asked him to come there to talk with her: at this, his mother started to revile them both. She said Clark had been responsible for her husband's wickedness and that he was now bent on ruining her son. My father said that this was not true. His mother then appealed to her friends, the mourners: she asked them if they had heard the son say that his mother lied, and they said yes, they had heard, and they had never listened to such infamy. She then screamed at him that she had loved him and tried to save him, she said she had done all a mother could do for him, and that he was an unnatural son. She told him he would have to choose between herself and God and "that actor," meaning Mr. Clark. She said if he did not do as she wished and go with her to Connecticut for the burial, he could get out of her house at once and that she never wanted to see his face again. My father waited until she had finished: then he told her he would go and that she could have her wish. Then my father left the house with Mr. Clark, and from that day he never saw his mother again. She went back to her home in Connecticut, she spent the rest of her life there, but she had not long to live: she died there three years later.

What spirit shaped this woman? Of what unknown elements was she made: Wrought by what troubled brain, what cruel heart? In all the chronicles of my life's rich journey there has been no one to be compared with her: we, with our fruitful cries, our warmth of love, our hate of hate, our depth of passion and of living, had strangeness and mystery enough for unbelief; but I knew the source we came from. But she would live for me like some legendary monster of some tainted earth, had I not proof of her existence: she coined the metal of her soul and flesh into the substance of her oldest child, her daughter, my Aunt Kate, with whom a portion of my youth was spent, and in whom I saw the spirit of this woman rise and walk. And my other proof lies bound up in a handful of yellowed letters which she wrote my father during these last years of her life. I have them yet: the faded scrawl upon those faded pages lives with a fierce eternity of hatred, a corrupt animation which no years nor centuries can wither up.

Whether he ever answered these letters I do not know, nor did I ever ask him. I believe he must have, since hers had been addressed to him at various stages in his wanderings, and I suppose she must have known his address from letters which he wrote to her.

That woman seemed to have all the books of the Old Testament committed to memory, and she used them as an almanac, a prophesy, a constant weather report of human earthquake and catechism: there was not an evil mischance which could befall mankind for which she did not have at once the corresponding warning in the gospel. As she said, "it has all been written down": she could see the hand of God, she could believe in His living presence only in some act of horror in the universe—the sum and confirmation of her fierce belief was suffering and destruction, and wherever she saw stricken men, wherever she saw grief and agony, her triumphant faith cried out that God lived and wrought and that his presence was abroad throughout the earth. As one reads these letters today, with their dense compilation of quoted prophesies, the immense and twisted erudition—with which instantly she could tag with prophetic doom the most trivial events—the death of a horse, the diseases of sheep and cattle, the intervention of lightning in the life of a child or a withered hag—the reader may have at first the sense of unbelief, a comic sense of something grotesque and droll. But as he reads, whatever quality of humor he felt will disappear: the woman emerges with a horrible intensity and reality, like someone we have never known but instantly recognize, a harpy screaming from the rocks of a separate, a stricken, planet, who belongs to no age, untouched by space or time, brought to this earth by what black charm, what evil incantation no one knows.

My father told me the whole story of his life with her only once, and I do not think I heard him speak of her, even casually, over a half dozen times in his life. He told me that he knew instantly when he left her that night that his feeling for her would never change, that he loathed her with all his heart and spirit, and that he would never see her again. At this moment of resolution all the tangled and bewildered dislike and resentment of years became clear and decisive: he knew exactly how he felt, he made a swingeing admission to himself, and thereafter he had no doubt about his feeling.

Yet, he told me, for years he was to feel the bitter indecision of self-mistrust: he could not change his feeling for her, nor say he had any love or affection for her, but her last words of reproach and indictment haunted him. He wondered if she had been right—if he was an "unnatural" son, if his feeling branded him a monster, if his lack of love for her meant that there was a deformed and twisted isolation in his spirit. He was only a boy of eighteen years, and there was no one to whom he could confide. I think it was during these years that he acquired the certitude and independence of spirit that he had thereafter, but he bought it with the intense and lonely pain of his youth.

This was his final comment: one Sunday afternoon a great many years after this, and at least ten years after his marriage, for I must have been eight years old or more at the time, we had as a caller at Bella's house, one of her friends, an actor named Grantham. Mr. Grantham was from Indiana, but he had not lived there for many years. Grantham's mother had died a week or two before and he had gone back to Indiana for the funeral: he had just returned to New York and now he was telling us about his mother. I think that actors as a rule spend as little time in thinking of their parents or kinfolk as any class of people I know: the reason for this, I think, is that the actor lives in a world that is unduly separated from the one in which he was born, and he constantly becomes more absorbed in one and more remote from the other. Yet, no one can talk more eloquently than an actor about the beauty of mother love: his eyes will fill with tears at [the] sound of a "mammy song," and he can weep copiously when he speaks of his love for a mother he has made no attempt to see in twenty years. Mr. Grantham was doing this now, and I think we all felt a little ashamed of him: everyone knew he had not been to see his mother for at least fifteen years, yet here he was saying that her death was the greatest sorrow he had ever known, that the thought of her and her teaching had inspired and guided him at every moment of his life, and that mother love was the most wonderful and beautiful thing on earth.

At length my father said: "I think you are very fortunate to feel that way." Mr. Grantham looked at my father in a sharp suspicious manner. I think he was uneasy about his own feeling, and had been trying to convince himself of his devotion and grief by talking of it. At any rate, he thought that there was something critical of him in my father's words.

"Fortunate?" he said. "How so? I only feel the way about my mother that all men feel."

"No," my father said. "I do not think so."

Mr. Grantham became a little excited: he still thought his beautiful emotion was being doubted, and he said:

"I loved my mother more than anyone else in the world. No one can say I didn't."

"I do not doubt you," my father answered. "I only said that all men do not feel as you."

"Oh, yes they do!" said Mr. Grantham.

"Oh, no they don't!" said father.

"Didn't you?" said Grantham, feeling that he had my father trapped.

"No, I didn't," my father said at once.

"Do you mean to say," said Grantham, slowly, "that you did not—love—*really* love—your mother?"

"Yes," my father said, "that is what I mean to say. I did not love my mother. I will go farther than that. I did not even like her. I had the most intense dislike for her that I have ever felt for any person, and I know she felt the same for me."

No one spoke. I think you could have heard their hearts beat in the silence. My own was pounding in my throat. As for Grantham, he was stupefied. At length he said:

"That is the most unnatural thing I have ever heard."

"Is it unnatural because I say it is or because I feel it?" my father asked.

"Because you feel it," Grantham said. "You would not say it unless you felt it, would you?"

My father's eyes had suddenly got black and smoky. He said:

"I would not go so far as that, Grantham. I think *you* must have known people who said things that they did not feel."

Mr. Grantham made no answer for a moment. My father looked at him. His face turned a fiery red. Then he said:

"But you really feel that way about your mother. Anyone can see you do."

"Yes," my father said. "I really feel that way. And I tell you,

Grantham, it is not unnatural. I tell you there are many men who feel as I do. Yes! I tell you there are men who even feel the most savage and unmitigated hatred for their mothers, and I do not blame them for it!"

We sat there in a hypnotic silence, and we felt awe and terror. My father's cheeks were burning with two badges of bright red. I saw his fingers tremble. In a moment he spoke again in a voice so low, so charged with some strange deep passion that it did not seem to be his own.

"But I'll tell you what *is* unnatural, Grantham. It is to say we have big feelings when we have not got them. It is to live by words when the words have no real meaning for us: it is to mock at love and mercy we have never felt."

No one said anything for several moments. All of us felt a kind of terror. Yet what he had said had cut like a sharp sword through all the falseness and hypocrisy. We knew that what he had said was the truth, but at that time few people would have dared to utter such an opinion: it was a blasphemy of the accepted and cherished sentiment. Suddenly our smooth Sunday tea had been shattered by an utterance which came up out of a burning depth of pain and wisdom none of us had known. Our spirits had shrunk away a little from him, because what he had said had frightened us, and none of us were willing to stand by him at that moment. I wanted to be near him. I loved him, and yet I was afraid to go up to him. Then, all at once he looked so lonely sitting there among us. I looked at him, and instantly he was revealed to me: I saw how lonely and silent his spirit was, and what dreadful depths it had known. I looked at the dark and potent beauty of the Jews, my mother's quiet and living faithfulness, and Bella's radiant power and opulence, and I saw that he had come to us as a stranger and a wanderer of the earth, and I knew now why he loved us, and I knew why we could never know each other. His secret and withdrawn spirit had a wall around it we could never break: my mother lifted her eyes to him and it seemed to me they looked at each other across a great and inseparable distance, and yet their look had the greatest love and loyalty in it I had ever seen.

As I remember my father now I always remember his lonely and secret spirit. Yet there was no one who loved the companionship of people more, and people always wanted to be near him. They wanted to be near him because it is the secret and lonely people who attract us most: we feel in them an integrity and power which other people do not have, we are drawn by a luminous mystery in them. Perhaps we feel that if we can pluck out the heart of this mystery we will find the wisdom and power we need in our own lives. It seems now that my father was always alone: even in a crowd he was isolated, the other people made a continent of life, they were bound together by great tides and rivers, but he dwelt among them like an island.

The remainder of my father's youth, after he left his mother's house, were years of exile and wandering. There was no poverty that he did not endure, no hardship that he did not suffer, no human crime or misery that he did not see. He knew the raw savagery, the brutal violence, the idiot cruelty of living as few people ever knew it, and his spirit remained fearless, uncorruptible, gentle, and innocent to the last, because such innocence as his belonged to the innate wisdom of the spirit, and could never be lost, no matter what he saw or did. The night he left his mother he went away with Mr. Clark, the actor. My father had no money and no place to go: Mr. Clark took him home with him, and kept him there until he found employment. At first Mr. Clark tried to help him find employment at some theatre, or in some show that was going on the road, but they could not find it. In a few days Mr. Clark came to him and told him he had a friend who was the manager of a small circus which was about to go on tour: he said he could get my father work as ticket seller with the circus if he wanted it. My father was glad to take the job, and in a few days he joined the circus and started on the tour with them. It was Spring: the circus had started in New England and worked westward and then southward as the Summer and Autumn came on. My father's nominal duties—for, in his vision, every incident, each face and voice and circumstance were blazing real as life itself—were those of ticket seller, but in this tiny show everyone did several things: the performers helped put up and take down the tents, load and unload the wagons, and the roustabouts and business people worked wherever they were needed.

My father sold tickets, but he also posted bills, and bartered with the tradesmen and farmers in new places for fresh food. He became very shrewd and clever at this work, and loved to do it—some old, sharp, buried talent for shrewd trading, that had come to him from his mountain blood, now aided him. He could get the finest, freshest meat and vegetables at the lowest prices. The circus people were tough and hard, they always had a fierce and ravenous hunger, they would not accept bad food and cooking, they fed stupendously and they always had the best of everything.

Usually, the circus would arrive at a new town very early in the morning, before daybreak. My father would go into town immediately: he would go to the markets and trade directly with the merchants, or with farmers who had come in for the circus. He felt and saw the purity of first light, he heard the sweet and sudden lutings of first birds, and suddenly he was filled with the earth and morning in new towns among new men: he walked among the farmer's wagons, and he dealt with them on the spot for the prodigal plenty of their wares—the country melons bedded in sweet hay of wagons, the cool sweet pints of butter wrapped in clean wet cloths, with dew and starlight still upon them, the enormous battered cans foaming with fresh milk, the new laid eggs which he bought by the gross and hundred dozen, the tender limey pullets by the score, the rude country wagons laden to the rim with heaped abundancies—with delicate bunches of green quilled scallions, the heavy red ripeness of huge tomatoes, the sweet-leaved lettuces crisp as celery, the fresh podded peas and the succulent young beans, as well as the potatoes spotted with the loamy earth, the powerful winy odors of the apples, the peaches, and the cherries, juicy corn stacked up in shades of living green, and the heavy blackened rinds of the home cured hams and bacons.

As the markets opened my father would begin to trade and dicker with the butchers for their finest cuts of meat: they would hold great roasts up in their gouted fingers, they would roll up tubs of fresh ground sausage, they would smack with long palms the flanks of beeves and porks: he would drive back to the circus with a wagon full of meat and vegetables.

At the circus ground the people were already in full activity. He could hear the wonderful timed tattoo of sledges on the driven stakes, the shouts of men riding animals down to water, the slow clank and pull of mighty horses, the heavy rumble of the wagons as they were rolled down off circus flat cars. By now the eating tent would be erected, and as he arrived, he could see the cooks already busy at their ranges, the long tables set up underneath the canvas with their rows of benches, their tin plates and cups, their strong readiness. There would be the amber indescribable pungency of strong coffee, and the smell of buckwheat batter.

Then the circus people would come in for breakfast: hard and tough, for the most part decent and serious people, the performers, the men and the women, the acrobats, the riders, the tumblers, the clowns, the jugglers, the contortionists, and the balancers would come in quietly and eat with a savage and inspired intentness.

The food they ate was incomparably masculine and fragrant as the earth on which they wandered: it belonged to the warm stained world of mellow sunwarmed canvas, the clean and healthful odor of the animals, and the wild sweet lyric nature of the land on which they lived as wanderers: and it was there for their asking with a fabulous and stupefying plenty. They ate stacks of buckwheat cakes, smoking hot, golden and embrowned, soaked in hunks of yellow butter which they carved at will with a wide free gesture from the piled pints on the table, and which they garnished (if they pleased) with ropes of heavy black molasses, or with the lighter free-er maple syrup. They ate big steaks for breakfast, hot from the pan and caked with onions, they ate whole melons crammed with the ripeness of the deep pink meat, they ate thick slabs of sugared hams, rashers of bacon and great platters of fried eggs, or eggs scrambled with calves brains, they helped themselves from pyramids of fruit piled up at intervals on the table—plums, peaches, apples, cherries, grapes, oranges, and bananas—they had great pitchers of thick cream to pour on everything, and they washed their hunger down with pint mugs of strong deep-savoured coffee.

For their midday meal they would eat fiercely, hungrily, with wolfish gusto, mightily with knit brows and convulsive movements of their corded throats. They would eat great roasts of beef with crackled hides, browned in their juices, rare and tender, hot chunks of delicate pork with hems of fragrant fat, delicate young broiled chickens, only a mouthful, a crunch and a swallow, for these ravenous jaws, twelve pound pot roasts cooked for hours in an iron pot with new carrots, onions, sprouts, and young potatoes, together with every vegetable that the season yielded: huge roasting ears of corn, smacking hot, piled like cord-wood on two foot platters, tomatoes cut in slabs with wedges of raw onion, okra and succotash, mashed potatoes whipped to a creamy lather, boats swimming with pure beef gravy, new carrots, turnips, fresh peas cooked in butter and fat string beans seasoned with the flavor of big chunks of cooking-pork. In addition they had every fruit and berry that the place and time afforded: hot crusty apple, peach, and cherry pies, encrusted with cinnamon, puddings and cakes of every sort, and blueberry cobblers inches deep.

Thus, the circus moved across America, from town to town, from state to state, eating its way from Maine into the great plains of the West, eating its way along the Hudson and the Mississippi rivers, eating its way across the prairies and from the North into the South, eating its way across the fat farm lands of the Pennsylvania Dutch along the eastern shores of Maryland and back again across the states of Virginia, North Carolina, Tennessee, and Florida—eating all good things that this enormous, this incredibly bountiful and abundant cornucopia of a continent yielded.

They ate the cod, bass, mackerel, halibut, clams and oysters of the New England coast, the terrapin of Maryland, the fat beeves, porks, and cereals of the Middle West. And they had, as well, the heavy juicy peaches, watermelons, cantaloupe of Georgia, the fat sweet shad of the Carolina coasts, and the rinded and exotic citrus fruits of the tropics: the oranges, tangerines, bananas, cumquats, lemons, guavas down in Florida—together with a hundred other fruits and meats—the Vermont turkeys, the mountain trout, the bunched heaviness of the Concord grapes, the red winey bulk of the Oregon apples, as well as all the clawed, the shelled, crusted dainties, the crabs, the clams, the pink meated lobsters that grope their way along the sea-floors of America.

My father awoke at morning in three hundred towns with the glimmer of starlight on his face: he was the moon's man, then he saw light quicken in the east, he saw the pale stars drawn, he saw the birth of light, he heard the lark's wing, then the bird tree, the first liquorous liquified lutings, the ripe-arred trillings, the plum-skinned birdnotes, and he heard the hoof and the wheel come down the streets of the nation. He exalted in his work as food-provider for the circus people, and they loved him for it. They said there had never been anyone like him—they banqueted exultantly, with hoarse gulpings and with joy, and they loved him.

Slowly, day by day, the circus worked its way across America, through forty states and through a dozen weathers. It was a little world that moved across the enormous loneliness of the earth, a little world that each day began a new life in new cities, and that left nothing to betray where it had been save a litter of beaten papers, the droppings of the camel and the elephant in Illinois, a patch of trampled grass, and a magical memory. The circus men knew no other earth than this, the earth came to them with the smell of the canvas and with the lion's roar: they saw the world beyond the lights of the carnival, and everything beyond these lights was phantasmal and unreal to them, it lived for them within the circle of the tent as men and women who sat on benches, as the ports they came to, and sometimes as the enemy.

Their life was filled with the strong joy of food, with the love of wandering, and with danger and hard labor. Always there was the swift violence of change and movement, of putting up and tearing down, and sometimes there was the misery of rain and sleet, and mud above the ankles, of wind that shook their flimsy residence, that ripped the tent stakes from their moorings in the earth and lifted out the great centre pole as if it were a match. Now they must wrestle with the wind, and hold their dwelling to the earth; now they must fight the weariness of mind and push their heavy wagons through the slime; now, cold and wet and wretched, they must sleep on piles of canvas in the flat cars in a driving rain, and sometimes they must fight the enemy—the drunk, the savage, the violent enemy, the bloody man, who dwelt in every place. Sometimes it was the city thug, sometimes the mill hands in the South, sometimes the miners in a Pennsylvania town—the circus people cried "Hey, Rube!" and fought them with fist and foot, with spike and stake, and my father saw and knew it all.

When the men in a little town barricaded the street against their parade, they charged the barricade with their animals, and once the sheriff tried to stop the elephant by saying: "Now, damn ye, if you stick your god damned trunk another inch, I'll shoot."

The circus moved across America, and foot by foot, mile by mile, my father came to know it all. It was rooted into his blood and his brain forever—its food, its fruits, its fields and forests, its deserts and its mountains, its savage lawlessness. He saw the crimes and violence of the people with pity, with mercy, and with tenderness: he thought of them as if they were children. They smashed their neighbors' brains out with an axe, they disembowelled one another with knives, they were murderers and lost upon this earth they dwelt upon as strangers.

The tongueless blood of the murdered men ran down into the earth and the earth received it. Upon this enormous and indifferent earth the little trains rattled on over the ill-joined rails that loosely bound the sprawling little towns together. Lost and lonely, sawings of wood and plaster and cheap brick ugliness, the little towns were scattered like encampments through the wilderness. Only the earth remained, which all these people had barely touched, which all these people dwelt on but could not possess.

Only the earth remained, the savage and lyrical earth with its rude potency, its thousand vistas, its heights and slopes and levels, with all its violence and delicacy, the terrible fecundity, decay and growth, its fierce colors, its vital light and sparkle, its exultancy of space and wandering. And the memory of this earth, the memory of all this universe of sight and sense, was rooted in my father's heart and brain forever. It fed the hungers of desire and wandering, it breached the walls of his secret and withdrawn spirit. And for every memory of place and continent, of enormous coffee-colored rivers and light touched miles of heady wheat, of Atlantic coast and midland prairie, of raw red Piedmont and tropic flatness, there were always the small, fecund, perfect memories of his father's land, the dark side of his soul and heart's desire, which he had never seen, but which he knew with every atom of his life, strange phantasmal haunting of man's memory. It was a fertile nobly swelling land, and it was large enough to live in, walled with fulfilled desire.

Abroad in this ocean of earth and vision he thought of his father's land, of its great red barns and nobly swelling earth, its clear familiarity and its haunting strangeness, and its dark and secret heart, its magnificent, its lovely and tragic beauty. He thought of its smell of harbors and its rumors of the sea, the city and the ships, its wine-ripe apples and its brown-red soil, its smug weathered houses, its lyric unutterable ecstasy.

A wonderful thing happened. One morning he awoke suddenly to find himself staring straight up at the pulsing splendor of the stars. At first he did not know where he was, but he knew instantly, even before he looked about him, that he had visited this place before. The circus train had stopped in the heart of the country, for what reason he did not know. He could hear the languid and intermittent breathing of the engine, the strangeness of men's voices in the dark, the casual stamp of the horses in their cars, and all around him the attentive and vital silence of the earth.

Suddenly he raised himself from the pile of canvas on which he slept. It was the moment just before dawn: against the East the sky had already begun to whiten with the first faint luminosity of day, the invading tides of light crept up the sky, drowning the stars out as they went. The train had halted by a little river which ran swift and deep close to the tracks, and now he knew that what at first he thought had been the sound of silence was the swift and ceaseless music of the river.

There had been rain the night before and now the river was filled with the sweet clean rain-drenched smell of earthy deposits. He could see the delicate white glimmer of young birch trees leaning from the banks, and on the other side he saw the winding whiteness of the road. Beyond the road, and bordering it, there was an orchard with a wall of lichened stone: a row of apple trees, gnarled and sweet, spread their squat twisted branches out across the road, and in the faint light, he saw that they were dense with blossoms: the cool intoxication of their fragrance overpowered him.

As the wan light grew, the earth and all its contours emerged sharply and he saw again the spare, gaunt loneliness of the earth at dawn, with all its sweet and sudden cries of Spring. He saw the worn and ancient design of lichened rocks, the fertile soil of the baked fields, he saw the kept order, the frugal cleanliness, with its springtime overgrowth, the mild tang of opulent greenery. There was an earth with fences, as big as a man's heart, but not so great as his desire, and after his giant wanderings over the prodigal fecundity of the continent, this earth was like a room he once had lived in. He returned to it as a sailor to a small closed harbor, as a man, spent with the hunger of his wandering, comes home.

Instantly he recognized the scene. He knew he had come at last into his father's land. It was a magic that he knew but could not speak, he stood upon the lip of time, and all of his life now seemed the mirage of some wizard's spell—the spell of canvas and the circus ring, the spell of that tented world which had possessed him. Here was his home, brought back to him while he slept, like a forgotten dream. Here was the dark side of his soul, his heart's desire, his father's country, the earth his spirit dwelt on as a child. He knew every inch of the landscape, and he knew past reason, doubt or argument, that home was not three miles away.

He got up at once and leaped down to the earth: he knew where he would go. Along the track there was the slow swing and dance of the brakeman's lamps, that moving, mournful, and beautiful cloud of light along the rails of the earth that he had seen so many times. Already the train was in motion, its bell tolled and the heavy trucks rumbled away from him. He began to walk back along the tracks, for less than a mile away, he knew, where the stream boiled over the lip of a dam, there was a bridge. When he reached the bridge a deeper light had come: the old red brick of the mill emerged sharply, and with the tone and temper of deep joy, fell sheer into bright shining waters.

He crossed the bridge and turned left along the road: here it moved away from the river, among fields and bridges, and through dark woods—dark woods bordered with stark poignancy of fir and pine, with the noble spread of maples, shot with the naked whiteness of birch. Here was the woodland maze: the sweet dense Yankee tangle of the brake and growth. Sharp thrummings, woodland flitters broke the silence. My father's steps grew slow, he sat upon a wall, he waited.

Now broke the birdsong in first light and suddenly he heard each sound the birdsong made. Like a flight of shot the sharp fast skarps of sound arose. With chitterling tricker, fast-fluttering skirrs of sound, the palmy honied birdcries came. Smooth drops and nuggets and bright gold they were. Now sang the birdtree filled with lutings in bright air: the thrums, the lark's wing, and the tongue-trilling chirrs arose now. The little brainless cries arose and fell with liquorous liquified lutings, with lirruping chirp, plumbellied smoothness, sweet lucidity.

And now there was the rapid kweet kweet kweet kweet of homely birds, and their pwee-pwee-pwee: others with sharp cricketing stitch, with their metallic tongues, a mosquito buzz, while some with rusty creakings, high shrew's caws, with every rasp, with harsh far calls—all birds that are awoke in woodland tangles: and above there passed the whirr of hidden wings, the strange lost cry of the unknown birds; in full light now, the sweet confusion of their cries was mingled.

Then my father rose and went along that road where, he knew, like the prophetic promise of a dream, the house of his father's blood and kin lay hidden. At length he came around a bending of the road, he left the wooded land, he passed by hedges and saw the old white house, set in the shoulder of the hill, worn like ease and habit in the earth. Clean and cool it sat below the clean dark shelter of its trees: a twist of morning smoke curled from its chimney.

Then my father turned into the rutted road that led up to the house, and at this moment the enormous figure of his uncle appeared around the corner, prophetically bearing a smoked ham in one huge hand. And when he saw him, a cry of greeting burst from my father's throat, and the old man answered with a roar of welcome that shook the earth.

Then the old man dropped his ham, and waddled forward to meet his nephew: they met half down the road and the old man crushed him in his hug, they tried to speak, but could not, they embraced again, and in an instant, all of the years between, the bad and bitter memory of his mother, the pain of loneliness and the fierce hungers of desire, were scored away like the scum of frost from a bright glass.

He was a child again, and he wept with joy, with sorrow, with discovery in his uncle's arms, he was a child that had stood upon the lip and leaf of time and heard the quiet tides that move us to our death, and he knew that the child could not be born again, the book of the days could never be turned back, old error and confusion never righted. And he wept with sorrow for all that was lost and could never be regained, and with joy for all that had been recovered.

Suddenly he saw his youth as men on hilltops might look at the whole winding course of rivers to the sea, he saw the blind confusion of his wanderings across the earth, the horror of man's little stricken mote of earth against immensity, and he remembered the proud exultancy of his childhood when all the world lay like a coin within his palms, when he could have touched the horned rim of the moon, when, heroes of a selfless passion, they enact the earth out in a lyric cry.

At this moment, also, my father's two cousins burst from the house and came running down the road to greet him. They had grown to be powerful and heavy young men, already beginning to show signs of that epic fatness that distinguished their father. Like their father, they recognized their cousin instantly, and in a moment my father was engulfed in their mighty energies, borne up among them to the house. As they ate breakfast, he told them the history of the last four years of his life and they told him what had befallen them. His mother had died the year before: this he knew; he did not know that two weeks after his father's death his uncle had come to New York to find him. His uncle found no trace of him, nor could get news of him from anyone: my father had vanished as utterly as if the earth had swallowed him—by that time, of course, he was wandering across the country with the circus. During this time his mother had lived with his uncle's family on the farm, but she had never given them any news of him, although she knew his address: when they had asked her if she knew, she had flown into such a storm of vituperation that they never asked her again. No one said very much about her, my father least of all: she who had lived on death now perished by the food she fed on. In the minds of all there was a quiet relief and thankfulness because she was dead, and a desire to forget her utterly, since there was no memory of her that was not filled with pain. They asked him why he had never let them know where he was or written to them: when he tried to answer them he could not. He knew now that they loved him dearly, and had always been his friends, but he had no tongue to utter the confusion, the desolation and doubt as well as all the fierce scourgings of a young man's pride which had restrained him: his soul had been in such a bewildered turmoil that he had feared, from pride and loneliness, to turn in his time of trouble to these people who would have done most for him.

But they understood what he wanted to say, but could not speak, and they surrounded him with love and lavish heapings of his plate, and my father knew the strange miracle of return to the dark land of their hearts' desire, which haunts men in their fathers' land, dreams but which many never know. Never before had he so felt the phantasmal strangeness of time and destiny, the living dream that is man's life: the sliding shadows of old time moved through the forests of his memory; years that had passed since he left this house, and all that had happened in these years, seemed the remote and half-remembered phantoms of a dream. The house drenched memory with a flood of light, and as if he had been there yesterday he remembered a thousand moments of his childhood, and each familiar object in the room recalled the presence, the exact size, shape, and color of a hundred other objects in the rooms he had not seen: and he watched, with the belief of a child, for these other presences in the house that he remembered—the foot of his father on the stairs, a word that was spoken long ago, his own voice and his own lost body—the child that had lived here long ago at that moment entering at that door, ready to touch him, to speak there at his shoulder.

They spoke with familiar and casual voices, with all of the little times and silences of men who have lived together, until their lives were like boulders in a stream's clean bed, and they spoke of the things they had known long ago. He asked about a neighbor, and one said he had seen him just the day before, he asked about a dog they had named Squire, and they said that Squire was dead; about a girl, and she was married, living in another town. Had the winter been hard, and were the apples and the cider good?—They answered all these questions as if he had been gone from home a month: the magic light of time played suddenly on forgotten things, and reduced the years between to powder.

My father spoke then of the fruit trees which he had that morning seen in bloom: he asked his uncle about "the cherry tree." His uncle at once began to talk with a passionate interest of the cherry tree, and in the story of this tree is written the legend of this wonderful family.

My uncle had many cherry trees upon his farm, but the one to which my father referred, the one in which his uncle's love was centered, grew in the yard a few feet from the house. It was a fine tree, with a thick trunk and large spreading limbs, and every year it bore an immense yield of big red cherries. As my uncle grew older and fatter, the tree gained a complete mastery over his affection: he spoke of it, of the quantity and richness of its fruit, and of its performances and prospects from year to year, with as much pride and love as if it had been his son. During the season when it bore fruit my uncle could think and talk of nothing else except this tree: he was obsessed by it, he observed every phenomenon of bud and bloom, his entire time was occupied by this alone. As the fruit began to ripen, my uncle would sit before the house in a broadarmed chair with a pile of stones beside him. Whenever the birds would approach to eat the fruit my uncle would arise and hurl a stone at them, at the same time shouting "Go Away!" to them. As he grew older this exertion proved too much for him: he had grown enormously fat and the constant excitement and the labor of hurling stones at the birds exhausted him. He could no longer throw a stone with any accuracy, and the birds no longer feared him: they began to get at the fruit and peck great holes in the plump bellies of the cherries while the old man looked on help-lessly, cursing with rage. His distress and fury were so great that it began to prey upon his mind. One day he collapsed and had to be carried to his bed: he was very ill for several days and the doctors warned his sons that he was in obvious danger of an apoplectic stroke. The boys were desperate: whenever they entered the room the old man would roar at them in a fury:

"Are those God damned little bastards eating up my cherries? Hey?"

He made them swear to him that they would keep the birds away, and my cousin John, who was the older, persuaded his brother Fred to sit before the house and throw stones when the birds came. Fred loathed the work: he felt that it was beneath his dignity, and made him look ridiculous, he had very fancy manners and had begun to go with the girls, and he was afraid his occupa-tion would be known to them. He would sit in the chair for hours, getting up to throw a stone at the birds when they came near. Then he would get uneasy and suspicious as time went on; he was afraid that John was playing a trick on him, and at length he would get up and go to find him.

"Look here, John," he would say. "How long do you expect me to sit out there watching those damned little birds?"

"Oh, it won't be long," John said, helpfully. "All you've got to do is sit there until the cherries get ripe, and then we'll let you climb up the tree and pick them."

"How long is that going to be? Will you please tell me that? I've been out there four days now and they're just the same as when I started."

"Well, they're a little green yet, Fred," said John. "It's early in the season and these things take time. Nature is a strange thing, Fred. God moves in a mysterious way, his wonders to perform. But you got nothing to worry about, son. Give 'em a few weeks of good weather and you won't know they're the same cherries."

"A few weeks!" Fred yelled. "What the hell do you take me for— Sitting Bull!"

"Why," said John, "I take you for one of the best cherry watchers in the world. You're always complaining about the work on the farm; I'm saying you're going to get away the first chance you get, and now look at the chance I've given you."

"Chance!" said Fred. "Why, you must think I'm a fool for certain, John. What kind of a chance do you call it making faces at a lot of damned little sparrows?"

"Now that goes to show that people never thank you for what you do for them," said John. "Here you've got the opportunity of a lifetime and you turn up your nose at it."

"Opportunity!" said Fred. "What opportunity are you talking about?"

"Why, the opportunity of being the world's champion cherry watcher and bird frightener," said John. "At the present time cherry watching is in its infancy, and here you are complaining when you're practically alone in your field. You're right up there among the leaders, Fred."

"Leaders!" said Fred. "Why you must be crazy! What leaders are you talking about?"

"Why, the leaders in bird-fighting and face-making," said John. "With that face of yours you ought to go far; I've started you off easy with a lot of little sparrows, but with a little more practice you could frighten the eyeballs off an owl. And here you are whining about it, when you've got a chance any other fellow would cut off his right hand to get."

"A chance!" Fred shouted. "Whoever heard of anyone getting anywhere by throwing rocks?"

"Well, that's how George Washington got his start," said John.

Fred got very angry: he accused John of making fun of him, and of telling his friends about it, and he refused to watch the cherry tree any longer. John asked him if he was going to let his poor old father die just out of his own stubbornness and pride; he told him it was only for a little while, and finally he so worked upon his feelings that Fred consented to go on. But John could not keep the secret. While in town he told another man, making him promise not to tell: then, in the same way, he told another and another. Presently people began to drive by the farm: neighbors would drive up to the house on any sort of pretext. When they saw Fred sitting in his chair they would ask him with an innocent air if he didn't feel well, and was there anything they could do for him. Then they would praise the cherry tree and ask him how much longer it would be before the cherries got ripe, and if he was not afraid the birds would eat them. "If I was you," they said [to one another], "I'd keep my eye on Fred there. If I had a tree like that I wouldn't let the birds come near it. You watch 'em, Fred."

Then they would go into the house to see his father and in a moment, to his anguish, he would hear his father's voice roar out:

"Yes. My boy Fred is watching them!"

One day, as Fred sat there brooding on his fate, he heard near at hand a slight choked sound. Looking around suddenly he saw John with another young man, the brother of one of the girls he went to see. They were grinning and nudging each other as they spied on him: They stopped as soon as he saw them, but the game was up. He was wild with fury, declared bitterly that he had been duped and cheated, and that everyone could go to hell. John pleaded with him to continue just for a little with the tree, but Fred was through. For the next day or two, therefore, John had to watch the tree: during this time he thought seriously and for a long time of their problem. He knew that some solution must be reached, or he saw for them a weary succession of days and weeks, year after year, while they sat and guarded cherries as they ripened. But in that great fat hulk of John's there was a lively and original spirit: his mind was more inventive than his brother's, and all at once, the answer to their difficulty came to him. It was a very simple one: he called for Fred, and when he told it to him, the two brothers danced for joy.

Fred drove furiously into town and purchased there a good-sized, full-toned dinner bell, a rope, and a pulley. When he got back to the farm, John climbed into the tree and hung the bell there in such a way that the full rich bosom of the tree concealed it. He tied the cord to the bell handle, fixed the pulley to the house above a window, and ran the cord across the pulley so that its end hung down before the window. There he waited till the birds came near the tree again: as they swooped down to settle, he pulled sharply at the cord and a peal of hidden bells burst from the centre of the tree. The startled birds shot up like bullets and soared away.

The brothers shook hands exultantly: then they went in to their father's room and got him out of bed. They took him to the window, and seated him in a chair. When the birds came again, they told him to pull the cord: he did so, there was a peal of bells, and the birds flew away.

The old man was wild with joy: for the rest of his life, whenever the cherry tree bore fruit, he did nothing but sit by the window all day long and ring the bell. This was my first and latest memory of him. When I was a child we used always to go there to the farm for a week at this time of year. As we turned from the main road into the road that led up to the house, our arrival would be welcomed with the sudden peal of the bell, the flutter of wings, and the bullet thrum of the birds. As we came up before the house, Uncle Bud would be sitting in his window with his great hand stretched forth on the sill below the cord. In this gesture, there was something calm and powerful that reminded us of the look of a locomotive engineer as he sits in his cab, waiting for the signal that will start his train.

And during the time of these wonderful visits to the farm, my memory is marked by the sound of the bell, and the sudden flight of wings. Wherever I was, stretched out on the floor of the dining room or in the hay loft of the barn, with a pile of books and magazines—*Leslie's, Harper's Young People*, and a book of pictures of the World's Columbian Exposition at Chicago—the sound of the bell came to me.

Uncle Bud and his two sons lived with a sole and simple intensity I have never seen to like degree in any other people for the pleasures of eating. All of them were huge fat fellows, and as they grew older they got fatter: it was not, however, their fatness which was hereditary, but their hunger. Nowhere else have I seen such quantity and variety of food, save at Bella's, and nowhere have I seen such eating.

During my childhood we always went there at least once a year: there was a period of about once a week when the shad were running in the river, and we were always there at this time. At this time tables were set up on trestles underneath the trees at the river bank, there was a grill of white hot wood coals, and my Uncle Bud, girdled in a long white apron, would broil the fish as fast as John and Fred could clean and dress them. The grilled shad were then served smoking hot upon big yellow platters, and pure cream from silver pitchers was poured over them. And as plate after plate of the smoking succulent fish was carried to the table, Uncle Bud would roar:

"Eat up! Eat up! There's more a' comin'! It only lasts a week!"

—As if we were engaged in a race with time and rivers and he expected us to eat without a pause for seven days. I remember Uncle Bud in many other acts and moments, but these two memories instantly dominate all the others: I see him as we drive up to the house, seated in his window like an engineer with his great hand ready near the bell, and I hear the sudden peal of the bell, and the churning of wings out of the dense red clusters of the cherry tree, and I see him by the river bank, with his fat cheeks pendulous and red with his excitement, as he dispatches plate after plate of smoking shad to the waiting tables. He died while I was still a child, appropriately after he had eaten a hearty dinner. He was then in his seventy-sixth year. When he was dead John said,

"Well, he dug his grave with his teeth, but it took him nearly eighty years to do it, didn't it?"

We all went up to the funeral. There was a great deal of excitement in the community because the undertaker could not get a coffin big enough to hold him. Finally, the day before the funeral, two carpenters were put to work: They constructed a coffin out of pine boards which was big enough. When they took it to the house, however, they could not get it through the door: accordingly, the door was widened—a section of the wall was taken out. And eight strong men could barely lift the coffin: they staggered below his weight.

Thus died my father's uncle. They buried him below an elm tree in the village graveyard: Now, if you go there, you'll see the grass is greener on his grave than on any other. He's heaved the earth up in great laughing heights of flowers.

Of this man's sons, John and Frederick Barrett, I shall often speak. They are occasional but enormous and beneficent visitors in the memory of my childhood: whenever they came they brought with them power and abundance. Neither of them ever got married. Neither of them was ever separated from the other. They both fell in love with Bella, and as far as I know this was the only time they were in love, and certainly the only serious trouble that ever came between them. They always kept their father's farm, but later they went there only in the summer: They built a big house in Brantford where they lived with a housekeeper and with Bella's child, whom they adopted. They were powerful and intelligent men with formidable wills: they created a great business and before their middle age they had become very rich. But they never lost in the slightest degree their intense and sensual love of life and the belly.

The gigantic figures of the brothers became famous throughout the state and in New England. Their table groaned with the produce of their farm, and throughout their lives they continued to do all their own marketing. They were up every morning by half past four, and at six o'clock they could be seen, each armed with an enormous basket, on their way to the markets. This regimen, Winter and Summer, was as certain as time, as punctual as the clock. John was a man with a coarse and robust humor—he was full of vulgarity and belly laughter, and he loved to tease his brother, Fred, who was somewhat more dainty, a fop in his dress, and often affected a florid speech and manner, but during this hour of marketing in the morning, both were solemnly intent and earnest: they made no jokes about food, and they allowed no levity to disturb the seriousness of their meditation.

As they entered the markets in the morning an air of gravity fell upon the place: the butchers, the fish dealers, the fruit and vegetable men awaited them with a brisk and attentive manner. The great fat jowls of Fred and John hung down ponderously, seriously, with gravity, they paused drawing upon the fragrant fruity air with a powerful breath of approval. Then they walked forward with their great baskets slung upon their arms, glancing about fiercely and suspiciously at the loaded stalls. They thrust in among the fruits, and with a sullen and solemn stare, they pawed at the roasts and poultry: John would poke at a shoulder of beef, and Fred would tweak the long and tender leg of a chicken; Fred would plunk a melon with his thick forefinger and John would turn the cabbages, the carrots and the turnips in his enormous hands with a look that was full of scorn and mistrust.

To all the oaths and arguments of the butchers and vegetable dealers they would listen with the same air of sullen suspicion: each morning a kind of passionate debate would take place, with John and Fred cast in the role of the suspicious interlocutor: the butchers would grow eloquent, and the vegetable dealers passionately inspired, as they held their wares aloft, smote roast and melon with a loving hand, and begged John and Fred to look at it, just look at it.

"Well, I'm looking," said John in a surly tone.

"O, a prime bit, Mr. Barrett! A lovely bit of meat if I do say so! Prime! Prime! Look at it now! Just look at it! Feel it! Go on, Mr. Barrett, feel it!"

Doubtfully, and with a slight sneer, John felt it.

"Well," he said, "I don't feel anything to get excited about."

"*Mister* Barrett!" the butcher cried reproachfully. "I tell you what!" he exclaimed with an air of sudden decision. "Take it along with you. If you don't say it's the best cut of beef you ever tasted, bring it back and—and—I'll eat it *raw*!" he yelled triumphantly. "I'll eat it raw before your eyes!"

At this point Fred would whisper something in John's ear: a muttered conversation would take place between them, punctuated with suspicious looks at the butcher, and at length, their decision made, they would buy generously, lavishly, enormously, going away with their great baskets loaded and their arms full.

The brothers were famous through the town, throughout the state. This morning ritual of food and marketing with its deep seriousness, the intensity and power of its hunger, and its earthly health brought all the world it touched closer to its exultancy and joy: men and children looking from their windows would see the two huge men go by, with laden baskets striding to the ponderous rhythm of their jowls. They would say, "Well, there they are!" and immediately it was as if they had just been born, full armed and lusty, shaking sleep out of their vital eyes, with hope, with hunger, and the smell of breakfast in their nostrils.

These men were more completely of the earth than anyone else I have ever known, and I know this is why they made their lives prevail, why people loved them, and why there was such a depth of love and wisdom in them. During my life I have seen so many people who have tried to make themselves less or more than other men, steering themselves into some poor mimicry of gods or devils, into aesthetical saints and melodramatic fiends, into unfleshed and dismal subtleties and unearthly cure-alls. There are two hungers that raven at the hearts of men: one is the mighty hunger of pain and fruitfulness that feeds on eating, that grows fertile with desire, that sprouts and blossoms in the deep earth of mighty men, and the other hunger is the terrible hunger of impotence—that shows these poor damned starvelings of the earth the vision of the great plantations which they can never touch, approach, or enjoy.

My uncles were New Englanders, there was something deep, buried, and withdrawn in their spirits that fortressed them about; they were enormous men, but there was something spare, clean, and delicate in them, they also came from the land of the great rivers and the mighty harvests: they were as great as rivers and as wide as the plains (it was the sea perhaps) and their hearts were deep and subtle as a vine. Therefore I never knew the barren land, I never saw a pinched or meagre element in New England: it had spare shoulders, but the bins were full: it was the place of the clean sweet rivers and of sharp October, ripeness was there, strong walls, and the full throat of the roaring fire; and men were fed there. Such are my father's folk, whose strange fortunes are so interwoven with my own, whose stories must be told as I tell mine.

My father never returned to the circus. That afternoon he drove over into Brantford with his uncle and his cousins: they saw the show while my father gathered up his few belongings and took his leave of the circus people, all of whom were sorry to see him go, and entreated him to stay. But he would not: All at once it was the circus, and this tented world, with all its warmth and pungency, that seemed remote to him—he had discovered the earth he came from, and now it seemed to him that he had never left it. His years among the circus people had slipped by like a dream: as he stood among them now, saying farewell, their faces were dark and strange, and there in their eyes he read the vision of all the loss and hunger that make men murderers upon the earth. He remembered every moment of his wandering with them, the whole vision of the enormous earth, inhabited with small elves' rings of canvas, with its infinite treasure of seed and harvest—he remembered all the pain, the labor, the misery, the unspeakable joy, and when he tried to speak to them he could not, for he had lost the language, he looked at them with love and sorrow over a wordless, timeless gulf, and he wondered in what lost world, and under what wild sorcery he had known them.

They pressed around him, they seized his hand with all their warmth and roughness, they knew all he wanted to say, and could not, and they said good-bye.

That evening he drove out of town again leaving the smell of evening food, the canvas and the tawny camel's reek behind him; the sun fell with a remote and ancient light, without violence or heat, upon the earth. Then the shadows walked across the land, the young moon glittered like a nail, night came and the sounds of the night rose out of the earth in a clear high mimicry. My father lay again below old rafters bedded at last in quilted sleep, in brown silence.

That year he lived there with them on the farm until late summer came. Meanwhile, he had written to his old friend, Walter Clark, the actor, who now was manager of a theatre in New York: in August, Clark wrote to him again and offered him a small part in a play which was to open in September. My father accepted: he went to New York during the summer, and for the next three years he was regularly employed by Mr. Clark, who had a stock company. By his twenty fifth year my father had established himself in his profession, and had a modest reputation.

During these years he worked very hard. Of formal education he had almost none, save a few years' schooling in his childhood, but he had learned much from his father—songs, ballads, and lyrical poems which he had committed to memory and spoken aloud, and the whole body of plays of Shakespeare, several of which he knew by heart. He had a prodigious memory, particularly for poetry, which he loved with a poet's love, and beyond this he had an understanding of what was living and beautiful on the earth that no amount of education could have given him. His sense had never been dulled or limited by schools, and everywhere about him he saw a thousand wonderful designs and forms: only in the theatre, which he loved, did he miss it. In the circus he had learned of the beauty that lies in balance and in that sense of timing which runs like a thread of gold through all the arts: it is an intuition rather than a calculation and it governs the movements of athletes, of cooks, and of poets, as I shall show you. But in the theatre he missed this rhythm, and he thought it was the theatre that most needed it. At this time the "serious" theatre was dominated by the spectacular figures of a few great tragedians: their monstrous and distorted shadows fell across the stage, ringed with phantasmal swarms of pygmy satellites. The great men walked the stage on stilts: they inhabited the silence with a ranting voice.

There was, however, at this time a great interest in the teachings of a Frenchman, Joseph Delsarte, who had died a few years before. His work was later so defiled by the charlatans and by people who claimed to have studied under him that his name became synonymous with a sickly and sentimental aestheticism. But what Joseph Delsarte had really taught was true and of the most lasting value: he believed there was as much music in man's flesh as in his words, and he thought the deepest feeling could be as eloquently expressed with the movement of the body as with the voice. He taught people the use of balance and posture, the meaning of rhythm. Now he was dead, but in New York his work was furiously discussed, and a few men gave instructions in what was known as the "Delsarte system." Among these men was a romantic and Byronic figure named Steele MacKaye: he was a man with a moustache and curly hair, a person of prodigious energies, a prolific writer of plays, one of which was *Esther Craig*, an actor, a designer of theatres, and an inventor of sinking stages, movable theatre seats, in which one could sleep or wake, contemplate the stage or the ceiling according to desire, with many other strange and wonderful things, some of which worked, and some didn't.

MacKaye had known Delsarte and had studied with him in Paris. Now he often talked to my father about Delsarte's work, of the great range and flexibility it gave to acting and how it enhanced an actor's power: he also spoke of his own life in Paris, and of his travels in Europe, and as my father listened a sense of powerful desire and joy was kindled in his heart: that terrible and undefined impulse which urges young men with a furious spur to "do something," to do something glorious and wonderful, was now focused and fused in a single word: "Paris." As Steele MacKaye spoke of his work, and of his life in Paris, each word he uttered, each casual reference he made to the streets, the boulevards, the cafés, the salons of painting, the "French," and the theatres, glowed for my father with a thousand wonderful shades and connotations. It seemed to him that he could see all of these things and people exactly as they were. He could close his eyes and see in exact detail that proud panoply of life, that glittering and beautiful carnival that men call "Paris," and over it all there played a strange and lovely light of legend and desire: the imperial and fabulous city rose from the earth like a form of magic, invincible, indestructible, and miraculous, more ancient than the earth it dwelt upon, and yet a golden myth remembered like a dream, tangible only to those who had themselves been touched by sorcery, a spot upon the surface of this earth—but a spot that no earthly road could lead to, that no earthly distance could define. There it was, then—Paris! A crest of earthly sorcery, only a stride away from those who had been entrusted to its magic, tangible, visible, apprehensible only to those in whom some magic dwelt, but never to be seen or touched at all by whatever toil of travel of earthbound men.

Paris! It was not a city, not a place—it was a fable, a vision, a state of enchantment, and a consummation of man's highest effort and desire. At this time my father could not have said toward what known goal his will was driving him, but it seemed to him that this word "Paris" gave the end and answer now to all the wanderings of desire, that all the wild unharnessed horses of his energy were reined and gaited to the bridle of this world, that here was the happy land he had sought so fruitlessly, and that here would he complete himself, fulfill his destiny. For, even to live in this enchanted place was glory enough, one breathed in greatness from the air about him, and everything else—the streets, the houses, the people, the language, the books, the conversations—conspired to the advancement of art and the production of genius.

My father resolved to go to Paris. He had no money: the money he earned in the theatre was barely sufficient to support him when he worked. But at this time the stage was crowded with plays which had been translated or adapted from the French. For a year, therefore, my father worked on these translations for Mr. Clark and other managers: he knew very little French, but he did the work doggedly with the aid of grammars and dictionaries, and succeeded because of his quiet intelligence and his sense of the theatre. The work was poorly paid, but it gave him some knowledge of the language, and by the end of the year he had saved a few hundred dollars. When he thought he had money enough he embarked at once. His hope, his hunger beat across the seas and burned upon that fabulous spot which dwelt in his vision like a living light of time. He was now twenty four years old.

VI

The Three Sisters

My mother was the youngest of three daughters: they came from a family of Dutch Jews, and were the children of a man whose name was Cornelius Goldsmith (or Goudsmit, as the name is spelled in Holland).

Cornelius Goldsmith had been born in Leyden and came to this country when he was a young man. Members of his family, whom I would visit several years after my marriage, still live in Leyden: they were forceful and cultivated people, they had originally come into Holland from Germany, and there were still branches of the stock in Germany and England. My grandfather was a graduate of the Leyden University and took his degree in law there. His younger brother also studied there: this man was a brilliant scholar and later was professor in jurisprudence at this university. They were people of considerable wealth for that time, and when Cornelius Goldsmith came to this country about fifteen years before the Civil War, he brought several thousand dollars with him. Moreover, he came as the legal agent for one of the Dutch navigation companies. Thus, he was solidly established before he came: he was a worldly and immensely capable man, bold and cautious, who left nothing to chance, and he was bound to get ahead.

When he had been here several years and knew enough people to assure his success, he left the company and set up in practice for himself. For years he had one of the largest practices in New York, but when the Civil War broke out he enlisted in one of the city regiments and served for the duration of the war: he was wounded at the battle of Chancellorsville, and was held prisoner by the Confederates for eight months, but escaped with several companions and got back to his own side safely after making a detour of hundreds of miles and travelling by night. In the years that followed the Civil War he was very successful: his practice was large and he made a great deal of money out of real estate. The time was particularly corrupt—it was the time of Gould and Fiske and Vanderbilt, of the plunderers of the Grant administration and of Boss Tweed and his gang: towns, cities, mines, forests, and the immensely fruitful wilderness lay open to their grab, and they robbed and looted like a set of drunken thieves.

In the midst of this debauch, Cornelius Goldsmith stuck out his scornful little mouth, and hewed precisely to the letter of the law, recognizing in that instrument a much more formidable tool than the crude clutching paw of the professional lootsman. No mud soiled him, but he belonged to Tammany Hall, and played the game with a dutiful completeness, and he prospered.

Also, he was well known to Dutch people all over this country and in Holland: many of his clients were Dutch people with business connections in America, he kept an office in Amsterdam, and he made a trip to Holland every year. On one of these trips he married and brought his wife back with him. He had known her for many years, and this marriage, of course, was a part of the life-plan he followed with unwavering calculation and which, in all respects but the most important ones, was completely successful. My mother and my aunt Mary were born in New York, but Bella was born in Holland one summer when my grandmother went back with him on one of these trips. There were only three children from this marriage: all were girls. My aunt Mary was the oldest. Bella, whose real name was Beatrice, was the second child: I do not know why people called her Bella, except that this was the name that exactly suited her, and the one she liked best, although a few of her older friends always called her "Bee." My mother was the youngest of the sisters: her name was Rebecca, which always seemed to me the most beautiful name a woman could have. The name is straight and sharp, there is silence and dark passion in it.

I never saw my grandmother. She died many years before I was born, but Bella told me she was a beautiful and gentle Jewish woman, faithful, docile, and loving. There was a suspicion that she had Christian blood in her: in Holland Bella heard that her great-grandfather had been half-Christian, but when she spoke of it later to her father he became furiously angry and forbade her ever to mention it again.

My grandmother never questioned her husband's word on any matter: he was a tyrant but she always obeyed him without hesitation. I have a picture of her—a little, faded daguerreotype, tinted with pale spots of color in her cheeks, made in what year I do not know but which always suggests somehow "1860." It is a gaunt, classical Jewish face: high boned, big visaged, with a powerful hooked nose, and a thin, wide, close-lipped mouth: a racial mask which seems to have been weathered in thousands of years of grief and pity. Most Gentiles would mistakenly call this bony visage harsh and cruel, because they have never seen its powerful and sensitive convulsions, its minute and instant transformations of feeling, and yet it is very similar to the bold, worn faces of the pioneer women. It is almost like a man's face, it is hard to say in what respect it is unlike a man's face, but it is a woman's face: gaunt, fecund, female, and powerful; recumbent, receptive, combative, ready for the plough. If a woman lived forever and never got old, this is the way she would really look—fertile, gaunt, and ageless like the earth: she would be strong, fierce and bony, with big lank thighs—the rest of it is brief, the magic of curve and breast, the velvet undulance, the creamy texture of the skin: this is a fashion of years, the hook fleshed with the succulent bait, part of their brief snare of harlotry.

My grandmother died before any of her daughters had grown up, and her early death was the most unfortunate thing that could have happened to them, and probably accounted for a great deal of the trouble they had later. But she unquestionably saved them from becoming stupid idle women: she was a maker and doer and she was fiercely attentive to her house, which was her kingdom. She taught them to cook in copper and in iron, and what to cook in each: she taught them how to get their rich Jew's tone and temper into cooking, to watch food with a loving and subtle intuition, to season, turn and mix with a delicate touch, never to be mean, dull, or sparing, and always to use abundantly the best of everything, together with the finest butter. These three sisters were the finest cooks on earth: there was no time in their lives when they could not turn in and cook a better meal than any of their servants. Later, I shall tell you what they cooked.

She also taught them how to shape and fashion with their hands: she taught them how to make clothes, and the clothes they made were more living and beautiful than any that could be bought in shops. This gift of seeing with their mind and heart, and of making with their hands came down to all of them, and had probably run back like a golden thread for hundreds of years. For they could see the pulse and cut of all things, great and small: the slant of a pocket, the set of a sleeve, the careful delicacy of well-made stitches, the color of faded brick or a paint-scaled wagon, the flight of a bridge, the hard lean cruel music of webbed steel.

My grandmother knew these things: she knew, as Jewish women know, finality and the end of hunger, the whole earth in a little room. She knew the synagogue, the markets, the feel of fat white-bellied fish, the closed kingdom of her walls. The Jewish women were final and complete: they needed no new worlds, they made their own within a little space, they got richer, deeper, and more populous, until the populous rich voices of their own earth filled the air in grief, in passion, in laughter, or in love. At length they were a field, a garden, the only universe they knew or needed, and of all things living that grew upward from the earth to heaven, they heard all, they knew all, they were fulfilled.

Did not her father seek and find them thus? Did he not know them after wandering? Did they not appease his fierce desire where starveling Gentiles had denied him? Did he not know their amber depth and sweetness, their warm recumbency, their complete fertility? Did he not hear their sweet henclucking Jews-cries (Oi!), their broken yolky beat: did the fiery lips not stop his mouth in darkness (Yes!), did they not receive him with deep-moaned darkling wholeness (aie, aie!), with velvety undulance, with satiable and entire fulfillment!

Bella told me that their life after her mother's death was unspeakably narrow, dull and lonely. They were allowed to see no one, to visit no one without their father's approval, and the only people he approved of were a few old and stolid Jews. Even a visit from these people was rare: he was an arrogant and secretive man, fiercely jealous of his household privacy, and he received visitors grudgingly and with great effort. It is likely that quality of secrecy is Dutch, but I suspect from other things that I have known and seen that it is. But part of it is also Jewish.

My grandfather did not think that anything or anyone was good enough for himself or his daughters. If he entertained people in his house, the food and drink he gave them was almost the best, but Bella told me that what he had for himself and the family when no one else was present was always better. My father told me that the old man had two kinds of cigars: one which he gave to his friends, which were very fine, and another which he kept for himself, which were just a little finer. These cigars were sent to him by one of his brothers who had a wine and tobacco importing business in Amsterdam: the tobacco was of Sumatra leaf and had a delicious fragrance. Bella said she thought one reason he invited so few people to the house (they then lived on West Twentieth Street), was that he was jealous of the comfort and luxury in which he lived and wanted no one else to share it, or know about it, because he thought it was much too good for them. Although he knew a great many people and had many friends, Irish, German, Jewish, Dutch and American, in politics and business, he would never bring these people home: if he wanted to entertain them he would take them to a restaurant or a club.

They lived in the most extravagant luxury: his daughters were not allowed to have friends or beaux, but they could have anything that money could buy. He encouraged them in wastefulness, their extravagance delighted him, and because they had no other outlet for their time and interest, they spent money with reckless indifference, and grew up with no sense of its value. They had horses, carriages, silks, satins, bonnets and dresses, bracelets and jewels—always "the latest thing from Paris," and he never questioned or checked them. He was mistaken in his own life, he set his value upon the wrong things, and he was wrong in almost everything he did for his children, and yet he loved them dearly and was bitterly disappointed in the way they used their lives. Like most worldly Jews, he was liberal with money once he had it, but he placed too high a value on getting it: he was purse proud and it was hard for him to respect or like people who were not successful. Even in the way he encouraged the extravagance of his daughters there was something arrogant and proud: whatever belonged to him must be the best and cost the most.

He died when I was about seven years old, but I remember very vividly his visits to us, and the way he looked and talked. He was a short little man with a very heavy figure, and a very proud, out-thrust, pompous carriage. He had a high, flat, and wide forehead, some sparse, reddish-brown hair, and great tufty side-whiskers. His face was very fat and heavy, but what seemed very remarkable to me was the delicacy of his features. In spite of the cushion of fat, they emerged as small and sharp as a child's: the nose was small and delicate and tilted at the end, he had a firm, decisive little mouth with a scornful, pouting underlip, and a sharply moulded little chin, and he had very bright blue eyes. His face was a beautiful tender pink from all the good living he had done: if anyone had touched it, his finger would have left a fading mark, but the set and cast of the face was choleric and proud.

The garments he wore were extraordinary: he was always spotlessly dressed, and his clothes were newly tailored, but they represented a style that was at least twenty years old. He wore long frock coats of beautiful broadcloth with big horn buttons, and he always wore white, stiffly starched shirts and a high, wide-open collar, tied with a big bow tie of heavy black silk. His waistcoats were very fancy: they were usually brown with a big checked pattern, and he wore a heavy gold watch chain strung through a button hole. He had a nice little belly neatly tucked away into these waistcoats, and when he sat in a chair, there was something withdrawn and scornful about his posture—one hand was usually thrust out resting over the top of a heavy cane with a smooth round silver head on which some letters were engraved.

There was something inarticulate and perverse in him that repelled affection even when it asked for it: he was scornful, arrogant, and hurt at the same time, he died a lonely and bitter man. I was afraid of him. All of his kindness had some scorn in it: once when he had come to see me, he tried to take me upon his knee but I would not let him. I shrank back and would not go to him. I think that he was hurt by this and at length he took a new shiny gold piece from his pocket and offered it to me. The beautiful coin, bright and golden, fascinated me: it lay there in his palm with a living weight I could feel myself. In a moment I moved forward to take it.

"You will come now, eh?" he said in his precise, somewhat foreign accent. "Now you will sit on my knee." He laughed shortly and scornfully, without opening his mouth. "Yes. Now you will come. It is the same with all of you. When you see gold you will sit on the old man's knee." He was mistaken. I would not go to him then. When he went away, he left the gold piece on the table. Then I took it.

When my grandfather thought his daughters were old enough, he sent them abroad to complete their schooling, because he did not think the schools here were good enough for them. All of them had been in Holland several times, and spoke Dutch because it was the only language he wanted to use at home. Probably he did not think that English was good enough, either, although, because he had to use it in most of his business dealings, he had learned to speak it accurately and well. But it was part of his obstinacy and pride to think nothing here as good as it was in Holland: he never ceased to feel that the life here in America was crude and barbarous, he often mocked at it, at the nasal twang and at many of the customs of the people, and yet he had managed to use this life so well that he had grown rich on it. But he would not talk what he called "Yankee Jabber" in his house; it annoyed him if his daughters spoke to one another in English, but because they resented his narrow tyranny and were bored with the life he made them lead, they often spoke English in his presence to annoy him, and they always spoke it among themselves.

After they had married and left him, they rarely spoke in Dutch again, although during my childhood Bella and my mother used to speak the language when they had something to say they did not want me to hear. I was always fascinated and impressed by this accomplishment on which they placed no value whatever: if they had spoken in French or German it would not have been half so strange to me, but Dutch was a language that did not seem probable. And yet, when I listened to them as they spoke it, it had a tantalizing familiarity as if I could almost understand it, as if its full meaning would come to me in another moment. And although I never learned to speak a word of it, it always seemed to me that Dutch had this familiar sound: if one would listen to a group of people speaking it, the sound, the movement, all of the little tones and implications are almost identical with casual American speech. I once asked Bella why she never spoke it any more, and she told me that she hated it. Yet all of her memories of Holland were pleasant ones. She told me some of the happiest years of her life had been lived there: if she hated to speak the language in later years I know it was because of my grandfather. Her relations with him had been so bitter and so hostile, and after his death she grieved and blamed herself for all of it, and wept when she spoke of him.

Of all his children, he loved Rebecca most: he knew nothing about her, he was troubled by something silent and implacable in her which once or twice he had encountered, but he did not know what depth and resolution dwelt in her, and how inflexible her decision was once she made it. This discovery, when at length it came, broke his heart. The oldest daughter, Mary, was docile and gentle like her mother: she was easily guided; he was very fond of her and felt she would always obey him. Yet she, too, thwarted his will in the end.

With Bella, however, he was constantly at odds. Sometimes they had bitter and violent quarrels together; sometimes they would go for weeks without speaking to each other.

On these occasions she would not go to the table when he was at home, and she would leave the room immediately, without speaking, when he came in. When he was not at home she would walk up and down the room impatiently as she talked to Rebecca:

"I have not spoken to him for a week. He never speaks to me any more. Do you think that's natural? I suppose I ought to remember he's my own father? I suppose I ought not to act this way? Do you think so, Beck?"

"Well, I don't think it would hurt you to speak to him," Rebecca said. "You know how stubborn and proud he is. After all, you are young and can afford to give in a little to an old man."

"Do you think so?" Bella asked eagerly. She walked up and down in silence for a moment. Suddenly she made a large unhappy gesture. "No, I won't do it. If he thinks he's going to have his own way all the time I'll show him he's mistaken. Why, good heavens, Beck," she burst out in a fury, "I think the man is mad. He thinks he's God Almighty. Why should we be always cooped up like this, and never allowed to go anywhere or see anyone? How does he expect us to spend our time? What are we living for? It is always the same—we get up and dress, we sit around and sew, we play cards, we read novels, we go shopping, we take a ride in the park. We get constipated. Always the same old ride, the same old shops—yes, and the same old constipation," she shouted, beginning to laugh. "Then we come back and sit at the table with him and watch him eat. God, I'll go crazy if something doesn't happen soon!"

"Well," Rebecca said. "I suppose we do the same things that most people do. I can't see that we're worse off than most of the others. What else would you like?"

"What else would I like!" cried Bella. "God, Beck, you're not so simple as to think we ought to be content with what we have. Do you mean to tell me you are satisfied to live like this. Of course you're not," she said impatiently.

"Well," Rebecca said, "it seems to me that Father has been very generous with us all. I don't think we can complain on that score."

"Complain!" said Bella. "I'm nothing but one huge mass of complaints. I don't complain: I howl. Why do you think he's so generous? Because he gives us all the money we can spend? You know why he does that—he thinks we are his property: he'll spend money on anything that belongs to him. Generous! Why, Beck, he's one of the stingiest and meanest people I ever knew!"

"Oh, Bella!" Rebecca said. "You're very unfair! You know he's not like that: he'd do anything in the world for us. He wants us to have the best and to do the best for ourselves. He is mistaken and narrow, but he means well. You know he's dogmatic and Jewish, but he can't help that: he's so afraid we'll get away from our race and religion."

"Get away!" cried Bella. "You can just bet I'll get away from them. I'll get so far away from them they can't find me with a telescope! I hope I never see a Jew again!"

"You'd better not let your father hear you say that," Rebecca said.

"I hope he does hear me!" Bella cried. "I'd like to see him writhe! God! How he's made me hate his race. When I see them coming I feel like starting a pogrom of my own!"

"Bella!" Rebecca cried. "How can you talk like that! Someday you may be married to a Jew."

"Married to one of them!" said Bella. "I'll be damned if I will!

They can boil me in oil before I do! God! I hate the sight of them! I hate their big noses and that come-on-please-hurt-me look they have. If I ever marry, I'm going to marry a Goy!"

"Bella!"

"Yes, I am! I mean it!" Bella said, suddenly beginning to laugh. "A nice blue-eyed, blond-headed uncircumcised son of a Goy! And so are you, Beck! You know you are."

"I have not thought about it," Rebecca said. "Anyway, we never get a chance to meet anyone but Jewish people."

"We'll get the chance," said Bella mysteriously. "You'll see. . . . Now, Beck," she said teasingly, "you know you've thought about it hundreds of times. You needn't roll your innocent eyes at me, old girl. You know you'd like to have a nice blue-eyed Goy make love to you. . . . It's what we all want."

"Bella!"

"Well, I would!" Bella cried. "And I'm going to have one, too! I'm going to get me a nice blue-eyed, blond-headed uncircumcised son of a Christian, and if he has freckles on the back of his neck, so much the better. Yes! And if he's been to Yale or Harvard College, so much the better! Yes, Beck, I'd like to have a nice fancy Goy name—Mrs. Cavendish Montgomery, or something like that—and bring up a whole flock of nice little tow-headed polo players!"

"Why, Bella." Rebecca said, "I believe you're just trying yourself to see how far you can go."

"Trying myself!" said Bella. "Why, I haven't begun to try myself yet. If I told you some of the things I really think about, I'd make your hair stand straight up on your head."

"Then I hope you never tell me," Rebecca said. "What are they?" she continued in a moment.

Bella laughed an open, joyful laugh, because she was young, proud with song, a girl.

"Oh, Beck," she cried. "I wonder if you know what a wonderful place the world is! You must have thought about it! My God, here we are starving to death in the midst of plenty! But we won't starve forever!" she said, flying her arms out in a powerful gesture. "Why has this hunger been put in us if we are never going to be fed? Sometimes I feel as if I could open my arms and crush the whole earth in my hug. If father only knew what goes on inside me! Sometimes I feel as [if] I could tear his whole little Jewish world to pieces as if it were a rotten cloth! And someday I will!" she said. "I'll knock his whole little house of cards to pieces! God! If these fools could know what goes on in us!"

She strode restlessly back and forth for a moment, then she picked up a book which her sister had been reading and opened it.

"Oh, listen to this, will you, Beck?" she said immediately, with a rising intonation of strong scornfulness, as she read the first line her eye fell on:

"The young girl turned her clear eyes upon Delano for a moment with a glance that was direct, pure, and full of great reproach.

" 'I am afraid you did not quite—understand, Mr. Delano,' she said simply.

"For a moment he said nothing. He stared blankly at her. Then, slowly, a flash of deepest red overspread his features.

" 'I beg your pardon,' he stammered. 'I assure you, Miss Josephine, I meant nothing—' "

"O rats!" Bella cried, hurling the book across the room. "He meant nothing! The poor fool! 'The young girl lifted her pure eyes,' *did she?* The lying young bitch, you'd better say. What she wanted to lift was her skirt! Beck, I don't see how you can spend your time reading such foolishness!" she burst out furiously.

"Well," Rebecca said. "It might not hurt you if you read a book sometime. You wouldn't prance around so. Did you ever try? Did you ever in your life read a whole book through from beginning to end?"

"I did not!" said Bella proudly. "Thank God, I've better ways to waste my time! Oh, of course, I've got no brain, Beck. I know that. But sometimes I think I have more sense than a lot of people who have brains. Why are smart people such big fools! They read and study all their lives and then they don't know how to get across the street! Don't you think it's queer, Beck? Here are all these wonderful brainy people who can settle the affairs of the world and everyone else, but they can't settle their own for five minutes? I have no sense, but sometimes I think I know more than any of them. Anyway, I know how to get across the street, and I know what I want. Good heavens! You wonder where these people spend their lives. Do they never learn anything? Do they never use their eyes? God, sometimes I wish that I could write a book! I'd tell them a few things that would make their eyes stick out, all right! You can just bet I'd tell them what young girls really think about! . . . I wonder what would happen, Beck, if a woman ever wrote the truth down in a book."

"Why, I suppose the other women would deny it was the truth," Rebecca said.

"That's it!" cried Bella. "That's just it! Of course they would! They're afraid to tell the truth! They think it would spoil the game for them."

"No, I don't think that's it," Rebecca said.

"Then why has none of them ever written about it: you know what I mean, Beck. Don't pretend you don't. You know this business of the young girl blushing is all bosh. Why don't they say so?"

"Perhaps they can't," Rebecca said. "It's not so easy."

"Well, I could," Bella said. "There are some things I'd like to tell them."

"What sort of things?"

"Oh, the most wonderful sort of things!" cried Bella. "The others can tell of what goes on in their heads. I have no head to tell about. I'd love to tell them what goes on between my shoulders and my hips! God! That would be a-plenty! It'd make juicy reading, I tell you! I'd like to tell of the slope of a man's shoulders. Don't you love the slope of their shoulders, Beck? And the way they carry themselves. God! I think the line of a man's back and the shape of his hips is the most beautiful thing in the world. The other day I saw a man digging a ditch. He was naked to the waist and as brown as a piece of leather. Honestly, I could hardly keep my hands off him."

"Bella!"

"It's the truth! I can't help it. I watched him as he bent and straightened up, and the way his muscles came and went was just like music. I felt my fingers itching to touch that strong salty skin. I got so close I could smell the sweat. Talk about your perfumes of Araby! I tell you, Beck, they were nothing compared—"

"Good heavens Bella!"

"Oh, but you haven't heard the half of it yet, old girl! I could tell you things about policemen and sailors that would curdle your blood!"

"Sailors!"

"Yes, sailors. Sailors are lovely. Why I adore them, Beck. It's those britches that they wear that does it. I can't keep my eyes away from them! Up and down! Up and down! Yes! And handsome young doctors! Oh, I'd love to have an affair with a handsome young doctor, Beck! God! If I can ever afford it, I'm going to be an invalid a large part of the time. I'd look at him with my pure innocent young girl's eyes in a way that would melt the heart of an iceberg. I have thought about it thousands of times: I can close my eyes and see it just the way I know it's going to be. I shall receive him all stretched out in a crimson negligee; I shall be pale and wan and tell him my throat hurts me. Something tells me if he ever gets a look at my tonsils, he's as good as mine already. He will be very strong and tender and handsome and when he bends over me I shall adore the way his head is set upon his shoulders! God! I think there's nothing more wonderful than the way a man's head is set upon his shoulders, Beck. Don't you think so? I wouldn't dream of marrying a man if his head and his shoulders didn't meet properly. I don't want any of these drooping, furtive, hang-dog Jews-heads! No thank you! Not for me! I like that proud, fearless, blue-eyed Christian look! They're the boys for Bella! I don't suppose they're so strong in the upper-story, but O! Beck, how I could love them! . . . I suppose I'll die an old maid. That's what usually happens to women like me. I've got a what-do-you-call-it—an *obsession*—for big blue-eyed, blond-haired Goys, and if I don't get one I suppose I'll never take anything else!"

"*Well*!" Rebecca said. "I must say, Bella, you've outdone all your former efforts today! I'm glad there's no one here to take you seriously. If you really believed all the things you say, I'd think I had a pretty wild sister!"

"You have, Becksie, but you don't know it! You don't begin to know it yet. But you will! I promise you that. I tell you what, old girl: I think I'm a bit of a whore, you know."

"Bella!"

"Well, where there's so much smoke, there's bound to be some fire. And God knows I'm boiling with smoke!"

"You're boiling with talk, you mean," Rebecca said. "You love to talk, that's all. As for your conduct, you have stricter morals than a rabbi."

"I don't know what morals a rabbi has," said Bella. "But I've got none at all."

"Oh, Bella! What a fib!"

"It's true, so help me God! Rabbi! That's it. You'd better say rabbit. I've got no more morals than a rabbit. Neither have you."

"You can speak for yourself," Rebecca said. "You're not speaking for me!"

"Yes I am! I'm speaking for every woman in the world. Look here, Beck, you know good and well that a woman doesn't care two raps of her fingers for morals. They believe what the men tell them they ought to believe—it's all only a kind of fashion or style as far as we are concerned: if the style changed in favor of going stark naked you know perfectly well we'd all be running around without a rag on in six months' time—yes! And we'd laugh at all the fool women who used to wear clothes in the old days!"

"Not I, Bee! You're not speaking for me!"

"Well, I would," said Bella, slapping her hips, and swinging her opulent figure with a happy laugh. "And be glad of the chance to show my wares!"

"Oh no, you wouldn't, Bee. No woman with any character could do a thing like that."

"No woman has any character," Bella said. "We have no morals and no character—no more than a wheat field. And I tell you what, Beck: we're all waiting for the plough. If we don't get that, old girl, we're alone in the desert. And I'm going to get it!" she said exultantly. "God! Sometimes I think I'd love to be a regular daughter of the regiment. I could take them as they came—whole platoons and companies of them all lined up—the dear little blue-eyed boys! Oh now, don't you worry," she said, noting her sister's alarmed expression, "I'm not going to. I'm not so big a fool. The game's not played that way! I haven't been brought up in a respectable Jewish household for nothing. If a man wants me he's got to marry me! As the Chinaman says, no tickee, no washee!"

At this moment a carriage stopped in the street, there was the slamming of a carriage door, and the sound of someone mounting the steps outside.

"Bella!" Rebecca said quickly. "There's father!"

"Well," said Bella, "there's one man I'll never have to marry, thank God!"

As he entered the room he stopped, for a moment his short figure was turned harsh and full against her; at length they broke the fierce stare of their unquiet eyes with a kind of hard effort, and Bella went past him out of the room without saying a word to him.

The reason for this bitter war was plain. Bella at this time was a completely innocent girl, but all of the fiercely sensual energy, the hot chemistry of her blood, her enormous hunger for living, fought savagely against the narrow cell of custom and convention in which her father tried to jail her. For her, at this time, the world glowed with a hundred light and sparkling colors, a furious swarm of desires and hungers, of tongueless expectancies and dateless fulfillments which beat like a drone of frustrate bees within her: There was nothing for her to grip in her devouring hug, no words that could utter her deep, driven desires, nothing at which she could hurl her strength. She sweltered in fury, in that maddening fury and bafflement of young people who feel within them enormous power and yet have no means of harnessing it, of focusing it, of expressing it. They do not feel that the delight they want, the life they desire, is intangible and amorphous: they feel it is as tangible as flesh or earth, but when they try to grasp it they cannot, even when they try to utter their desire they cannot—they are devoured by their own hunger, and they have no words to utter the desire that feeds upon them. Their energy is torn asunder and diffused by the wild, unyoked horses of desire, they are maddened by the concrete immanence of wonder which is yet just beyond their touch or utterance; they try to speak, and in their fury they strike their fist vainly into the air, or beat their flesh, in a gesture of bafflement and fury. At no other time in life does one have such lucid and terrible flashes of wisdom—in a second the magical and irrecoverable moment is struck by lightning, the youth knows instantly all that can be known of the human destiny and of man's brief wink of sentience in time—he sees the moment go forever.

Suddenly he understands that such moments, that a single marvelous day, may not be repeated a dozen times in his life—and that all he lives in hope of finding and possessing may, even if the supremest fortune smile on him, be found, possessed, and relinquished in ten minutes. A kind of madness of desire overwhelms him—the desire to possess the moment as it may never be possessed, to feed hunger in an absolute fashion, as it may never be fed: at such moments he has constantly the sense of starving to death in the midst of plenty, of perching unfed in the greenery of life, of being made impotent by abundance.

Of course, it is true that very few people ever feel this hunger with such intensity, and most people would think this description of it, which only moderately and inadequately describes it, a wild exaggeration. Most young people, indeed, would condemn this statement of the youth-hunger and would deny that it represented their own feelings. But if youth is wonderful and rare and lovely, most of the young people are not, and youth is wasted on them. Youth is lonely, wild, and beautiful—it falters, it is blind, it is usually foolish and ridiculous, it is often afraid, it is almost always mistaken—but if all the poetry of all the mighty poets who ever lived and wrote in praise of youth, was bound together in one great book with words of living gold—yet the sum of all these priceless numbers would be paltry compared to the true excellence and beauty of youth. The reason men love youth is because they know it is so lovely and because they know, however wrong and foolish all of its actions may be, it is the truest and loveliest spirit on earth.

The true friends of youth, again, are the old men. Most young men are stupid, barren, fearful and gnawed by bitter envy: if they see hunger, they mock at it, they say it does not exist because they have no hunger in themselves. They must have something to ridicule, because they fear that ridicule will be turned against themselves, and this they cannot endure. They are afraid to be alone: therefore, they hate youth with the consuming hate of men who have no power to live within themselves. Youth goes alone, but young men go in crowds: they want to be safe, they want to be fashionable, they have no power of belief or disbelief in them, they know what they do not know, they live upon the lives of truer, bolder spirits, their words are hedged with fear, measured by timorous calculations. The young men are treacherous and disloyal, they betray one another, but they are united in their betrayal of youth: they hate its power, its faith, its loneliness, and they try to destroy it by ridiculing its follies and excesses.

For a young woman like Bella, who feels this savage hunger, the release is harder than for a man. For a man is a wanderer; he reels, he staggers, he gropes blindly across the earth, but he moves, strives, actively seeks and searches: his power is often foiled and wasted, but from this labor of defeat he comes to know himself upon the earth and at length to believe in fences. A man is nothing until he stands alone, a man alone may be a hero or a poet, but a woman alone is nothing. A man must invade and try to conquer the earth for himself, but a woman must be conquered and invaded before she can make her life prevail in any way. Her body is like the earth: she must be ploughed and sown before she can yield a harvest. Even in its physical structure her body resembles the earth: the likeness has been observed and written about by many poets. John Donne, in a magnificent tribute to his mistress, addresses her as "O my America! My new-found land, my king-dome, Safliest when with one man man'd"—he likens himself to an explorer and begs license for his "roaming hands, and let them go, Before, behind, between, above, below"—etc. Similarly, in "Venus and Adonis," Shakespeare has Venus petition young Adonis in these words:

'I'll be a park, and thou shalt be my deer;
Feed where thou wilt, on mountain or in dale:
  Graze on my lips; and if those hills be dry,
  Stray lower, where the pleasant fountains lie.
'Within this limit is relief enough,
Sweet bottom-grass and high delightful plain,
Round rising hillocks, brakes obscure and rough,
To shelter thee from tempest and from rain:
  Then be my deer, since I am such a park;
  No dog shall rouse thee, though a thousand bark.'

It must be obvious that these splendid metaphors are not the product of a rich but wayward fancy. No. The poet has meditated them deliberately and he pursues the analogy of the earth with opulent detail.

Everyone must have observed the truth of this for himself: in its contours—its curves, slopes, hollows, mounds, its music of flowing rhythms, and its legend of fecundity, a woman's body resembles the earth much more closely than a man's. Moreover, many women have had an illusion of physical union with the earth—of being joined to the earth and a part of it, particularly during the period before the birth of a child. Finally, most women

are much more beautiful in recumbency, in a position of languor-
ous receptivity, than when erect.

Thus, like Shakespeare's Venus, Bella saw her desire before her
and could not grasp it. Before she could possess, she must be possessed, before she could hold she must be held: sometimes a frenzy
of desperate energy would seize her—she felt that she could push
her finger through a wall of brick, that she could tear the world
about her into rags, that in an instant she could grasp the palpable warm treasures of the earth she wanted. But always the word,
the way, the moment slipped away, and she was left like a wave
that breaks upon the shore. At length she would release herself in
moments of explosive destruction: she would storm through the
house like a fury, hurl books across the room, knock over chairs,
sweep stacks of music from the piano to the floor—attack whatever
came within reach of her angry hands.

"Bella! In heaven's name! What's wrong with you? What do you
want?" Rebecca said.

"I want to get my hands on something and smash it up!" said
Bella. "I'd like to get my hands on him!" she cried, thinking of
her father. "I'd like to shake him till his teeth rattled! God! Beck!
Sometimes I think I'll go mad if I don't get out of here! I wish I
were a man! Think of the fun they have: when I see them passing
on the street I want to call out to them, to tell them they don't
know how lucky they are, to make the most of it! God! What fools
they are not to do more with it. They can do what they like without asking. Think of it, Beck! They can go where they please and
no one will stop them. They walk along the streets smoking big
cigars. They go into saloons and order drinks, they stand up to
the bar and talk to the bartender, they tell dirty jokes, they eat in
restaurants, they go to the Fifth Avenue Hotel, they spit in spit-
toons—like this—Hock! Ptoo! They work on ships, they ride on
trains, they drive wagons and cabs, they ride in them, they curse
and fight, they belong to clubs, they go fishing, they live in flats,
they go to the theatre and sit in the front row, they make eyes at
the girls, they loaf around on street corners, they build houses,
they run machinery, they sell meat and groceries, they go to the
bank and count their money, they pick their teeth in public with a
private gold tooth-pick while a boot-black shines their shoes, they

go down to the Bowery, and they go to the houses where those women are. . . . I've heard that some of these places are very high-toned. All the men are perfect gents and all the girls are perfect ladies. . . . Beck, do you suppose I'd be any good at a job like that? Maybe we could go into business together. You could be the lady of the house: you could give it tone. We would cater only to the better class of people. Why, there's our chance, Beck: many a poor girl got her start in life like that—we might pick off a couple of Society Swells from Newport. I've been told that some of them go to those places."

"Well!" Rebecca said. "I must say, Bee, that for a girl who grumbles about leading such a shut-in life you certainly gather very spicy information. How on earth do you ever hear such things?"

"By asking questions when I get the chance and by keeping my eyes open. I tell you, Beck, there's nothing like asking people questions. If you want to find out anything about them you've got to ask them questions."

"I shouldn't think it'd be so easy," Rebecca said. "I should think they'd hate to tell you things about themselves."

"Hate it!" Bella cried. "They love it. Once you get them started you'd have to strangle them to make them stop. Why Beck, don't you know there's nothing people like better than to talk about themselves? . . . I talk to everyone, Becksie, and everyone talks to me. And I could tell you some very strange and interesting things, old girl, that I bet you'd never learn from reading Tennyson and Longfellow. We go along the streets and we pass whole blocks of tenements or brownstone houses and all of them look alike. But inside everyone is different. When you go down a street at night, it's very peaceful looking, isn't it? But I want to tell you something: the silent watches of the night are not so very silent as you think. Sometimes there are some very gay doings: you'd be surprised to know what goes on down the street at number 31 on the last Friday night of every month! I mean that pretty little doll-faced Christian, Mrs. Crawford—butter wouldn't melt in her mouth, would it? Oh, no! And isn't she just devoted to him: did you ever see anything like the way she hangs on his arm? It's a pity he's got to leave her for a minute, isn't it? But he has—the factory is at Hartford and he's got to go there once a month. . . . If you want to know what happens when he's gone you want to get acquainted with Mrs. Madden: she's the cook."

"Good heavens, Bee!"

"Oh, the private life of doll-faced Christians is not always dull, my dear! . . . There's the home-life of Italian fruit merchants—that's worth looking into, I can tell you! Mrs. Scarsati has told me all about it! . . . Her husband beats her, Beck—he beats her once a week, and, what is more, she likes it!"

"What does he beat her for?"

"Oh, for one thing or another," Bella said. "One time he beat her because she took a bath. . . . He was really mad that time . . . the Italian men don't like their wives to bathe, she says. . . . It spoils the way they smell. . . . But, usually, he just beats her for fun!"

"Well, he's a low brute if he does—that's all I've got to say!" said Rebecca angrily. "Somebody ought to beat *him*, and beat him good! I don't see why she stands for it! Why doesn't she call a policeman and have him arrested?"

"Why Beck, you *are* a goose! Why should she call a policeman? Most of the police are married men, anyway. They've got wives of their own to beat. How do you think the tired working man spends his time Saturday night? You don't think he spends it playing checkers, do you? He's got to have some rest and relaxation, hasn't he? If he doesn't beat his wife, what's he going to do?"

"Well, it's a dreadful thing, if it's true," Rebecca said. "If that's the kind of life you complain of missing, I think you're better off the way you are."

"Yes. I suppose you'd call it dreadful," Bella said, "but it's—God, Beck! it's so beautiful!" she said. "They get their hands on one another! Oh, I can't tell you how it is!" she exclaimed with a sudden half-checked gesture of fury and frustration. "It's like getting a hold on something! It's like finding a single word that would make the whole thing clear."

She paused: for a moment she stared somberly at the window.

"Do you know what I'd like to do?" she said abruptly. "I'd like to give a great party and invite everyone I know to it.—I'd like to have Mr. & Mrs. Scarsati, and old lady Witzenstein, and Ed O'Hare, and Miss Hilda Berniker, the dressmaker, and old man Berniker, and Bertha, and the two Rosenzweig boys and George Innes, and Mrs. Madden, and Hunter and Post, the grocers, and their families, and Captain Groen, and Jim Earnshaw, the horse car driver, and Wayne Mears, and Mr. Norodny who runs the tobacco shop, and Mr. Haddad, the rug merchant, and old Doctor Purefoy, and—"

"Why, Bee!" Rebecca said. "You can't mix people up that way. Do you think anyone would come to a party like that?"

"Would anyone come!" said Bella. "You mean, would anyone stay away? Why, you couldn't keep them away with a shot-gun. Do you think people are going to refuse a chance to have some fun for a change? They'd come in flocks and droves: I'll bet you that for every one who failed to turn up there'd be three new ones who weren't invited. We'd have the house full, never fear!"

"But how would they pass the time after they got here?" Rebecca said. "What could they do?"

"They could eat!" cried Bella. "That's what they could do! They could begin by eating and drinking, and you can be sure they'd get around to talking and singing together later on."

"I wonder what we could give them," Rebecca said reflectively.

"I've thought about that," said Bella. "My idea is, it would be a mistake to serve them hot food—I mean an elaborate cooked dinner. I think if we gave them something cold—some light refreshments—and let them mix around together and help themselves, it would be better."

"We might give them chicken salad," said Rebecca.

"Yes," Bella said. "That's the very thing! I'd thought of that. Then we might get Else to cook a ham a day or two before and stick it full of cloves. I thought we could lay it all out on the dining room table in a tasty manner and let them help themselves."

"Oh, the table would be much too small for all these people," Rebecca said.

"Why, no," said Bella. "It's big enough. We'd pull it out and put in two or three extra leaves. No one would sit down anyway: they'd move around and help themselves. It would all be very informal. I thought we could put Else's ham at one end of the table, and perhaps a cold roast turkey, or a duck at the other end—I thought we might have a great pyramid of all sorts of different fruits in the centre of the table: I've thought of it many times, I can just see how it would look, it would be beautiful. Joe Scarsati told me he would furnish the fruit himself—I thought we could have pears, oranges, bananas, raisins, plums, tangerines, and big red apples with maybe a few pineapples around the base and some bunches of Concord and Malaga grapes. Joe would arrange it so it would knock your eye out: the way he does it is a marvel—he's an artist at it. Honestly, it's a pity to spoil it after he gets through building it up."

"Oh, Bee, we couldn't let him," said Rebecca. "Why-he-he *spits* upon the apples, to make them shine."

"Oh, he does not!" said Bella, beginning, however, to laugh heartily.

"Why he *does!*" said Rebecca. "I've seen him do it!"

"Oh well, it'd be all right," Bella said easily. "I could arrange all that—just tell him in a tactful manner not to spit. He'd understand. . . . Now I think, Beck, we ought to have some cold meats, too—say, a cold sliced tongue and a roast of beef. We could also have some plates of little sandwiches—I think some dainty little sandwiches—caviar and cucumber and cheese, you know—and then we could have hot chocolate and coffee for whoever wants it. After all, people don't expect a great deal: once you get them started talking and laughing they're not going to pay much attention to what they have to eat. Of course, we'll have to have ice cream and cakes for the children: Jim Earnshaw said he'd take care of the ice cream—he'd freeze it, and Mr. Hunter will send assorted candies—I think it would look nice in all these little silver dishes: we could set it about in various places on the table and on the sideboard."

"I could make a big cake," Rebecca said.

"Yes," said Bella. "I think one of these frosted layer cakes you make, with nuts in between the layers and an edge of maraschino cherries and some strips of lemon peel would be nice. Of course, we could have some little ones, too—cookies, ginger bread, wafers, and things like that—the children like them."

"It would be nice to do," Rebecca said. "It would be fun. . . . But of course we couldn't!" she added regretfully, but decisively.

Bella was silent for a moment: her vital, generous features smouldered for a moment with a sullen, a resentful energy.

"I will! Someday I will!" she said.

For a few moments, gripped by the excitement of desire, the sisters had forgotten that such a party as they planned was only a hopeless wish: they had believed in its reality as they planned it, and now they were left with nothing but a sense of the full joy that somehow lay within their sight, beyond their grasp.

Rebecca, the younger sister, bore herself more patiently and quietly than Bella at this time, but her hostility to the life they were forced to lead was as implacable, and her determination to escape from it as fixed. She had a more contained and enduring soul than Bella's; she could endure to be alone, and she could wait more tranquilly, with patience. But Bella's hunger for the earth and for people was imperative: as limited as her life was, she fed fiercely on the colors and movements of the earth, on every human relation. She talked to everyone who came within the confined circle of her life—to cooks, grocers, coachmen, cab drivers and horse car drivers, newsboys, street urchins, to the Jews, the Irish, the Italians, the Germans, to passengers on ships and to Dutch sea captains—and they responded, revealing their lives to her with instant confidence because they knew and understood her at once.

She loved the city. The rock of life bordered between its gleaming tides, mast hemmed, exultant, was the richest earth her heart had ever known. Even the years she had spent in Holland with her uncle's family, living a life that was immeasurably freer, more generous, and more gay than she had ever known in her father's house, she had felt inexplicably the sharp, the piercing ache of nostalgia for Manhattan, with its cold wet jaws of ocean running waters. Even then as now, as always and forever, a fabulous light of time fell over it—it was its own legend, a living sorcery, and as she thought of it from the humid flatness of Dutch fields, its myriad sights, its shapes and swarming motions, the harsh din of its million voices, were sunken and seductive as the seanotes of a dream. Fenced with its delicate forest of young masts, it glittered in enchanted light, bent in upon the under cheek of an incredible earth, remote, wistful, savage, young and unspeakably exultant.

It was the fabulous place, the timeless city, and as Bella remembered it from the smooth, suave reality of Holland, from the subtle and secret opulence of Dutch life, which is the most desolate and sophisticated life on earth, she felt a deep and wordless longing to return to it again. Her vision pierced through the soft, grey, humid enervation of the foreign air, a thousand scenes and memories of the city she had left returned to her, she heard again all its familiar sounds, she saw its brawling pageantry of life, and all of it seemed

This book started in Paris June 6, 1930 from notes and fragments which have been collecting for two years. Now I hope, with all my heart for courage and strength enough to see it through to its end, on paper as it is in my spirit, to make it as good as I can, + to do it day by day no matter where I am no matter what despair or loneliness I may feel + at no matter what cost of flesh or blood or spirit.

Wolfe recorded this pledge on the inside front cover of one of the early "October Fair" ledgers. (By permission of the Houghton Library, Harvard University)

With these conversing I forget all time

The Immortal Earth
The Good Child's River
Antaeus
Faust & Helen
The October Fair

The Good Child's River

By
Thomas Wolfe

" By night on my bed I sought him whom my
soul loveth: I sought him, but I found
him not "

The Immortal Earth
One generation passeth away, & another
generation cometh; but the earth abideth forever

Faust & Helen
And I gave my heart to know wisdom, & to
know madness & folly: I perceived that
this also is vexation of spirit

Wolfe inscribed the title and attendant quotation for his projected work early into his writing of "The October Fair" manuscript. (By permission of the Houghton Library, Harvard University)

Handwritten annotations across top: *Part I 1926* · *Book* · *The Good Clocks Have* · *The Time that is lost —* · *Penelope's Web* · *Used cut*

```
                " Long, long into the night I lay-"
                            (One')
                " Long, long into the night I lay awake-"
                            (Two')
                " Long, long into the night I lay awake, thinking how I should
        tell my story'"
                " (One, two, three, four'   One, two, three, four')
                            Time'
                O, there are bells and that is time:
                    What time is that?
                That was the half hour that the bells were striking,
                    A nd that was time, time, time.
                And that was time, dark time.  Yes, that was Time, time, that  dark
        hangs above our heads in lovely bells.
                Time.  You hang time upon great bells in a tower, you keep
        time ticking in a delicate pulse upon your wrist, you imprison time
        within the small coiled wafer of a watch, and each man has his own,
        a separate, time.
                            One'
                Now in the dark I hear the boats there in the river.
                            Two'
                Now I can hear the great horns blowing in the river.  Great
        horns are laughing in the harbor's mouth, great horns are lowing in
        the gulph of night, great ships are putting out to sea.
```

Edward Aswell, Wolfe's editor at Harper's, crossed out Wolfe's original titles, adding "Book" and "Penelope's Web." Throughout this portion of the manuscript, he indicated material that was to be used or cut from the final edition of The Web and the Rock. *(By permission of the Houghton Library, Harvard University)*

An early draft of a portion of "The Time That Is Lovely." The handwritten manuscript captures Wolfe's intentions regarding the dramatic characterization of Joe, Esther's father. (By permission of the Houghton Library, Harvard University)

Daddy began to talk at once
ed God!! I was ~~so embarrassed~~, I just
didn't know what to say, "Major"
pulling at my dress
Daddy said, 'I want you to meet the
Princess Arabella Clementina /
Sapolio von Hoggenheim; the prin —
cess has appeared both in the flesh
ed by proxy here ed abroad d
before all the crowned heads
Drop, Drop, Drop, Drop, d
~~Drop~~ " " O Daddy!" d
said "I have not!" God!
~~was embarrassed~~, I didn't know
what to say, I was afraid the
old man would believe it . "Don't
listen to her, major!" Daddy
said, "She'll deny it if she can,
but you mustn't believe her. The

This page and the three that follow are from Wolfe's final handwritten draft of "The Bridgebuilder," from "The Time That Is Lovely." (By permission of the Houghton Library, Harvard University)

"HOWS THE BRIDGE
GETTING ON TO DAY?"
Daddy Holland
" Very well sir " the fellow out
NELL, TIE UP THEM LOOSE
CABLES, WE DONT WANT

this powerful magnificent voice, and he could do all sorts of things with it; he could throw it like a ventriloquist and make it come from somewhere else, and he could call out in a tone that made the whole room tremble. "HELLO OVER There! IS THAT YOU?", then he would answer in a funny little voice that seemed to come from miles away; "yes, sir"; "WHO GAVE YOU THAT BLACK EYE?" Daddy said, then the little voice said: "a friend of mine"; "CATCHING ANY FISH?" Daddy hollered: "no, sir", the little voice said. "WHAT'S THE MATTER?" Daddy hollered

" they aint bitin' "; the little voice
said

IN THE PARK

(A chapter from The Good Child's River:
The October Fair: Part IV.)

by

Thomas Wolfe

Title page from the typescript of "In the Park." (By permission of the Houghton Library, Harvard University)

us: ~~you know nearly all the guns are Catholics;~~ and Mr.
Gates talked to him and gave him some money, and Daddy joked
with him and made him laugh, and then Daddy showed him his
police badge and asked him if he knew Big Jake Dietz, and
told him he was ~~Uncle Jake's secretary~~ one of Joke's best friends at police headquarters, and then I was so proud to see the way the cop came
round. Copied off here

   And the cop said for us all to go into Central Park
and we could ride all we damned pleased for all he cared,
but you wouldn't catch him in one of ~~them,~~ those things) they'd blow up
on you at any moment and then where'd you all be? And Dad-
dy said he hoped we'd all be in Heaven, and what's more
we'd take our own priest with us, so there'd be no hitch in
any of the formalities, and we all got so tickled and began
to laugh and the cop did too, and then he began to brag about
his horse and God.' it _was_ a beautiful horse and he said give
him a horse always, that they'd never make one of those things
that could go faster than a horse. The poor fellow.' I wonder what he'd say now.'

   And Daddy teased him and said the time would come when
you'd have to go to the zoo to see a horse and the policeman
said by that time you'd have to go to a junkshop to see a
motor car, and Daddy said, "The trouble with us is that we're
anachronisms." and the policeman said well, he didn't know
about that, but he wished us luck, and hoped we all got out of
it alive.

   So he rode off and we drove into Central Park and God.'
but it was beautiful, it was just the beginning of May and
all the leaves and buds were coming out, they had that tender

familiar things begin to live with
a fresh and living glory. Almost
my first memory of Bella was
of her smoking a cigarette; I was
sitting on the floor of our back
parlour, and it was Spring,
and suddenly I looked up and
I saw Bella looking at me as
she lit a cigarette, I can
see her slow rich smile
with the faint shadow of her
dimple appearing as she looked
at me with the deep and living
sparkle of her eyes that was
so mocking and so tender, I
saw her face dip toward
the lighted match, and her
mouth pucker, I saw her

A passage from ledger one of "The Good Child's River," which depicts Esther's first awareness of Bella's magical personality. (By permission of the Houghton Library, Harvard University)

his lonely and secret spirit.
Yet, there was no one who
loved the companionship of people
more, and people always wanted
to be near him. They wanted to
be near him because it is
the lonely secret people who attract us
most; we feel in them an
integrity and power which
other people do not have, we
are drawn by some luminous
mystery in them. Perhaps we feel that if we
can pluck out the heart of this
mystery we will find the wisdom
and power we need in our own
lives. It seems now that my
father was always alone; even in
a crowd he was ~~but an island~~ isolated,

This page and the three that follow are from ledger one of "The Good Child's River" and help to illustrate how Wolfe "reinvented" his material into new forms. He changed the beginning and the ending and edited the text, thus creating the short story "His Father's Earth." Note Bernstein's initials, in her own hand, on the page stamped "404." (By permission of the Houghton Library, Harvard University)

the other people made a continent
of life, they were bound together
by great tides and rivers, but he
dwelt among them like an island.

The remainder of my father's
youth, after he left his mother's
house, were years of exile and
wandering. There was no poverty
that he did not endure, no
hardship that he did not suffer,
no human crime or misery that
he did not see. He knew the
raw savagery, the brutal violence,
the idiot cruelty of living as few
people ever know it, and his
spirit remained fearless, incorruptible,
gentle, and innocent to the
last, because such innocence

104

(The image of the circus at his
Father's Earth) caps

⊂ℬ

there will his

And as the boy stood looking
at the arms with his brother
there came to him ~~in~~, ~~two~~
~~with a magic at~~ an instant
~~congruence~~, two images, which
had haunted his childhood
at the life of every boy that
ever lived that were now for the first
time seen together with an
instant and a magic congruence, And
these two images were the images
of the circus at his father's
~~thought~~ earth,

as his belonged to the innate
wisdom of the spirit, it could
never be lost, no matter
what he saw or did.

The night he left ~~his~~ mother
he went away with Mr Clark, the
actor. My father had no money &
no place to go; Mr Clark took him
home with him, & kept him there
until he found employment. At
first Mr Clark tried to help him
find employment at some theatre, or
in some show that was going on
the road, but they could not find
it. In a few days Mr Clark came
to him & told him he had a
friend who was the manager of a
small circus which was about

484

Joe thought of them, he knew they flashed the curves, the depths, the deep throat-tone and warmth, feel and smell of dark, potent, living Jewesses — they were incomplete, infertile, lovely and in their pestures, but the old fantasy returned that he would one day enrich and complete them, make them what they might become, "put," ~~as he felt~~, "the curves in them",

Suddenly the deep toned clocks were striking out above the city the metes and measures of our mortal time, and when they thought to seven, and then but surge trembled out upon the air

A page from the chapter "The Theatre," from ledger two. Wolfe wrote extensive running commentary across the sides of several pages during this period. (By permission of the Houghton Library, Harvard University)

On the inside cover of ledger three, Wolfe made a detailed outline for his projected novel, "The Good Child's River." His references to Monkey Hawke reflect his increasing distraction with other projects and characters. (By permission of the Houghton Library, Harvard University)

(For Chapter I(C) (Begining)
My cousin Robert Sat — etc)

Chapter —
Even Such Is Time

As the curtain fell — a mar-
vellously woven curtain which
was said to have cost five
thousand dollars, which really did
cost two, & which, among
other sensational novelties in
this new theatre, had been a
subject for the public
gape & stare for at
least a week — Joe hurried
to his dressing room, tore off
the costume that clothed
the movements of Atticus
Apple, & got ready for the
street as quickly as he

Title page for the chapter "Even Such Is Time." (By permission of the Houghton Library, Harvard University)

A page from ledger three of "The Good Child's River," from the chapter "White Fokes." (By permission of the Houghton Library, Harvard University) you describe her?"

"The sensual woman is the woman who never changes," Harriet said. "She is the woman who is always the same"

"Is there such a woman?" said Joe "I thought the accepted notion was that she is never the same"

"Yes, I know," said Harriet, "But haven't you found, Joe, that the accepted notions and the true fact hardly ever agree? One thing we learn as we grow older is that almost all the maxims that are given us as gospel truths, when we are children, are false in the light of experience. For example, the French are not romantic, the English are

A page from Wolfe's lengthy fragment "Aunt Hugh," from ledger three of "The Good Child's River." (By permission of the Houghton Library, Harvard University)

got the loveliest clothes for me, we went around for weeks looking at materials & then we made them ourselves. God! I was excited, I'd never had so many things to wear before, it was the first time I'd ever been away like that & when we got there it was so lovely; it was along in June sometime & everything was still green & beautiful, & as we walked across the Yard they were hanging out the Japanese lanterns & there were all the young fellows & their girls, & he ~~said~~ was walking along with me, & we passed some of them & he whispered in my ear "You make them all look like a crowd of washerwomen, Esther."

500

On the final pages of ledger three, Wolfe recorded a poem, Joe's letter to his daughter Edith, and an outline for a projected series of chapters from Joe's point of view. (By permission of the Houghton Library, Harvard University)

" A little farther, get a little
farther, ~~follow~~ O my child! follow
along the footpath that my steps have
made ; ~~for~~ so shall come at to the level
Safety of the beach

The way was long, it was no perilous
among the rocks, my ~~throttle~~ throttle sobbed out
with all my fear and labor there among the
rocks, I heard the howling of demented winds,
and far below the cruel moving of the sea
~~about the b—~~ among the rocks

at yet my feet had taken me where
no other feet but his had ever gone, I was
the last ~~that~~ that lived along that broken road
I ship ; had not my toes bent in to
grip the fueless stone had not my
fingers clung to places ~~where~~ no other had
lived grip of seacaves old

" To the pleasure of the toy at level beaches,
the mule sting at undutiful sea
" To the plsrs of the ruled smile, the
good home smell of smile, the sea bone
robust smell
It ~~to the~~ apple tree the very at the gold

One of Joe's Letters to Edith

" — My dear child, enjoy yourself,
tell us what you want, if we can get
it, you shall have it. Please study hard, too,
get all you can out of your work: we are
proud of you, my darling, we ~~love~~ all love
you so much."

— these words, which may seem to the reader
to be the familiar and sentimental clichéd phrases of most
parents, ~~although perhaps~~ ~~sure to be the~~
most ~~foolish letters as~~ in no way
~~schooling~~ or to be distinguished from thousands
of similar letters — unless, perhaps, they are sincerer
and more tender than ~~pitiful letters~~ usually are —
were nevertheless the simpler indications of the
whole depth and meaning in Joe's spirit now, of
a vision of life which seemed at length to have
emerged clear and wholly, and ~~to~~ which his own
life was now devoted.

Joe   Chapter I   — Doctor — Nest — Childhood — Youth Etc
           Chapter II — Bella at Birth
           Chapter III — Paris note
Frat ~~half?~~ Chapter IV — The Doctor — Esther's death
    Mode   Chapter V   — The Bar — The Cutters
           Chapter VI — on the Road
           Chapter VII — The Doctor — The Ocean Freight Grandfather
           Chapter VIII— the Beverly House   etc
           Chapter IX — The Voyage to East
           Chapter X   — East — East 16yh — etc
           Chapter XI — Return — Paint House — 8th St.
           Chapter XII — Rebecca's Death — the Cutters — Etc

lost and sunken in a dream. She saw the island with its forest forge of masts, and its nose thrust out into sea-running tides, she saw its vast sliding traffic of boats and lighters, its immense and joyful ugliness. She saw its solid decent blocks of coffee-colored brown and its streets of young thin buildings, packed, ragged, grimed with work. She saw the jaunty lines of horse cars along Broadway, the jammed confusions of wheel and hoof, the curses and threats of drivers, the shrill harsh cries of the dirty newsboys as they charged in among the crowds flaunting the latest rag of thrill and scandal, and she saw its crowds again, rude, hoarse, thrusting, pushing, swarming—visibly thickened year by year by new tides and dumpings from abroad, with its brawling arrogance of Irish, its proud dark potency of Jews. Here it was, again, the fabulous city, the great encampment, rootless, save for the rock it rested on, unbounded, save by the gleaming bracelet of bright sea-running waters that girdled it forever—a threat, an insolence flung like a cry into the maw of the all-taking ocean. The blare and glitter of loud hot brass, the full loud coming-on of drums, the hard grain of marching music in the bright air, the tramp of marching men, the roar of the crowd, the love of parades and pageantry, the crude, gilt splendor of the millionaires, the teetering of proud, groomed horses in the park, the rubber flash and rumble of rich carriages, the rich men's wives and daughters in the park, the coaching hacks with their style of whips and reins, the prim, the smug, the murderous, the threat and swagger of the rough; and all over, life, cursing and shouting out of doors, foaming across forbidden places, bursting out of bounds, swarming, thronging, pulsing, spreading by moments of perceptible growth—over all the litter, refuse, rickets, shambles, dives and diggings, over all the immense indifference and carelessness of this shifting encampment of a city, which was the stupefaction of ugliness, and yet the most exultant and beautiful place she had ever known.

VII

Esther

She hated school with a deep-rooted and constantly growing hatred which she dared confess to no one, and which she was unable to articulate even for herself. Curiously, this hatred of school went hand in hand with a perfect diligence and punctilious service to the thing she hated: she was never tardy, never absent, never late or unprepared with work which had been assigned. Her loathing of the whole school ritual, in fact, manifested itself in a feeling of sickening terror lest she be remiss in some detail of her duty. For several years during her childhood this terror had grown to such proportions that Bella had at length become alarmed and called in a physician. In some way it seemed to be related to that nameless, dreamless, unpalpable horror which woke her out of sleep screaming with terror, unable to speak, unable to know or tell its cause. Her greatest fear was that she would be late for school in the morning: she was never late, had never been late, yet the fear grew until she was obsessed by it.

When she went to bed at night, her heart would pound with dread as she thought of the possibility of being late the next morning; she would go off to sleep at last with this uneasy fear grown dull but not quiescent, coiled like a snake at the edge of her brain. At length she began to awake suddenly in the morning fully clothed. One morning Bella, who had been troubled by her increasing nervousness and unrest, and by something nameless and terrifying of which she would not speak, awoke to hear her stirring in her room! It was not yet six o'clock. Bella got up quickly, flung a wrapper over her shoulders, and went softly down the hall to Esther's room. When she entered, the girl was sitting on the edge of her bed, completely dressed for school, save for her shoes, which she was putting on and now began to lace rapidly with impatient trembling fingers. By the dim light Bella could not see her plainly, but, surprised and shocked, she called out sharply to her.

"Esther, what on earth are you doing out of bed at this hour?"

Instantly, as soon as she had spoken, she saw that Esther was asleep. As she spoke, the girl's hands faltered at their work, a strong sigh of weariness and slumber stirred her, her eyes opened and for a moment rested on Bella with a blank stricken stare. Then with a tone and movement of deep agitation she cried:

"Is it time? Did I sleep? Am I going to be late?"

"Why child!" said Bella, going toward her. "In heaven's name! It's not six o'clock yet. Esther!" she exclaimed, noting at once the girl's distress, her delicate trembling hands, and the breath that panted in her like a bird's, and feeling as she sat down beside her a great warmth of love and tenderness for her youth and misery.

"What is it? What is wrong with you?"

Esther flung her arms about the other woman and suddenly began to sob convulsively.

"I hate it! I can't stand it any more! If I have to go to school another day I'm going crazy!"

"Well, you don't have to go to school," said Bella quietly. "You never have to go another day if you don't want to. You mustn't worry about it. You shall do as you please. I want you to take off your clothes and go on back to bed! You must get some sleep."

"Oh no!" Esther cried in an alarmed tone. "I couldn't do that!"

"Why not?" asked Bella.

"Oh, I'd be late!"

Thus, in spite of all of Bella's efforts to dissuade her, she insisted on going.

It was after this discovery that Bella had called a doctor in to determine the cause of the girl's nervousness, and the fear which made her dress herself in her sleep. After many questions and much examination, the learned physician concluded that the cause of this deep trouble of the spirit was "cold lunches." Accordingly, Bella made arrangements to provide Esther each day with hot food during the midday recess. Near the school on the corner she found a German couple who owned an ice cream "parlor" and candy shop, and whose only daughter went to school with Esther: these people agreed to provide the girl with hot food every day, and for the remainder of the year Esther went here for her lunch. Although she disliked the place, the heavy cooking, the general untidiness, she concealed her strong distaste from Bella and told her the change had helped her, and that she no longer felt the old nervousness and fear of being late. As a matter of fact, she was really better after this, because as a result of her aunt's concern, and the conversations she had for the first time had with her about this trouble, her reason and sense of judgment had asserted itself and she saw her fear was an unreal phantom, that, even if she were "late," neither she nor the school would perish, that "lateness" was not a very heinous crime. Nevertheless, as long as her schooldays lasted, she never recovered completely from this fear of lateness: she always awoke early in the morning with jumpy nerves, the old constricted paleness of the heart, the queasy stomach and the lack of appetite.

She had usually finished all the breakfast she could eat—the half of a buttered roll and a cup of scalding milk meagerly thickened with a dash of coffee—a good hour before school-time, and from that time on she was in a state of increasingly prancing nervousness as she tried to hurry Georgia Barnhill from her placid table, her leisurely consumption of fat greasy bacon. As the girls started for school Esther worried about her larger, calmer companion like a terrier, trotting ahead in her excitement, coming back to pluck the other girl by the sleeve, saying,

"Come on, Georgia! Come on! I *know* we're going to be late!"

The only result of all this nagging was finally to draw from Georgia this drawling, but somewhat nettled answer:

"All right, then. We'll be *late!* That's all there is to that."

The calm decisiveness of this usually served to quiet Esther for a few seconds. Then, her nervousness increasing, she would say:

"But Georgia, you don't *want* to be late, do you?"

"No," drawled Georgia, "I don't *want* to be, but if I'm goin' to be, I'm goin' to be, so what's the use of gettin' yo'self all worked up about it?"

Then for a moment she would survey Esther's smaller, more alert and active figure, her flushed excited face, with a look of good humored sarcasm and contempt:

"My land!" she said. "The way you go *prancin'* around beats all I ever saw. Anyone would think you belong to the fiah department to look at you. They ain't no fiah, Esthah. We ain't goin' to no fiah, y'know. I ain't seen no fiah wagons about."

"Oh, but I'd hate it so if I was ever late to school."

"Why, it'll keep, honey," Georgia drawled. "The school will be right there in the same old place where we left it in when we get there. They ain't nothin' goin' to happen to it; if I thought somethin' *would*, then I might hurry. But they ain't nothin' goin' to happen to it. I wish it would."

"So do I!" said Esther suddenly and emphatically. "I'd like it better than anything in the world." It was, in fact, because of these conversations that Georgia was finally aroused from her lethargy: each morning as they approached Fifty-fourth Street, the two girls would pause, glance nervously and eagerly at each other, and, at the call of "Now," race at top speed the remainder of the way to school, simply to see "if anything had happened to it."

"What do you suppose *could* happen?" Esther asked, as their speculations took the form of delightful concrete possibility. "What do you suppose would have to happen to make them close?"

"Well," said Georgia reflectively, her thought run easily to arson, "they might have a fiah. . . . One of those stables across the street might ketch on fiah: they're full of straw and hay, they'd burn like tinder."

"Oh, no, that wouldn't be any good," said Esther. "Everything's made of brick. You can't burn brick. If there was a fire it'd have to come from the inside."

"And then it wouldn't do any good," said Georgia. "That's the trouble of bein' in a great big place like New Yawk. If one school *did* burn down, they'd only send you on to one of the othahs. I reckon they must have about a thousand. In the town where I come from down South we only had *one* school, an' that was a little ole thing made out of clapboa'd wood. Law! if we'd evah a-had a fiah there, I don't reckon we'd evah have gone back to school." She said this as if stating another of the fundamental advantages and superiorities of Southern life, and for a moment after was lost in a delirious fantasy of this glorious but unrealized possibility.

"Well, fire wouldn't do *us* any good," said Esther. "It'd have to be something else. It'd have to be somebody getting sick or dying."

"Well, they wouldn't shut down just because somebody got

sick," Georgia said. "Not unless it was somethin *ketchin'*, like one of these epidemics, an' then we *all* might get sick. Pshaw! I'd just as soon be in school as in bed all the time."

"Well, then," said Esther, "it'd have to be somebody dying. That's the only thing I can think of."

"That's what I think, too," said Georgia. She meditated the idea for a moment. "But it'd *sho* have to be somebody mighty big," she said. "These fokes up heah wouldn't shut down fo' just *anyone*."

Then, with hunger, with strong eagerness, they fell to considering appropriate deaths.

"There's Miss Brill," Esther said. "Do you think we'd get a holiday if she died?"

"Why, *Esthah*!" Georgia said with a scornful rising intonation. "Miss Brill ain't nothin' but a little ole common school principal. Why, honey, they grow on bushes: you kin find plenty of them. You're not simple enough to think they'd shut down school if *she* died, are you?"

She laughed slowly, richly, with derision.

"No, *suh*!" she said with positive assurance. "It'd have to be somebody a whole heap biggah than *that*! It'd have to be somebody who was *sho-nuff* big, I tell you! It'd have to be somebody lak Pres'dent Cleveland or the Mayah of New Yawk."

Nevertheless, the wild final breathless dash that brought them panting up before the school had now become part of their morning's habit. But nothing happened. The school stood ready to receive them, harsh, solid, angular, and red: the day's ritual proceeded with punctual monotony.

One morning, however, as the girls dashed round the corner they saw something which brought them to a sudden halt. Before the school a dense crowd of boys and girls had assembled, the number grew greater at every moment as other children dashed up from every direction: even as they looked there was a flurry in the crowd; a wild cheer, fierce, exultant, burst from them, and in a moment the boys were tossing their caps up in the air with a brave free motion, and the girls, less confidently and more subdued, were swinging their books around in circles by their straps. As Esther and Georgia came up they heard repeated again and again everywhere around them, these wonderful magical words which have brought exultant joy to children everywhere, when they have heard them:

"No school today! No school today!"

Already, some of the children, laughing and cavorting, had begun to go away, but another group was gathered before a sheet of white paper which had been tacked to the closed doors of the school. The notice read: "Owing to the death of the Hon. Philip I. Becker, Superintendent of City Schools, school is dismissed for the day."

Esther had never before heard the name of Philip I. Becker, but the news of his death brought her the greatest happiness she had ever known. She turned to Georgia with a look of joy and wonder, and she said:

"Georgia! It *did* come true!"

And Georgia, with her slow ripe negroid humor, said: "Yes, suh! It sho did! It just goes to show there is a Gawd settin' way up theah an' listenin' to ouah prayuhs." Solemnly, drolly, she read again the notice: "The Honnabul Philip I. Becker! Uh-uh! . . . Well, bud," she said, "I don't know who you ah, an' I don't know wheh y'ah, but I sho hope you ah happy!" She looked around for a moment at the crowd of cavorting, shouting children, then laughed shortly and vulgarly:

"Man!" she said. "This is sho a prime crowd of moanahs. They are suttenly all to'n up about it." Slyly, she nudged Esther, and deftly indicated a boy whom they knew named Reuben Feinberg, who lived near them on their block: he had an immense hooked putty-colored nose, and his mouth now curved up under it in a great half moon of grin: "Gawd!" she said. "Now *theah's* a hot Christian if I evah saw one! I reckon they's not much he can't smell with that nose of his: if I had one like it I'd paint it green."

Esther laughed: she had no real feeling of inferiority because of her Jewish blood, in her brief life she had rarely been rebuffed or wounded on this account, and her feeling toward people was very simple, healthy, natural, and eager. Moreover, the world which she had known was a remarkably warm, generous, and intelligent one: she knew, of course, how much more beautiful, joyful, and comfortable the life at Bella's house was than at the houses of most of her companions, but she thought the difference was one of degree, and not of kind. She concluded that the lives of most children were not very different from her own, and that people everywhere were like the people she saw at her aunt's house. And yet, in a single evening at Bella's, after the theatre, there might be present such an assorted company as Richard Mansfield, her uncles John and Fred Barrett, Fay Templeton, the light opera singer; the painter, George Innes; two Catholic priests who were friends of her father's, Henry Dixie and De Wolfe Hopper, a bartender who sang sad songs; Miss Josephine Beaufelt, an actress who dressed like a man; her fat cousin, Fred Goldsmith; a Dutch sea captain; her aunt Mary; old lady Witzenstein and Mr. Hodges, two of her oldest boarders; as well as a circus trouper, a baseball player, and a Jewish silk merchant. In a gathering of this sort, whatever decisions or arguments might disturb it, differences of race or religion played no great part. Moreover, all of these people had been gathered by Joe and Bella in the most natural and spontaneous way: this great and sometimes comically varied acquaintance had come through their warm hug on life—there were people who had been met and known through a thousand acts of living: the case of Innes, the painter, was typical of this. He had first come to the house when Esther's mother was still alive, and this was the manner of his coming: Rebecca was celebrated among Joe's friends for her cooking, and particularly for the pies she made. The hungry actors would come home late at night with Joe, and Esther, whose room was above the dining room, could hear them plainly as they went in to eat their supper that was always laid out for them. In Esther's room there was an iron furnace grating, and by sitting near this she could hear plainly all that was said among the people in the room below. Night after night, she would sit in the dark listening to their conversations, drinking in eagerly everything they said, rocking with laughter not only because of the things they said, but because coming to her in the dark with vibrant hollowness, they seemed even more funny.

". . . What is this, Beck? Ham? Well, as I live, it's ham. . . ."

"Don't give him any," another voice said. "It's cannibalism. He can't eat his own kind, you know."

"Well," the first voice said. "I'd rather see than be one. . . . Anyway, cut me off a piece of it."

"Becksie, by God!" a voice full, feeling, choked, exclaimed a moment later. "This is the finest pumpkin pie I ever tasted. I never thought I'd live to see a pie like this in New York City. . . . Say, I know a fellow who'd give his shirt for a piece of this. His name's Innes: he's a friend of mine. . . . He's crazy about pumpkin pie, Beck: he told me the other day they didn't know how to make it any more. . . . God, I'll bet the sweat would break out on his forehead if he got a look at this. . . . Say, Beck, do you suppose I could take him a piece of it?"

There were derisive shouts and laughter, and then another voice said: "Don't you believe him, Beck. . . . That fellow's been eating his way across the country with that yarn. . . . Eat! Why, God! Beck. He could eat his way across the Pampas from Rio de Janeiro to Buenos Aires without ever stopping to draw breath. . . . Out in the Hay belt they call him Bottomless Bill, the Crop Destroyer. . . . He's worse than a plague of locusts, Beck. . . . After he's passed through a town they have seven lean years to follow. . . . Innes! Why, Beck, he never heard the name before tonight. . . . The last time I heard the story the name was Sniggins: he worked on the feelings of an old maid out in Keokuk until she cried right out of her glass eye. . . . I saw her give him two hams and a bacon to take to Sniggins. . . . Honest, Beck, that fellow could get a handout from a wooden Indian."

"By heaven, Beck, they lie," the other voice now cried with passion. "As God is my witness I speak truth. . . . I do know a man named Innes, and he likes pumpkin pie."

"Well, Bill," Rebecca said. "You can take a whole piece to him if you promise to bring the plate back." She sent the pie and in a day or two Bill returned with the plate. On it Innes had drawn a wonderful picture of a pumpkin field: among dried shards and on the frosty clotted earth great pumpkins ripened in the foreground.

VIII

White Fokes

The character and temper of the two girls were sharply and deeply contrasted: Esther, small, brisk, vital and dutiful, obsessed by her constant ravening fear of "lateness"—Georgia, large, slow, indolent and indifferent, still definitely "Southern": immensely vain and ignorant, negroid, sensitive and stubborn in resentment, but incapable of deep penetration of the spirit, as ripe and sensual as a peach. It was as if not only her spirit but her flesh was dyed in those deep colors of place and climate, as if her life was soaked in the weather of the South, and as if all its qualities—its near-tropic heat and indolence, the lush fecundity of its thick red clay, its guarded sense of a smouldering and volcanic passion, abrupt and fatal, just below the surface of its life, and its terrible lack of memory—in which it seemed the continuity of life was destroyed moment by moment by the murderous and present instant, even as the swarming life of the tropics eats and is eaten, conquers and dies, perishes, past hope, past honor, past memory, in the idiot prolif-eration of the jungle—had worked their potent insoluble chemis-try on her, soul and body.

For it is this, exactly this chemistry, this weather of the soul and body, and not anything traditional or consciously remembered, that gives to Southern people whatever quality of difference they have: in the slow and impenetrable ways in which their lives have yielded to this infiltration there is something of mystery and deep strangeness—they have yielded to warmth even as New England-ers have yielded to cold—in each there is something secret and remote, unpalpable and strange—but the chemistry of warmth has wrought something which outwardly, at least, is more agreeable: ease, indolence, rich colors, and a powerful humor that is of nature, witless and devastating—a belly laughter that surges from the earth.

In the city and the tropics, alike, memory is destroyed, but from different causes: the city memory is drowned below the rush and glare of the days, the stamp of a billion feet, the dusty violence of ten thousand shocks and changes, but the tropical memory swirls into the level tides, the full blank samelessness of yesterday and forever.

The affection Esther felt for this Southern girl at this time was deep, positive, active: for a time their companionship was warm and constant, although later it was to dwindle out into indifferent apathy, and finally into total separation—with Georgia, because alert purpose and the intelligence of direction were distasteful to the lazy sprawl of her soul, because even now, the absorbing interest of her life was in "the boys," in having "lots of beaus." It was a pattern, a tradition formed years ago out of the structure of the only life she knew, and she had never questioned it, nor dreamed of any better one: there was only one standard of success for women—to "have lots of beaus" and finally to "get a man"—a kind of benevolent scapegoat vaguely described as "a good husband" to whom at length she could turn for sanctuary and support when the last possibilities of flirtation and coquetry had been exhausted. In this picture of a ship-worn and paved-over matrimony she saw nothing distasteful: her vision of the future was fixed, tawdry, banal—but she desired no better one. She saw herself as an accomplished flirt with a dozen unhappy suitors dancing on her string, as having not one, but two, three, a half dozen "dates" in the course of a prize evening, bestowing her time and interest with queenly graciousness upon a host of hot, jealous, amorous, competing slaves, but its consummation, forever balanced dangerously but superbly above seduction, but finally maintaining what she thought of, without humor, as her "virginity."

The final separation between the two girls was therefore inevitable. Esther's nature was profoundly romantic, Georgia's merely erotic. As time went on Esther began to be vaguely distressed and annoyed by Georgia's erotic obsession—the fixed monotony of her desire. For Esther at this time the physical world was expanding before her waking sense with a thousand magnificent designs and colors she had never seen before. Each walk to school or through the streets revealed new intensities, new unsuspected glories, and in her passionate and vital spirit a fierce though obscure hunger was now awake—the hunger of a creative spirit for all the beauty in the universe, ravenous, insatiable and at its beginning, cruel, because it has found no means of articulation. In her excitement, she was constantly speaking of these things to Georgia, but the other girl answered her only with a sleepy and dull attention, slothful, without perception. One day, however, she did say in a tone that was good humored but that had a note of impatience in it:

"Esthah, you can spend *mo'* time lookin' at some dirty ole piece of junk than anyone I evah saw! Who wants to spend their time lookin' at a dirty ole ice-wagon?"—for it was this that Esther had indicated.

"Well, I never said that it was pretty," Esther replied. "I only said it was painted a wonderful color."

"*Colah*!" Georgia shouted derisively. "Why, it was nothin' but a dirty ole yellow!"

"Oh, you don't know what you're talking about," Esther said angrily. "It was a lovely color. You just don't look at things."

"I know I don't!" said Georgia with a note of anger in her voice. "I know I don't look at *things*. I look at *people*! I want to see what's goin' on! Some fokes I know," she added pointedly, "might do bettah if they spent less time on *things* an' *mo'* on *people*."

"Yes, I suppose so!" said Esther ironically. "Especially people in *livery* stables!"

She was sorry the moment she spoke for what she had said; but it was out, and they were as near now to an open quarrel as they had ever come. For some time past Georgia had been carrying on a flirtation with a man who worked in one of the stables on the street. No word had been spoken, but now the man was waiting for them every day as they came from school: he was a young man, well-fleshed and muscular with thick straw colored hair, blue eyes, a thick red neck, and a bold high colored face, sensual, wide-lipped and brutal. He always wore riding-breeches and leggings and he stood in the stable doorway with his legs apart, and his hands thrust into shallow pockets, with a look that was bold, foul and insolent. A strong odor of the stable—animal-hide and hair and horse—hung round him: his glance explored their bodies fully with a quality that was almost as palpable as the touch of a hand. Speech—crude, shameful, and slimy—seemed forever immanent. Esther hurried by with averted eyes and with her heart thudding in her throat. Then she became aware that Georgia did not wish to hurry, suddenly aware that there was something in Georgia's walk and manner that answered with equal eloquence, with the same foul potent silence. It spoke out of her sensual flesh, with a sly and evil tongue, it spoke indefinably yet unmistakably in every gesture, it spoke in something loose, exultant and inviting, like the phantom of obscene laughter in her face—yet apparently, in all this strange sensual eloquence of their flesh, she never glanced at him, never gave him any visible sign. The next day as they came from school Esther said:

"Georgia, let's go down the other side. I don't want to go by there. He'll be waiting for us."

"Who?"

"That livery stable man."

"What you got against that po' man," said Georgia good naturedly. "He ain't done nothin' to you."

"Oh, I don't know," said Esther. "I don't like the way he looks."

"Don't like the way he *looks!*" said Georgia. "Why, child, you don't know a good-lookin' man when you see one."

"You don't mean to say you think *he's* good-looking!" Esther said incredulously.

"Yes, suh! I sho do!" said Georgia emphatically; a flag of color, hard and angry, began to rush in her cheeks. "He's the best-lookin' man I seen aroun' these pahts! A sho-nuff man, I mean!—not one of these little dried up Jew-boys that you see!"

Esther made no answer: in the last words she now recognized an intention that was harsh, wounding, malicious—when they had gone by the man again, and turned the corner, her face was flaming, not with resentment, but with a sense of deep and wordless shame; but whether she felt this for herself or for her friend she could not say. They did not speak to each other on the way home, and when they reached Georgia's house they did not linger but said goodbye abruptly and formally.

A sense of disaster, immanent, foreboding, pressed like a weight upon her heart: she kept thinking,

"What will her people say if they find out? What will they say?"

A memory of grand dignities, of noble families, of high untarnished prides, of fiercely arrogant poverty, of "death but not dishonor," of an ancestral line of gentlefolk, brave, high, and rare, that ran straight back into the past with the gleaming strength of an unrusted and unbroken lance—all this, evoked through Mrs. Barnhill's assertion of a remote, princely, and awful antiquity—swept through her mind now like a curtain of dark and tragic splendor against which Georgia's infamy was made to seem more complete and terrible than if this panoply of past time had not existed.

Although she still called for Georgia on her way to school, the other girl avoided her on their return, and she accepted the evasion willingly: she understood now that her old friend did not want her company on the way home, and for her part, she was glad that she must no longer suffer the lewd loose foulness of the livery man's stare. For she knew he had no interest in her whatever: now that she was alone, she could pass the stable without being noticed.

One day, when she had left school late, she saw, as she approached the stable, the man and Georgia talking to each other. He had one hand stretched forth and leaned against the open door, the other was upon his hip, and the girl was indolently swinging her books by their straps as she talked: her manner was casual, bantering, hesitant—his was insinuating, sly, easily careful—the look of a man who is feeling his way. Before Esther had come near, the other girl glanced up, saw her, bade the man goodbye, and went on down the street alone. The man's grin, reflective, loose, went after her: then he shook his head decisively, laughing, dropped his hand, and turned back into the stable.

As Esther hurried by, she was aware of a circle of grinning faces gathered about him: he stood, with his back turned—a back in whose carriage boastful confidence was legible—and she heard one of the men about him say:

"Y'ought t'be ashamed of yerself! Robbin' the God-damn cradle!"

Esther hurried by.

"Ah! he won't get nowhere!" another said. "I know that kind— a little teaser, she's laughin' up her sleeve at him right now."

"She is, eh?" the hero said: his tone was hard, quiet, confident. "Say: I want to tell *you* something—if I don't have that little son-of-a-bitch up the pole within a month you can kick my God damn a—all over the stable!"

There was a burst of laughter, harsh and derisive, and their speech, a replica of millions of others, pursued unweariedly its twin topics of horses and women.

Yet, if Georgia could have heard them it is not likely she would have been repelled or displeased. Her true desire—a fantasy of what she wanted most—had little that was sentimental in it: she did not even trick it out with the morals and fancy manners of romantic fiction—her lust, her version of "good-lookin' men"—was animal, save for a caste of color, negroid: she wanted the thick red neck, the muscular buttocks, the coarse vacant regularity of the face, the complete full hunger of a brutal energy.

"I wonder what her mother would say if she knew," thought Esther, and suddenly, it seemed at once, the conviction came to her that Mrs. Barnhill would say, would care, nothing. The sum of their actual lives, as she had herself witnessed them, with all that was trivial, disorderly, impure, slothful, of low desire and aspiration, and which formerly had weighed nothing against the sum of their grand assertions, now shattered in an instant that iridescent bubble of romantic and gentle ambiguity in whose reality she had believed. She thought of the kitchen and the slatternly negro girl with her dirty, unheeled white stockings, her run-down shoes and the strong black smell, thick and salty, niggery, which soaked out of her, the litter of unwashed dishes, unscoured pans, the bucket of decaying garbage, the strong blue buzz of flies, the most actual sign of force and purpose in the room; and then the house with its assortment of rickety furniture, its inept souvenirs of the past— its burnt-wood trinkets, with bows of dirty ribbon, its ancient calendars, its dilapidated beds, warped blistered dressers and untidy sewing machines, with their cigar boxes filled with loose unmatched buttons, threads, thimbles, swirls of wool and ribbons, its odd collection of chairs, squeaking rockers, and finally she remembered the day she had for the first time gone into Mrs. Barnhill's own bedroom on an occasion when "company" from the South was calling, and when Mrs. Barnhill did not wish any let or hindrance to impede the full flow of envenomed gossip:

"You children go somewheh's else to tawk."

The old sagging bed had been rudely made: its soiled counterpane was awry and rumpled, its pillows unsmoothed. Upon the dresser there had been a strewn wilderness of hairpins, soiled powder puffs, brushes chocked with hair, and thickly gummed combs; and under the bed, both visible and odorous, a full chamberpot, swimming, rancid. And from below the woman's insistent, incessant monologue:

"They don't know white fokes when they see 'em up heah! . . . These fokes don't cayah who you ah. . . . No, suh! . . . All they think about is makin' money. . . . An ig'rant! My lan'! . . . These ole fawr'ners that you see! . . . Why, it's awful! Ha'f of them c'aint read ner write. . . ."

Now, suddenly, as Esther remembered all these scenes and moments, a laugh, short, explosive, angry, burst from her: she felt tricked and cheated, resentful, and when she got home, she flung her books down angrily, and began to wander sullenly and indecisively about the room.

"What's wrong with you?" said Bella.

"Nothing," she said morosely.

"Is everything all right at school?"

"Yes. Look here," she burst out suddenly, in an exasperated tone. "If the Barnhills are such a wonderful old family as they say they are, it looks like they might try to keep that house better. Why it's *filthy*!"

Bella laughed. "Oh *it's* the *white fokes*!"—this was the name, the inevitable name she always called them by. "White fokes don't have to wash. Don't you know that yet? It's only Jews and niggers who get dirty."

"Oh, white fokes!" Esther muttered. "They make me sick!"

"What's the matter with you? Have you and white fokes had a falling out?"

Esther made no answer: she went over to a chair and sat down wearily and dejectedly. At length she said in the same sullen and dejected tone:

"I don't care."

Bella looked intently at her for a moment:

"I knew this would happen," she said at length, slowly, and with a kind of triumphant, although not malicious, emphasis. "I knew it!" She paused for a moment. "Well, let me tell you something," she continued. "You haven't lost anything. . . . You may think you have, but you haven't. . . . You're better off without these people."

Later on the same day she told Joe about it:

"She's had some sort of trouble with the white fokes. I think it's all over between them."

"I wondered how much longer it was going to last," he said.

The sense of freedom that Esther now felt, however, also carried with it the sense of loss. She felt, even more than the feeling of repulsion and disgust that Georgia's conduct with the livery man had caused her, a feeling of bitter resentment, a feeling that was touched with jealousy. She thought of Georgia's slow maturing charm—her peachy perfection of skin, her languid ripeness, her warm calm eye, the unutterable ease of the careless and slothful spirit that dwelt in her—and she felt frightened, stripped by her loss of some essential, some inestimable support. There was no doubt that the feeling was strongly physical: among women, when their feeling for each other has not been envenomed with a sense of rivalry or jealousy, there is a quality of affection which is unlike the affection men have for each other—it is intimately physical, caressing, and somewhat lesbic. Esther had almost a lover's tenderness for Georgia's physical beauty: she liked to put her arm around the other girl, to embrace her, to nestle in to her, to stroke with a sense of affection and wonderment, the velvet and perfect texture of Georgia's skin.

This was the only time she played a lover-like and suitor's role with another woman. Curiously, as she grew older, and as her own beauty, which was delicate and ripe, matured, she inspired in other women the same feeling that she now felt for Georgia. These other women were always much larger physically than Esther: one was a nurse, a big, gaunt, raw-boned woman, with hands as large and strong as a man's; another was a powerfully built Russian woman—a masseuse; and another was a tall, handsome, and passionate Jewess—a rich young woman devoured by a stupid fury and pride of possession: for her it was not enough to share with others a friend's love—she had always to be a dominant and over-shadowing first, to hold off rivals at an outer wall. For her, possession died by what it feeds upon—glutton and niggard in one breath, crafty, insinuating, trivial, and meanly contriving, and beaten at length by its base stupidity.

All these women later lived to put their hands on Esther: the strong gaunt woman stroked her face and forehead, and the rich woman held her in her arms and kissed her. She loved affection: as one saw her rich and delicate figure clothed in splendid robes upon a couch, her rosy and beautiful face bloomed like a pansy, and her whole body seemed to yield itself up gratefully to the tender stroking of the strong gaunt hands like some rare and splendid flower expanding toward rich warmth and light.

As one saw Esther thus in later years, one's feeling toward her would not have been tinged with any repulsion: one would have had, on the contrary, a good and tender feeling for her because her attitude as she responded to the caresses of these women was plainly innocent, sensual, and hungry as a child for affection. As for the women, the strokers and caressers themselves, one's feeling might have been tinged by repulsion, anger, and disgust: as old Rapp, her great frame dried and withered now by loveless and sterile years, a web of insane and degrading illusions (such as: that lustful men were pursuing her constantly, with intentions of rape and defilement, so that now, past sixty, with her rusty hank of hair all dyed a dry harsh red, she nevertheless wore three pairs of drawers to protect more securely what she was pleased to think of as her "honor")—on whose lank scorned visage as her great-knuckled fingers gently stroked the flowering pansy of the face below her, was legible a look of hypnotic contemplation in which an expression of tender love was mixed with a quality as repellent as a senile male lechery. And yet this quality itself was at once denied and complicated by a dozen other elements: a sense of noble tenderness, devotion, and changeless love as she spoke of Esther, of her childhood, and of her beauty as a young woman— a quality of love and profound understanding which played marvelously upon the lank leathery yellow of her features a luminous radiance. Thus, her mind, old, broken, and diffuse, caught hopelessly in a web of manias and impossible persecutions, would be focused suddenly upon some memory of Esther's youth, and for a few moments, with a convulsive and splintered coherence, she would speak of her:

"That time!—O! . . . I shall never forget it. . . . I want to tell you . . . I was thinking about it the other day. . . . In all your life you never. . . . If you could have seen her! (Here she drew her breath in with a rusty intake.) O! Her *little* feet. . . . I lifted her like a child. . . .

'Why' (I cried!) Her *little* toes so straight. . . . And O! That great hunk of a thing inside her tearing her to pieces! . . . Why! Enough to make you hate the sight of men! Yes, and *him*!" she said scornfully. "Playing cards! When she asked him for a drink of water . . . one time we were all sitting on the stoop. I've never had any use for him since. Do *you think* he would! I could have told her then." (This in a mincing tone of envenomed bitterness.)

"Rapp, Rapp," said Esther gently. "That was before."

"But O! the birds . . . outside. . . . O *my* no! . . . He was too fine a gentleman. He said, 'Get it yourself!' " This in a curt blunt tone. "But it was the longest night I ever. . . . For fourteen hours she was. . . . I'll never forget . . . a lovely young . . . these Germans. . . . Always despised them. . . . Things they did in the war. . . . *Think of that*. O! do you remember what you kept saying all the time? . . ." She began to laugh in a rusty and clumsy manner, holding a few large gnarled fingers loosely over her mouth.

"Yes," said Esther. "I remember your face as you bent over me: it kept going in and out like a concertina. . . . I kept saying 'Rapp, you mustn't do your face so funny! I don't like it!' "

"O yes! I remember!" Rapp screamed rustily, rocking slowly back and forth. "But you kept saying 'For *who* would fardels bear! For *who* would fardels bear!' "

"That's what I said!" said Esther. "God, it was hot! And just at day all of the birds began to sing! Don't you remember!"

"O! if you could have seen her *then*!" cried Rapp. She drew in her breath with a sort of rusty ecstasy. "Her little hands and feet! . . . Her slender little body. . . . In all your life you never. . . . O! I thought! . . . She was the loveliest little. . . ."

"Rapp! Rapp!" said Esther gently, lightly stroking the great hand upon her forehead. "You must stop it now. You are going to make me cry in a moment."

For a moment, in fact, Esther's eyes were full of tears, and her delicate rosy face seemed steeped in a memory of lost and irrevocable years, of the terrible mortality of flesh and beauty, of the vast and poignant sum of moments that could not be recalled, and of the merciless stroke of time which could not be stayed. And as she placed her strong delicate hand upon the old woman's big gnarled fingers, one was conscious at this moment of a unity of love and loyalty which led them back among the scenes and persons of a buried life and a lost world, a unity that was like a living crimson thread and that was beyond life and death and beyond the terrible rush and glare of ten thousand city days, the hot blind insanity of change and movement. And instantly, one felt the same sense of bitter regret and pain that these two women felt over the loss of Esther's youth and the passing of her beauty: under her crown of greying hair, and the webbing of her eyes—now tired and venous—one saw at once that her face had not changed at all since her childhood: the child's face was indestructibly legible in the woman's face, and the pain, the regret, the resentment was a child's feeling over a loss it could not accept, a defeat it could not condone.

And suddenly, it was as if through the rich and living unity of her marvelous life she had bridged all the depth of sunken years, and through the warmth and actuality of her living touch had led one (me) back into the midst of unrecoverable moments, had made one so certainly a part of a buried and unvisited life that it lived again with every color, every tone and shading, every casual atom of the scenes which the mind forgets, so that the substance of a million buried moments are ours again, with all their freight of sound and movement, as actually as the scene before us. It was as if, through the union of her flesh with buried time, she took one back until he was able to recover the buried life as men in India through an intensity of contemplation are said to unravel their lives day by day back to the moment of birth, and then to merge their memory and their identity with the unlived past.

For, had not this same familiar voice uttered familiar words so long ago? Was not the seed of all this vanished time mingled and diffused within this living flesh? Had these eyes not looked on ten million moments of the buried life, and could one not, through the unity of this flesh, this life, this love, have inured oneself into the lost days, the buried years, until the sound of their voices, each moment's flow and shift of movement, passed before him like this moment's presence, like all the dusty tumult of this morning's pavement.

Yes. The magic of time and memory was true: suddenly a vast nimbus of dead faces was blooming around Esther—the faces of people dead and gone as they swarmed along the pavements, as they thrust and jostled in great crowds, as they walked toward us through the delicate webbing of the Bridge, or as, with painter's nostrils, they rushed through heat to the place of the murdered man, to the salty smell of hot spilt blood, here they were in all their heavy dignities of dress, the derbied mustached men, the women with their dusty length of skirts, their clumsily muttoned sleeves, their stiff precarious hats, their hard sensual corsettings, and yet beneath the ornate and sculptured conventions of these fashions, with something sly, potent, and female, like ornate and decorous concubines in temple dances. Around Esther was the smell of proud dark woods, of bitters and of orange peel, the fast and easy slatting of the wicker doors, and a style of easeful feet upon a polished rail, piled iridescences of gleaming thin-shelled glass behind the proud dark woods of bars, and the foaming and hoppy fragrance of pungent beer, wet, tidal, rolling. The shout of the children playing in the street, the cold and frozen rasp of sawn ice, and a sound of quiet voices, of the near and the far of laughter, on summer nights; the rustle of the leaves was there. The small jeweled flicker of bicycle lamps, the great vital thrum of a thousand wheels, the stamp of the hoof at night on mellow board, and the odors of hoof, of gleaming hide, of proud and costly leathers, the odors of horse and bit and rein, and of all the sweet rich sultriness of sweat-cured harness, and the fabulous and fragrant woods superbly turned and shaped: the craft and cunning of fine hands in hub, spring, axle, brace, shaft, and crossbar, in sills, panels, felloes, spokes, in woods as hard as lignum vitae, and in delicate tender woods as soft and spicy as pared cheese. The imperial princely union of fine horses and fine women: behind the trotting velvet rumps the women leaned and nodded in luxurious leathers—love mixed slowly with a tinge of ice around the heart, a spell of desire, exultant, trembling, stirred across the loins, and the smells of the trotting rumps, the leathers, and the ripe slow-smiling women were all good: in the freckled light of the leaves, the lovers bolted, they went across the daisied warmth of fields into the woods, they came out slowly as a waning sun, with smiles luxurious and tender, with heads uplifted to their crown of hair, pulling a burr from the hem of their long full-figured dress; and their laughter welled in darkness soft and deep. Always there was the smell and stump of the horses, in the streets ammoniac, in ten thousand stables thick and warm, and the hoof and the wheel struck forth its lean and lively music in the night. Always there were the horses, sweet-breathed, smoke-throated in the wintry air, huddled below their blankets, stooped dejectedly below all the savage and persistent cruelty of heat and cold—and Esther remembered them, as if they had been people, in a thousand scenes and attitudes.

She saw the lank and weary steeds that trotted along between loose climbing traces on the horse-car tracks: their lean heads tossed and nodded to the jaunting of their bells as if the laborious rhythm of their lives had warn itself into the structure of their flesh, and their heads turned toward each other constantly in a gesture that was mournful and resigned, steeped in all the infinite grief that finds acceptance in those who labor on the earth.

And there were the droppings of great beasts upon the cobbles, the ponderous truck teams, slow footed and sway-backed, mottled with solid greys, the drivers standing in their wagonbeds, cursing, the heavy sweating police cursing, the hot air sown with thick cursings, the vein swelling, the neck swelling, the thick snarl of the simian upper lip, the thick sweated brutishness of the corrupt and unspeakable Irish, the foul brown sensuality of the unwashed Italians, the stale rancid smell of pallid sweaty Jews, oozing with a desperate and deathless tenacity, the weary load of centuries beneath their bales of cloth, and these the faces of the lost Americans, the thousand styles of faces each with a quality of baffling similarity, a quality that was recognizable and lost. —What was it, token of all our wordless and incongruent hunger that one saw here, that has never been expressed, that was so imminent, so exasperating, so impalpably near, as if the opiate of finality we had sought for our exacerbated nerves, the complete nurture we needed to stop the jaws of Cerebus was here almost within our grasp, an inch away from hope, a hand's breadth off from certainty.

Here were the faces of the lost, the dead, the buried men as they came toward us on the Bridge, as they streamed past us on the pavements, as they shifted, glanced, and passed in a thousand streets as dead, as lost, as buried as themselves: here was the lost world, the starved world, the world with all its blooms of time and magic as it grew outward now in all its myriad and magic evolutions from the rich annotation of Esther's small, opulent and triumphant flesh. And suddenly, in this vanished world, we saw all that had not changed in us: we saw upon the faces of dead men what we could hardly see upon our own, we saw, through this permanent dimension of time done and cold, of moments finished and secure, the whole dark legend of our destiny, the vision of our hunger—as actual then as now: the vast loneliness of our inarticulation, the vast incongruence of our desire, the stupendous weight of our godless, wingless, formless, and undiscovered fears that press upon us from immense and lonely skies, from the piled masses of inhuman architecture, that comes to us like an invisible effluvia from all the tiny atoms of the man-swarm, lost, like ourselves, in the weariness of heat and distance, in a broad unsufferable light that beats and glares upon us till our earth is enclosed in that thick pocket of our impurity through which we struggle toward one another as through a marine consistency of foul depthless waters—drowned, our hope, our belief, all of our inner dignities—drowned deep in the thick stifling depths of weariness, horror, and stupendous triviality. Thus, these incongruent monsters of our fear, impalpable and immense, that hover over all our innocence and nakedness and that are mingled with all our wild exultancy and joy, had left their shadow as legibly on the faces of these dead men as on us: they, too, were guarded by this obscure and savage hunger, and they, too, must have felt that wordless but powerful desire to articulate some image to which these wild and restless longings of the spirit might be emitted and by which they could be assuaged, to articulate mighty and recognizable forms out of that unmistakable material which, we know, is everywhere around us, as certain as the joy, the exultancy, and the fear that springs from it.

This picture that she had of Georgia that day before the stable returned in later years, long after it had lost its power to awaken resentment or revulsion, to haunt her with a memory of pity and piercing wordless regret. For it is so with time and memory: the seed of our deepest feeling is buried under the rush of a momentary and violent one, there is in all feeling a quality of deception and evasion, and the meanings of the spirit become evident only in the light of a dispassionate distance. Thus, in later years her memory of Georgia was always attended somehow by one of the most evocative and moving memories of her life: this was the memory of men coming across the Bridge—she could not say what it meant, but she remembered their faces with a sense of loss and finality, as, poised high above the gleaming tide of water, they passed between two points in space two moments in lost time, and were gone forever; and yet she felt she had met them and knew in an instant all that could ever be known about them: the total legend of their destiny. So, later, when she remembered Georgia, that memory was mixed and shadowed by the Bridge: she remembered her as she stood talking to the man before the stable, and her clumsy indecision, and half-shy gesture as she swung her books by their strap, a gesture that was bewitching, awkwardly bold, and pitifully knowing—evoked in Esther later a vision of all that is wistful, stumbling, and moved by a shy and clumsy eagerness in youth. As the years passed, Esther's sharper and more personal memories of Georgia, and of the relation of their ages, faded, until, mothered by memory, a woman looked with pity and compassion at the clumsy figure of a child, and before the child was the old red brick of stable, the stamp of vanished hooves, the odor of dark worn leathers, the fading light of a morning sun graining with golden dust before the stable door, with all that was sad and exultant in its wordless connotation, and all the forgotten words, the lost faces, the remembered footfalls of a buried life—a child who, now that all bitter memory of an evil moment was forgotten, had become the type of youth everywhere, its destiny caught in a flitting moment as permanently and completely as that of men who cross a bridge—caught with all of the universal hopefulness, clumsiness, cheapness and stupidity of youth.

As that Spring advanced they saw each other less and less frequently, until their relation dwindled almost to complete separation. Finally their companionship was utterly broken; when they saw each other they nodded, or spoke curtly: in Georgia a sullen and resentful pride smouldered even more stubbornly, she thought: "Well, if she's goin' to act like that, I'm not goin' to run aftah her." And Esther, although her stronger and deeper spirit was in later life not much troubled by the distorted vanity of such "pride," which is really a kind of weakness and fear, a childish desire to out-wait and out-stare the other person, and not to be the first to speak—(Esther's almost complete lack of such folly was one of the chief elements of strength in her direct, forceful, and healthy temperament) — was restrained from speaking a dozen times when she wanted to by a sense of indecision and doubt: later, she remembered this feeling, and wondered why she had not spoken.

Meanwhile, a rumor of disaster impending in the Barnhill family had spread throughout the street. It seemed to be a perception, an omen of ill fortune, which, without direct communications, had passed into men's knowledge. One day Bella said to Esther:

"I understand the Barnhills are going to move."

"Why?" Esther burst out sharply, and then regretted she had spoken.

"I don't know," said Bella. "I don't think things have gone so well with them." She paused a moment, then with an air of irrelevance, added:

"That poor man! . . . I wish there were something we could do for him. I feel so sorry for *him*."

This feeling of sympathy for Barnhill seemed general among the people in the street, there was a sense of tacit agreement among people about him, and yet no one could have explained just why he was sorry for the man or why, in this communion of regret, the name of the woman was never mentioned. There was almost nothing about the man that could be remembered, no atom of personality to awaken either dislike or affection, and perhaps it was this very fact — that every element of personality had been stripped from him, that he had been spiritually caponized and every color of manhood, every mark of character taken from him, which awakened in people a sense of pity and shame. The little man with his wing collar, his drab clothing, his straggly sandy moustache, his feeble and polite laughter, and his soft colorless drawl which had never uttered a word that people could remember, cherish, or deny, remained, nevertheless, in the memory as someone who had been shamed and broken, and their hearts were with him. As one saw him come along the street and turn to mount the steps into his house, he seemed to pause and hesitate timidly, and then to enter with an air that was resigned and lost, and by which he seemed to surrender the last light of day, the last faint glimmer of personality. And, indeed, when the door had closed behind him the sense of his annihilation was complete: the front of solid and untelling brown had engulfed him as completely as an opening in the earth engulfs a rabbit, and until he again emerged into the light, every vestige of his identity was lost.

And then, as if to intensify this sense of his disappearance and engulfment they heard at night, one voice—the woman's high drawling and insistent voice, addressed to him, but they never heard him answer: they could only judge from the brief infrequent pauses in her harangue that he had spoken a word or two. And even more than the things she said, the sound of her voice, which was not loud, but which had a drawling resonance that carried clearly through stone walls into the street, over the shouts of the playing children, between the lapse of the horse's hoof, or entering into quietness and darkness with a quality that was naked, wet, and unclean. And these city people who had heard without warning so much that was hard, bitter, and violent—the curse of a drunken Irishman and the screams of his beaten wife, the threats and abuse of truck drivers, the jeers of the roughs, the constant mockery of disbelief and cynicism—these people who had accepted all this with indifference or laughter turned away with a sense of convulsive shame from the sound of this woman's voice:

"... I *knew* it! I *knew* it! I knew it the first time I saw yo' haid!"

At this time phrenology was still alive and flourishing and Mrs. Barnhill's judgments of people were always touched by the size and shape of their "haid."

"My mothah tol' me but I wouldn't listen: she tol' me the first time you evah cume to see me that you couldn't expect nothin' from a man with a haid like that. . . . She tol' me no man with a haid no widah than you got between the eahs would evah amount to a hill of beans. . . . She said, 'As sauh as you live, if you go an' marry that man you'll cuss the day you ever laid eyes on him.' I *knew* it! I *knew* it! But I wouldn't listen. . . ."

Here, briefly, there was the pulse of silence: perhaps the man had made some answer no one could hear; but in a moment, the naked and near penetration of the shrew's voice took up its tirade again, insulting darkness:

"She said, 'You c'aint make somethin' out of nothin', an' he just ain't got it. . . . I nevah saw a man yet with eyes that close togethah who was with powah enough to kill him. . . . There nevah was a man yet' (she said) 'whose eyebrows grow straight across his haid like that who had sense enough to come in out of the rain. . . . Don't you know what the Barnhills *ah*?' (she said). 'Don't you know that evy'body in And'son county considahs them nothin' but low-down po' white trash? . . . If you marry that man, I'm bettin' you right now, you ah goin' to bring disgrace on yo' family. . . . The Tolly's ah the best people in this part of the state' (she said). '. . . We got a long line o' high-up people—leuoyahs an' preachahs an doctahs an' all like that' (she said). '. . . yo' gran'fathah would tu'n *right* ovah in his grave' (she said), 'if he knew you was plannin' to marry one of them little ole two-by fo' Ba'nhills. . . .' "

There was another pause, during which the man apparently made no answer whatever, for suddenly she burst into a long sneering laugh, loaded with a full envenomed hate, a choking desire to slash and maim:

"Look at him! . . . With his po' little peanut of a haid, pretendin' he can read a *papah*! . . . Yaie! Go on! Read yo' papah. . . . You won't undahstan' what you read, noway. . . . You ain't foolin' no one. Why, pshaw!" Here she laughed long and sneeringly. "You po' little *sorry* excuse fo' a *man*! . . . *Pretendin'* you can *read* when you ain't got sense enough to spell 'cat' an' 'rat'! . . . When I think of the chances I had, an' the real *sho-nuff* men I tu'ned down in awdah to marry a thing lak you, I could beat my brains out against the wall. . . . *You!* . . . Why, you po' little countah-jumpah! . . . You *cheap* little fifteen dollah a week ribbon clerk—fo' that's all you evah been—the on'y reason you evah got this job was because I went down on my knees befo' my frien's to get it fo' you. . . . I might have *known* you wouldn't have get-up enough to hold a *real* man's job. . . . I might have *known* the only thing *you* was good enough fo' was checkin' in some *cheap* little dry-goods sto'. . . . Well!" she screamed suddenly. "Ah you goin' to *tawk*? C'aint you *say* somethin'? Ah you goin' to sit thah lak a dummy? Do you know what we're goin' to do *now*? . . . Have you thought what's to become of yo' wife an' chile? . . . Do yo' know wheah nex' month's rent's to come from? . . . Have yo' money enough to pay the fayah back home, or do we have to wawk? . . . Ain't you got nothin' to *say*?" she screamed.

There was only the dark listening silence: far off the vast brooding murmur of the city rose, the cars clambered by on Broadway, there was the delicate briskness of hooves, but in the street it seemed that life had been fixed in a strong hypnosis, a fascination of disgust and loathing, as it paused to listen. At length, more quietly spoken, but carried even more clearly in the astonishing resonance of her voice, came the final words of shame and grief. It was as if, goaded by some deep madness of fury and frustration, to a foul liberty of speech she had never taken in a more familiar place, and finally maddened because what charm of youth and sex she once had possessed had long since vanished in the general ruin of all her other hopes, she was emboldened now to publish in this alien place (whether truly or falsely no one ever knew) a news of foul infamy that would strip from him the last ray of dignity that remained to him. Her voice, calm, hoarse, broken between words as if she panted to get breath, still carried an amazing resonance:

". . . You say we ain't goin' back. . . . No, I know that. . . . I know we're not. . . . An' I'll tell you why. . . . We ain't goin' back because they won't let you come back. . . . We ain't goin' back because they's no one in that town that would give you a job. They won't give you a job because everybody knows why you lost yo' job at Ivans' (Evans) sto'. They know you lost yo' job because you'd been stealin' from Ivans fo' yeahs. They knew you'd been takin' Ivans' groceries an' sendin' them home without payin' fo' them. . . . An' I tell you somethin' else. . . . they know you ain't comin' back because you ah afraid of Charley Brissey. . . . They know that Brissey slapped yo' face and kicked you out in the street when you went an' tried to get money from him. . . . They knew you tried to get money from him because he'd been goin' to bed with yo' wife fo' yeahs, an' you wasn't man enough to do anything about it. . . . Yaie!" she screamed. "I was his woman, I went to bed with him, an' I'm proud of it. . . . I had me a man, a *real* man, fo' once . . . not a little good-fo' nothin' rabbit. . . . Yaie! Good-fo'-nothin'. You weren't even good enough to get a chile of yo' own. . . . Yo' own chile is Charley Brissey's, an evy'body knows it, an' I'm proud of it. . . . God-damn you, I hate the sight of you, you good-fo'-nothin' pimp, that's all you ah. . . ."

Her speech broke into hoarse incoherent sobs, and at length there was silence in the house again, a movement of life along the street. A man knocked out the red cake of ash from his pipe against the stone railing of a stoop:

"Christ!" he muttered, rising from the step. "I hope he smashes every God damn tooth she's got into her throat!"

And Bella, standing in darkness, her face pooled beside a film of curtain, spoke briefly and quietly through a mouth puckered with ruralism:

"White fokes!"

And someone said: "I wonder how much Charley Brissey misses her," and laughed softly, bitterly.

And Esther turned and went into the house that had no depth of darkness deep enough for the concealment she desired.

Early Summer, late June: the beginnings of blazing heat, the summer persistent, timeless, an immeasurable weariness—the sweltering stifling blanket of the insistent and merciless heat: at ten o'clock the glazed murky light, the weary murky sky, the mournful acceptances of impure and tormented heat that sank nauseously to the entrails:

"Looks like another scorcher today." "Yep: It's going to be hot. It's not the heat I mind so much: it's the humidity." "Oh well! It's not so bad, taking there's only six weeks of it. August's not a bad month: the nights are always cool."

It was a lie.

"Yes: by the middle of August it's all over. September's a good month."

It was a lie, a lie, and Esther, looking out into the weary forenoon glaze, knew that it was a lie.

Some of the horses wore a body netting, some wore straw hats through which their ears pricked rakishly, beneath which their long heads and enormous mottled eyes stared with their comic and mournful wisdom: the horses suffered horribly, they died by hundreds in the heat, in the deceiving gloom below the elevated structure, the raw horsecar nags were unhitched and rested; drivers with thoughtful faces appraisingly threw buckets of slopping water on the smoking trembling flanks of horses.

Heat, thick glazed heat, humid and sweltering heat: from day to weary day the man-swarm thrust and jostled in this heat until all their memory and hope—all brilliant recollections of bright-nailed cold, of the frozen and immense solitude of stars, of the piercing exultancy of wind and frost, of the cry that leapt out in the wind—were lost under the thick dense envelope which pressed soddenly upon man's spirit, and which shut him off from every memory, swift, soaring and exultant that joined him to cold lonely space;—heat that melted him out in hopelessness, that leveled out the keen and sharp defiance of self, the lean and secret architectures of vanity, beyond private dignity into a general nucleus of wet, weary and hopeless flesh, an uneasy atom in its world and inter-flux with a degrading identity of melting gropings, unmemoried and unmindful of anything but the uncaring moments, interfused of one drab stuff of rootless, quivering and impotent life. Hope, belief, joy—every strong and sudden energy that goes leaping through the blood and that makes life valuable drowned miserably in the glazed swelter of that heat, and Esther, who hated its miseries particularly, now felt a sense of exasperation and dislike for people themselves, as if they accepted this ugly and uncomfortable existence because their sense and aspiration were both too coarse to want (she knew not how or where) some better one: she resented the misery and discomfort of their sweltering lives, the fetid cells they lived in, their rancid body smells—and, with a sort of hatred for her own race, the rancid stench of Jewesses with unwashed armpits—as if these people had in some way willed and desired the wretchedness in which they dwelt. And then, with only the stay of a moment's breeze, some seconds' pause and flutter of a tired belief, a feeling of pity and wonder would surge back into her heart as she saw, below the dull greasy yellows of their disturbed and contorted faces, a look that was, in all the base indignity of their shabby, sweaty lives, patient, tenacious, dogged, and wistfully enduring—and suddenly the wonderful enigma of living, the sad, terrible, patience of living, came to her: suddenly she saw that man, out of the full sum and multiple of his twenty thousand miserable, sweaty, vile and loathsome days, might wrench ten hours of joy and ecstasy—ten moments, if he were lucky, when an almost perfect joy might not be fouled and mutilated by the infinite little diseases and destinies of his flesh, the itches, aches, and vague discomforts of his paltry body, of the insistent rasp of his tortured nerves, the pressure of his ragged and inept memories with their grotesque swarm of fears, hates and duties—and that it was only in hope of these ten possible moments that he lived or desired to live, that this and this alone, this mirage of some future and impossible bliss made him endure the desolation and horror of the existence he was forced to lead, kept him alive in all this sweltering misery from which he rarely gained a moment's respite.

A sense of horror and desolation which seemed too much for her to bear swept over her suddenly: it seemed to her that life was unendurable, and she hated people for enduring it as it was and for not resenting its ugliness and misery. It seemed to her that these people with their inept, confused, and frenzied lives actually loved the discomfort and ugliness in which they weltered—as if the horrible weather of these hot glazed skies, with their nausea of steaming heat, was also the weather of men's souls, and as if she could no longer draw her breath in peace in a world where such things and people lived. In herself she felt only the desire for joy, wonder, and exultancy—for the discovery of an earth which had once seemed wonderful but had now betrayed her: she felt herself drowning, the only fish that could not swim or breathe in this sea of abject grey misery and dullness of mankind.

Heat—and misery; and in the midst of this the Barnhills were moving. The cavernous maw of an enormous moving van stood backed to the curb to receive the dingy furnishings of the house, and in the street two powerful grey horses dropped their great heads doggedly before the heat, dug heavily at the pavement, and stiffly brushed their rumps with coarse dry whiskings of their tails. At length it came—upon the shoulders of three sweaty Irishmen: it came endlessly and horribly, the accumulated trash of a lifetime—the cheap dressers, with warped and blistered drawers, their mottled glass, the dirty stained mattresses, the rickety and dilapidated chairs, the long, rattling wide-width pictures, the rocker with carpeted seat, the fancy pincushions with their borders of dirty ribbon, the calendars, the organ with broken and sunken keys, the stereoscope, the accordion hat-rack, the grit and grease encrusted kitchen pots and pans, the chamberpots, the bedding— it all came out under the eye of the merciless sun with a sense of shameless and degrading exposure—as if the poverty, the lunacy, and defeat, and the dirty confusion of these lives was made legible and published nakedly in the ill-assortment of these possessions.

At length, the last piece was roped into the end of the bulging and loaded van, the great horses strained and pulled off slowly, and

Barnhill, his wife, and a little later, Georgia, came down the steps, and left the house. Esther waited at the window, and for a moment she thought Georgia had glanced in her direction and would come to speak to her. Esther's heart was thudding fiercely, her legs trembled, she felt a wild impulse to rush out in the street, call to the other girl, and embrace her. But she didn't. After a moment Georgia turned and walked slowly down the street behind her parents. They all turned south on Broadway, and vanished from her sight. The street seemed empty when they were gone, inhabited only by the fierce glare of the sun. They were lost in the heat, the glare, the searing confusion of the city. She never saw any of them again.

Appendix A

FRAGMENTS FROM

"THE GOOD CHILD'S RIVER"

LEDGERS

I Even Such Is Time: The Theatre

As indicated in the outline at the end of Appendix B, section II,
Wolfe probably intended this material to be part of his projected
fourth chapter, entitled "The Theatre—Esther's Birth," which
was written from Joe's point of view. As Wolfe had researched his
subject extensively, the information about the play Hazel Kirke
and the new and innovative Madison Square Theatre was
correct.

This segment is the most fragmented in "The Good Child's
River" manuscript; segments begin and end seemingly without
connection, and several passages are recorded for several pages
along the sides of already written pages. The characterization of
Joe Barrett mirrors this chaos, for at one point he suddenly
becomes Monkey Hawke reflecting on his southern past and at
times he is even Wolfe himself—Wolfe scratched out Joe's name
and replaced it with "I" when raging against a variety of evils in
society, particularly the abuse of alcohol. Moreover, the cynical
approach to the actors and their behavior seems to approximate
more closely the author's own view of the world of the theatre than
that of Joe Barrett.

The theatre in which *Esther Craig* was being played had been
opened only a year before. The event was notable. At the time,
the public interest in the theatre itself had been so great that comparatively little notice, and that of an almost perfunctory quality,
was given by the newspapers to the play which opened it. And yet
Esther Craig had already enjoyed a run of about a year, and was des-
tined to run so long that its name would be famous in the annals
of the American theatre long after Prince's Theatre had been out-
worn, antiquated, and destroyed—a part of buried Troy, a fragment of that sunken world, that buried city of which the whole
impulse, and only some few mouldering shoals of house remain at
once, everything and nothing.

For a brief period the theatre was almost a national monument,
an object in which a people that measured itself pugnaciously
against other peoples in terms of the size and modernity of its pos-

sessions could take pride and comfort. The newspapers when they described the theatre assured their readers that there was "nothing in Europe to touch it."

From cellar to roof every fixture and device represented what was most up-to-date theatrical construction, and there were, in addition, several notable improvements which no other theatre had ever possessed. There was a balcony, cunningly suspended in mid-air, from which a hidden orchestra discoursed aerial music to an enchanted audience which said "Where? Where?"; there were sliding and adjustable seats, calculated to give the spectator the comfort almost of his own bed (this device had later to be abolished); there was a courteous and capable staff that refused tips and dispensed free ice water during the intermissions (this courtesy was noted in columns of print); and finally there was the wonderful elevator stage which could sink swiftly and noiselessly into a vast basement, where it could be instantly detached with its whole freight of scenery, rolled off along a track and dismantled while another stage, already set for the next scene, rose swiftly into place behind the footlights.

These marvels had been described so lavishly in print that people all over the country knew about them, and one of the first things strangers visiting the city for the first time wished to see—along with the almost completed East River Bridge, the Vanderbilt houses on Fifth Avenue, and the Elevated railways—was Prince's Theatre. And this curiosity was by no means confined to country visitors. The city people, if anything, outdid the rustics. Everyone went to see *Esther Craig* during that first year of its run, or rather, as a journal of the period remarked:

"We've all seen *Esther Craig*, a young lady who has, as we all know, her *ups and downs*—Now couldn't we all go some night to see what really *happened* to the girl? We assure our readers she doesn't spend *all* her time rising out of the infernal regions. The play itself is well worth seeing."

The public fascination in the mechanics of the theatre was predicated in unmemorable puns, jests, and cartoons. One drawing in particular which caused considerable amusement at the time was called "The Rise and Fall of Esther Craig"—and it showed a bewildered looking maiden rising out of the lower depths on the ascending stage, with her hands clasped and her eyes uplifted in a gesture of entreaty to a mustachioed villain above—himself a recognizable caricature of Malcolm Keith, the builder of the theatre—and saying to him piteously:

"Spare me. I will do whatever you desire if you only let me see the light of day again. This is the seventeenth time this week you've sent me to the cellar."

There were other caricatures, some more biting and less friendly. The best of these showed Thalia, the muse of Comedy, sitting among a litter of contrivances such as elevator stages, theatrical mill wheels, railway trestles, locomotives, lighthouses, thunder-making machines, calcium glares, and so on, in the attitude of depiction and contemplation in which Durer has drawn his figure of *Melancholia*. The legend below read simply:

"*Real* thunder? Well, I think I have known better."

Another, which bore the title "The Future of the Drama," represented a beak nosed manager enthusiastically congratulating a dramatist on the merits of his latest manuscript. He is represented as saying:

"It's superb, my boy. How you must have lived and suffered to have produced a thing like this! In three acts you have managed to have four storms—rain, hail, thunder and lightning—two train wrecks, a sinking ship, a burning building and three brigades of firemen! This time we'll show them what we can really do!"

Another caricature which was obviously directly aimed at the famous "old mill scene" in *Esther Craig*, in which the heroine hurls herself into the water below the wheel and is rescued by the hero, represents a woman in a box saying to her male escort:

"But what was her motive? I can hardly believe she'd do a thing like that."

To which the escort answers:

"Of course, she did it. You can see for yourself—it's *real* water!"

The owner of the theatre, Prince, was shrewd enough to capitalize instantly on this publicity. He responded to the general curiosity by opening the theatre, the stage, the cellar, the operation of the complicated lifting machinery for public inspection: visitors were allowed to enter the building in the morning between ten and noon and after the matinees, and there were guides to conduct them.

The public prowled and poked about backstage, they stood

on the stage with gaping jaws and sank gently and slowly into the basement—they intruded, gaped, and stared into the regions which hitherto had been private to the stage crew and the company, and these people, although compelled to maintain an appearance of good nature and courtesy toward the visitors, were rasped by these intrusions into a state of controlled exacerbation and nervousness which finally turned into a feeling of bitter dislike toward Prince, the owner. And this dislike Prince returned with all the hardness, tenacity, and meanness of his tight and bitter spirit.

Prince was a dry little man in his fifties with a small, mean acid face. His voice was nasal, tart and disparaging: it was with difficulty and grudgingly that he yielded assent to any opinion, even a pleasant and harmless one; he was by nature surly, by birth a New Englander, and he had made a fortune in New York from real estate, and the rustling of innumerable papers through his dry parched fingers. He had been by profession an attorney, and the land on which the theatre was built, formerly occupied by a block of brownstone fronts, had been his property. And, as a result of the passionate enthusiasm of Malcolm Keith, who had come to him with pockets bulging with his plans and profits for a theatre, and even more, of course, as a result of his own hard and intense conviction, after minute and searching inquiry, that the affair would be profitable to himself, Prince had given the land, and produced the money for the construction of the theatre. It was his first and only connection with the theatre: he had no knowledge, no liking, and no respect for the stage, or for the people on it.

Moreover, he had used the talent, the energy, and the labor of Malcolm Keith mercilessly to his own profit, and now, having collected a liberal supply of golden eggs, he was preparing to get rid of a goose that was becoming troublesome. It was Keith who had planned the theatre and supervised its construction; the improvements, innovations, and inventions which had excited so much public wonder were all Keith's; Keith had written the play, engaged the cast and rehearsed the company—and it might reasonably be thought that a man with talent, energy, and intelligence enough to execute so formidable a labor was, at least, a remarkably shrewd and clever person (the newspapers called him a "genius," "an eccentric genius," "an extraordinary genius")—but the plain truth of the matter is that Keith was a fool. He was a fool, however, that the actors liked much better than they did the grey but cunning little fox who had used and cheated him: at this very moment, within less than a year after the golden enthusiasm of the opening, the relations between Prince and Keith had reached an open break, and in this quarrel the sympathy and support of the actors—if so feeble a manifestation as they dared make could be called support—was all for Keith, but for the most part it manifested itself in handshakes, muttered assurances of friendship, lusty undertones of a timorous and quiescent indignation.

Joe still had much of the quick and eager passion of his youth, the warm tongue, the ready loyalty: he had never stood in fear of a job or an employer—his fears and apprehensions were innumerable, bewildering and complicated, but the question of money seemed not to trouble him at all. He was perhaps as indifferent to money as any man one is likely to meet in the course of a lifetime: it came to him as colored strips of paper which might be exchanged over counters for desirable things—his whole contemplation of life, with its incredible freight of memory, its constant and painful struggle with the swarming complexity of the physical world, his vision burning with a thousand dreams, memories, and prophesies of horror or joy, seemed utterly remote from the idea of money. And it was an idea that he had never understood, that had always seemed fantastic to him as the following story will show: a year or two before his marriage he had found himself without money one day when he was a member of a travelling company which was then appearing in Boston. It was several days before pay day, and there was only one man in the company whom he knew well enough to approach for a loan. But this man confessed that he, too, was without money. In the conversation that followed, this man asked Joe if he had, or had ever had, a bank account. Instantly Joe remembered that he had at that moment over thirty dollars on deposit in a bank in New York City. His companion immediately told him that his difficulty was solved—that the manager of the company would cash his check, or vouch for him with the hotel cashier, who would cash it. And this is what happened. The manager took him to the cashier's window, explained the matter, and offered to stand good for endorsement. But when the cashier asked Joe to make out the check, he discovered he had no checks on the bank in which his money was deposited. The cashier, who was a woman, thereupon pushed a book of checks bearing the title of a Boston bank under the window and instructed Joe to cross out this name and write in along it the name of his own bank. He did this—his bank was the Corn Exchange, he knew it was one of the strongest and richest banks in the country, but as he began to write its name laboriously, with an aged, encrusted, and splintered pen that shot its spray of minute ink particles upon the paper with every scrawling stroke, it seemed to him that such a name was fantastic and unsafe—that such a name was not proper for an institution which should be as sound as established government, but rather that it had a bonanza, wild-cat, and speculative flimsiness. Also, the ink in which he wrote the check had a faded and watery color, and when he finished and thrust the check back through the window it seemed to him that he was trying to get money through false pretenses—that, in short, he had perpetrated a fraud and a forgery. Meanwhile the cashier took the check up in her dry money-counter's fingers and read it. She was a severe and ugly looking female with a large red nose, a skin of remarkable freshness, redness, and delicacy, and a hard maidenly face of an almost cruel and muscular primness: Her face, like the faces of many people in New England, resembled the soil and physical topography of that region: her surprisingly delicate and reddened cheeks resembled the thin soil with its hardy gristles of hemlock and of pine, and its green and fertile presence, while her powerful nose, her cheekbones, the craggy mountains of her face, reminded one of New England's worn and craggy coast, and the great grey roots that push their noses through swart rocks. She wore glasses that gave her eyes a hawkish glitter and when she lifted her head she looked at him over her glasses in a way that somehow reminded him of an old judicial horse, and with a glance of such formidable and wintry sternness that his heart quailed.

"How will you have this?" she said at length in a disapproving tone, although the amount was only ten dollars. He told her, and as she pushed the money out to him he felt that both her glance and the glance of the manager who stood beside him were fixed accusingly and suspiciously upon him. Suddenly he turned to the manager and stammered out impulsively and earnestly:

"I *know* this is all right. . . . I am *certain* about it. . . . If there should be any trouble . . . if you will let me know. . . . I. . . ."

"Why should there be any trouble?" the manager said, eying him sharply and with surprise. "You have money in the bank, haven't you?"

"Oh, of course!" said Joe hastily, wishing already he had kept silent. "I am *certain* about it!" Although now that he said so, doubts began to torment him: *did* he have money in the bank? *Could* he have withdrawn it at some time and forgotten it? Was the amount, as he thought, over thirty dollars, or? — Nay! Could he be certain now that he had ever had money in the bank? Was he the victim of some powerful delusion? Or had he not deliberately lied to others, and to himself, knowing all the time in his secret heart that he had nothing, had never had a penny in the bank?

During the remainder of his stay in Boston he went once or twice to the cashier for small sums, and each time he imagined that the woman was looking mistrustfully and suspiciously at him; and each time, as he got real money — spendable, lendable money — in exchange for a piece of paper, crudely and clumsily scrawled upon, the old feeling of wonder, disbelief, and guilt returned.

The mystery of money, therefore, was very much a mystery to Joe: he had no desire whatever to save or hoard it, ten dollars in his pocket satisfied him at the moment as completely as a hundred, and in his fears and calculations for the future the question of money played an almost negligible part. Moreover, when he thought back over his life and saw how large a proportion of his money had been spent for food and drink, he was so far from having a feeling of guilty depression that he actually felt a surge of triumphant and exultant satisfaction. Suddenly one day he realized that the money he had spent this way — in eating and drinking — was money he did not regret at all: his miser's hoard was not pieces of gold, but the memory of countless good meals, of hundreds of bottles of good wine consumed in France and Germany, of the full toned and potent ale and steaks in London, and succulent foods from some of the best restaurants on earth.

Thus, in a spirit tortured by almost every kind of uncertainty, confusion, and lack of assurance, in a Faustian soil still struggling like a mad man with the blind horror of amount and number on this earth, groping at times like a drowning man upon the sea-floor of life, strangled and engulfed, it seemed, in the insensate multitude, the barren fecundity of nature, where men were like drops of water, humanity like the foaming welter of a river's tide—this memory of the food he had eaten, the wine he had drunk returned to fortify him with a sense of triumph, of certitude and perfection. He felt assured, with a conviction that was immovable and unassailable, and that was anchored in his spirit like a great rock round which the dark and stormy waters of disbelief and confusion were beating constantly, that no one on earth could surpass him in the appreciation of these things, and that no one in his (my) own nation of one hundred million people could surpass him (me) either in appreciation or in the quality of his experience. Joe (I) felt, in short, with a belief that was an obsession that he (I) had enjoyed food and drink as well as anyone in America. It was a curious delusion—if delusion it was, for could any certain evidences have been secured to test the validity of his belief, it would surely have been found that his belief was not wholly illusory: it would surely have been found that among the hundred million people in the nation his position among the eaters and drinkers would have been a very high one—it is inconceivable that there could have been found even fifty thousand who had enjoyed food and drink as well as he (more than I);—it is likely my position would have been within the first few hundred.

Moreover, this golden chronicle of his (my) bodily hunger and thirst was not distorted by the romance of distance: it seemed to him, on the contrary, that not only his taste but his experience had grown finer as he grew older, so that some of his most wonderful memories were the most recent ones. For, no matter what dark confusion, mistrust, doubt, and labyrinthine twistings his spirit had gone through in its protean conflicts with the world, he was assured of the power and richness of man's material life; of a subtler, wiser, and profounder understanding of sensuous experience. . . .

He was assured of their subtle and mature value, of a subtle, wiser and profounder understanding of sensuous experience, so that in this respect they were better and finer people than most Gentiles. For example, Joe knew that most Jews would not stand for bad food: he had seen them protest warmly and indignantly many times at the quality and preparation of food that most Gentiles would have swallowed without complaint or discrimination. Again, in restaurants where he had witnessed these Jewish protests, he had often been interested to observe the sense of communion—a communion of scorn, hard and vulgar, barren and destitute—with which a Jewish family greeted the appearance of badly cooked food. They would stare at it with an expression of strong disgust, the powerful and sensual volutes of their nostrils would tremble and curl with distaste, and then they would glance at one another with a bewildered and uncomprehending look, as if to say: "What is it? Does anyone know what it is?" Then one of them would say something to the others that was apparently vulgar and clever, for it would be accompanied by the vulgar and cynically worldly look that often accompanies their potent humor, and they would all then burst into rich, mocking, and rather loud laughter. Then they would call the waiter, speak to him earnestly, indignantly, and scornfully, until he took the food away. On several occasions when this happened, Joe would be accompanied by a companion who very often made some such comment as this: "You see, that's just like a Jew! They've always got to attract attention to themselves when they come into a public place like this. They're so afraid they won't be noticed! They were taking advantage of that man because they knew he was a waiter and couldn't talk back to them. That's what I don't like about them! They are so loud and noisy and when they think they've got the upper hand they run all over people."

To this comment, at first, Joe made no answer, but it stuck in his mind and returned to his reminiscent and contemplative memory at one of these times when he lay for hours on his couch brooding upon the whole rich, passionate, dense, and complex tapestry of experience, while the vast and murmurous sound of the city, of men in a million lost unseen moments, rose like the core and essence of all time, the distillation of eternity, above his life. Suddenly he understood that this comment—the criticism his friend had made of the loudness and arrogance of the Jews—together with other criticisms of the race which are most frequently heard, was not at all true—was not at all true in the sense that these qualities were uniquely possessions of the Jew: on the contrary, he realized with a feeling of violent anger that these qualities—arrogance, loudness, and the desire to domineer over those who must obey and cannot answer, were even more qualities that belonged to the native American. Thus, he thought, as between the two—American Jews or Americans of the native stock—the Jew was more likely to behave himself with quietness and decency. Joe had seen this demonstrated again and again in foreign countries: the American travelling in Europe was likely to be loud, arrogant, overbearing, and anxious to draw attention to himself—in other words, to be guilty of just these vices of which he accused the Jew. On the other hand, the Jew who travelled abroad was very likely to travel quietly, intelligently, and unobtrusively—to act like a man of sense and not like a rowdy and disagreeable child, and to adapt himself readily to the flow, use, and habit of the countries he visited.

Therefore, it drove me mad at times to see the shameful offenses of people all around me against peace, repose and happiness and the plain priceless simple glory of man's appreciation of sensual joy. As Joe (I) reflected, his (my) face began to burn with anger, and a thousand shameful memories returned—of men and women who had met as friends in public, to eat and drink and to enjoy themselves in fellowship and affection and who so debauched the simple decency of good fellowship that they abused one another foully with curses, jeers, and threats until the spectator was torn between the desire to vomit or to hurl them bodily into the street. Even in their laughter there was no warmth, no kindness, and no solid belly mirth: Even their laughter was harsh, final, and jeering—its forced tones, its harsh unnaturalness, its deliberate brutality, together with the lewd and stupid boastings, the foolish threats, were governed somehow by this general terror, the acrid and nameless fear. And these memories produced countless others even more shameful and hateful—of men without dignity, pride or justice—the traitors of alcohol, the swine of the bottle, the real enemies of perhaps—the greatest instrument man has found for happiness and the good life—this foul, jeering rabble who dared to swallow down their filthy throats the glorious god of the bottle— a desecration as unspeakable as would be, to believers, the knowledge that jeering infidels had dared through communion to partake of the body of Christ. And as he thought of them, he saw them in a hundred places, along the mellow polished sweep of splendid bars, or in the dreary back rooms of cheap sordid saloons, or reeling along the streets through all the barren and brutal shambles of Saturday Night, with its smell of blood and vomit, its odor of acrid fear, in which the weary sterility and dulness of a million tones released itself in darkness, shame, ugliness and horror. Here were the enemies of splendor, the goat cry, love and proud potent joy, and wherever they saw it, they could neither be a part of it nor stay away from it—like envenomed eunuchs they thrust themselves upon it polluting the air with their foulness, their sterility, and the acrid odor of fear. And from where did it come—this barren and impotent fear, this congealer of fruitfulness, this enemy of the joy he knew and felt was everywhere. How had they been so corrupted, and for what reason? Fear pressed upon them from the skies, it came from nameless sources, it ran like ice through all the conduits of their blood—it hovered above, almost like a grey, shapeless, impalpable and terrible presence—but why, why?

He had felt it himself a thousand times, he had observed it a million—in the weary, sterile, and exacerbated faces of the people on the streets, in the abuse, the threats and curses, and the boastfulness of the drinkers, in countless other ways—and now he hated this grey, nameless and shameful thing because he knew it was the false and corrupting element in life—the trickster and the cheat that stole men's lives away, duped them out of joy and sent them into dusty death beaten, disgraced, tricked, and swindled—food for the eyeless worms, lives for the adders and the asps.

How many of his own sweet store of golden days had been thus swindled and polluted by this dirty cheat? As he thought about it now he began to choke with his fury and resentment because he saw from the thousand incontrovertible evidences, that exultancy and joy were real forever, that the incomparable fruits of this earth were glorious past description, past belief, and past imagining, and that the enemy to all the treasure was this lying cheat of stark fear.

And this lying cheat was always the same—this lying cheat that put grey and corrupted fingers on the pulse of life: it was the same whether it made its appearance in the roots of the flesh— in these foul-mouthed, sterile, and intrusive dark-millions, who struck their fangs with hate into the heart of joy—or whether it made its appearance in the roots of the spirit, even more deadly than their brother vermin because it seemed to him—how, why he knew not—a cruel and incredible power had been given into their barren gripe: these enemies of joy had been made the guardians of all its grandeurs and sources, so he thought; with a corrupt and deathless vitality of hate they kept the glory and the gold from its rightful heirs.

He was obsessed, of course, and maddened out of tempered judgments. But the fierce love of life, such as Joe (I) knew, is an agony: in it there is neither contentment nor restraint. It is a gluttony of the flesh and spirit that knows no appeasement, that grows from what it feeds upon, and that burns with as much fierceness and tenacity at the hour of death as at any moment of its life. It demands nothing less than all the joy and glory of the earth—there is not food enough to feed it, not wine enough to slake its thirst.

At times Joe felt the presence of incomparable joy, of possession, assuagement, and complete fulfillment everywhere around him, and yet, Tantalus like, it slipped away from his grip just at the moment when he felt that he must capture it. He felt that it was tangible, yet he could not quite touch it, that it could be described and uttered, and yet he could not find the word for it; but it sang out at him from the air, it glittered in proud flashing tides, and in the bellied lean of sea-borne sails, in the slant of a diving wing, in the potent exhalations of the street, in the vast rude lyricism of the earth: Exultancy and joy forever: It was, and was everywhere, beyond denial, beyond belief—it lived in ten thousand days and minutes, in a million sun-flicks of desire and memory, as piercing as a wound, as impalpable as the flight of a hawk, soaring across the earth like music, and when he lifted up his head to trick it he could not, when he opened his mouth to utter it he could not—it filled his throat with a wild hot tongueless cry of pain, joy, ecstasy, and regret. Thus, in his frenzy—his sense of frustration and loss— his feeling turned, at times with a bitter and murderous rancor, against the people he felt were the enemies of richness and joy on the earth.

And one of the chief of these was Prince. For, what Joe had long ago perceived, as one result of his swarming and universal observations, was that this hostility toward glorious and magnificent living lay like a curse, a pestilence, upon the nation, it included most of the people who thronged the streets, it comprised almost every race except the negroes, and it identified to a central emotion—

an emotion of shame and sterility—people who thought they had nothing in common with one another.

Thus, old Prince's true kinship was not only to the millions of others of his own kind, to the millions of old men and women with dry, fruitless and venomous faces, but also to the ugly and abusive drunks, to the whores who sold themselves without joy, and who, with a kind of hated shame, deliberately made the act of love as harsh, as profane, as revolting as possible, to the sterile and abominable Irish, and to the murderers. And why? Because over them all like an impending doom beneath whose menace they had always covered long this grey shapeless weight of shame and fear— a shame and fear that embraced ugliness and horror—that condoned murder, corruption, and theft, and that turned with hate against all free and generous living. It was a poison working in their veins, it united them, and made them comrades—the brutal cursing whore, the Irishman who murdered his wife, the foul and sterile drunkard, the young street roughs with their loose pustulate mouths, and old Prince. These were the enemies of life, and as Joe thought of them, remembering them in a thousand shameful and degrading moments, remembering how their pollution had tainted life and drawn all the brightness from the day, hatred burned in him like a hot coal, his great paws curved and he felt their necks distil in yellow putrefactions below his grip; he felt that if all their flesh had been compacted in one loathsome body, he could gladly have twisted the neck from the shoulders with one movement of his hands.

Everyone is familiar with Macaulay's definition of a Puritan as a man who hated bear-baiting not because it gave pain to the bear but because it gave pleasure to the spectator. Perhaps this is not a good or just estimate of a Puritan, but it is one of the truest and shrewdest things that has ever been said about people. It describes with biting accuracy the feeling of millions of people who would not fit most of the definitions of puritanism—prostitutes, criminals, thugs, roughs, the whole sour and rowdy turmoil of the streets—as well as the millions of others who would: poisonous old hags on Brooklyn Heights, and elsewhere, the futility people and the huggers of sterility generally, the mournful intellectuals, Jew and Gentile, as well as all other eunuchs, sour and stingy,

virgins, Protestant ministers, men in the uniforms of petty insolence—ticket takers and conductors (but not the engineers)—and
embittered wives. And the definition fitted old Prince like a glove.

During the first year after the opening of the theatre, he had
attempted to establish a complete dictatorship over the habits
and morals of the actors. He forbade them to drink, and even
attempted to force them to sign a "temperance pledge" to the
effect that they "would not touch alcoholic beverages in any way,
shape or form while a member of this company." Joe, who had for
months now made no effort to conceal his hostility and dislike for
Prince, had refused to sign this pledge, although he was told that
the punishment for disobeying it would mean dismissal from the
company. The other actors, however, did sign it; and, of course,
continued to drink as usual—at home, in their dressing rooms,
before and after the show in any one of the numerous and splendid bars that were just around the corner—that is at the Hoffman
House, the Fifth Avenue Hotel, the [Albermark], the St. James,
Kirks, Delmonico's, or wherever they could afford to go or were
invited. Prince also began immediately to investigate the private
lives of the actors. He had, of course, the prevailing opinion of an
actor's life—that it was dissolute and inured, scaled with glittering
sin. He found enough to satisfy his worst and greediest hopes. For
one thing, he discovered that Gifford, one of the older actors, had
been living for years with a woman to whom there was no record of
his legal marriage. When he questioned Gifford about this, Gifford
admitted he had not married her.

"Well," said Prince, in his tart mean voice, "I'm not going to
have anything like that in *my* company."

Already he referred to "my company" as if the actors had been
live stock belonging to his farm.

"You'll either have to leave that woman, or get out."

"Leave her!" Gifford said. "Oh, I can't do that! She's my wife."

"Your wife!" said Prince in an exasperated tone. "You just told
me there never was no weddin' ceremony."

"Well," Gifford answered, "she's the same as my wife. I can't
leave her. We're just the same as married. That's the way I look
at it!"

"Well, it's not the way I look at it!" said Prince tartly. "And you
wouldn't look at it that way either if you'd led a different sort of

life. . . . Now I've said all I'm goin' to say to you," he said curtly. "You can either leave that woman or leave the company."

Gifford was silent a moment.

"Look here, Mr. Prince," he said suddenly. "How'd it do if I married her? Would that fix it up all right?"

Prince was stupefied. The possibility of such an event had never occurred to him. Probably some measure of self-interest tinged his surprise: if a woman was foolish enough to give herself away for nothing, why should a man later grant her that reward which is usually reserved for virtue?

"Marry her!" he exclaimed. "Why, you don't want to marry a woman like that, do you? You've been *livin'* with her."

There was something about this answer that seemed so comical to Gifford that he had difficulty in keeping his face straight. Then he saw the ominous closure of Prince's mouth, the drawing down of his thin lips—the harbingers of stubborn disapproval. It had just occurred to Prince that there was something very immoral to Gifford's proposal—that is, that what he was willing to do apparently seemed pleasant, easy, and agreeable to him—and he was rapidly deciding not to be a party to the act: he would not condone immorality. Gifford quickly saw the turn events were taking, and instantly he regretted having spoken so glibly and easily. He saw that he would have to act quickly now, or all was lost. Indeed, Prince had already begun to speak in a surly and obstinate tone:

"No," he said, "I don't want anything like that in *my*—"

Here Gifford interrupted him with a very earnest look, and began to speak in a dramatic manner.

"Mr. Prince!" he said. "Give me a chance—that's all I ask of you. I'll show you I mean to do the right thing. I know I haven't done the right thing by her, but if you say I've got to marry her, why,"—here he paused, swallowed hard, as if the decision came very hard with him—and then burst out in a resolute tone—"Why, I'll *do* it!" he concluded.

He pressed hard along this track, and at length persuaded Prince to yield a grudging consent. When he told Joe what had happened, Joe was incredulous and angry.

"Do you mean to tell me you're going to get married just to satisfy that old skinflint?"

"What else can I do? If I don't, I lose my job, and I don't see a chance of getting a new one in a hurry."

He was sore and angry about it—as particularly angry as Joe had ever seen him, and yet, beneath all of it was his constant bitter resignation—his weary cynicism of a man who seemed to have known nothing but defeat and who seemed to Joe constantly to be saying, in answer to a younger man's passion, hope, despair, and belief, "I know! I know! I've heard it all, I've thought it all, I've felt it all—but you'll wind up someday by feeling as I do. It's no use!"

"I'd see him in hell before I did it."

"No you wouldn't. Not if you'd been in the show business as long as I have. You'll find there are not any soft spots in pavements—not when you're tramping around looking for a new engagement. Who wants an old trouper like me anyway? If I died tomorrow do you think Booth would deliver the funeral oration over my remains? Not by a long shot! There are ten thousand like me—we are not very good, and not very bad, and if we drop out no one will miss us. There are hundreds of others who could take my place; he doesn't need me and he knows it, so if I can hang on to my job by doing a little thing to oblige him, I'm going to do it."

"Do you call getting married a little thing?"

"In my case, it is, and I know Kitty won't mind. We've been together so long now we've both forgotten that we were never properly joined, anyway. And God! To hear this fellow talk. . . . I sort of hate to speak to her about it, though. You'd think I was living with some fancy little chippy! Why couldn't he leave me alone?" he said, somewhat resentfully. "What harm were we doing? We were both getting along all right—this thing makes it look dirty. I know now what it meant by saying Adam and Eve first knew sin when they ate the apple. Well, Prince is the apple—and a damned rotten apple too, if you want my opinion."

At any rate, Gifford got married and thus retained his job: Joe, Ella Blair, Street, and one or two others were present at the ceremony. Gifford, with a stroke of solemn cynicism, invited Prince to attend. And with a sour and graceless humor, Prince refused. Thus did he have his will. At length, however, he was faced with an obstinacy as great as his own, with a rebellious spirit that he could not subdue. And the circumstance that caused it was, apparently, much more trifling than the Gifford affair.

From the outset, since the opening of the theatre, Prince had watched with a bitter eye the conduct of the women members of the company. He watched them meanly, with the sterile and bitter morality of envy, and in all his effort to preserve them in a state of decency, there was a feverish gnawing of desire. And yet, as the members of the company well knew, he had himself been involved in a disgraceful and discreditable affair with a young actress only the year before. The story was this: the girl had had a small part—the maid's part—in *Esther Craig*. Although she was paid only twenty dollars a week, she dressed well, and even expensively, drove to the theatre in a hansom, and lived in a large room at a hotel farther up town, on Broadway. This hotel belonged to Prince: it was well known as a place in favor with the "sporting people." Its standards were light and easy, and its reputation unsavory. To those who knew Mr. Prince well, there was nothing at all surprising in the fact that so fair a Christian should run so foul a property, for this citizen whose sight was so sharp and whose smell was so brisk that he had telescopic powers of detection when another man's dirty linen was fluttering in the breeze, was afflicted with almost complete myopia when his own was exposed: his left hand was not only able to ignore what his right hand was doing but could even have denied with complete assurance that the right hand belonged to the same master, had it been caught picking someone's pocket. As a result, Mr. Prince was able to own some of the filthiest, foulest, wickedest and most profitable real estate ever inhabited by the human cesspool, and still to rest convinced of his own righteousness, and the incomparable superiority of his own nation, as he often maintained, in happiness, morals, physical and spiritual well being, to any other nation on earth. Among Mr. Prince's possessions were rotting tenements swarming with dirty and drunken men and women, with filthy unfed children, as well as with criminals, prostitutes, rats and lice. Here were the smells of cabbage, both boiled and rotten, of stale dry urine and of human manure, of garlic, and the thick, rancid, unspeakable odors of unwashed human flesh. And always in these dark corridors, in these ragless depths, there was a sound of water, of a single developing drip that somewhere fell in darkness, with its punctual and crescent monotony—and that was ominous, unperturbable, as detached as judgment, and as remote as time, time, time! Here on Saturday nights, as Mr. Prince's happy working people came homeward to repose, to simple cheer and Sabbath pieties, were heard occasionally the voices of the eagle and the dove—the drunken scream of the Irish wife, and her husband's soft retaliation: "God damn ye, th' dirty whore, I'll kill ye!"—and then the sounds which are dear to the ears of the unspeakable and the apelipped Irish, the smash of a splintered chair, as well as softer, subtler sounds which only a practiced and cunning ear could distinguish: there is, for example, the sound of a blackened eye, which is soft and ripe like a well-poached egg, or as if a plum had fallen to the earth; the sound of a broken nose is somewhat harder—it has in it the numb ground scrunch of a powdered cartilage and the voice is somewhat thickened later with the sweat and gluey flow of blood, while the sound of the smashed mouth is one of the nicest sounds of all—it is soft and yet it has the sound of good meat in it, it evokes a muffled grunt, and it is punctuated by the hard grain of a few teeth spat softly, pulpily out upon the floor. The sound of concussion and the sound of flowing blood, as Joe was later to discover, are subtler still; concussion is solid, yet has a long resonance, the head is full of rockets going off, the brain is loosened from the skull and floats, one feels light and dizzy, and as for blood—it thickens softly in the veins like cavalry, it rides fast upon dark feet, it comes with muffled rush,—and then it falleth like the gentle dew from heaven, it courses sweetly, coolly at first like rain, it branches out its brilliant hue across the forehead, it seeks the curves, the hollows and the channels of the face so that at first it is like pouring rain—one thinks the marvelous and million footed rain is falling, one lifts one's head to let the blessed rain fall over it—all of one's hair and face is wet with sweet, cool, falling and caressant rain, and then one lifts his fingers up to feel the rain and when he takes his hand away, suddenly he feels it wet and warm there on his fingers, it gets sticky: suddenly he knows it is not rain. And now he tries to breathe and it is pouring in his nostrils, wet and warm, he opens his mouth to breathe and it is smothering him with its warm, wet flow, he swallows it: it is no longer wet and cool, it is warm and gluey, it chokes one—

Finally, there was the sound of murder—a sound that grew familiar in Mr. Prince's houses, as it had long since grown familiar in the city. Sometimes it was the swift drawn knife, a body falling in the dark: no doors were opened. But usually it was not so cleanly done, murder in these houses was not nice or poignant, it was red and blurred as Mr. Gregin's face, brawny as corned beef, a mask as clumsy as a policeman's fist—the skull was splintered with a club, the man groped out of darkness to welter in his brains upon the step. Thus morning found them: the pure and delicate light of morning in America with its incomparable lilac freshness, sweetness, and purity came cleanly down, and stamped with its clear perfect light, and with its joy, this sharp mechanic world, these brown and aquiline streets, that harsh, cruel unmemoried, and somehow exultant city. It fell, with swift and flashing light, upon cold potent filth-destroying tides, which with their clean measured sweep into the bay and seawards seemed every morning to have washed the city free from all its foulness with a sucking glut: the rivers were like mouths that drew away the venom from the snake-wounds of the city. Now this pure light, so delicate and immense, at first is melted into fading night until the air is frail and lilac; then it tinges, potent, deep, into grey-blue, and then for a space there is the essence of pure light, cool, crystalline, colorless, and of transparent purity. Then the light is rosed incomparably: an immense contrast of rose light appears upon the east: the colors of dawn appear at first invisibly, a cloud goes by, far up, and it is bathed like magic in this unearthly and delicate light; then the first rose light falls on the highest objects—on the wooden water towers, on all things gaunt and high, and yet with this magical, remote, and unearthly quality—without violence, without heat, without body—like an echo, a hope, and a spell. The light conspires with water: the rivers, the lakes and the sea have at first the same clear, cool purity as light, the same immense exultancy, and the thickset form of wharves and docks around the island, with their immense gaunt and thrilling ugliness, their pungency of sharp magical odors, compacted of the smells of forty years, their incredibly nostalgic message of the voyage which drove straight at the heart its thorn of longing. Then this rosed delicacy of light touched water also: instantly the tides were flashing with a million diamond points of iridescence, the shining tide was broken with a million scallop-shells of waves, rose hued: the harbor burst into life, the tugs slid out, thrusting at their tow of barges and lighters, the air was broken with their sharp shrill cries, and suddenly there was the long deep shattering laugh of a departing liner.

Softly, gently, without a ripple on her lip, a clipper, stripped to bare poles, was going out under tug, and then the fast ocean goers, the princely products of the *Hamburg American*, the *Cunnard*, the *North German Lloyd*—the seven day palaces—began to blow from tetherings at quarantine, and to come in, rosed with light across the morning harbor, crossing the cleavages of tugs and barge, braking the blunt speed of the hooded ferries, which were parked with their dense wedge of faces, as always, it seemed, patient, silent, upturned, and somehow mournful, like a vision of time and judgment. Then instantly, it seemed, as if fit compliment for this immense happiness of air and water, all of the odors of the wharves—a mighty, potent, and subtle compost of perfumes—was released and rushed out into the air about the city: the pungent, sultry, incomparably fresh odor of ground coffee, and all the odors of thin, spicy crates, of citric rind and tropic fruit, of fresh briny fish, of tar and molasses, together with thousands of tons of sweet dewy lettuces, beans, peas, tomatoes, as well as crated and barrelled grapes with their layers of sawdust, apples, a few rotting cabbage leaves, and the warm feathered odor, loamy, sensual and vulgar, of live crated hens and pullets.

In the city now, along those streets still bare and barren, and on the cobbles, which had a swept, clean look, and past the doorway in old Prince's house where the murdered man was lying, life began again with its first spare and lovely notes, its lean message of a thrilling and vital joy—the sound of the hoof and the wheel along bare cobbles, the banging of tin, proud, harsh, and clangorous, upon the pavement, the sound of a foot, and a sodden voice, at once lost, lonely, and familiar. And within the houses also there were all these familiar, simple, and wonderfully poignant sounds which have never changed—the sound of doors that were opened, of windows that were raised, and the sounds of the first words spoken in the day—words of greeting or observation, quiet, familiar, and affectionate—the flat, casual, friendly Yankee tones.

And for Joe, who had seen all these things a thousand times, who had remembered them a million, this great vision of morning in America returned again and again to fill him with a sense of triumph, to restore hope, belief, and joy to his spirit, crushed in the horror of noon, drowning in the endless flood, the sickening immensity of amount and number, the dusty, murky, howling and annihilating chaos of the man-swarm, so dreadful in its power to drown out every leaping hope, all proud belief, that to walk along a mile of crowded pavement sometimes seemed like drowning without death, smothering without extinction, plunging into fathomless depths of grey horror and weary futility without hope either in the return of pride or any meaningfulness, and without hope even of the moment's pain, passion, and victory of death.

A thousand times he had seen this wakening of life, this restoration of light again to the immortal Earth, and a thousand times he had wakened for a moment just at this time—he had wakened in proud harsh brown, among dark woods, with the whole pure clarity of first light upon his window—square and instantly, through the possession of this minute square of light and a few sweet familiar sounds of life upon the streets, he had become a lord of the morning, an eye, a wing, a spirit that enhanced the earth. Instantly, with superb conviction, he seemed to inhabit life, to know all that men were doing at this moment, and his spirit soared exultantly, in a moment the horror of confusion, weariness, and staleness, the brutal drunken chaos of night, the desolation of cold harsh streets and of lights from which all brightness seemed to fade, and which burned through smears of blood against loud, sterile and encrusted browns, was forgotten: he saw nothing but triumphant morning, and it seemed to him that all mankind was bound together in the repetition of abundance, in a congress of simple and familiar acts, in a unity of rich and fruitful life.

The hoof and the wheel upon the street below now echoed down the streets of ten thousand towns, the familiar accent of one voice became the voice of morning throughout the nation. And now, too, up through the dark and potent browns of the house, up through warm glooms and misted beams of yellowed light, the fragrance of the kitchen was ascending: he knew the negress, Sarah, was at work, he heard the sharp and homely clatter of the pans, and smelt the first deep pungency of coffee, the thick sharp fragrance of frying sausages, the smell of bacon and of buckwheat batter.

Instantly, as if these elements of pure light, food, and morning had made the city a living and organic creature, he felt and knew the life that was going on everywhere around him: behind two hundred thousand brick and brownstone fronts these sharp ecstasies of breakfast were arising. He saw the rich men, the merchants and the bankers, rising in rich walnut glories, he saw their proud monied faces, bearded, or tufted with the decent pomp of sideburns: and these proud whiskered faces, these grave, thick, and sideburned visages, which seemed themselves to wear the solemn proper clothing of position, looked strange and ludicrous across the light of morning; below them he could see their rich and crowded rooms, now vacant, with a smell of woods and velvets, lonely, closed and odorous, in subdued morning lights whose yellowed sunbeams contended with dark browns, their crowded reception rooms, parlors, and the thick warm fragrance of conservatories, the lavish and bewildering confusions of cushions, canopies, crossed spears and Turkish shields: of bric-a-brac and their teetering shelves, of ferns, palms, potted plants and flowers; of ornaments of gilt and clocks below glass covers—enclosures of dark time, of gilded, crowded, brown, bewildering, precious splendor, measured in dark yellowshrouded morning quiet only by the small punctual ticking of a clock; and then Joe saw the servants, the proud wives, still bedded in their dark rich airless rooms, the chamber pots encased in walnut with thick marble tops: and then the girls, the lovely girls, the rich man's lovely daughters, the future wives of the counts and dukes, the travellers abroad, with their young, thin, lively, early Gibson-girl faces. They lay there in that proud and lavish brown like flowers that were alive and slept, they lay in all the casual and careless attitudes of sleep in lovely abandon and with printings of crisp rose nipples on their gowns, their fine heads bowed upon the sweet stalk of their necks, with arms slender and like satin, roped with floating hair, and with dewy sweetness on their lips: they were young, lovely and unploughed— as yet untainted by the vulgarity in which they dwelt—a promise of beauty, the curve and fecundity was in them, and the germ of harshness, sterility, arrogance, and bitchdom: as Joe thought of them he knew they lacked the curve, the depth, the deep throat-tone and warm feel and smell of dark, potent, loving Jewesses— they were incomplete, infertile, lovely only in their freshness, but the old fantasy returned that he would one day enrich and complete them, make them what they might become, "put," as he felt, "the curve in them."

Suddenly the deep toned clocks were striking out above the city the metes and measures of our mortal time, and when they thronged to seven, and their last surge trembled out upon the air, the year came suddenly into his mind with its miracle of "now": he heard the sounds, the present practical sounds of life upon the street with a sense of strangeness, magic, unbelief, and suddenly the proud potent words were ringing in his brain: "Eighteen hundred and eighty one," and as the ponderous bell-notes trembled on the air the words were lulled to a rhythm, they went ringing through his brain like proud ponderous strokes of time with deep urgency and golden reverberations and the rhythm that they made was "Eighteen hundred eighty now, and one; now, and one; now, and one; eighteen hundred eighty now, and one!"

Already his memory of past time, so vivid and particular, so fresh, was touched by magic and destiny: it seemed far and lost. He [Monkey Hawke] remembered the day only sixteen years before when some of Sherman's stragglers had come into Libya Hill; he could still see old man Foster sweating up the road between two grinning Yankee troopers; and he could still hear the roar of laughter from the soldiers as the Captain sniffed him, and then cried,

"Yes, by God—he told the truth boys:—Turn him loose! He's a nigger!"

In the proud presence of living time, below the ponderous and decisive strokes of eighteen hundred and eighty one, he saw it all, remembered all his childhood, but it was as if he saw it through misted and enchanted vistas, heard it, like faint spells of music, through a sea depth of lost time. Now "1865" made lean and lonely music in his ear: it was the young day of the earth, the child's age, the lost and lonely time, and suddenly Joe saw the faces of the lost Americans, but it was all as if they had been long in the wilderness, as if they were all lost and buried in another time, and as if all vestige of them had vanished long ago. He heard them like lost voices upon the dark and mournful air of the desolate South, and the sound of their tongues, the laughter of their throats, was as sad and broken as the memory of the rustling of a leaf, a memory of cowbells in the valley, a memory of a cloud that made its floating shadow in lost Southern hills a hundred years ago.

Walled, thus, at morning in deep, lavish brown, upon the lip and edge of bright actual time, Joe saw the lost South over again, as he had known it in his early youth. He saw it with the clear intensity of a vision, but dark light was on it: it was a lost world, and brightness came to it through sunken depths. Would it ever be morning in the South again? His powerful subtly toned imagination, which now saw places and events by color, mood and tone, reached all the effects of involved and subtle reasoning through some single telescopic tone of meaning, some forgotten songs of old lost time—cloud shadows floating on a hill, the frosty broken voices of the birds at dusk, a smokey lamp which cast its ring of tottering light into the darkness of a country store, a man walking down a road between the wide, dry sweep, the brown and brittle stubble, the dry bolled sterility of picked cotton—and the memory of these things evoked a history, a time, a past, more accurately than all the books of the historians.

Thus, now he saw the South, lost, lonely, and he heard the voices of negroes singing from the smoking lamp light of a little shack, and, as if evoking some fragment of a dream, he seemed to hear the stamp of boots far off, measured, rhythmic, the twanging banjo's notes, and a heavy rhyme of drunken voices: there was the smokey lamp light, the gloomy dark of country stores, the smells of gingham, cheese, and kerosene, and a wheel that creaked along a lonely road.

The voices of the South returned to him again—the voices of the poor whites, the little farmers, the mountaineers, the negroes—and these voices were all lost in darkness; it was dark, evening dark, and the vast and mournful desolation of the earth engulfed them. He heard them, far, faint, and casual, out of the smokey distant lamps of country stores; he heard them, lost and casual, for a moment, over the halt of a train: their feet milled and shambled round the yellowed drabness of a country station, their voices, soft, casual, and mean, were mixed with the soft panting respiration of the engine, the sporadic clatter of the telegraph, they were remote from all bright movement in the earth, and the luminous and attentive night engulfed them. . . .

Suddenly Joe turned to Gifford and began to speak to him in an excited and earnest fashion:

"Gifford," he said, "I want to be left alone by these bastards. I have come here to drink, laugh, talk and enjoy myself with my friends: now, God damn it, I will do it, and no drunken son of a bitch of an Irishman, no, nor anyone else, will keep me from it."

Gifford spoke to him quietly, in a mild, remonstrative tone:

"Oh, come on," he said. "Everything's all right. You take these things too seriously."

"Seriously!" Joe exclaimed, in a thick hoarse voice. "You're God damned right I take them seriously! Why are you here, Gifford? Are you here to enjoy yourself or not?"

"Why, of course I am!" Gifford said. "I'm enjoying myself. Aren't you?"

Two men had begun to talk to each other at the other end of the bar—they were drunk, they had never met before, and in their greeting now there was something belligerent, hostile, fearful, and boastful. As Joe looked at them, a kind of fury choked him, he began to mutter:

"Look at them. Will you look at the swine. The whole world to move around in, but do you think they can leave each other alone? We will now presently begin to hear some choice bloodthirsty talk of what bad, mean, wicked, rough-and-tumble men they are: O deary me now! Sh—!" he said in a mincing and sneering tone. Joe: (excitedly, passionately)

"—At this moment do you *know* there are millions of people all over the country talking to one another? What are they saying, Gifford? Could we understand them if we heard: Do you think so, heh?"

Gifford:

"Why, Goddamn it, man, you know the English language, don't you?"

Moreover, May's story, as she told it, was further complicated by these obscure references to "Him," by which however,
it was easy to assume she meant Prince because of the expression
of dislike and disgust with which she pronounced the word, and
other references to her own father whom she would mention in
the same breath as "Him," and yet in tones of endearment and
reverence. Thus:

"*Him*! Yes! and my father was as fine and decent a man as ever
lived. Never touched a drink after he was fifty! Yes! and by Jesus I
never heard him say a cross word to my mother in her life . . . as
fine people as ever walked the earth, both of them . . . and *him*! . . .
never missed a day rain or shine goin' to Mass for thirty years . . .
a real American . . . none of these dirty foreigners that you see
. . . that went the whole way through the war walkin' down the
street every Fourth of July with the flag on his shoulder . . . too
good to wipe his feet on the likes of *him*! Yes!" she paused, hoarsely
breathing. "I had the best mother that God ever created . . . as
sweet an' pure a woman as ever walked upon the earth. . . . She was
a saint if ever there was one . . . too good for this earth, I guess
that's why God took her."

May was sobbing hoarsely and convulsively now and it was obvious that the actors were deeply stirred, as they always were, by
these references to someone's mother.

"If she'd been here I'd a led a different life. . . . The last words
she ever spoke to me, I was sittin' right beside her bed holdin' her
hand when she died. . . . She turned to me with the *sweetest* smile
an' said, 'May. . . . Don't have nothing to do with a man unless he
means to marry you.' . . . If I'd listened to her I wouldn't be where
I am today. . . . When she died I lost the best friend I ever had. . . ."

May lapsed for a moment into a somewhat drunken revery. Then
she continued:

"Yes. . . . they're the best friends we'll ever have. . . . There's
nothing on earth as pure an' sacrid as a mother's love. . . . Am I
right, or not?"

The actors agreed warmly that she was right and in a moment

more, without transition, without a sense of contradiction, May had passed from this mood of sentiment to one of hard, snarling cynicism:

"Him!" she said contemptuously again. "Oh well, I might have known! . . . They're all alike. . . . All men ahhe! . . . When you know one you know them all!"

Here, Street objected mildly, saying that *he*, at any rate, was not like all other men, but May hushed him aside emphatically and cynically:

"Yes, you are! . . . You're like all the rest of them! You're all the same. There's no difference among you. . . . I know! I know all about it!" She nodded with hard drunken wisdom. "You're all looking for one thing. . . . That's all you want from a woman. . . . When you get that you're through with her. . . . She can go to hell for all you care."

For a moment she brooded before her with a hard drunken stare:

"All men are alike!" said May conclusively. "And every woman," she announced sensationally, "is a whore."

Again, there were protests at this, but May continued inexorably:

"Yes, they are. They may never do anything about it, but they're all whores at heart."—etc.

Joe, who had heard these people engage in dozens of conversations of this sort, was surprised now, as always, to see how solemnly such preposterous stuff was listened to, and how, in part, the actors seemed to give agreement to it. The fact that after her apostolation to the saintly purity of motherhood, and of her own mother in particular, May had passed immediately to a blanket indictment of all women as whores, did not seem strange or illogical to anyone. On the contrary, it fitted neatly into all the grooves of accepted platitude which stood with them for "knowledge of the world." There was not one of them who was not convinced that he was wise and knowing, and yet life seemed to have taught them nothing. His feeling veered sharply between pity, anger and disgust. At one moment he was sorry for them as one would be for foolish children, at another he was so exasperated at this silly pretense of knowingness, and glib unearthing of this welter of sentimentality and cynicism, both of which were false, that he could have taken them by the scruff of the neck to shake them. Again, he looked at them, and he hated them, for their lives seemed so cheap, mean, vain, and venomous—a foul compost of hate, slander, jealousy and cheap vanity: they stank in his nostrils, and his look embraced them with such loathing that his face was controlled by it, although he did not say a word to them, his glance said plainly: "You swine! You foul pustulant swine—you make me want to vomit!"

But often, when he was away from them, he seemed to get a more just and generous picture of them: he saw that these foolish and sentimental talks they had together were only replicas of the speeches they had had to say upon the stage—"God above!" "Better poverty with virtue and a good man's love, than all the tainted luxury your guilty passion offers, Rudolph Montague!" and so on. Yes! At such times he saw them again like people whose real face was sunk below a mask, and whose tongues were dumb although they were given many words to utter: below the mask the eyes of the actors seemed to look out with something dumb, hungry, and pleading—as if they did not know how to utter the words they wished to speak, or express the emotions that they felt.

The end of May's story was this: she had been discharged and put out of the hotel, she at length admitted, because Prince had found out she had taken a man to her room a few days before.

"The dirty old sneak!" she said. "He's been having me watched ever since I went in there: I couldn't turn around—if you went to go you-know-where for a moment," she broke out with an angry vulgar laugh, "there'd be one of them snooping around after you. . . . Now that's a fine job for a grown man, isn't it? How'd you like to do that for a living—chief Whiffer and Sniffer in a ladies' room?"

Suddenly she burst into a rich hearty laugh.

"You know what I did one day? I knew he was standing just inside—I said, 'It's all right, dear: I don't think much is going to happen to-day' and then—" she screamed—

"What?" shrieked Ella Blair—

"And then," she gasped, "I let him have it!"

They roared with laughter: Gifford bent over feebly, holding his head against his stomach, baring his blackened teeth:

"Was it a good one?" he asked.

"Oh!" she screamed. "It was a beauty!"

In a moment she continued:

"What if I did ask one of my friends up to my room? It's the only home I've got! Where's a girl going to receive her friend in a place like New York? You can't meet them out in the street all the time. I don't see anything wrong in that, do you? 'Evil be to [the one] that evil thinketh.'" The actors agreed with her warmly, but later on Ella Blair said to Gifford:

"It may be all right, but I'll bet May never took him there to say his prayers."

"Maybe she wanted to show him her embroidery?" Street suggested.

Gifford, as usual, was more charitable: he said surlily:

"I can't see whose business it is. If Prince was running a decent place it might be different. But everyone knows what kind of joint it is." He laughed a short and surly laugh. "God! but this is rich! They allow everything up there except arson and murder, and here they put a girl out of her room because she takes a man to it!"

And this, too, was one of May's causes of grievance:

"It's not as if I were the only one," she said. "At any rate, I've always acted quiet and decent. You all know that! I've never raised a row. But the things that go on up there would make a monkey blush. You can hear them running along the halls and slamming doors until five or six o'clock in the morning."

"Does Prince know about it?" Joe asked.

All the actors looked at him angrily and derisively, and May said incredulously,

"Does he *know* about it! Do you think he's blind?"

"Sure he's blind!" said Gifford cynically. "He can't see any farther than a tomcat in the dark."

"Let me tell you something," May said decisively. "He sees everything he wants to see. There's mighty little that gets away from *him*, I can tell you! Does he know about it!" she said contemptuously. "You should see him sometime when he's going over accounts with the cashier! Just try to keep a penny from him, and you'll see how quick he knows about it! One of the worst dives in town and him passing the plate and sitting in the amen corner every Sunday! Yes! and his own brother preaching sermons to them about the terrible conditions of vice and everyone knows he's half owner in it!"

Prince's brother was minister of a Madison Avenue church: he was a very wealthy man, and it was true that he was associated with Prince in many of these real estate affairs.

"God!" May cried bitterly. "I wouldn't trust the two of them together as far as you could spit! . . . Running a rotten joint like that, and then they have the gall to ask *me—me*!—to start actin' like a lady! . . . Wouldn't it make your tail want buttermilk!" she said vulgarly. "It's enough to turn the stomach of a goat!"

As often happens in such quarrels, Joe noted that the deepest cause of grievance was frequently obscured by her memory of a comparatively trivial circumstance. The fact that the hotel clerk had told her to "start actin' like a lady" before she was forcibly ejected seemed now to rankle in May's heart: she returned to this consistently and bitterly, and all her vague and almost incoherent references to her father and to the saintly purity of her mother, her insistence that she "came from good people," that her own people were "the finest folks that ever lived—everyone who knew them will tell you the same," and so on—all this seemed to conform to the same hurt, resentful, and stricken feeling of inferiority—some desire to establish herself before the world as in every way worthy of its respect, as in every way "as good as anyone," and the actors, who listened with grave and attentive faces, nodding agreement and approval from time to time, believed it too, and some were so moved, even to the point that they had tears in their eyes. And yet the same people, Joe knew, would later on make cynical jokes and laugh about these very things that moved them now—as if embittered by the mockery of their own sentiments, made more harsh and cynical by their own falseness. It was the enigma of their nature which he had seen so often and which disgusted and yet touched him. This was ridiculous, as everyone knew, as May was a woman of very easy virtue, and had more lovers than it would be easy to count. All of the actors knew this perfectly well, and May knew that they knew it, and yet so strong was her conviction at the moment, so consumed was she by the rush of her emotion, that she probably believed what she was saying.

During the performance that afternoon, she wandered about

backstage, refreshed herself frequently with strong pulls at a black bottle, got in the way of the stage hands and stood drunkenly in the wings, encouraging the actors audibly and affectionately with comments such as, "Good! It's a beautiful piece of work you're doin', dear!" laughing loudly in the wrong places, applauding drunkenly and with startling effect in the middle of a speech, or a tense scene, and sobbing hoarsely over all the bits of heavy and hackneyed sentiment she had heard so often.

Suddenly, May was discharged from the company. She was given her pay and her notice one Saturday night: there was no explanation beyond "Your services will no longer be required after tonight's performance." Further, when she returned to the hotel that night she was refused her key at the desk or permission to enter her room unless she paid immediately her bill which, with arrears for back rent, was in excess of two hundred dollars. She protested that she owed no rent. She said:

"You can see Mr. Prince about this: you know he has always taken care of this," to which the clerk answered stubbornly:

"I don't know anything about that. All I know is, I've got my orders. You can't use your room service until you've paid the bill."

Then the girl asked permission to enter the room in order to remove her belongings. The clerk told her she could not do this—that her baggage would be held until she paid the bill. May began to weep and threaten, she demanded to see Prince; she became abusive and profane and screamed:

"I know the reason the old bastard's done this! And so do you, you dirty pimp!"

She was then seized and forcibly exited from the hotel, still screaming threats and accusations.

On Monday, May returned to the theatre again and told her story to Ella Blair, Gifford, and one or two of the other actors. She had been, as they all knew, Prince's mistress, and it was understood that her quarters at the hotel were given to her, along with other concessions, rent-free. This part of it she admitted boldly, without much evasion, although with some sentiment, such as "You know what a bad time a girl has in this city alone. You know how hard it is for her to have a decent life, no matter how much she wants to," etc.—all of which was mixed freely with tears and the emotions of enraged womanhood, together with the intimations that the cause of her "shame" was Prince, and that she was an innocent girl before she met him. All of this, moreover, was in a somewhat pointless and meaningless fashion interspersed with apostrophes to her family—"As fine people as God ever let breathe," pugnacious assertions that she was a "lady," glancing around belligerently and saying—

"If there's anyone who says I'm not! If there's anyone that knows a thing against me—just let them look me in the eye and tell me so, and not go sneaking around with these dirty lies behind people's backs. I *hate* a hypocrite! A hypocrite is the lowest thing on God's green earth! *Him!*" she cried explosively and indignantly. "With his face of a little dried up monkey, pretendin' butter wouldn't melt in his mouth. We all have our faults," she said profoundly. "What I say is, none of us is perfect."

The actors nodded gravely, with agreement and understanding.

"What I say is we're all the better for a little yooman weakness. Am I right or wrong?"

They nodded.

"It makes us all more—*yooman*! Y'know what I mean?"

Again they nodded, signifying that they knew what she meant.

"I got my faults as well as any one," said May magnanimously. "But there's one thing no one can say about me: " 'Start actin' like a lady,' he says."

She paused and glared about her fiercely. "No son of a bitch alive can say I'm not a *lady*! I won't take that off of no one. Am I right!"

Again they nodded to signify that she was right. Joe and Street went suddenly out into the hall.

"If they say that, they're telling a goddammed lie, and they know it!"

III Even Such Is Time

Although this fragment bears the title "Even Such Is Time," it is unclear whether Wolfe intended to incorporate this material into "The Theatre" chapter of his projected book about Joe, or to use it in his earlier writings on "The Good Child's River." At the top of the first page of manuscript, he wrote "(For Chapter I (?)) Other Book (Beginning My Cousin Robert Sat—etc)."

As the curtain fell—a marvelously woven curtain which was said to have cost five thousand dollars, which really did cost two, and which, among other sensational novelties in this new theatre, had been a subject for the public gape and stare for at least a week—Joe hurried to his dressing room, tore off the costume that clothed the movements of Atticus Apple, and got ready for the street as quickly as he could. He tossed his flaxen wig upon the table, and ruthlessly shredded away the extravagantly tufted sideburns that framed his gaily painted mask. Then he swabbed roughly at his face for a moment with a greasy muslin cloth, and began to dress himself in his own garments. Outside the actors were going along the passage to their rooms and as she passed his door Ella Blair called out to him:

"Joe: Are you coming with us tonight?"

"No," he yelled, craning at his cravat. "Leave me alone, won't you?"

"Yes, indeed!" another voice, probably Gifford's, said. "You've got to leave Poppa alone now: the chee-ild needs him."

Joe made no answer, but continued dressing: Slyly, quietly, they opened his door, and stood there, a pool of bewildered faces, a circle of smiles, regarding him.

"Begone you fools!" he said, still without a glance at them. "I've got no time to waste on you tonight. Begone, I pray thee."

He tugged hard at his cravat: then, with gravity, he turned to look at them: when they saw his face they burst out laughing. He was surprised.

"Huh? What is it? What's the joke?"

The others made no answer, but Ella Blair said,

"Just look at your face in the mirror."

Joe stared into his mirror for a moment: his raddled visage still kept the brilliant stiffness of leaded lash and brow, and his rude swathings had left his face barred with bright strips of color, harsh, zebraic.

"Father's all broke out in a rash, isn't he?" said Gifford. "I never knew it did that to you."

"Father missed three cues tonight. I know that much," said Ella Blair. "Look here, Atticus, are you going to do it again? I'm glad you don't have a baby every day."

"Begone! Begone!" Joe said in a lofty and indifferent tone: he rose, thrusting on his coat, and fumbled for the buttons.

For a moment longer they regarded him, silent, grinning, sly and attentive. The girl stood with arms akimbo, plump, observant, with a woman's smile, ambiguous, tender. "Look at him," she said in a quiet and confidant tone. "Trying so hard to be cool and calm when you can hear his knees rattling together. "Here, you poor thing," she said. "I'll button you." She fastened the buttons of his coat for him. "You *men!*" she said, with pity, with patient mockery—"God, but you're wonders, all of you! Right now, I'll bet his wife will have to baby him along with the other one when he gets home. Go on, baby! Go on home to mother now. She'll look after you." For a moment more, a fleeting fraction of a second, she allowed her warm and loving palm to rest carelessly on his shoulder and in that moment of communication he knew instantly that he could have her when he liked.

"Oh," said Gifford in a mincing tone, "but you women don't know what we suffer at a time like this. The first time it's so hard," he whined. "No woman could ever know what we go through!"

"You get out of here! I'll kill you!" he yelled, and scampering in frisky play and laughter, they left him. In a moment more, after a final hasty glance around him in which, unconsciously, the sensitive nostrils of his full straight nose trembled and dilated as they breathed in that thick familiar odor of the dressing room—warm, oily, mixed of suave buttery creams, pigments, alcohol and ether, with a faint tinge of escaped gas—he jammed on his hard derby, with the deep flaring curve of the brim that was then in fashion. For almost a year, at least nine times a week, he had observed a punctual ritual of entrance into this room, of departure from it and return to it as he came and went from the stage; and he had never entered it without a feeling of strong exultancy and never left it without an obscure and wordless feeling of regret. When he had entered this room for the first time, the theatre had been new, and every object and detail of the room's appearance and equipment— the line of shelves that ran along its sides, the varnished partitions of thin latticed wood that separated him from the occupants of other similar rooms, the dressing tables, the mirrors, the chairs— had glittered with their fresh unused newness. Now everything in the room looked old and worn: the shelves were obscured behind a thick drapery, mixed, undulant and gay, of hanging costumes, the woods had darkened, the tables with their litter of small jars, pots and bottles, looked worn and mellowed, even the rich and oily compost of cosmetic odors seemed to have worked and engrained themselves into material objects.

"Father missed three calls tonight. I know that much," said Ella Blair. "Look here, Atticus," she continued, with an abrupt but good-humored gravity. "Are you going to leave that poor girl in the lurch again? And *what* a place you picked for it, too!"

"I know!" said Joe, laughing. "You kept saying 'Speak, Atticus, speak!' and I didn't know what the hell to say: I had forgotten whether it was Act One or Act Four."

"I could have killed you!" Ella said. "I kept yelling at him to 'Speak, Atticus' and all he could do was to goggle at me like an idiot! And there I was with a shadow on mah womanly honor, and the audience hanging on the edge of its seats to see it if was true, and still the damned fool wouldn't speak!"

"Why, Atticus!" said Gifford reprovingly, "I'm amazed! If you're going to have these lapses of memory, son, you've got to pick a place where it won't hurt."

"Go on!" said Joe. "It was an inspiration: it came to me all at once. I don't believe it hurt a bit! They were eating it up: you could hear them hold their breath. Everyone's heard so much about the virtue of Esther Craig, it would be a relief to hear she had a vice! Why!" he exclaimed, with an air of sudden conviction, "We ought to try it. It'd give us a new lease on life. The girl's too damned good to live: I believe the public's getting sick and tired of her. I believe we'd be good for another year if we just tawdried Esther up a little with a few good juicy sins!"

Slowly, sadly, Gifford shook his head from side to side.

"Did you ever hear such blasphemy!" he said quietly. "It's a wonder God doesn't strike him dead! Our Esther with a sin! By heaven, no!" he cried with sudden energy. "Let it never be said," he continued piously, "that the great American peepul would support a spectacle that glorified sin or condoned the degradation of an innocent woman."

"Hear, hear!" said Street softly.

"No, Atticus," Gifford continued, after a moment, "You speak in the ignorance of your youth. The public is paying to see a virgin, my boy, and by gum!" he said emphatically, "that's what we're going to give them. Am I right, Ella?"

"Of course you're right," she said. "If they've got to come all the way to the theatre to see one, we're not going to disappoint them."

"If we do," said Gifford with a sudden touch of grimness, "we'll be walking the cold hard streets before long looking for a new engagement! And God! How cold and hard these streets can be when you're out looking for a job!"

"I know they are," said Joe. "I've been there."

"You've been there, have you?" Gifford said. "Hell!" he continued with gruff contempt. "You haven't been properly weaned yet. I'll bet you can't even tell me how many cinders make a mile. You haven't even crawled across your first trestle yet. You couldn't tell me how long it would take a good ham to walk from Albany to Troy.—Now could you?"

"No," said Joe. "You've got me."

"And he calls himself an actor!" Gifford said. "What does he know about our art! He still thinks it's natural to eat."

IV Aunt Hugh

*Written in the upper left-hand corner of this manuscript was
the notation "For London." Wolfe was probably referring to the
projected chapter "England—Aunt Hugh," recorded in the
outline for Joe's story at the end of the third ledger (see outline at
the end of Appendix B, section II). The "Aunt Hugh" material
was written in three separate blocks of manuscript in the third
ledger; these blocks were out of order and had to be pieced together
like a puzzle. As with the theater segments in "Even Such Is
Time," Wolfe wrote several portions of the text on the sides of
pages. This method of writing may reflect Wolfe's growing
agitation and confusion concerning the focus and outcome of his
work. Once again, the third-person point of view is used, but in
this fragment a more formal presentation of ideas seems to be
established.*

*The discussion between Joe and Harriet about the creation of a
"true" woman character is unique throughout Wolfe's works. It is
particularly interesting in the light of his attempt to create such a
character himself in Esther Jack (see fragment, item 824, from
The Web and the Rock manuscript).*

Esther's aunt, Harriet Bergman, was a Jewess of the Goldsmith
branch of the family which had settled in England. The family
was rooted all over Europe, but it was generally agreed that Holland was the source of all these other migrations. The family had
a remarkable solidarity: they corresponded with one another constantly, visited relatives in various countries, and always knew what
was going on in Holland.

Harriet Goldsmith had been in the East End of London, and
was the daughter of a jeweler. Curiously, the family had come to
America in the Seventies, and the jeweler had set up a business
in Grand Street, on the East Side, but he failed either to make a
success of his business or to develop a liking for the new country. After two years he took his family back to England where he
remained the rest of his life. Harriet had thus known Bella and
Rebecca Goldsmith in America when they were children (she was

several years older than either), but she had come to know them even better, later, in Holland.

Harriet's father, the jeweler, had been more of a poet than a business man: he loved music, he was a very fine violinist—When he died he left scarcely enough to pay his debts and the expense of burial. Shortly after, Harriet had married a young Jew named Bergman: he, too, was a musician—an orchestral violinist. They had one child, a son, born two years after their marriage: three years after their marriage Bergman developed tuberculosis, and from then until his death two years later, he was a bed-ridden invalid. Harriet was thus faced with the necessity of supporting her family: she had a quick and humorous mind, a light touch, and a great gift for telling a tale—she decided to earn her living by her pen, and after a time got a commission from a publisher of popular fiction to produce at so much a word. The pay was miserable—for a complete novel she at first got less than one hundred dollars, and the amount of work she was required to do was stupendous: in one year she had written as many as six books. In spite of the brutal haste with which she had to write, the stories are written with remarkable grace and naturalness and with a degree of skill that grew constantly and was in itself an extraordinary instrument. It is true she had only one plot: on the instruction of the publisher—a completely illiterate man whom she called "The Butcher"—she always told the same story, but in each retelling she gave it a remarkable tinge of freshness and variety. The story was this: it was always about a girl who was poor, young, beautiful, and unhappy. The story invariably opened among scores of the most sordid poverty and squalor, in which the purity and loveliness of the unfortunate heroine blossomed like a lily from a dung hill, and the story invariably closed in a scene of opulence, romance, and titled gentry. Although the girl apparently was poor, there was somewhere in the world an immense fortune and a title waiting for her, and tied up to that future and that title was a beautiful young man. Sometimes he was simply a young lordling going around the world seeing that justice got done to beautiful girls (in this case there was always an accidental meeting in the first chapter when they dash into each other coming around a corner in the slums, and he knocks the apples from her hands and then cracks his head against hers as he bends to help pick them up: this is always very comic and charming, and it always paves the way for the scene later on, when the plot thickens, and he looks at that beautiful face again, saying: "Strange! I could have sworn— But no! impossible!"—and that final satisfying flash of illumination when he leaps up shouting, "By George, I have it! Apples!").

If, however, the young man is the "guardian," everything is very beautiful and tender: there is always a bitter misunderstanding and a quarrel, and she goes away, but he always finds her at the end, and tells her that "at last he is free to speak."

Finally, there is always a power of darkness, a kind of continuing villainy, a sinister force which plots to do the girl out of her fortune and her title, or keep her from ever getting it: this force uses as its instrument a beautiful but evil creature dominated by jealousy and the determination to possess for herself the handsome hero—her name is the Lady Maude, or the Lady Gwendolen, or the Lady Elinor—there is always a smashing scene between her and the heroine, and a smashing end to villainous plots.

This, in its essential elements, is the plot that Harriet Goldsmith used in over sixty novels.

As time went on, and as the long list of her books grew longer, she discovered a curious fact. She discovered that books which made use of the "guardian" motif were almost always more successful than those in which the young lover appeared accidentally in a chivalric performance of roving knighthood. In these "guardian" books, with their long drawn-out and melting tenderness, their spotless purity, their sweet and secret heartbreaks, their nobilities and renunciations, the delicious agony of their inevitable misunderstanding and the delicious gulp gulp quality of discovery and renunciation, there was a quality of titillation, and the public found this irresistible: they lapped it up with a maddened hunger, and the more they got the more they demanded another helping. In her earlier books Harriet always contrived to make the guardian a young man in his twenties. To her surprise, as she went on, she discovered that her readers preferred an older lover—that, in fact, if the man were in his late forties and had greying hair, the purity of his relation to a heroine of twenty was touched with a greater poignancy. In fact, there was something in this relation of a grey-haired man who strove to maintain a fatherly relation while his heart was aching with love, and of a girl who strove to be filial while she was heartsick with a more romantic feeling that exerted a hypnotic fascination over readers, particularly over women. Accordingly, in her later books, Harriet invariably made use of these two characters—the young girl and the aging but not-too-old guardian. When Joe remarked on this and asked her if she knew the reason for it, Harriet, an admirable and rather stern-minded woman, whose spirit was founded in an utter honesty, said:

"Yes, I know the reason, but I am not going to tell you what it is—you would think it obscene. But I tell you this: there is not a more consciously pornographic writer in England than myself, and, with the exception of one book—which is the only moral story I have ever written—my reputation for propriety is unassailable. Spinsters with parrots adore me, the Scotch let their daughters read me after church, I make wet Sunday afternoons in Leeds endurable for thousands of honest people—all over England constipated ladies read my books—and compared to me Casanova was a colonistic pamphleteer. . . . It's funny, isn't it?"

She wrote under the name of Hugh Strange, supposing there was a more popular prejudice among the public in favor of male writers than of female ones. The name of Hugh Strange is today forgotten by most readers, but at this time (1888–1890) she was at the peak of her renown and success, and was one of the best known and best paid writers in England: she was as well known, for example, as Wilkie Collins, and made more money; she was certainly better known to the general public at this time than George Meredith, and vastly more prosperous.

It is a curious fact that although in basic originality of plot, characters, and development of story her books were in no important degree superior in quality to those of Mrs. E.D.E.N. Southworth, the Duchess, or any one of a dozen other women writers of the period whose production and sale were enormous, the belief was rooted in the mind of her public that she was vastly superior to these writers—that she was, in fact, a remarkable writer whose work was distinguished by a high literary quality. Thus, her readers, in addition to getting just as complete a satisfaction from her story—with its perfect finality of rewards and punishments, its completely romantic triumphs of virtue—as they could get from any of the Duchess' books, were rewarded also with a thrill of cultural superiority, a conviction that their tastes were "above" those of ordinary readers of cheap fiction: they could even say, with the indifferent loftiness of a superior cultivation—"No: I never read Mrs. Southworth. Really, I can't read such stuff. . . . I should think you'd get tired of reading it: when you've read one you've read them all. Why don't you try Hugh Strange? It costs no more, and you'd really be reading something worth-while."

It was an extraordinary achievement—this adroit infusion of housemaid fiction with a literary quality—and it was not the result of any chance: it was managed and determined as deliberately as the plot of her story, it was one of the best assets, one of the elements of her success. No one, probably, reads the novels of Hugh Strange now—with the exception of one remarkable book of which we shall speak later—but an examination of some of these volumes today yields an astonishing result: the reader turns page after page with fascination and interest, and in his excitement and surprise over the freshness, the naturalness, the observing and accurate tone of the dialogue and setting, he is likely for a time to forget the mechanical and meritorious artifice of the story. At first, the reader wonders "Why have these books been forgotten? Why has the name of this writer passed into oblivion?" And he is convinced for a time that there has been a serious error in critical judgment, he is thrilled with a sense of discovery and determination to right this wrong which has been done to the memory of a talented writer.

Then, as he continues, he will see that the books got the reward for which they were written, that no real injustice has been done to them, that their essential quality was not worth saving. It is as if the writer had been furnished with every gift except the important one—the deep and passionate seriousness of an artist. All of the garments of truth are here—a wise and accurate observation of men and living, a superb ability to record the look, the shape, the forgotten words of men as they walked in the streets of life with a living and magical touch, but the truth itself is lacking: the garments clothe a dummy figure. This is a judgment that Harriet Goldsmith herself would at once have sanctioned: she was a brave, honest, and resourceful woman, and she had no illusion about the final merit of her work.

But what are the exact and admirable qualities that the reader discovers in her books even today? They are chiefly an observation of life in the East End of London, a power to make poor people talk in their exact and natural accent, a description of the lives, the dress, the speech and gesture of the humble which surpasses, in certainty and skill, the work of any other writer of the time who dealt with like scenes. In every book, there are a dozen or more casual supplementary figures who walk across the scene, furnish it out with living time, and give a strong semblance of reality to the cheap artifice of the story: frowzy drunken women, abusive shrews, ferret-faced cockneys, barmaids, river barge men, gutter urchins, pawnbrokers, housemaids, thieves and femmes—a vast and varied army of the poor, the lowly and unkempt, who are made to live in a few lines as surely and naturally as if the whole source and mystery of their lives were rooted in the author's brain and heart so that she could instantly produce them, living and speaking, in any circumstance or situation. Yet, it is obvious in these books that the author of these superbly living minor figures always keeps them carefully in check: certainly the full and naked brutality of their lives, their lusts, their cruelties and woes was known to her, but she never gave it, cleverly measuring reality to the tender palate of a sentimental public. Thus, with these interesting and abundant minor variations, her story repeated itself through five dozen books.

There was one startling exception. In 1886, two years before the visit of the Barretts to England, and at a time when Harriet's reputation was so firmly established that a large and devoted British public eagerly awaited her new books with the blissful certainty that they would always be the same, there appeared, without warning, with the explosive suddenness of dynamite, the remarkable book to which she gave the title: *The Heart of Mile-End Mary*.

The excitement and consternation which this book caused on its appearance was one of the most interesting facts in the literary history of the time. From her own public, after its preliminary stupefaction, there rose up a howl of bewildered agony and her mail, which always contained several letters from her following, now grew fat and thick with hundreds of other letters which heaped reproaches on her. The general tone of these letters was as follows:

"We have read your books for years and there was no writer whose works we cherished more. When we opened a novel in which your name was printed it was always with the certainty that it would contain nothing that could not be read with perfect propriety by our daughter or any other modest young girl. Your latest book, however, has been one of the most painful surprises we have ever experienced. Why, why did you write it? —you who have given the world so many beautiful and elevating stories, you who have brought joy and happiness and an aspiration for finer things to so many thousand readers? Dear Mr. Strange, you have a great talent, a great power for doing good in this world: please, we beg of you, do not ever again misuse this great and beautiful gift as you did in writing that ugly and revolting book *The Heart of Mile-End Mary*. The fact that such terrible things as you describe in that book may actually exist is no excuse for your having written about them: the sewer has no place in letters. All of us see enough of the sordid and unpleasant things in our daily lives, we don't want to be told about them in books: when we open a book we want to read something that will take us out of ourselves and show us the real beauty and joy of living. Therefore, please give us no more books like this last one, our dear author: return to your former manner and give us some more beautiful novels like *The Young Duke's World*, *Lord Barrister's Heir*, or *O Saw Ye Not Fair Innes*."

This was the general and more moderate tone of most of the letters, but there were others which denounced her violently and announced the sender's intention of never buying her books again.

So much for the effect of the book on Harriet's own established public. Its career with the other and more critical reading public was even more sensational. For the first time in her life Harriet found herself considered seriously by the cultivated minority—the appraisers and judges of literary values. The book aroused a storm of comment, debate, protest, denunciation, praise, and critical disagreement comparable in tone and intensity to the fierce discussion that was to take place a few years later, upon the appearance of *Jude the Obscure*. For the most part, the critical opinion was bitterly hostile. McCaulay remarked that few spectacles were more edifying than that of the British public in the throes of one of its periodic attacks of morality, and the attack from which it suffered at this time was particularly virulent. The more conservative critics, while sometimes admitting the power and skill with which the book was written ("it is deeply to be regretted that such a talent was not expended to a higher cause"—etc), denounced it with the most violent abuse—"a filthy and revolting book," "a disgusting travesty on English womanhood: could anyone in her right mind possibly imagine that any English girl ever behaved or talked as the unspeakable Mary behaves and talks in this book?" One savage reviewer remarked:

"It seems the afflicted population of this island is to be spared nothing in this year of terror—not even the latest and most malodorous benefits of French civilization. Here is naturalism at the lowest and most unnatural state it has yet achieved: the refuse of the gutter is explored with a patient and degraded thoroughness that describes the movements of the smallest maggot and misses the glimmer of the largest star. Even a cesspool may catch reflections from the moon, but the cesspool of this author's mind has never been disturbed by the tiniest gleam. Monsieur Zola at his dreadful worst has never approached the triumph of obscenity that defiles these pages; the master is dethroned; he must give way— the great struggle for the supremacy of the sewer is at an end, and the victor is—a woman! Le roi est mort! Vive la reine!"

Some of the notices demanded the instant suppression of the book.

There was, however, a more moderate group of critics who, while deploring some of the things in the book, defended others, and felt, on the whole, that the attack had been needlessly violent and the charges of indecency exaggerated.

Finally there was a small group of younger and more "modern" critics and writers who espoused the book with passionate enthusiasm, hailed it as a masterpiece, and answered the charges of hostile critics with counter-charges of hypocrisy and prudery, with juicy references to British morality and an utterly unfavorable comparison of the life of the artist at home with the life of the artist in France.

In this stormy turmoil, at whose troubled centre she suddenly and unexpectedly found herself, Harriet kept her head admirably. She neither allowed herself to be overwhelmed by the violence of her attackers nor swept off her feet by the fervor of her defenders, who willingly might have established a cult with Harriet as the object of central devotion. But she looked at this latter group of young people with a good-natured but somewhat skeptical eye, judging shrewdly and correctly that their enthusiasm for her book was not so great as their enthusiasm for their own opinions and their desire to flaunt conservative tradition, and that within six months they would have forgotten both her and her works in their zeal for some other stalking-horse of rebellion and liberation.

Moreover, she knew very well that when the excitement had died down she would be exactly where she was before, forgotten by the great and faced in addition with the hard necessity of winning her way back into the favor of the unenlightened but profitable audience she had formerly made her own.

This, finally, was a very serious matter: she might view the commotion she had caused in the literary frog-pond with humor but she could not trifle with the harsh necessity of living which, as a widow with two children to support, she had known so well and so long.

She expressed her feeling at this time accurately in the following letter to Rebecca:

". . . I assure you it has not been as hard as you think. There have been some very bitter words in high places, but a snob might cherish being snubbed by a duke, and certainly not every hack can say he has been cursed by the *Times*. Of course, the kind words of my partisans have been pleasant, too, and help to make life easier. . . . I am very grateful to them all, but really, what worries me most of all now is my bread-and-butter people"—this was her name for her following. "I must retrieve my position with them quickly—I've got to do something 'very beautiful' or all is lost. . . ."

She did something "very beautiful" within six months. It was called *It Fell Upon the Mountains* and it was a triumphant success: all was forgiven and Harriet was restored to the heart of her great family, where she continued to flourish the remainder of her life.

But the uproar had been so great that her anxiety over its effect on the public that bought her books became acute: concern was practical; it always kept the butcher's bill in mind; she had no intention whatever of becoming the martyred saint of a cult. Accordingly, when the excitement was hottest she wrote several letters to the press, in which she took issue with assailants and defenders alike, and sharply and tellingly pointed out, citing word, page, and instance, that her new book had in no respect violated the most rigid standards of propriety—that it was in every respect as "moral" as any book she had ever written, that in it the good were gloriously rewarded, and the evil terribly punished, and that the real course of its plot and narration was in every essential identical with the story in every book she had written. At this, her savage critics and her zealot defenders paused, took note of her assertions, and discovered at once to their utter stupefaction that it was all exactly as she had said. Abruptly the excitement ended, the matter was dropped, her name was heard on the lips of the mighty no longer, the show, to her vast relief, was over. The book was forgotten, its name and memory passed into oblivion. It has been only in recent years that it has been recovered for the reader, and this recovery has been chiefly due to its publication a few years ago in one of these libraries (of which there are a good many) of "the world's best books." The recovery has been apt and good: we can now appraise the book at its real worth, and it remains, in spite of its final and essential fault, one of the most interesting books of that time and in many respects one of the most remarkable books a woman ever wrote.

The Heart of Mile-End Mary is a book about a woman by a woman: these are the two primary facts about it, and before we discuss it further the following conversation between Joe and Harriet may be useful. One morning after his usual late breakfast, he was sitting in the back parlor reading while she answered letters and attended to her household accounts. Suddenly he looked up from the book he was reading, and rather abruptly said, "Harriet, has anyone ever written a good book about a woman?"

For a moment she did not answer him, meditating his question as she continued to write. At length she said:

"Do you mean a good book about a woman or a book about a good woman?"

"Oh, there are plenty of books about good women," he said, "and bad ones, too. I don't know what you'd call this one," he said, lifting the volume in his hand. "The woman in it sins, so I suppose she is a bad one; but," he added in a somewhat exasperated tone, "she is the most saintly, virtuous, sinned-against sinner I've come across in many a long day. And unlucky!" he exclaimed. "I've never heard anything like it in my life! If there was just one small pox germ floating around in the entire universe, that girl would walk right out and get it!"

"What is the book?" asked Harriet curiously. He showed her: it was *The Return of the Native*.

"Oh, *that* one!" she said. "Well, that poor girl never had a chance anyway: every big gun in heaven was pointed straight at her, and if they wouldn't go off themselves, the author pulled a revolver from his pocket and shot her."

"Yes," said Joe, "and if that misses he hits her with a brick. God, but that girl has a bad time: if that's the way they treat the women over here I should think they'd all be trying to get passage on the first ship over to God's country."

"But all the same," said Harriet, "isn't the book good? You can see him laying plots and pitfalls for her all along the line, you don't believe anyone ever had such a constant run of disaster without having a little good luck here and there—it's not in nature, it seems deliberately unfair and contrived by the author—but in the end doesn't the book convince you? The man's average is all wrong, he has no sense of probability, fate doesn't thwack people with the unvarying precision of a pile-driver—but in the end, they *do* get thwacked, don't they?—That's why the book convinces you in spite of everything: he tells the truth about human disaster."

"Yes," said Joe. "It's a good book. But it's not the kind of book I meant when I asked the question. This is a good book with a woman *in* it—he calls her a "true woman faithfully presented." I simply mean a book about a woman: do you know the kind of book I mean?"

"Yes," said Harriet, "I think I do. Did you ever read a book called *The History of Moll Flanders*?"

"No. Who wrote it?"

"A very great writer named Daniel Defoe."

"I've heard the name," said Joe, "but I never knew he wrote anything besides *Robinson Crusoe*."

"He wrote a great deal besides that," Harriet said, "including two or three magnificent books about women. *Moll Flanders* is one of them: it's the life story of a woman who is made by chance a prostitute. But what it really is—is the story of the sensual woman, and the sensual woman is the woman you are talking about."

"Oh, no!" he protested. "I never said that."

"But it's true just the same—because the sensual woman is the real woman: she's the one you want to read about."

She paused a moment slowly.

"And really, Joe," she said, with an air of the deepest conviction, "I think she is the only woman worth writing about."

"Then why don't you write about her?" he asked.

Again Harriet was silent for a moment. Suddenly she laughed:

"I'll tell you why," she said. "I'm not man enough! I would to God I were!"

"Then you think only a man could write such a book?"

"It looks that way," she said. "Only men have succeeded in writing them so far." She paused reflectively. "I can't think of a single exception: wherever a woman has been written about truly, a man has done it. We seem unable to write the truth about ourselves."

"Go on!" he said. "There have been plenty of women who wrote the truth about themselves: what about Jane Austen?"

"Oh, that's an entirely different matter," Harriet answered. "Of course, that woman was a superb artist, and what's more she wrote and thought like a woman: you won't find *that* combination often. She had a deep and truthful vision of the earth and of the people in it: she saw them in drawing rooms, at parties, by the fireside, in genteel domestic privacy—but that is the way they were given to her, and I suppose that is as good a way of seeing them as any other. She shows us woman as a comedian, a social minx, a contriver—there was never a writer who describes better the social comedy, with its intrigue, cruelty, humor, and its deep, but guarded, emotions; she is the most feminine writer that ever lived and in one sense, she knows all about women. But she could no more have written the kind of book you have in mind than she could have built St. Paul's. And the distance that separates her from *Moll Flanders* is greater than the ocean that separates you from America."

"What about George Sand?"

"She comes much closer to it," Harriet replied. "But she certainly proves my argument that no woman can ever do it truthfully and successfully. With her you find woman as the lover and mistress: in a way she writes about the sensual woman as frankly as any woman has ever written—but then she is always romantically mixed up in it herself: she appears under various disguises in almost all her books (she wrote forty or fifty of them)—but then she can never see herself clearly, she is a sort of female Byron, a magnificent woman who believed in the eternity of all her passions for three months at a time. All of her work, her entire life's work, is really a sort of triumphant vindication of a romantic personality, a pageant of the person she believed was herself in a hundred different poses—but she, too, was far from writing such a book as you have in mind. At one of these Byronic moments she exclaimed: 'My heart is a graveyard'—and do you know what one of her former lovers said when he heard it: 'No—a necropolis.'"

"Then I don't see what you mean by the sensual woman," Joe replied. "How would you describe her?"

"The sensual woman is the woman who never changes," Harriet said. "She is the woman who is always the same."

"Is there such a woman?" said Joe. "I thought the accepted notion was that she is never the same."

"Yes, I know," said Harriet. "But haven't you found, Joe, that the accepted notions and the true fact hardly ever agree? One thing we learn as we grow older is that almost all the maxims that are given us as gospel truths when we are children are false in the light of experience. For example, the French are not romantic, the English are. I give you my word it's not restrained, we Jews do not love money, and you Yankees are certainly not a practical people. In the same way, women are not really variable: they are the same yesterday, today, and forever."

"In other words," he said, "human nature is always the same?"

"Not at all." said Harriet. "I never said that and I don't believe it. That is another false maxim. Human nature is certainly not always the same, it changes constantly—particularly masculine human nature."

"You think, then, that men are more variable than women?"

"Most certainly," she answered. "If I am sure of anything I am sure of that. There have been hundreds of kinds of men—in every generation there is a new kind. But there has only been one kind of woman. A man is a great provider of creatures, a woman only one: a man is a poet, a philosopher, or a child. In every age he unites himself with some image of belief and worship. He extends his own experience and suffering to embrace mankind, he has had a thousand schemes of salvation, and he has believed them all. In less than ten centuries here in England since the Norman Conquest we have had a dozen types of man: At one time he is the knight, at another the rebel, at another the poet and prophet, at another the man of science. At one age he is going to save the world through chivalry, at another through conquest, at another through rebellion, at another through patriotic nationalism, at another through conformity, at another through patriotic internationalism, at another through religious belief, at another through skepticism. At one time he swears by tradition, restraint and the so-called classical virtues, at another he is in bitter revolt against it and in favor of any form of liberation; at one time it is God, at another Evolution through natural selection; at one period he is corrupt, urbane, cynical and sophisticated, at another he swears by the simple life, the natural man. And all this on one little island within eight centuries!

"Don't you think it's incredible? Suppose we could go back, live ourselves in all these years, do you think we would find it anything at all like history? Suppose all the dead that are buried on this little island could swim up out of their graves. Why, history is a childish fairy-tale! It's like going back through the wilderness, through growing forests and swarming jungles of forgotten things, of moments and utterances that are lost forever. It is the danger lurking at the bottom of the sea."

Harriet's thought of all the buried dead swimming upward from their graves awoke in Joe's mind countless men.

"And yet you men have the effrontery to call women changeable!" she said indignantly. "Why, by comparison, we are as fixed and immovable as the Rock of Gibraltar!"

"Well," said Joe, laughing, "what have you women been doing all that time? Have you not changed, too?"

"Not a bit!" she said emphatically. "Not one tiny little bit. How can one know, how can one tell," she continued earnestly, "what men were like even three hundred years ago? When I think of them now, when I try to imagine them as they were, I find everything about them strange and remote. They are the ghosts of the universe: the lonely of heart, the unfixed, the phantasmal wanderers. The sound of their voices is lost, the words they spoke and the way they spoke them—all is lost. Listen!" she said, and for a moment they paused as hooves trod briskly by on wooden blocks as through the moist and heavy air, the sound of London, murmurous, fogged, illuminable, came to them. "The sound of the horse is the same as it always was, the look of the horse is the same, his movements are the same. But what of the movements of men?"

"I am sure they are also the same," said Joe.

"Then try to think of the knight as he stood looking out the window! Or can you see him with his back turned to the fire, with his hands behind him! Imagine men five hundred years ago suited in chains with legs crossed, or try to think of London merchants in the evening with their families. Can you see the citizen as he passed by in the street? Did his arms swing as he walked? Can you see the crowds—the plain, obscure, forgotten faces of all these dead men—as they moved through the streets of the town? Are they not lost? I have seen so many men and watched their movements, I know how they walk, sit, and gesture: I have seen them in a thousand places, in a thousand casual postures, I know the whole style of their movement— A stick for one hand, a pocket for the other—but the movements of dead men long ago are lost. I cannot see them."

"But what of women? Do you know any more about them? Can you imagine how they looked any better?"

"Yes. I know exactly how they looked. I can see them in any situation because their bodies are shaped for movements that never change: they have the hills, the slopes and valleys of the earth in them. They have always been the same."

"And yet they change the style of their dress with every season."

"They change their styles but they do not change their souls. The reason they have a new style every season is not because their souls are variable, but because they are immutable. Do you think that it is for themselves that they change these styles? Tell me: if all the world was female (which God forbid!); if the last man on it died, do you think the women would bother to dress up for one another? Do you think that these ridiculous and obscene little kidneys called bustles, which they hitch on to their rumps nowadays, were invented because of some wayward fancy? No! Where there's a buttock there's a bustle, and where there's a bustle—there! the eye of man will follow also. . . . Isn't it true?"

"Perhaps it is, but it is not very moral."

"Morals! What does a woman care for morals. She has no more morals than a rabbit. She believes what she is told to believe: what she *really* believes is another matter! But if the masculine fashion in morals is for modesty and the blush of shame—then she is modest and blushes. If the fashion is for boldness and lewdness, then she is bold and lewd. Nowadays you hear a great deal about our modesty and innocence—we are affronted by female nakedness—yet if men decreed that classic nudity was the thing, we would walk down Piccadilly without a stitch to cover us."

"Even the Queen?"

"Yes, the Queen, too—God bless her! . . . I tell you, Joe, they have never changed—I can see them eight hundred years ago locked up in chastity belts, or trussed up later on in steel corsets, or loaded with lace, ruffles, ornament, wigs, powder, or in a plain gingham dress—and they are the most constant creatures that ever lived: I know exactly how they have always been and they are not a bit different today from what they were in Elizabeth's time. All the variety and changeability of women, of which you have heard so much, is really a constant quality: it is like the vanity of nature which rises, falls, and returns upon itself. It is seasonal and rhythmical, it has ten thousand shades and subtleties, but if all these could be known and understood it would be seen that there is nothing bewildering or capricious at all about woman's character—that it moves with the logic of nature: like a river which changes with every second and yet is always the same, or like the earth which changes with the seasons and yet is always the same, or like the earth which changes with the seasons and yet remains the earth. The real woman has always been the same because she is the sensual woman."

"But you haven't yet told me what you mean by the sensual woman."

"Well, then," she said. "The sensual woman is woman between her shoulders and her knees. It's woman in the position that becomes her most, to which her body is naturally adapted—on the flat of her back with her knees up and open. What that woman really feels and desires has never been uttered, but I assure you it has nothing to do with all the pretty notions you may have about her."

"You mean it is ugly and revolting."

"No: it is not ugly and revolting—except perhaps in the minds of wicked and sentimental people, and most people are wicked and sentimental. But it is terrible, and it frightens us, and that is the reason we avoid it."

"In what way do we avoid it!"

"By not speaking of it, by not recognizing it, although we all know that it exists. I have found this to be true: we avoid what we know is so. It is not only the knowledge of death that men avoid, but the knowledge of life. The common notion is that most men are superstitious and ignorant—people think it is this that enslaves them, and that if knowledge could be given to them they would find freedom. It's not true. There is more knowledge in men than we are prepared to admit: in all of us there is the knowledge of life and death.

"Around us all we feel and know the presence of these destinies: it is as if there were great walls about us which we recognize but behind which we do not dare to look—not from ignorance and blindness but because we understand so well what is there. And all men know this: in a way all of us know all that can be known. . . . Have you ever been in a crowd, Joe—just an ordinary crowd such as you find every day in the street—and felt suddenly between yourselves and all these other men a flash of recognition and communion?

"Sometimes you may have stopped to listen while some speaker harangues them: then perhaps you all laugh suddenly at something he has said, and in the little pause that follows there is a moment of silent and complete wisdom among you. Then you go away, the crowd disperses, you never see any of them again, but in that moment you have come to know them. Have you ever had that happen to you?"

"Yes," he said. "That has happened to me often."

"It means, I think, that we all know the human destiny," said Harriet. "We are not duped by all our lies and our follies, so blindly as they say we are. No. There is something deliberate about the fables we tell ourselves: we believe them because we want to believe them, we must believe them or face the ruthless horror that bends over us."

"Do you think that that is what we do with women, too? Is our belief in them a deliberate fable?"

"Most certainly," she answered, "and nothing could more easily be proved! . . . Do you suppose, for example, that anyone—even the critics who harped so much upon the purity of English woman-hood when they tore my poor *Mary* into tatters—ever believed in the reality of the heroine of most of the present fiction? That absurd impossible sawdust doll with her blushes, her ridiculous modesty, her impossible purity of thought and speech! Do you think that there was ever anyone under the sun who resembled her? Do you believe in her reality?"

"No," he said. "Of course not."

"Of course you don't! Good God!" she exclaimed. "She doesn't even possess the reality of a good wax figure at Madame Tussaud's. It's like being bitten with a set of artificial teeth. And everyone knows it! Everyone knows that no woman was ever like that. Yes—and this woman we are talking about—the real woman—everyone knows what she is like, too: she is really not a mystery to anyone—but no one has ever dared to describe her."

"Then why don't you?" asked Joe.

"I can't," said Harriet. "I tried it—and I failed."

"In your book."

"Yes."

"The critics seemed to think you had succeeded—from the howl they made."

"But I didn't. I came as close as any woman could. But it is not in us to tell the truth about it: even when we know what we want to say, when we open our mouths something else comes out—a lie, a fairy-tale. There's something in us that won't let us tell the truth even when we want to: we're afraid to give ourselves away."

"Tell me, Harriet," he said abruptly. "How much of that book was true? Was any of it based on your own experience?"

"Yes," she said. "A great deal of it—most of it. . . . I don't know why I wrote it," she added, after a moment's pause. "I have never been able to find out."

"Neither did your devoted public, did they?" he added.

"No, neither did they. Everyone who had read my other books was astonished. That book almost ruined me: I had worked like a dog for years to build up a reading public, and then, almost over-night, I lost them. But, really, I did not do it deliberately. I was as much surprised as anyone by the book. When I started it I thought it would be exactly like the others. The strange thing about it is that the story is practically the same. Mary does not marry a titled guardian as she does in the other books, but she is about to marry a fine young fellow in the city who is making money hand over fist when the story ends. Furthermore, although the book was denounced for its obscenity from one end of the country to the other, there is not one word or phrase in it that anyone could object to."

He was surprised at this. "That was not the impression I got," he said. "I remember it as being extremely frank and outspoken."

"Yes—that is the impression they all got: but there was not one single word in it that could give offense. I challenged the critics to find one: when they tried, they failed."

"Then how do you account for the scandalous impression it made?"

"It was solely and simply a matter of implication. It was the presence of that wall of silence of which I spoke. It was not in what was written down that they took alarm but in what was suggested. . . . Do you remember a scene in which the mourners are assembled around the widow of the dead man before the funeral?"

"Yes. I remember very well. That was one of the scenes that aroused the greatest protest, wasn't it?"

"Yes. In that scene I showed poor people as they are when someone dies. They are filled with a horrible eagerness and hunger for death beneath their mourning: they gloat over the body as if they were present at a feast."

"But, as I remember that scene, you did not convey that by suggestion—you actually said it."

"Oh, yes. That is really written down into the book. But that was not really the thing that made the public yell. That was the thing they picked on, but you will find that people protest at one thing when they really mean another. The thing they protest at is usually not at all the thing that alarms them."

"What was the thing that alarmed them?"

"It was the relation between the man who died and his wife. . . . Do you remember that?"

"Yes," he said. "I remember it very well."

"How did you feel about it?"

"Well, I suppose I felt more or less as the other readers did. . . . There was something very disturbing . . . almost terrifying, about it."

"But *why*? Why did you feel that way? Was there actually anything on the printed page that justified your feeling as you did?"

"No," he admitted. "I don't think there was. As a matter of fact the woman is represented as a faithful and loving wife who had struggled against poverty for years and taken care of her husband with her own earnings when he was sick."

"Yes. That is certainly what is written down. Then, what was it that you felt, Joe? What troubled you?"

He was silent a moment. "Well," he said, "I think I felt that the woman was really glad when her husband died. I felt somehow that she was waiting for him to die and that at times she hated him because he hung on for so long a time. And it seemed that he knew she felt this way about it and was mocking her—hanging on as long as he could in order to baffle and disappoint her."

"To disappoint her in what way?"

"I don't know. But I felt that she was a healthy and passionate woman and that she wanted to get rid of this invalid and to . . . to . . . start her life over again."

As he uttered these words he was surprised to find how painful and difficult it was to utter them, and how something in him twisted about like a trapped animal and made him avoid words that were even plainer and more painful for him. But what he was now really thinking with a sense of horror and bitterness was this: "She wanted that poor devil to die so she could get some husky brute to go to bed with her—someone who could 'really satisfy her,' as they say! Really satisfy them! God! has there ever been one of them since the beginning of time that any man could 'really satisfy?' Poor, weak, delicate, fragile, helpless little woman! Isn't it just too bad about them! And yet there's not one of them—even some little ninety pound wench—who could not make a wreck out of John L. Sullivan any time she wanted to!"

And now it seemed to him that he stood before a vision of life that was naked and terrible, and that was adorned with no assuagement of glamour and romance to soften it. Each word that was uttered now came like the confirmation of a dreadful and prophetic dream; he was sure now—what he had only dared believe before— that he would hear for the first time from the lips of a woman a confession of desire and hunger that was without mercy, memory, or deceit. He waited: Harriet's long dark face brooded in an intent and sombre thoughtfulness. In a moment she spoke.

"Did I ever talk to you about my marriage?" she asked.

"No: I don't think I ever heard you speak of your husband over three or four times."

"Do you remember him?"

"Not very well. You know I only saw him once or twice when you came to New York; after that you took that trip to Colorado. When you came back to New York I was on tour."

"That was just a few months before he died. Of course, you never knew him as he really was. He was sick of living when you saw him—already a dead man! And yet he would not die!" She spoke these words with a sudden and passionate emphasis that had in it almost a quality of indignation, and he looked at her surprised.

"It must have been a very painful experience for you," he said. "I remember you seemed very unhappy at the time."

"Yes. I was unhappy," she said bitterly. "But not for reasons anyone might suspect. I was unhappy because he would not die."

And now he had it, and he could not speak.

"I thought you loved him," he said at length.

"Yes. I did love him," she said. "When I married him I was mad about him. That first year of our marriage was the happiest time of my life. When he was taken sick two years later it seemed I loved him more than ever. I seemed to have the strength of forty people, I felt equal to any task; I thought I could endure any hardship if only he would get well. And I believed I could make him well: I loved him so much I felt that I could blow the breath of life back into him, heal him, give him part of my own strength. I had the baby to take care of as well, and I had our living to make. It was as hard a task as anyone ever had to face but I was glad to be able to do it. No one will ever know what I went through that first year. We were living in two rooms in Bloomsbury, we had no money for a nurse, I took care of him hand and foot, and ground out fiction at the rate of three thousand words a day. When I had to go out to take what I had written to the publisher, I got the woman downstairs to come up and stay with him. And then every night I worked in the front room until three o'clock in the morning. Then one day I saw that he was going to die—that there was no longer any chance of his ever getting well. The doctor told me that his right lung was completely destroyed, and that the left was being eaten away inch by inch. His coughing became incessant: at night when I wrote it made a kind of horrible accompaniment to my work. My heart and my mind were sick with horror and nausea and a sense of uselessness, but I had to keep on covering page after page. Sometimes I would go back and sit with him, there was nothing I could do, he was coughing his life up at every breath, and he clutched my hand with a kind of desperate energy as if by holding on to me he could somehow hold on to life. He looked at me with an expression of silent terror in his eyes I shall never be able to forget as long as I live: his eyes seemed to grow larger and brighter as his flesh withered until at last there was nothing left of his face except these two great living eyes and his big Jewish nose. His hands were nothing but claws: as he clutched my hand his hot grip seemed to burn right into the marrow of my bones and his great staring eyes pleaded with me with a kind of silent terror to tell him it was not true that he was going to die. But when I tried to tell him this I could not because we both knew it was a lie. Now I was obsessed with the thought of his death: there was not a moment of the day when I could escape from it. Everything on earth seemed colored by death and horror: it got into the sunlight, into the smell of the air, into the look of the streets, the houses, and the people. Then the winter came, and you know what winters here are like: the choking fogs began early in November that year and lasted on into the New Year. And then the rain, the sodden wetness, the gloom and misery seemed to soak right through the brick walls of the buildings and to pierce right through my heart. It seemed to me the sun would never shine again, I could scarcely believe it had ever shone before, and as I looked at the people swarming through the streets of London, enduring all this wretchedness, dirt, and misery I hated them. And yet I did not hate them so much as I hated my own life and my home. It seemed to me that such melancholy and despair as I had was greater than anyone else had ever known before, and for the first time it seemed to me I had become so morbid because I was a Jew, and I began to hate myself for being a Jew and to wish that I were something else. And then I began to hate him because he was a Jew and would not die: I got so I hated to be near him, I hated the sight of his large ugly nose, his white withered face, and his little rotten emaciated body. He had become so weak he could hardly raise himself from his pillows—yet at times a horrible and impotent sexual animation would seize him, and he would attempt to embrace me, fondling my legs and breasts with his hot claw like hands, kissing me with flabby hurried kisses, breathing his hot foul breath upon me, and entreating me to lie down beside him on the bed. At first I tried to do as he wished, but I could not go on with it: I got sick, nauseated and would have to leave the house.

"When he saw this he suddenly understood how I hated him. Then he began to hate me: the light in his eyes that had been so pleading and terrified was now full of a hard and bitter mockery, and hate. He hated me because he saw I wanted him to die, and because I was young and healthy and he knew that after his death I should lie down with another man. I was afraid to be alone with him: there was something so naked and terrible about our silence— it said everything more plainly than speech could ever say it, and there was no escape from it. Every day his body seemed to waste a little more, his eyes got brighter and larger, and they stared at me with a constant bitterness and hate. He seemed to be able to read every thought that flashed across my mind, he knew every desire that consumed my spirit, and although we never spoke of it there was nothing I could conceal from him. His little Jewish smile seemed to mock at me, I knew he had set himself to thwart me by living as long as he could, and his hatred seemed to give his little scrap of life a terrible tenacity and endurance.

"Sometimes I would be driven almost mad by physical desire. I began to look at men in a way I had never before observed them. I looked at their arms, their legs, the set of their shoulders, their hips and buttocks—if they looked anything like my husband, if they were small, pale and Jewish-looking, I despised them: if they were tall, strong, fair and English-looking I lusted for them and dreamed they were lovers. In my mind I committed whoredom a hundred times—sometimes with an ideal Du Maurier sort of nobleman, and sometimes with soldiers, carters, butchers, laborers, handsome young Anglican clergymen, and police constables. And often in my desire I lay with the doctor who came to see my husband: he was a young Scotchman, a tall, lean, rugged man. He had a high boned face with sunken cheeks and a square jaw, he smoked a pipe and there was always an odor of tobacco about his clothes: his hands were large and long and if our fingers touched when I helped him lift my husband in the bed my knees got weak and my legs began to tremble. And my husband knew what I was feeling and desiring and he looked at us both with eyes full of hate, although I spoke scarcely a word to the doctor and never looked at him directly. And I think he too saw what was going on at length, because when we were all together in that room there was no escape from that terrible and naked silence, it seemed to tell everything without mercy or evasion.

"One night I was writing at my desk when suddenly I felt that if I did not get out into the street at once I would go mad. The fog and wetness had got into the house and it seemed to give the horrible old plush furniture and the curtains a disgusting and suffocating odor. I went to the door of my husband's room and listened, he seemed to be asleep: I told myself I would just go out for a little walk of ten minutes—I thought I would just go as far as Bedford or Russell Square and take a turn about the square and come right back. When I got out into the street I saw that the fog had come down so thick that one could see nothing: it was impossible to see even the houses just across the street—it was a real 'London Fog.' The fog was yellow and heavy, and it blotted out the earth and deadened all sound like a fall of heavy snow. Once or twice a cab went by me in the street: I could not see it, but I could hear the horse's hoofs as they passed me as if they had been wrapped up in layers of felt. And when I passed under the street lamps the gas made a great murky yellow flower of light. Sometimes people would pass very close to me: they emerged out of the fog so suddenly I could almost have touched them before I saw them. Their steps made no more sound than if they had been walking on thick carpets and they disappeared at once into fog and total silence.

"The fog closed in between me and that accursed house immediately, and when it did I felt that I had escaped forever and need never go back to it. It seemed to me that this fog which would be death to him was life to me—I felt a sense of joy and mystery and power such as I had never known before. The entire magnificent and mysterious earth seemed ready to receive me: I felt it below my feet, I felt it all about me hidden but waiting in the fog. I felt London there like a mighty and glorious presence, and my spirit swelled with such a feeling of exultant power and triumph that I seemed to embrace all London, and then to embrace all England, all the earth.

"I could see London, and then I could see the dark country out beyond, the fields, the forests, the hedges and the roads of England in the dark. I could see a hundred little trains as they rushed across the earth with their momentary flares of fire and smoke, and then I saw there in the dark the immortal and exultant coasts of England broken with splendid flashing lights and stormed at by breaking seas. I felt the whole earth under me as if it had been my ship—yes! even the whole continent of Europe beyond—and it all seemed to have been framed for my joy and glory. As in a dream I seemed to inhabit the earth, to be its brain and centre, and to be rushing toward a meeting with some mighty lover, who was waiting for me. Yet all this time I was only a poor half-demented wretch walking through fog past all the dreariness of Bloomsbury, along the illimitable distances of London streets.

"At length I came to Oxford Street and walked along it until I came to Regent Street. I turned down Regent Street and walked to Piccadilly: a man passed very near to me; he looked at me and I returned his look with a bold and lusty stare. He disappeared, but in a moment he came back and spoke to me. He was a young man, tall and fair; he had a little moustache and I think he had been to the theatre. He wore a long overcoat with a fur collar and he was dressed for the evening. He said he had rooms nearby in St. James and he asked me if I would go there with him. I said that I would: we went there, he was very nervous and embarrassed—he told me later he had not had much experience in accosting women on the street, and that he had spoken to me on a sudden impulse—that was the reason he had come back after he had passed me. I think this was the truth: he was certainly very much surprised to find anyone like me—I must have seemed far different from any street woman he had ever spoken to, and he kept saying in a somewhat dazed manner that it was extraordinary.

"For my part, now that I was faced with just the situation I had so often imagined, I had become as cold and calculating as a rattlesnake. The hot desire I had so often felt seemed to have left me, but I was more than ever determined to go through with this thing. And so far from feeling remorse or regret I was filled with eagerness and impatience: I wanted to consummate this act of physical infidelity at once because I felt I could in this way at once establish my freedom and independence, and also pay off some of that score of bitter and ruinous hate that I felt toward my husband. As for the young man, I was merely using him as a convenient instrument to help me achieve what then seemed to be my destiny—I think he felt something of this, and was terrified by me. Poor fellow! It must have been like being compelled to go to bed with one of the Greek Fates or Furies. I have thought of him often since, I would not know him if I met him, I stayed with him that night until two o'clock in the morning—far longer, I suppose, than he wanted me to stay—for I think by the time I left he was really terrified. He could not understand what I was or what I was about, but he did see that I was not the typical prostitute: when I got ready to go he did not know whether to give me money or not—but he could not quite look me in the face and pay me; so he put a guinea on the edge of the table quickly and muttered something incoherent. I snapped it up, I assure you, as if my life depended on it: I was not ashamed to take it, it was money I was proud of. Then I left him.

"When I got out in the street, the fog had almost disappeared. The air was still heavy, wet and misty, and strong wisps and sheets of fog were drifting through the streets like drowned seals and all at once the mystery and the glamour seemed to have vanished with the fog, I felt unutterably weary and sad all at once. I saw a hansom going by. I stopped it, got in, and told the man to go to Gower Street. When we got there, I got out and paid the man his fare and waited until he drove away. The street was completely bare save for the cab, and the sounds of the horses' hooves were like the sounds of time, and when the cab had turned a corner and the street was empty there was nothing but the wet and heavy pavements, the gas street lights, and the houses staring at the street. I stood for a moment on the step and it was like looking down into forever.

"In the front room upstairs the gas was blazing brightly. I remembered I had turned it low: I waited on the stairs and listened but there was no sound within the house but the sound of silence and of time. Then I went upstairs softly and opened the door.

"He was standing in the centre of the room facing me, and the door which I had opened as slowly and quietly as possible seemed to have opened as an apparition. He was no longer flesh and bone: already he seemed to be transformed into an unearthly substance, corrupt but immortal. The color of death was on him, he did not seem to stand so much as to be borne up, supported by some inhuman and demoniacal vitality. Only his eyes were living; they burned with a reptilian glitter in which was a depth and eternity of hatred such as I had never before witnessed. The whole lost flame of his life seemed to go out into that look of hate, and as I saw it my own hatred welled up to meet his: I stood at the door and answered him and as I did he saw instantly, because it was written in my bold and triumphant posture, in every atom of my flesh, what I had done. He took a step toward me and as he did I raised my hand which held the coin the man had given me and flung it at him. Instantly a scream of hatred and madness so horrible and unearthly it might have come from a spirit damned in hell was torn from him, he plunged toward me with his fists raised over his head and as he did, a torrent of blood burst from his mouth and nostrils at the same moment. I ran toward him, and I think at that moment I felt the deepest and wildest sense of pity and regret I have ever known. I caught him in my arms as he fell, but I think he was dead before I got to him: I lifted him up and carried him to his bed, he weighed no more than a bundle of dead and rotten sticks. It was a wonder he could have had so much blood in him. The moment I lay him on the bed I knew that he was dead, and all my hate and lust had died with him. And I bent over him and wept bitterly."

"Because you were sorry for what you had done?" Joe asked.

"No. Because I remembered how much I had loved him at first, and because it all seemed so long ago and with a different person. The thing that makes me weep is the memory of time that can never be brought back again. I was not sorry. We are not really sorry because our lives go wrong. We are not sorry because we made mistakes. We are only sorry for these things which we did feebly and half-heartedly. Whatever in us has burned out fiercely, whether love or hate—whatever we have done because we could not help doing it with a whole heart—we do not regret. The great, the unspeakable crime against life is not that we have lived mistakenly or badly, but that we have lived cautiously and half-heartedly, and without belief. I know that now!

". . . And that's the story." She paused, and as he was silent, she continued. "Do you think a woman who could act like this was a monster? We are all monsters, then."

Appendix B

FRAGMENTS OF PROJECTED

CHAPTERS FROM

"THE OCTOBER FAIR,"

"THE GOOD CHILD'S RIVER," AND

THE WEB AND THE ROCK

1   Fragments from "The October Fair" Ledgers

This is one of the earliest fragments of Esther's recollections of her early life, told in the first person. It appears in the ledger shortly after Wolfe first copied Esther's "melody": "Long, long into the night I lay thinking how I should begin to tell my story."

O God! if I could turn time backward like a clock! Once upon a time, there was a tiny little girl, and she was a mighty sweet lovely little girl, too, and "O Daddy!" I said (I could hear it ticking in his pocket). "What is that?" "Daughter of Des-o-lation," he said. (O he was so wild and beautiful, you would have loved him!) "That is a watch, and that keeps Time. . . . And if it stops!" he said in a strange wild whisper, "Time Stops! Gone! Ended! Done for!"

(Here he snapped his fingers, staring at me in the strangest way till I got frightened): "No more time!" I was so frightened I began to cry, to think that time would stop.

To think that time would stop! O God! if it only would, or if we could run life backward like a motor car. Now there are bells again, how strange to hear the bells in this great city: now in a million little towns small bells are ringing out the time. O my dark soul, my child, my darling, where are you now, and in what land and at what time: O ring sweet bells above him while he sleeps, I send my love to you upon those bells.

God! what a tragic lot we are! to keep time ticking out our lives in our vest pockets, to put time up in great bells in a tower, to print time in vast letters on the sky so we can look up there and be reminded of our death. I've got a clock here ticking in my breast, I've got a better clock than any you can buy: it's beating out in love for you, it's telling me I've got to die: it beats so hard I think it's going to stop. I wish it would.

This brief episode deals with Joe's shrewish sister, Auntie Kate, based loosely on Aline Bernstein's real-life Auntie Gert, with whom Esther and Edith lived for a short time after their father's

death. Wolfe wrote this below a note that reads: "Auntie Kate:
She would drink all kinds of patent medicines instead of booze.
Esther, Auntie Kate, Uncle Ed—the Jews and the Christians."

"That child looks just like a Jew," she said. "Do you know where your father is?" she said. "Well, I'll tell you where he is. He is in Hell, being punished for his vile sinful wicked life. He is being burned with flames of fire."

Sometimes he would come up to my room late at night and wake me.

"Sh-h!" he whispered. "It's your sinful uncle. Are you ready to go to Hell?"

"Yes," I said. "I'd love it."

"Do you ever think of anything except your belly?" he asked.

"No," I said. "I think of it practically all the time."

One time she caught us and she was furious.

This fragment recounts Esther's courtship and engagement to a
young man at Harvard who died prematurely. Wolfe periodically
refers to this material in his outlines as "The Boy at Harvard."

But, so far as there can be any critical design and story in these reveries which, touched off by some chosen word, or made suddenly luminous by some buried connotation that we cannot fathom, Mrs. [Esther] Jacobs at this moment was thinking of the following incident, which had flashed swiftly through her memory as she told the story of her uncle: At about this time, when she was sixteen or seventeen, she had been engaged to marry a young Jew who was a student at Harvard University. It is probable that these two young people were not deeply in love, although she told herself now that they were; but they were very fond of each other, and had known each other since childhood—they belonged to that wealthy and cultured community of Jewish people that establishes itself in a great city, and maintains itself from one generation to another through all the growth and swarming change of the city's life. The "engagement" of the boy and girl was probably more or less tentative, it was something that had been suggested and fostered by members of the two families, who would have been pleased by the marriage, but who would not have made a very stubborn resistance if the two young people had changed their minds. Marriage, at any rate, was years away: the young man was to attend the law school for three years after his graduation from college, and then he must establish himself in his profession—everyone, including the boy and girl, realized the many possibilities of new changes and formations in their youthful plans; but in the middle of his senior year at college the boy had suddenly died. Now, of course, as she thought of it, her whole relation to this boy seemed much more definite and decisive to Mrs. Jacobs than it really had been: she was convinced that their engagement was rigidly fixed, and that she should certainly have married him had he lived.

That year, she was thinking, I had lived with Uncle Bob and Auntie Kate, it must have been just the year after Daddy died, I guess I was about sixteen. God, I was a beauty, I was just like peaches and cream, you never knew anything like it in your life, I'd have knocked your eyes out! So then when I asked Auntie Kate if I could go with some of the other girls who were going she said no, I couldn't go without a chaperone, I wasn't going to fly around by myself like a little chippy, not if she knew it! Gee! she was mean to us, she did the most dreadful things after all the promises she made to Daddy, I don't see how anyone could act like that to their own flesh and blood: so then I almost had a fit when I thought I wasn't going to get to go, I cried so about it, and I went to see Bella, and she said, "Never mind, darling, you're going just the same: you'll go if we have to strangle that old bitch," and then she went to see Auntie Kate and they said the most dreadful things to each other, I got so frightened!

Auntie Kate said she wouldn't let her brother's child be hauled around the country by a dope-fiend and a drunkard, it was the first time I knew what was wrong, poor Bella cried about it later, but she had her way, she was a wonder! But—God, the nerve of that woman saying these things to Bella, a hell of a lot she cared about her brother's child, didn't she? When she used to go away and leave us in the house for days without a bite to eat, and then spending all the money Daddy left us, it makes you sick! God, these Christians are a swell lot, aren't they?: they do such nice things to each other, I'll take my chances with a Jew any day. So then I got to go and Bella got the loveliest clothes for me, we went around for weeks looking at materials and then we made them ourselves. God! I was excited, I'd never had so many things to wear before, it was the first time I'd ever been away like that and when we got there it was so lovely: it was along in June sometime and everything was still green and beautiful, and as we walked across the Yard they were bringing out the Japanese lanterns and there were all the young fellows and their girls, and he was walking along with me, and we passed some of them and he whispered in my ear, "You make them all look like a crowd of washerwomen, Esther," and God! I was proud: he took Bella and me up to his rooms for tea, and he smoked his pipe, and he had all these pennants, and guitars and fencing foils, and he had an enormous champagne bottle with a ribbon tied around it and some beer steins with things written on them and some whiskey bottles on the mantel with candles stuck in them, and Bella said, "Well, well! I *am* surprised! What a drunken young man you are!" and Gee! it was so funny, he sort of leered at us and tried to look so wicked, the poor kid! I don't think he'd ever had a drink in his life, but God! I was impressed, I just. . . .

This fragment comes near the end of "The October Fair" manuscript. It is interesting to see how many themes and melodies Wolfe incorporated into this brief passage. Wolfe made Esther thirty-nine in this passage, which begins in 1925.

Mrs. Esther Jacobs was fair, she was fair, she had dove's eyes; and in all the world there was no one like her. Strange time, dark time, strange tragic time was flowing by her like a river. Delicate time was ticking out its small sharp pulse upon her wrist; but she had the flower face. The ponderous strokes of time are surging in great towers (*one* two three four), but the element threads the bones of buried lovers. . . .

11   Fragments from "The Good Child's River" Ledgers

Ledger 3, pp. 48–52, presents this note about Esther. It seems to deal with the similar kind of night terror that she experienced in the "Esther" chapter, and perhaps Wolfe intended to incorporate it into this material.

Esther

She seemed to be three people. She could feel her child inside her, and she seemed to be a child herself who bore this child, and then she thought she was another person who stood apart and saw them both. (Her dislike of her physical appearance too.)

In her sleep the old terror of her childhood—the black terror that brought her awake screaming at the presence of something dark, nameless, ruinous—had now returned. Only now this terror did not come with dreamless sleep, as when she was a child: it came always with a dream and always the dream was the same. In this dream Esther watched herself enter one of these long streets of brownstone houses of which New York was chiefly made: the street was empty save for herself, and the strange brown timeless light of dreams was over everything. Before her, right and left, without a break, without a difference, with the monotony of insanity, the brownstone fronts stretched away—each with its high stone stoop, its high angular regularity, its tall bleak staring windows. Nothing moved here, nothing stirred, there was no sound of life save the sound of her feet upon the pavement. As she advanced along the street her terror grew, because she was searching for the house in which she lived and could not find it: it seemed to her that she had lived in one of the houses in this endless street, but now she did not know which house it was.

She did not know what meaning this dream had—it was before the surmise of the analyst had been imparted to readers—but she was sure it had to do with her grief and distress, and she felt, wordlessly but profoundly, that the life in which she was caught and the deepest desires of her spirit were alien to each other.

This fragment, which appears in the final pages of ledger 3, recalls Esther's successful attempt to have Bella buried in a Jewish cemetery.

"What's the name?" he asked.

"McLean," said Esther. "Mrs. Beatrice McLean."

The man laughed harsh and short:

"You come in here with a name like that!" he said. "To a synagogue! You try to tell me that anyone with a name like that could be a member of this congregation?"

". . . I know about your case," he said suddenly. "The woman went outside her own religion. That was the way she chose to live. Very well. That is the way she must die, as well."

This fragment appears in ledger 3. In An Actor's Daughter, *Aline Bernstein makes reference to the beloved nurse who cared for her mother in the months before her death.*

The Russian Nurse

Where she came from, where, finally, in what lost cell or shoal of the memorial man-swarm she was lost forever from them, Esther never knew. In her memory the woman emerged and vanished with the same complete abruptness: for a year before her mother's death she was with them, white, tall, a music of powerful curves, passionately beautiful. After her mother's death she vanished: they tried to keep her but she would not stay. For years, whenever Esther went downtown to the great shopping and amusement districts near Madison Square, she always had some sense of hope, an imminence of expectancy, that one day among the millions of moving faces she would find her. But she was lost.

Her name was Anna: they called her Sister Anna—her full name was Anna Sur. One day, however, when Esther had spoken to her, she paused and said abruptly, kindly and gently,

"You must not call me Anna any more. Not if you lof me. Do you lof me?"—her tone was tender, droll, insistent.

"Yes," said Esther. "I love you, Anna. . . . What must I call you, then?"

"You must call me by my *real* name after this."

"I thought Anna was your real name," Esther said. "What is it?"

"My real name is *Annushka*—for those who lof me. Now, *you* must say it," she commanded.

Esther tried to say it, but failed to pronounce it correctly: then Anna made her say it many times until her pronunciation was better.

"Now you must always say it to me just like dot."

"I'll try but it's an awfully funny name—Annushka!" said Esther, laughing.

"Vait! You will see!" Annushka said with a knowing and mysterious air. "It will not be so funny later."

"But why do you want me to say it?" Esther asked. "I think Anna is a nice name!"

"Because de ozzer means a different t'ing," Annushka said.

"What does it mean?" said Esther curiously.

"It means Anna, but it means something besser, too. It means to say 'Anna—my leetle darling!'"

As she uttered these words, she smiled in a droll, eager, and comically cunning manner, and Esther burst out laughing because this great strong woman should want anyone, particularly a child, to call her "my little darling."

But what Annushka had said was true: the name, which at first had seemed so foreign, so difficult and unnatural, soon came smoothly and readily off the tongue, and it had, particularly when uttered by the thin small voice of a child, a tender and familiar quality which the other name did not possess. Soon everyone in the house was calling her by the new name, and it was obvious that Annushka was enormously pleased by the change.

Esther thought Annushka one of the most beautiful women she had ever seen. The child had an unerring perception for whatever was strange, rare, and beautiful in the form, design, color, quality, and texture of men and objects—the shape of a leaf, the stamp of a coin, the set and pattern of a garment, the texture of cloth, the cut of any small rare ornament, as well as bold, rare, beautiful designs and harmonies in lines and colors. In her the rare gift was innate, sourceless, unlearned: few people ever have it, most who have must come to it through toil and painful error. She always knew what was beautiful; she never paused at prettiness, which is a kind of thin belief, a semblance snug and cozy, a rootless pattern, a congruence of thin agreements, fixed, obdurate, a dramatic monotone, which most men must cherish out of want and impotence, and which, accepted, must shut out the quality of strangeness that is the living heart of beauty. However—such stamps of custom as "the American girl," "the Gibson Girl," "the Follies girl,"—and all the others, dark, fair, brown, blonde, light or middling, but forever the same, whether on magazine covers, show-posters, in "society" stories, or tooth-paste and constipation advertisements. . . .

On p. 501 of ledger 3, this poem was written.

Under a timeless sky, over a timeless and unvisited earth
forever traversed on bright wheels, the immensity of the
    solid
continent of earth below me:

"A little farther, yet a little farther,
O my child! follow along the footpath
that my steps have made, for we
shall come out at the level safety of
the beach."

    The way was long, it was so
perilous among the rocks, my breath
sobbed out with all my fear and labor
there among the rocks, I heard the
howling of demented winds, and far below,
the cruel moaning of the sea among the rocks.

    And yet my feet had taken me where
no other feet but his had ever gone. I was
the last that lived above that broken wreck
of ship: had not my toes bent in to
grip the faceless stone, had not my
fingers clung to places that no other hand could grip
    Father of seacaves cold

    "To the place of the long and level beaches,
the wide shining and unbountiful sea

"To the place of the inland earth, the
good home smell of earth, the sea borne orchard smell
The apple tree the singing and the gold."

*On the last page of ledger 3 is an outline in Aline Bernstein's
handwriting that gives a chronology of the places she stayed at the
various stages of her life. This is an indication of the lengths
Bernstein went to assist him while he was writing about her life.*

Born 34" St.
Lived—217 W 44—Boarding house
201 W 44—Nana's house
6½–8½   Europe—
            Barrett House few weeks—8" St.
9–15   218 W 45"—Mama died here
15   Bristol Hotel for one winter
            13 West 8" St
20   One winter in the country-
            near Elizabeth N.J.-
            I went to live with Auntie Gert
            68 W 68" St. Daddy died here
            Lived with Annie Lobo at 237 W 71" St. part of time
            Cousin Harry Amy Frank
            111 W 88" St.—
Teddy born Lived 391 West End Ave—
            342 W 71" St.
            Cedarhurst L.I.
            252 W 74
            233 W.E. Ave
            333 W 77" St.
            270 Park Ave
            Hotel Wyndham
            Armonk

*Also on the last page of ledger 3 is a fragment entitled "One of
Joe's Letters to Edith."*

"—My dear child, enjoy yourself, tell us what you want, if we can get it, you shall have it. Please study hard, too, get all you can out of your work: we are proud of you, my darling, we all love you so much."

—These words, which may seem to the reader to be the familiar and somewhat hackneyed phrases of most parents, and in no way extraordinary or to be distinguished from thousands of similar letters—unless, perhaps, they are warmer and more tender than fatherly letters usually are—were nevertheless the surface indications of the whole depth and meaning in Joe's spirit now, of a vision of life which seemed at length to have emerged clearly and wholly, and to which his own life was now devoted.

This outline, located in the bottom corner of the final page of ledger 3, seems to be the only one of Wolfe's countless outlines of "The Good Child's River" indicating that he intended to include the passages written from Joe's point of view in ledgers 2 and 3 as a separate part of his book.

Joe	Chapter I—Doctor—Feet—Childhood—Youth—Etc.
	Chapter II—Bella & Beck
First	Chapter III—Paris Meeting
half	Chapter IV—The Theatre—Esther's Birth
of	Chapter V—The Bar—The Actors
Book	Chapter VI—On the Road
	Chapter VII—The Doctor—The Poison Draught—Grandfather, etc.
	Chapter VIII—The Boarding House
	Chapter IX—The Voyage to England
	Chapter X—England—Aunt Hugh—etc.
	Chapter XI—Return—Barrett House—8th St.
	Chapter XII—Rebecca's Death—The Actors—Etc.

III Fragments from *The Web and the Rock* Manuscript

In item 817, folder 2, pp. 146–52, of the manuscript, material dealing with the quarrel scene, Wolfe recorded this fragment about the death of Esther's mother.

My father was sitting at his desk in the room which he used as a study. When Bella and Auntie Kate went in he was leaning forward across the desk with his face buried in his folded arms. I had a feeling of shame and horror when they approached him: I was afraid when he raised his face that he would be weeping and I felt I could not bear to look at him if he was. But when Bella touched him and he lifted his face, [he was not.] Suddenly I noticed that the room seemed to be divided in two separate groups of people, in two groups of people who had come from different planets, from separate universes. The Jews and the Gentiles drew off into separate camps as if drawn there by some powerful magnetic force of nature.

The actors stood near Daddy with a respectful and embarrassed look on their faces: all of a sudden they seemed like little children to me, awed and frightened by something they could not comprehend, and wanting to get away from it.

I remember the powerful dark convulsive faces of the Jews, the women rocked back and forth gently as they wept, and their grief seemed to have in it something that was universal and immortal: they wept for the world's woe, and it was as if a demon had settled in them, and as if they knew the whole story of grief and pain and death since the beginning of the earth.

Suddenly it seemed to me as if they had borne up the body of my mother, had reclaimed her and drawn her into their circle again and my father and the little group of actors looked forlorn, wistful, shut-out, and afraid.

In item 823, folder 2, of the manuscript, Esther remembers her early life with her sister Edith and the family.

And then I remembered a street in which we played as children, the sound of the hoof and the bell again, the budding of a tree in May, and rooms in all the houses we had lived in. Once she had taken an apple that she wanted from a boy, he fought and struggled but she took it from him without a word, with her grave eyes full of quiet life and interest, she could not speak a dozen words together, but her look was truth, her word a sacrament, and when she drew a needle through a piece of cloth a magic touched it. We had been so brave and beautiful as children, we were so strong, so faithful, and so full of love: I thought of the vexed weave and fabric of our childhood which had been so rich, so full of pain and joy, and so uncertain. I thought of my father and my mother, and of our lovely Bella, they were so lost and beautiful that it seemed now we had been the parents of our parents, the mothers of the children that begot us. We had been so young, so dear, so unperplexed, so richly gifted: the gift of structure and of beauty was alive in us, and everything we made was good.

The earth was ours because we loved the earth: we had the touch and gift of nature in us, we saw the life that all things have in them—the life that slowly beats its pulse out of the thickness of an old brick wall, the life that hangs wearily in the set of an old warped door, the life that lives in chairs and tables and in old knives with worn silver handles, the life of all things that a man has used and dwelt in—a coat, a shoe—the set of your battered hat, these old felt tramps that had such ease and casualness in them, and the magnificent life in clean hard bolts of cloth.

And then these streets and weathered heights at which your soul shrank, these swarms and movements where your heart grew faint! "The earth!" you said. "Give us the earth again!" I tell you that the earth is here and that we knew it. This is the soil, the harvest and the earth: I tell you there has never been an earth more potent and more living than these streets and pavements. Perhaps, as you have said, there's something in my rich Jew's blood that loves a crowd: we swarm with honey, we like laughter, richness, movement, food, and the fullness of a crowd. This was my meadow: I knew it and I loved it, I walked about in it, these faces were my blades of grass, I understood the life that dwelt in it—the tired but happy life of streets when crowds have left them in the evening, the brooding calm of buildings breathing after use and labor, the quiet sounds of the day's end and the smell of the sea and shipping that comes forever from the harbor, the last red earthless light of the sun that falls remotely without violence or heat upon the ancient red of old brick buildings—these, and a million other things, I knew and loved.

Therefore, I knew this land was as good earth as the hills and mountains of your childhood land.

In item 824 of the manuscript, within unnumbered manuscript on the last two pages in this folder, Wolfe relates his purpose in creating the character of Esther. These comments are significant in the light of Joe's discussion with Aunt Hugh in Appendix A, section IV.

As to the character of Esther Jacobs, the writer is unable to judge what impression it will make upon the public—whether there will be outcries from some that woman-hood has been insulted, from others that such a figure is incredible and that "no woman was ever like this," from some, the familiar and foolish complaint that better art would be more reticent, from others again, the false contemptuous urbanity of shocked respectability, which states that such a book is dirty, but says that it is dull.

Over these possible judgments he can no longer have any control: he can only assert his intention to record, by the intensest use of the creative memory, and with a completeness and freedom he does not remember to have found in his own reading, the life of such a woman as has lived upon this earth, as she lived and felt and acted. This woman he has called Esther Jacobs, he has made her half a Jew by blood and birth, and perhaps, in all these qualities which make her so rich, lovely, and passionately beautiful, wholly a Jew.

Esther Jacobs is not presented as one of fiction's "noble women," "pure women," "true women": she is not a fictional heroine, a figure of wires and jerks, a creature of crass impulse and of balanced. . . .

Bibliography

Bernstein, Aline. *An Actor's Daughter*. New York: Alfred A. Knopf, 1941.

——. *The Journey Down*. New York: Alfred A. Knopf, 1938.

——. *Three Blue Suits*. New York: Equinox House, 1933.

Donald, David Herbert. *Look Homeward: A Life of Thomas Wolfe*. Boston: Little, Brown and Co., 1987.

Field, Leslie. *Thomas Wolfe and His Editors: Establishing a True Text of the Posthumous Publications*. Norman: University of Oklahoma Press, 1987.

Halberstadt, John. "The Making of Thomas Wolfe's Posthumous Novels." *Yale Review* 70 (Autumn 1980): 83–86.

Kennedy, Richard S. *The Window of Memory: The Literary Career of Thomas Wolfe*. Chapel Hill: University of North Carolina Press, 1962.

Klein, Carole. *Aline*. New York: Harper and Row, 1979.

Lanzinger, Klaus. *Jason's Voyage: The Search for the Old World in American Literature*. New York: Peter Lang, 1989.

Nowell, Elizabeth. *Thomas Wolfe: A Biography*. New York: Doubleday and Co., 1960.

Reeves, Paschal. *Thomas Wolfe's Albatross: Race and Nationality in America*. Athens: University of Georgia Press, 1968.

Stutman, Suzanne, ed. *My Other Loneliness: The Letters of Thomas Wolfe and Aline Bernstein*. Chapel Hill: University of North Carolina Press, 1983.

Wolfe, Thomas. *From Death to Morning*. 1935. Reprint. New York: Charles Scribner's Sons, 1963.

——. *The Hills Beyond*. 1935. Reprint. New York: New American Library, 1941.

——. *The Letters of Thomas Wolfe*. Edited by Elizabeth Nowell. 1946. Reprint. New York: Charles Scribner's Sons, 1956.

——. *The Letters of Thomas Wolfe to His Mother*. Edited by C. Hugh Holman and Sue Fields Ross. Chapel Hill: University of North Carolina Press, 1986.

——. *Look Homeward, Angel*. New York: Charles Scribner's Sons, 1929.

———. *The Notebooks of Thomas Wolfe*. Vols. 1 and 2. Edited by Richard S. Kennedy and Paschal Reeves. Chapel Hill: University of North Carolina Press, 1968.

———. *The Story of a Novel*. New York: Charles Scribner's Sons, 1936.

———. *Of Time and the River*. Vols. 1 and 2. 1935. Reprint. New York: Charles Scribner's Sons, 1971.

———. *The Web and the Rock*. 1939. Reprint. New York: New American Library, 1966.

———. *You Can't Go Home Again*. 1940. Reprint. New York: Dell Publishing Co., 1960.